RANDALL STEPHENS

SAMUIL
AND THE
LEGENDARY
SNOW OWL

978-1-965552-31-5 (Paperback)

Library of Congress Control Number: 2025913778

BOOKWRIGHTS
HOUSE

admin@bookwrightshouse.com
☎ (213) 286 6700

In memory of Mom and Dad

Enjoy your journey.

Go to Samuil's Facebook page (Samuil Fedorchak) for
a peek into the sequel, *Samuil and the Dark Prince*.

CONTENTS

CHAPTER 1

Killing Of The Bear

Samuil "the Fox" Wolowitz stared into the gloomy predawn. The silence of the night covered the land like a blanket. Moonlit mist gunpowder and smoke swirled across the cold hard battleground as animals from the forest were being sucked into a dark shadow fog that drifted out of the Black Sea.

Samuil watched as the souls of dead warriors rose from the battlefield and were pulled into the fog. Once regenerated, they stepped out to fight again. Demons from the netherworld atop flaming beasts raced out of the fog to lead the reborn. Throughout the gloomy forest, ghostly silhouettes drifted just above the ground, looking for souls to take as death slithered in the darkness, awaiting its next victim.

With his heart pounding, Samuil peered into the fog. With heightened senses and a clenched jaw, he strained to hear. Almost imperceptibly, the forest groaned. "The Fox" sensed something evil afoot. Listening, he heard faint footfalls crackling along the edges of the burned battleground. Quickly, Samuil turned and ran to warn his sleeping friend P'etro.

He stopped abruptly when he saw three ghostly, glowing, hooded figures with red-black swirling eyes mysterious step out the eerie dawn forest and encircle P'etro as their cloaks blew in a windless wind. They raised their hands to the heavens and blue, red, black, green, and white colors of magic flared like fire from their fingers as they touched P'etro's forehead. Then circling, and swirling they exploded into the dawning sky and vanished.

Samuil's sandy blond hair fell in his face as he knelt beside his sleeping friend. First, he saw a white feather and then he saw the silver-blue sparkling aura surrounding P'etro Fedorchak. When Samuil touched the aura, it sparked and dissipated. P'etro's eyes shot open, but he wasn't yet awake. So, Samuil nudged P'etro into awareness.

"Wake up, little friend. Wake up."

"What?" P'etro asked, staring into the emerald-green eyes of his friend.

"The enemy's here."

"What?"

"The shadows are coming. Come on, little friend; we must go. Soon it will be time to resume the fight."

Seventeen years old and stout, P'etro jumped up, stretched, and ran his fingers through his thick black hair. Samuil noticed his hazel eyes were gleaming.

As Samuil and P'etro ran through the predawn light, they saw the eerie reflections of shadow soldiers and beasts moving covertly along the perimeter, attempting to cut them off. Dodging saplings, ducking under branches, and jumping over boulders, the two friends raced through the forest. They had to deliver an urgent message to their comrades.

Before they could reach the front line, the battlefield burst to life. Canon fire lit up the predawn battlefield as it streaked through the sky. Cannonballs exploded around them, saturating the forest with dirt and smoke. Rifles flashed, filling the night with bullets that tore into flesh. Sabers shimmered in the moonlight, dripping blood. Chaos and death spread like a plague as the cries of dying men filled the air. Samuil cringed but steadied himself.

Suddenly the enemy forces swiftly fell upon them from every direction. Hordes of gray monsters, red demons and dark Nephilim raced from the shadow fog. Some had protruding horns, others huge claws, some sharp teeth and all had extra ordinary strength. Encircled and outnumbered, Samuil and P'etro fought beside their Russian-Ukraine brothers. Shoulder to shoulder, the two blood brothers stood their ground against enemy soldiers and hordes of demons.

Samuil heard a bellow of rage as the red-bearded Dimitri "the Bear" Popovitch, came roaring into the battle. Samuil watched as a glancing blow hurled Dimitri's helmet across the war-torn ground. With red curls blowing in the wind, Dimitri slew soldiers and beasts and demons.

P'etro yelled, "Dimitri!"

Then he yelled, "Bear!"

The mountain of a man looked up, and Samuil saw his threating glacier blue eyes.

"Over here, Dimitri! Over here! Hurry! The shadow creatures have broken through the line and are falling upon us like hungry wolves!"

Samuil watched Dimitri fight his way toward his friends in the morning light. The enemy before him were chopped down like weeds. Their bodies formed a bloody cobblestone path to his friends. United, the brothers fought side by side like wild men. With a fierce effort, the army beat the overwhelming enemy back into the woods.

A shadow fog twisted the dead enemy into it, soared into the sky and dropped them reborn back into the battle. A shadow cloud thundered into the sky and demon riders atop dragons and phoenixes dripped into the dawn sky. They were met by an equal number of Russian riders on phoenixes with Ivan "the Boar," leading them into battle atop Major. The frontline roared with the voices of dragon, demons, beasts, and solders. Death fell like rain across the battlefield. The enemy swiftly and brutally pushed the allied forces back.

In the chaos of the heated battle, Dimitri, Samuil, and P'etro were forced to run for cover. Coming across the skeleton of a broken-down wagon, they stopped and knelt beside it to catch their breath. A moment later, "the Fox" fisted his sword and set his jaw.

"Follow me!" He yelled.

P'etro and "the Bear" momentarily locked eyes and grinned.

"For the Brotherhood!" "the Bear" shouted.

"For the ancestors!" P'etro yelled."

They charged into the roaring battle with weapons in hand. Red-faced and yelling like ancient warriors blinded by bloodlust, they smashed into the front line. Amid the dizzying pandemonium, they fought back-to-back in hand-to-hand combat. Though strong, proud, and courageous, the ill-equipped allied army began to buckle. The breached Russian line crumbled, and the three blood brothers were surrounded.

Hearing a battle cry from an unknown Russian soldier gave them courage.

"For comrades, for family, and for the Brotherhood!"

At the sound of the pledge, the three blood brothers looked up. Sitting tall in the saddle of his flying white steed, Major, Ivan "the Boar" soared above the foot soldiers. With bulging muscles and his black hair blowing in the wind, Ivan raised his blood-streaked sword and grinned. After saluting his friends, the chocolate-eyed Ivan jumped to the ground and carried the fight to the enemy.

Filled with the strength of godlike heroes, the three brothers surged forward, fighting shoulder to shoulder. They slowly carved their way to Ivan, leaving a trail of blood and death in their wake.

P'etro heard a scream above the forest canapé and saw the shadow of a huge bird racing toward him and then over him. A white feather the length of P'etro's arm fell to the ground. Kneeling, he picked it up and stared. The omen gave him courage.

"For the Brotherhood!" He yelled.

Again reunited, the Brotherhood Four fought like madmen in the most ferocious skirmish of the war.

As the hazy sun eased its way through the morning sky, the Brotherhood found themselves cut off and flanked by the enemy. Though vastly outmanned and exhausted, the four fought on in the raging battle but soon became separated. P'etro and his comrades fought long, hard, and bravely. P'etro, exhausted from the battle that would not end, heard a familiar bloodcurdling yell, and looked up. "The" Boar was once again astride Major, in the air, shooting arrows. As the fighting intensified, a beastly shadow soldier lassoed Pegasus and pulled him to the ground. "the Boar" drew his sword and leaped into the enemy horde.

P'etro dodged bullets and clashing swords in his struggle to stay alive. He'd lost sight of his friends, and though fearful and disheartened, he knew they were more than capable of taking care of themselves.

In the heat of battle, a bullet struck P'etro. A hot, searing sensation flashed through his exhausted body. His wounded leg gave way, and he fell, bleeding and yelling in pain. Helplessly, he looked over the smoking battleground as a shroud of darkness began engulfing him. His mind gently faded into the shadowy recesses of nothingness.

Feeling dazed, P'etro floated into a no-man's-land where everything was fuzzy and just out of reach. Hot shooting pain brought him back to momentary awareness. Confused, he wondered what was happening and where he was.

Pain … Oh, the pain. Why is the light moving away? What is that sound? Music? Laughter?

Smiling, P'etro blacked out.

P'etro heard a boy yell.

"Hurray! The circus has come to Moscow!"

He smiled at the thought of the circus and saw children rushing out of shanties and shacks into the dirt streets. Boys and girls were yelling, singing, and dancing as the circus parade rounded the corner. Music blared from a marching band wearing colorful costumes and funny feathered hats. Oxen pulled painted wagons with caged lions, tigers, and bears. The smells of roasting meat and spices filled the air.

P'etro raced through the streets of cheering children and down the country road that led home. While taking a shortcut through the forest, he abruptly slid to a stop. He stared at the large white feather in the path. He picked it up and watched it change from blue to silver repeatedly before it disappeared in a plume of smoke.

A breeze from the forest brought him back to the moment, and he ran. When he arrived at the family homestead, he heard a voice call.

"P'etro!" Fedir, his older brother yelled.

"You're late for chores. Come on!"

"Okay, don't be so bossy."

Fedir was a year older, an inch taller and a little heavier than P'etro, but as far as P'etro was concerned, that didn't make him the boss. Fedir wasn't shy, but he was quiet in a crowd.

"P'etro, you're going to make us late for the circus!"

"Leave me alone!"

"Faster, little brother! We still have a lot of chores to do."

"Oh, Fedir has a girlfriend waiting that likes his curly black hair."

"No, I don't."

"Fedir has a girlfriend. Fedir has a girlfriend."

"All right, you are going to get it now."

Fedir ran toward P'etro, but P'etro couldn't run for laughing. Colliding, they rolled in the dirt.

"Boys! Boys! Stop it!" Papa Danio shouted as he stepped out of the barn.

"Go clean up. I'll finish up here. Go on now, or you'll miss the circus."

"Thanks, Papa," P'etro answered, getting up from the ground.

"Yes, thanks, Papa," Fedir echoed.

Entering the family's cabin, they quickly washed up. P'etro slid his trousers on and dusted off his scuffed books. He found his collarless, knee-length white shirt and pulled it over his head, tied a leather strap around his waist, and ran out the door.

In town, they pushed through the crowd and made their way toward the ring at the center of the circus where the ringmaster was shouting.

"Friends! Neighbors! Come! Gather round!" The ringmaster shouted waved his hands and stirring up the audience.

"Who's next? Who's brave enough to step into the ring with the devil bear of the Southern Forest? Who will take up the challenge and become the new champion? Defeat the bear and receive this golden championship medallion as a badge of courage and victory!"

As the Ringmaster started again P'etro poked his brother.

"Go on, Fedir, you can do it," P'etro teased.

"Do I look crazy? Look at all those beaten and bloody fools who tried."

"Come on, Fedir. I dare you."

"You do it, P'etro. I dare *you*."

"P'etro!" someone yelled, breaking the tension between the two brothers.

P'etro turned and saw his friend Ivan. Ivan was as stout as a boar and built close to the ground like one. He could also be as mean as one.

"Ivan! Where have you been?" P'etro asked.

"I was helping Papa."

"Wrestling boars I bet. Maybe we should rename you Boss boar. You're short, stocky, stronger than any pig I know, and you stink like one," Fedir teased.

"Fedir, I'm going to beat you into the ground."

"Ivan, wait—you wrestle boars all the time, so why don't you take on that bear and be a champion?" Samuil suggested.

"I will, but Dimitri is ahead of me."

"Oh, no," P'etro whispered, feeling a chill come over him.

Quickly, P'etro ran to find his friend Dimitri to dissuade him from wrestling the bear. He desperately pushed and squeezed his way through the crowd to reach his friend. P'etro finally reached the ring. Although he was out of breath, he ran up to the ropes and pleaded with Dimitri to stop his foolishness. Dimitri smiled at his little friend.

"Dimitri, what are you doing? You'll be killed!"

"You have always been the most protective of the Brotherhood. P'etro, little friend, I know what I am doing."

"I know you are as big as a bear, but please do not do this."

"P'etro, the bear is muzzled, and his claws are cut off."

Dimitri waved at the beast, which lay panting in the corner of the ring.

"Besides, he's breathing heavily and is tired from all the other matches. All I have to do is stay on my feet and knock him off his."

"But a thousand things could go wrong!"

Dimitri smiled down at P'etro.

"Little friend, everything is all right. You'll see. Samuil and I watched all the matches. Samuil has come up with a plan for me to beat the bear. You know how crafty he is. Nobody in all of Russia is as sly or sneaky."

Turning around, P'etro saw Samuil walking toward him with his fox-skin hat and a grin as the ring master introduced Dimitri.

"P'etro, you look like you have lost your best friend." Samuil said greeting P'etro.

"No, but I might real soon."

"Oh, come on, little friend, don't worry. Everything is going to be fine."

"Samuil, Dimitri is our friend."

"You worry too much. Come on—let's watch Dimitri fight the bear."

When Dimitri entered the ring, the crowd went wild chanting his name.

"P'etro, the bear's first move in every match has been to stand, swat, and circle, when he does, then Dimitri will…"

P'etro turned to the ring and saw that the brown bear was as thick as an ox, as muscular as a grizzly, and angry as a wounded wildcat. P'etro's heart lodged in his throat as the ringmaster let loose the furious beast. With white teeth shining through his muzzle, he attacked Dimitri, drooling and wanting fresh blood.

Just as "the Fox" had said, the bear stood, lurched forward in a flash, and swatted at Dimitri. The crowd roared, hungry for excitement and thirsting for blood. The yells of the animated crowd thundered through the circus grounds. With great determination, P'etro blocked out everything around him except his focus on Dimitri.

P'etro's heart pounded, and his head spun as he stood, lost and alone, in the blood-crazed, roaring crowd. All he could hear was the roar of the bear. All he could feel was fear for his friend. All he could see was the ring of death. A knot of emotion was stuck in his throat, and screaming demons were in his head. His body shook.

A sense of dread engulfed him as he helplessly stared at the ring. His eyes were transfixed on his friend, and he watched what he didn't want to see.

The bear lunged, swinging his massive paw. Dimitri ducked and came back with a lightning-fast punch that surprised, stunned, and stopped the bear dead in his tracks. The crowd filled the air with chants of excitement for their beloved champion. "Dimitri! Dimitri!"

Quick as a blink, Dimitri hammered the bear with a second blow that would have made Thor smile with pride. The blow rocked the bear, and the crowd gasped in anticipation. As the bear wobbled, they cheered.

"Dimitri! Dimitri! Dimitri!"

The bear stumbled and fell to all fours. Dimitri kicked the beast in the side of his head, ripping off its leather muzzle. As the bear shook his head violently, the tattered muzzle flew into the crowd. Free, the bear roared with such vehemence that a bone-chilling fear fell over the crowd. He roared showing his large, sharp canines. The crowd gasped, fell silent, and collectively held their breath in disbelief as the bear stalked its prey.

Madly, the bear charged on all fours and lunged for Dimitri. Dimitri sidestepped and kicked the bear in the rump. In a crazed rage, the bear spun and was met with a roundhouse kick to the jaw. The crowd cheered, encouraging their champion on to glorious victory.

The bear lunged, intent on trapping Dimitri in a bear hug. Dimitri stepped backward and spun. As the bear plowed into Dimitri, both sailed out of the ring. They hit the ground with an earth-shaking force and rolled through the crowd.

Back on their feet, Dimitri and the bear continued fighting. The ringmaster wrestled his way through the panicked people. In the center of the crowd, he tripped, fell, and was trampled by the crowd.

The beast slapped Dimitri, who stumbled and rolled—but not far enough. He staggered to his feet as the bear rose. The bear grabbed Dimitri in a smothering bear hug. Back on his feet, the ringmaster fought his way through the hysterical crowd to Dimitri.

The beast roared and opened his massive jaws, still holding Dimitri in a bear hug. His teeth flashed in the sunlight as he positioned his giant head to bite and crush Dimitri's skull. P'etro gasped and rushed to the aid of his friend. Samuil was right beside him. Fedir and Ivan "the Boar" tore through the crowd from the other direction.

Overhead, a blue cloud full of silver flashing lightning appeared, and out of the forest, a blue fog twisted into the circus, blanketing the whole area. Everything became deathly quiet as the cloud descended and the fog rose. Gradually, the two combatants became one swirling, tumbling, blue-silver hazy mist. P'etro gasped.

From the misty cloud, P'etro saw an old man with a long white beard and a mangy old wolfhound beside him. As he stared at the old man's catlike bright-green eyes, they turned silver. In one hand, he held a flashing blue crystal and in the other, a glowing silver saber. The old man and hound slowly descended from the mist to the center of the ring. A blue mist snaked around his feet and a silver light swirled around his head.

Mouth open, P'etro walked to the ring. Stopping outside the ropes, he stared. It was the most amazing thing he had ever seen.

"P'etro, P'etro, P'etro," the old man called.

"You shouldn't allow your friends to play with dangerous beasts. No, no, no. Dangerous, dangerous, dangerous. Shame, shame, shame."

P'etro opened his mouth to speak, but nothing came out, so he grabbed the ropes and climbed into the ring. Stepping into the blue mist, he stiffened and stopped. He tried to step closer to the old man and his wolfhound, but he couldn't move.

The old man smiled through the mist, which was wet and cold. "However, I do see the thrill in it. Yes, yes. I do. I do. It's adventurous and all. Yes, it is. Yes."

P'etro's jaw dropped. All he could do was stare and hope that he wasn't drooling on himself as he began floating in the buoyant cloud.

"I've stopped in for a quick fix. Quick, quick. My old wolfhound warned me this would happen. Yes, he did. Yes, he did. But what do old hounds know? What, what? Well, this time he knew what he knew. Or did he? Oh well, even a blind hog finds an acorn occasionally. Indeed, indeed."

Afloat in the mist, P'etro fought to move. Unable to move, he struggled to speak. Finally, P'etro asked the question ablaze in his mind. "Who are you?"

"Oh, how rude of me. I am Nikolai of the Caves, and this is my hound, Wolf Killer."

Samuil looked at the huge gray wolfhound with its scarred muzzle and gnarled ear. He was scraggly but lean.

"Did you come to save Dimitri?" P'etro asked.

"Well, well. You see, it's like this—Dimitri doesn't have a Brotherhood name, and he needs one. Yes indeed, he does. Yes, yes. Plus, he still needs to rescue you."

"What?"

"Yes indeed. Yes, yes. What, what? You sound like Wolf Killer. Always asking what, why, how, when, and so on. But it's time, P'etro. Time for me to go. Yes, yes. Go, go. And time for you and the town to wake up. You will remember what you remember unless you forget to remember, or you keep remembering to forget. But everyone else will not remember. No, no."

P'etro frowned. The old man was confusing him.

"Until we meet again. Whenever we meet again. Wherever we meet again. And however, we meet again. Yes, yes. Until then. Until, until."

Suddenly, blinding silver lightning filled the sky and struck the fog, which burst into hundreds of silvery blue flares. P'etro saw that Dimitri and the bear had been separated, and both were encircled by the flaring mist.

Once again, the crowd began to chant for their champion.

"Dimitri "the Bear"! Dimitri "the Bear"! Dimitri "the Bear!"

Still dazed, P'etro looked down and saw that he was floating several inches above the ground. Now aware, he quickly dropped with a thud. In the sky above the ring, he saw the last remnants of fading silver light, which flickered one last time and then vanished as the blue mist disappeared back into the forest.

"The bear has won again!" the ringmaster yelled.

"No!" the crowd roared.

"The bear hit the ground first! Dimitri won!" someone from the crowd yelled.

"Dimitri is disqualified for being outside the ring." The red-faced ringmaster yelled.

The enraged crowd quickly became a mob, and if they hadn't feared the ringmaster's bear and the quick wit of the magistrate, they would have had the ringmaster's head.

Ivan grabbed Dimitri, and they all ran through the crowd to the forest. Stopping deep in the timber, they collapsed and gulped deep breaths of air.

"Dimitri, you're crazy!" P'etro shouted.

"Samuil, I should choke you! And Ivan, thank you for getting us all out of there!"

"Did you hear the crowd?" Dimitri asked.

Ivan laughed then said, "Did you see the ringmaster's face?"

"Dimitri won! I knew he could do it," Samuil added.

"Yeah, and the crowd chanted his new name! Dimitri "the Bear"! Dimitri "the Bear"!" Ivan said with pride.

"Did anyone else see a cloud?" asked P'etro.

A whisper encouraged P'etro to fight his way back from the shadowy world of unconsciousness. As he began to fight, the whisper developed into a hum that quickly became an echoing melody. The strange melody was everywhere and nowhere. It rang out from beyond and near. He had heard this—no, he had felt this—before.

"It is time, P'etro. Yes, yes. Time. Wake and fight; wake and fight, my son. The battle still rages, and the enemy is upon you. Wake up, wake up."

He'd heard that voice before.

Whose voice is that? Why is the ground shaking? Why can't I move? I smell the Black Sea. And I'm surrounded by the forest.

Suddenly the pain of his bullet wound surged through his body, making him wince. P'etro blinked, trying to force his eyes open.

It's the 1840s. It's the war. The Allied Shadow War. I have to wake up, or I'll die.

Softly, the distant voices of ancestors called to him. As he listened, he jerked and struggled against the murky haze that flooded his mind. Squinting one eye open, he saw the shimmering silvery figures of his ancestors, swarming in a blue mist. With a concerted effort, he gasped in a lungful of air and forced his way back to consciousness.

Able to move, P'etro grimaced from the throbbing pain in his leg. He willed himself to stand; then he stumbled. With the helping hand of a comrade, he stood and looked around. The air was filled with the sounds of bombs and bullets and the screams of the dying. Fire and smoke from cannon blasts rose from the demolished forest. All around him, dead soldiers and horses littered the bloody battleground.

P'etro realized that while he was unconscious, the skirmish had escalated. The intense life-or-death struggle was raging out of control, randomly taking whomever it willed. P'etro and a handful of weary soldiers were fighting for their lives.

"Stand and fight, men! Stand and fight!" P'etro shouted.

Regrouping, they stood in a circle, fighting with pistols, swords, and knives. P'etro stubbornly fought with every ounce of his

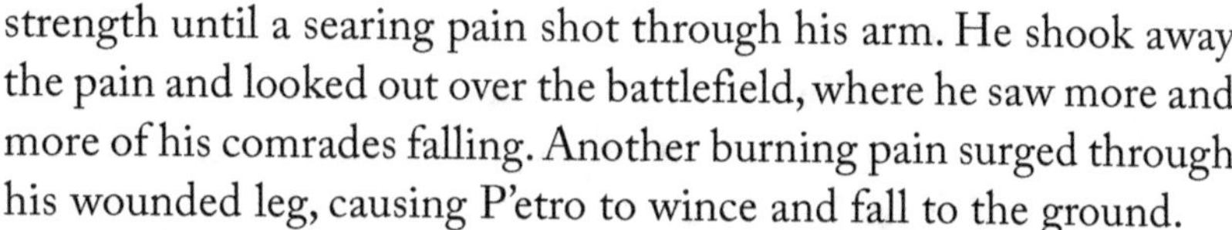

strength until a searing pain shot through his arm. He shook away the pain and looked out over the battlefield, where he saw more and more of his comrades falling. Another burning pain surged through his wounded leg, causing P'etro to wince and fall to the ground.

Though injured, bleeding, and barely conscious, P'etro heard an old familiar yell. A blood-curdling roar thundered in his ears. P'etro looked up and saw Dimitri racing out of the woods toward him. Blood streaked the air like rain as the enraged Spartan of old ran to the rescue of his friend. With saber in hand, he sliced through the enemy hoard rushing to P'etro's side.

Dimitri kneeled beside P'etro and winked.

"On your feet, little friend! Hell hath burst open, and we're going to catch a ride out of here on wings of fire!"

With that, "the Bear" reached down, scooped up P'etro, hurled him over his shoulder, and ran. As he raced through the raging battleground, he yelled from the depths of his soul. With one hand he steadied P'etro, and with the other he whirled his sword. Before him, the enemy bled; behind him, they died.

"For family! For Russia! For the Brotherhood!" he yelled as bodies fell about him.

Like Achilles at Troy, he taunted and slashed his way through frightened beleaguered demon warriors. Running, he shouted—red-faced, arm pumping, blood and spittle flying.

"Bleed and die, you heathen vermin! Bleed and die!"

P'etro spotted a rocky path to the forest and pointed it out to "the Bear", who quickly ran for the safety of the trees. Suddenly, P'etro was tossed through the air. With a bone-crushing thud that took his breath, he hit the ground. P'etro rolled over, wincing in pain and gasping for air. Sitting up, he looked around and saw "the Bear" on ground, gasping in pain. P'etro moaned and crawled to his side. The mighty Bear had fallen. In a split second, everything transcended into a peaceful silence. The two eternal friends lay face-to-face on the cold, bloody ground behind a bolder.

"P'etro, we all knew you were too young for military service … but I'm glad you're here." "The Bear" clutched P'etro's arm and then continued.

"Thanks for not listening to me."

"Dimitri, you know I have always listened to your advice."

"Yes, but"— "the Bear" gasped for air — "you never took it."

"Although you and the rest of the Brotherhood are older, I've always been smarter."

"The bear" laughed and coughed and choked to a stilled silence. P'etro no longer heard the cannon blasts, the gunfire, or the agonized screams of the dying. In a fleeting crucible of time, their eyes met. In that moment, the souls of the two friends locked together in unspoken communication. Everything that needed to be said, plus things never said before, were spoken without a word. When "the Bear" winced in pain, the mysterious stitch in time broke. "The Bear" closed his eyes.

Deaf from the roar of war, crushed from the thought of losing his friend, and isolated from his allies, P'etro shook with a cold chill. In the smoky bullet-filled air, his frayed emotions roared.

"No, Dimitri! No! You can't go!" He pleaded.

A fiery anger burned through P'etro's grief-filled soul.

"Dimitri! Get up, Bear! Get up!" He yelled.

P'etro looked away from his friend's pain-stricken face. Choking at the idea of "the Bear's" demise, P'etro shook him.

"Come on! We have to go! Come on! Don't make me carry you out of here!"

P'etro helped the crippled Bear to sit up and lean against a bolder. P'etro knelt beside him.

Dimitri looked endearingly at P'etro and spoke with the broken and coughing and choking voice of a fallen hero.

"Little friend …", "The Bear" paused.

"I'm afraid we'll not be riding out of here."

"Of course we will."

"No." Dimitri coughed, spitting blood.

"Hell's flames have turned on me. Never trust a deal with the devil."

P'etro opened his mouth to speak, but nothing came out. Deep within his wounded soul, he felt his own fire go out. Impassioned but immobile, he stared at Dimitri, unable to believe what he was seeing.

Dimitri coughed, and a smile on his battle-stained face slowly rose from the corner of his mouth. He winked.

"Forgive me." Dimitri begged.

"For what?"

"For not being able to save us."

P'etro's heart surged with emotion at the impending loss as he looked into the fading eyes of his friend.

"Don't worry, Bear. Everything is going to be all right."

"Sorry, P'etro."

Dimitri winced in pain and his breath was shaky.

"I can't even save myself."

"What are you saying?"

"I'm saying—"

"No! You are the champion of Russia. You're the great and terrible Bear of Moscow. "The Bear" may have fallen on the soft fat belly of the enemy, but I know he will bounce back up again. Just like you always have. Like you did at the village circus when you were christened with a new name and emboldened with a new nature."

In a heroic voice, like that of a battle-hardened warrior, P'etro said, "I'll save us both, Bear."

"No, P'etro, you must save yourself."

"No!"

"P'etro, look after my family."

"The Bear" paused, took a painful breath, before continuing.

"Take care of my beloved little girl Lena."

"All right."

"Keep her from charlatans."

"But—"

"Promise me."

P'etro couldn't believe what was happening.

"The Bear" gripped P'etro's arm and spoke softly.

"I am dying, little friend."

"No."

"Promise you'll care for my little girl."

Wincing, P'etro fought to maintain his composure.

"Promise me."

"I promise, Bear. I promise."

The gut-wrenching vow pierced P'etro's heart like an arrow.

"Thank you, little friend." Dimitri coughed.

"Tell Marina I love her. She's the best wife a man could have."

"I will. I'll tell her, and I'll see to Lena as well, my friend. I promise. I swear by the blood of the Brotherhood."

As P'etro gave his vow, "the Bear" sighed and slipped away. P'etro closed Dimitri's eyes, softly whispered a goodbye, and choked on his breath as memories of his dear friend flooded his mind. A cannon blast shocked P'etro back to reality. Gasping, he looked around the battlefield.

"This is war, I'm in a battle. Dimitri is dead."

P'etro looked at "the Bear" lying on the cold ground and sighed. His heart hurt more than his leg and arm. He struggled to his feet, but then felt his leg buckle, and he fell back to the ground.

P'etro knew the shadows would be back soon, and he needed to be prepared. In his condition, he knew he couldn't face them head-on. So, he decided it best to barricade himself, buy some time, and maybe help would come.

In the distance, the sounds of war thundered. In the air, there was the stench of death. P'etro heard the roar of combat all around him. The enemy was rushing his way. P'etro could feel them coming; the very earth was vibrating with their strides. The battle-scarred terrain screamed of danger and death.

They're coming. I can feel them. I can smell them.

Cannonballs exploded all around him as lead filled the air. Urgency and danger filled his mind. Fear, pain, and sorrow rushed through his veins. Swiftly, his battle training broke through the barrier of his shell-shocked mind and wounded heart. P'etro tried to stand but fell back to the ground, groaning.

CHAPTER 2

Staying Alive

With shell fragments and lead in his leg and arm, P'etro crawled out of from behind the bolder and limped into the forest. When the shadow of a large bird crossed his path, he stopped, looked around, and saw a tree had fallen across a dry creek. He made his way to the tree, lay down in the creek, and relaxed. A breeze rustled the leaves of the forest, making him flinch. He sat up and listened. Closing his eyes, he concentrated. In the rustling of forest leaves, he heard the voices of the ancestors. In a whisper, they warned of coming danger. But there was something else in the air. Like a lazy breeze, something was subtly moving through the forest.

P'etro squinted and stared at the timberline. Though he didn't see anything, he heard a faint sound that made the hair on the nape of his neck stand up. Peripheral movement made him flinch. Closing his eyes, he reached into the forest with his senses, searching for what was out there, but there was too much residual mayhem from the battle.

A twig snapped nearby, and P'etro's instinctively jerked his head in that direction. Whatever was out there was closing in. He grabbed his rifle; then, slowly and quietly, he maneuvered into a more secure position. Now, he had both a better view of the tree line and a better shot. Settling down, he listened and watched.

Again, a twig snapped in the silent forest, making P'etro flinch. He stared in the direction of the sound, but he was unable to see through the dense grove of oaks. Moments later, there was a rustling in the undergrowth. P'etro stared intently as anxiety knotted in his stomach.

I know you're there. Come a little closer. Easy does it ... closer. Let me see what you are.

Something in the forest moved toward P'etro. It carefully darted from tree to tree. Patiently, he slowed his breathing, prepared for the shot, and waited. The brush rustled, sending chills through his body. Slowly, he steadied himself, took careful aim, and got ready to fire.

The stalker suddenly moved. P'etro wiggled to relocate himself for the kill shot, which sent searing pain through his leg. He grimaced, steadied his pain-riddled body, and repositioned himself. Ready, he waited for his pursuer to make a wrong move and give away his location. Taking a deep breath, P'etro tightened his squeeze on the trigger. Ready to take the shot, he waited impatiently.

An unfamiliar sound rose on a forest breeze startling P'etro. From beyond the periphery of the tree line, notes sounded. Then, from somewhere within the forest, a faint melody crackled. P'etro tilted his head. Concentrating, he was still at a loss as to what the stalker was.

"A bird?"

Then an exploding cannonball shattered the still air. Startled, he jumped and remembered he was still on a battlefield. He knew that birds didn't sing in the heat of a battle. Besides, the birds had been silent since dawn when the battle began. So, what was that sound?

Again, a hooting call sounded from the forest but closer this time. Exhausted and in pain, P'etro listened and realized that he had heard that call before. A memory of "the Fox" flooded P'etro's mind. P'etro had often sat by a creek, struggling to master the secret birdlike Brotherhood identification call. This one was familiar.

"The Fox." He's here. I know he is.

P'etro hadn't seen "the Fox" since the twilight raid when they were separated. He couldn't believe that this could this really be Samuil.

Is he's still alive. But how did he find me?

Slowly, "the Fox" stood up, silhouetted against the dark trees.

"Samuil!" He whispered and began to move cautiously toward P'etro.

The thought of his old friend standing there in the forest made P'etro momentarily forget about everything else. Again, the roar of battle filled the air. and P'etro yelled over to Samuil.

"Dimitri is dead! I'm wounded and can't walk! Go for help!"

P'etro prayed that "the Fox" could hear him.

"Samuil! Go for help! Hurry! They're coming!"

P'etro shivered, leaned back on the fallen tree, and closed his weary eyes. His wounded body throbbed, his mind swirled with anxiety, and his disillusioned soul was in a dark place. He felt trapped and haunted by the howling wind. It was like a gale that shattered his resolve into shards of hopelessness. The thunderous storm of war was threatening to destroy everything. Dimitri was gone, Ivan was missing, and Samuil was in jeopardy.

P'etro fought against slipping deeper into the murky void of nothingness until pain surged through his leg like a hot iron. He realized that the bullet was embedded and must come out.

"P'etro," a soft voice called.

The sound of the voice broke the depressing trance P'etro had fallen into.

"P'etro," the voice called again.

With shock, he looked up.

"Samuil, you're here!"

"Yes, little friend. I am. I saw you and Dimitri in combat, and I fought my way here as quickly as I could. It was slow-going. And as you know, the enemy is relentless, and the shadow creatures are everywhere. But I got here as soon as I could."

Samuil pulled off his shirt, folded it into a pillow, and gently placed it under P'etro's head. Quickly, Samuil went to work rewrapping P'etro's wounds. P'etro looked at Samuil's scruffy beard, bulging biceps, and upper-body strength, and he couldn't believe how much he had grown up. He wasn't a wiry boy anymore.

"Thanks, Samuil. I'm glad you are here."

"I've been trying to get back here since we were separated this morning."

"Yeah, it's been a dreadful day. Have you seen "the Boar"?"

"No, not since daybreak."

Samuil pulled the wrapping tight around P'etro's leg, making him wince.

"P'etro, remember the day we all enlisted?"

"Yes, I remember. I was too young to enlist."

"Yeah, remember our solemn oath to leave no one behind?"
"Yes."

"All right, then, you're coming with me, even if I have to carry you out of here on my back."

"What about "the Bear"?"

"We'll come back for him as soon as we can. First, I have to get you out of here. This battle can't last much longer, and when a ceasefire comes, we will come back."

As bombs began exploding all around them, "the Fox" helped P'etro to his feet and put his friend's good arm around his neck. Then they began to trudge through the woods. P'etro's injured body screamed in revolt, and his head swam from nauseating pain. Resolute, Samuil struggled, tugging them ever forward. They limped through the cover of the forest, moving as fast as P'etro's battered leg would allow.

"How did "the Bear" meet his end, P'etro?" Samuil asked in between awkward steps.

In detail, P'etro related the brave and heroic feats of "the Bear"'s last stand. Coming across an abandoned ammo wagon, the pair stopped. "The Fox" leaned P'etro against a wagon wheel while he inspected their new transport.

"P'etro, stay out of sight. I'm going to steal a horse."

"What?"

"Shush. I have a plan."

P'etro glanced at Samuil and frowned. Samuil smiled, but P'etro shook his head in disbelief.

"You're mad, Samuil."

"Yes, that's why you like me. Right?"

"The Fox" winked at P'etro and then disappeared into the trees. P'etro assessed the wagons munitions and found several rifles and pistols. They were English weapons and fine ones at that. P'etro loaded them, lined them up for firing, and stuffed his pockets full of ammunition. Then he settled down behind the wagon, readying himself for whatever came his way. Silent and hidden, P'etro waited anxiously for Samuil to return.

Gunfire rang out in the forest. P'etro jumped. Steadying himself for what could be his last stand, he took aim in the direction of the uproar. Then he heard the pounding of hooves rumbling through the woodland. A second later, "the Fox" burst from the tree line on a shining black stallion that looked like the mount of a general. The shadow demon cavalry crashed through the forest in hot pursuit. Samuil rode like the wind on his black steed. Jumping the wagon, he reined in the horse to a sliding stop. When Samuil and the stallion were clear, P'etro unleashed a storm of hot lead making the carvery ride for the cover of the forest. Moments later the cavalrymen regrouped and charged their barricaded position with lightning fury.

"Here!" P'etro shouted as he tossed Samuil a rifle.

P'etro fired and hit his mark—a cavalryman and mount fell. Samuil fired; another man fell. Discarding the rifle, P'etro grabbed a loaded one and fired. "The Fox" did likewise.

The next few chaotic minutes seemed like an eternity that unfolded in slow motion. The bloodthirsty enemy kept coming, the duo kept firing, and the enemy kept falling.

Overrun by the enemy, P'etro pulled two pistols from the wagon and fired. When their ammunition was spent, he tossed them aside, drew two more from his belt, and fired again. Yet the enemy continued to charge like a pack of hungry wolves from the shadow cloud. With his adrenaline pumping, P'etro dropped the guns and then drew his saber to face the horde. With one good leg and one good arm, he cut the enemy down. Grimacing from his wounds, he steadied himself while the cavalry regrouped. Quickly, he reloaded rifles while Samuil reloaded pistols; then he leaned against the wagon with rifle in hand, prepared to meet the next wave of attack.

Above the ear-piercing conflict, a familiar war cry resounded from the forest. It was a battle cry that P'etro knew from the fields of his childhood. It was the war cry of the Brotherhood as they got ready to fight their imaginary enemies.

"Ivan!" P'etro yelled.

"The Boar" has come to rescue us from the enemy!" Samuil shouted.

"Ivan is alive! Give them hell, Ivan!" P'etro shouted.

Ivan "the Boar" guided his magnificent white stallion through the air, followed by a dozen others. They were engaged with shadow demons on dark horses with tusks. When Ivan spotted his friends, he flew to their rescue. He landed with a pistol in each hand and charged the ground cavalry.

Like a madman, he thundered through the killing field, filling the air with lead. He tossed the empty pistols aside and drew his saber—and Pegasus soared. They circled above the forest and crashed back into the heart of the enemy. "The Fox" handed P'etro another loaded rifle.

Then, suddenly, they were joined by the battling sky cavalry as they brought their fight to the forest.

P'etro considered their situation.

There is very little ammo, no food, no water, and the horse attached to the wagon is dead.

Pegasus raced forward, leaped over the wagon, and slid to a stop. Ivan dismounted in a swirl of dust and grabbed the rifle tossed to him. Together, the trio fired volleys of bullets at the enemy.

"P'etro, cover me while I hook Pegasus to the wagon so we can fly out of here."

"All right. Go."

Ivan dashed to the wagon while Samuil and P'etro returned enemy fire. Quickly, he unharnessed the dead horse, removed Pegasus's saddle, took off his bridle, and yoked him to the wagon.

Pegasus snorted, and "the Boar" winked at P'etro.

"Ready, little friend?"

"Ready."

"Hold on tight, Samuil. Pegasus is about to fly!"

With that, "the Boar" slapped the reins, and the white steed flew through the bombs and bullets that filled the air. On all sides of them, the bloody war waged on. Behind them, the ground and sky enemies pursued at a hot pace. With blistering speed, Pegasus thundered onward, flying toward the Russian encampment. The wagon jerked behind him, bouncing in the air.

P'etro noticed blood on Samuil's back. In horror, he rolled his friend over. Samuil flinched in pain, barely conscious and moaning.

Samuil motioned for P'etro to come closer.

"Give them hell, little friend. For the Brotherhood. For Dimitri "the Bear"." He whispered in a weak voice.

"Yes, Samuil, I will."

P'etro got Ivan's attention and pointed with his eyes to Samuil. Ivan "the Boar" frowned. P'etro took a deep breath, exhaled, and steadied his nerves.

"Hold on, Samuil; hold on. We're nearly to the encampment."

An enemy shell exploded near the wagon, causing it to tumble in the sky. It hit the ground, rolled, and began breaking apart. Planks and splinters shot through the air like arrows. Samuil, P'etro, and Ivan rolled across the war-torn ground.

P'etro pulled himself up to a knee and looked around. He saw Samuil lying nearby and called out to him. When Samuil didn't answer, P'etro crawled to him. Samuil was unconscious. P'etro looked up and saw a rushing horde of soldiers and a blood-soaked Ivan, standing defiantly. With a pistol in one hand and a sword in the other, the wide-eyed warrior rushed headlong into the pursuing cavalry. Ivan yelled and fought like a madman.

"Come on, you heathens! Time to meet your ancestors!"

P'etro tried to watch Ivan fight, but he blacked out. Yet somewhere between consciousness and unconsciousness, he heard the faint call of angels. The call became a rhythmic hum. The humming grew into chorus. The singing filled him with peace, and P'etro wanted to fly away with the angelic choir. Out of their majestic tones of heavenly bliss, a reassuring voice softly whispered. The whisper danced in P'etro's head until it became as clear as the morning sky.

"Get up, little friend. Get up. It's time to fly away. You must go now. Go to your friends. Goodbye, little friend. We must go."

As the angelic voice faded, trumpets sounded in the distance, shocking P'etro back to awareness. It was the sound of the enemies' trumpet. The trumpeter was calling for a final crushing assault on the Russians.

A bloody, stallion appeared, stepping through a cloud of gunpowder and smoke. He stood gallantly and pawed the ground. P'etro knew Pegasus was the only hope of getting back to the safety of the Russian encampment. He struggled to his feet as Pegasus slowly walked toward him. He was amazed that Pegasus seemed oblivious to the all-out attack.

He pulled a bloody, delirious Samuil from the ground and leaned him against his tired body. The regal steed, without saddle or bridle, lowered himself to the ground at P'etro's gentle coaxing. After wrestling Samuil onto Pegasus, P'etro mounted the stallion. He marveled at the brave beast who was so calm in the raging battle.

"The Boar" reappeared, stepping out of the smoky dust, armed to the teeth with rifles, pistols, sabers, knives, and ammo. Ivan walked up to P'etro and grinned.

"Friend or foe, solider?" Ivan asked.

"Foe, if you don't get out of the way, Ivan."

"Far be it from me to get in the way of a commanding general, his mission, and his wounded help atop my horse."

"Come with us, Ivan. Let's all ride to safety."

"No, I still have varmints to eradicate and nemeses to destroy."

"But—"

"Go now, ride like the wind to the Russian encampment. Take care of Samuil and yourself, little friend."

"Godspeed, Ivan."

"Go on now; ride out of here while you still can."

Ivan slapped Pegasus on the rump, and away they dashed. Pegasus skillfully weaved through trees, maneuvered around fires, jumped over the fallen bodies of soldiers, and leaped into the air. P'etro marveled at the speed and agility of Ivan's majestic stallion as they rode on the wings of the wind. P'etro felt that Pegasus was the mightiest and smartest steed in the world.

With a handful of horse in his left hand and the belt of his best friend in his right, P'etro rode the magical steed into the clouds.

CHAPTER 3

Wounded Body And Soul

Pegasus carefully and quickly flew to the medic's tent as if he had traveled there a hundred times. When the stallion stopped, P'etro lowered his weary head onto the horse's muscled neck.

"Easy boy. Easy. Good boy," P'etro mumbled, barely conscious. Looking down, the ground below him spun.

"Help," P'etro whispered, even though he tried to shout.

"We need help!" He spoke in a louder voice.

When no one responded, P'etro wondered if they didn't hear or if they were just too weak from their own injuries to respond. Exhausted yet determined, P'etro called out once again.

"We need a doctor. We need help!"

P'etro slumped back down onto Pegasus's neck, drained and defeated. Pegasus neighed loudly as a nurse walked into his view and paused.

"Who called for help?" She asked.

Startled, P'etro sat up and fumbled for words.

"My friend is hurt badly, miss. He needs your help."

The young nurse beckoned two men, who walked over and helped Samuil and P'etro down from their mount.

"Thank you, miss."

"You're welcome. We'll take care of your friend and send someone for you."

"Thank you. What is your name?"

"My name is Nadia."

As they walked away with Samuil, P'etro leaned against a log. He sighed with relief, knowing that finally "the Fox" would be taken care of.

P'etro noticed that Pegasus had already disappeared. He smiled, knowing that the stallion was racing to the aid of his master, Ivan. In his mind, he saw the majestic steed gracefully flying through the sky. When he closed his eyes, he saw "the Boar" as an avenging angel, thundering victoriously through the sky, striking terror into the hearts of the enemy.

Now alone with only his nagging thoughts, P'etro found a bench and lay down next to a tent. Around him, the camp bustled with energy—men ran in and out tents; horses pulled carts or carried riders down the main lane. Inside the tent, he heard two injured men playing cards. Following their game of cards, their laughter and badgering eased his mind.

"Soldier!" yelled a brusque voice.

P'etro jumped to his feet to salute, but his injured leg gave way, and he collapsed to the ground in agony. Searing pain shot through his body. As he lay on the cool ground, clutching his bleeding leg, the shadowy figure of a huge man bent over him.

P'etro saw the concerned, weathered face of the officer.

"Are you all right, comrade?" the burley officer asked in a gravelly voice.

"No, sir! I was wounded in battle this morning."

The officer stared at P'etro in shock.

"This morning?"

"Yes Sir."

The officers face reddened as he shook his head in disbelief.

"And you have yet to be seen to?" He asked in a voice laced with exasperation.

"We just arrived, sir. Been killing the enemy all day, sir."

"Oh, good Lord!" the officer declared in a surprised tone.

"Come on, soldier. Let me help you to your feet. We're going to find a medic."

The officer hoisted him upward, and P'etro moaned. His muscles ached, and his wounds were painful. Wobbly and lightheaded, P'etro steadied himself as the grizzly but kind officer wrapped P'etro's arm around his neck, and they began to limp away.

As they neared the medical tent, the officer saw a crowd of soldiers around it.

"Out of the way, men! Wounded soldier coming through!" He yelled.

Like the parting of the Red Sea, the soldiers moved away, opening a wide path to the medical tent.

"Medic! Medic!" The officer cried out.

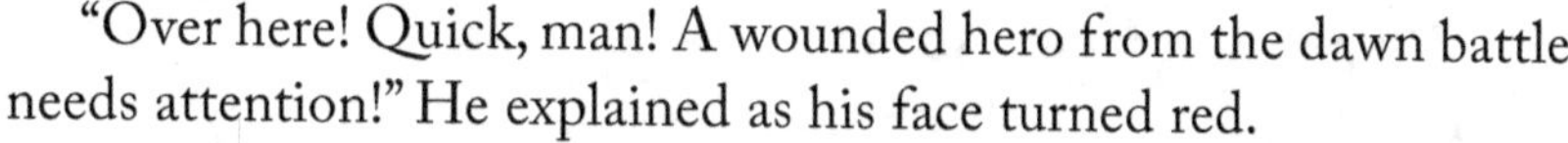

"Over here! Quick, man! A wounded hero from the dawn battle needs attention!" He explained as his face turned red.

"From dawn's battle?" Someone from the medical staff murmured.

"They said no one survived that battle," a doctor announced.

"Well, this soldier did. Come on; the hero needs your medical attention."

The staff quickly scrambled about, making accommodations for the wounded hero.

P'etro woke abruptly in the dimness of a strange tent to the sounds and smells of dying men. Above the moans of the wounded, he heard the faint deadly echoes of war in the distance. His pain-riddled, confused mind raced. He didn't know where he was or how he got there. Disoriented, he jumped to his feet and fell as his wounded leg gave way. Lying on the dirt floor, he saw stained white sheets draping wooden cots.

"Easy, solider. Let me help you up," a nurse with an angelic voice said softly as she hurried over.

Her sweet words swirled through the tent and pirouetted in his mind. Staring into the darkness, P'etro saw a lovely creature with the face of an angel, smiling in the dim candlelight. He tried to shake his head and focus, but it only made him dizzy. Then a light appeared out of nowhere, and the sweet, angelic voice spoke again.

"I'm here, soldier. Right here. Everything is going to be all right. I'll take good care of you," the nurse reassured him.

Coughing and choking as he tried to speak, P'etro finally formed words.

"Where am I?"

"You are in the medical field tent."

"Are you an angel? Am I dead? Is this heaven?"

She took P'etro's hand in hers.

"Now, now, soldier, you are very much alive, and I intend to keep you that way."

"Good."

"What is your name, soldier?"

"P'etro."

"P'etro. I saw you earlier with your friend Samuil."

"Nadia?"

"Yes, it is me."

"How is Samuil?"

"The doctor is taking care of him. Lie back and rest now."

"But—"

She frowned and dabbed his fevered brow with a wet cloth.

"Rest now." She said with a smile.

P'etro heard her soft voice, but the cobwebs in his fuzzy mind were beginning to spread as he struggled to focus.

Dimitri is dead, Samuil is critical but being cared for, and I'm wounded.

Nadia leaned into the light, and P'etro smiled at the most beautiful face he had ever seen.

"Thank you for saving me, Nadia."

"Oh, but I'm not saving you. I am only mending you so you can go home."

"Well, thank you for the patching up, then."

"You are quite welcome, P'etro."

Slowly, P'etro faded away into a restless sleep until the distant roar of cannons echoed in the predawn, waking him. The screams of dying men resonated in the night, arousing the soldier deep within him.

"I must get back to the battle. I must avenge Dimitri and help Ivan. It's time to fight. My saber? Where's my saber? My rifle? For the Brotherhood, for Dimitri, for Samuil. Where is Samuil?" P'etro mumbled.

"Easy, P'etro. You have been hurt. You were wounded in battle. Remember?"

Nadia's voice soothed him, but he wrestled in his mind with what she said. For a long time, his foggy mind couldn't comprehend.

"Wounded?"

"Yes, you have been wounded. I understand how you feel, P'etro, but I have my orders."

"Orders?"

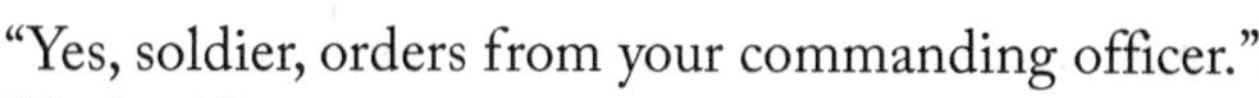

"Yes, soldier, orders from your commanding officer."

"Orders?"

"Yes, your orders are to stay here and rest until morning. Then a company of men will follow you into the battle."

"Yes, sir." P'etro coughed as he struggled to get to his feet and salute.

Before he could get up, Nadia placed a hand on his chest.

"At ease, solider. You need to save your strength. Rest now.

"Yes, sir."

Now that he'd heard his new marching orders, he began to relax.

The next morning the intense sounds of war woke P'etro. The noise of scurrying soldiers, neighing horses, and officers shouting orders confused him. He painfully struggled to his feet and carefully inched his way through the dark tent. He bumped into something in the dark; he looked up and saw the familiar face of the brass-chested officer, just as his knees buckled. He hit the ground and tumbled into frightening nightmares.

In his feverish mind, P'etro engaged in an internal struggle that he feared he could not win. Fiery dragons and evil monsters charged out of the forest and onto the killing field. Trapped in an endless night, he fought the demonic powers of the underworld with his knife and saber. As the earth erupted, the ground beneath him cracked open, and P'etro fell through the darkness of a fiery midnight. He fell toward the open jaws of a dark demonic world. Falling, falling, falling. In a start, his eyes shot open, and P'etro realized it was a nightmare.

He struggled to reorient himself as he lay in bed. The dream had seemed so real. Looking around in confusion, he wondered where he was. Sensing danger in the air made his skin crawl. He grimaced once he recalled his wounded condition. He told himself it was best to just lie still, collect his thoughts, remember, and try to focus. But he felt an uneasy darkness rising through his soul, filling his mind, saddening his heart, and gripping his body like a vice.

A blanket of mist, thick with moisture, covered the encampment. A dark ankle-deep shadow fog rolled out of the forest and drifted through the morning mist toward P'etro's tent. Inside it smothered the lamp light, creating an eerie atmosphere, and slid onto P'etro's cot covering him from the waist down. The fog was both hot and cold. From somewhere within it there arose unnerving groans that sent chills through P'etro, but he was shocked back to reality by a booming voice that made the fog dissipate.

"You're awake! Good." The brass-chested officer said striding into P'etro's tent as the shadow fog disappeared.

"It is about time. I have been waiting for you to come around. We must hurry. Someone is asking for you."

"Who?"

"His name is Samuil."

"Samuil is alive?"

Joy flooded P'etro's heart when he heard this news.

"Yes P'etro. I'll take you to him."

"Oh, thank you, sir."

He tried to rise but winced in pain. The officer reached out with a callused hand and helped him up. The officer then served as a crutch, enabling P'etro to keep all the weight off his injured leg. Together they wobbled out of the medical tent and into the smoky air and then into a nearby tent.

"What is this place, sir? And what is that noise?"

"I'm sorry, P'etro, but this is the tent of the dying," the officer replied.

P'etro's heart began to ache.

Oh please, not Samuil.

"Come, soldier, step inside, and see your comrade."

P'etro entered the large tent. The odor of blood and death filled the air. He looked around and saw crude hand instruments, medical containers of minerals, and even an old saw. As he walked along the tent, he saw long rows of wooden beds, cots, and gurneys filled with dying men on bloody sheets. His heart sank when he heard the mingling death sounds of moaning, crying, sobbing, and yelling— the worst sounds he had ever heard. Stunned, he walked down the long row of beds filled with broken men. Some seemed at peace, others cried out in agony, and still others sat quietly mourning the life that they would never live.

Near the end of a row of wooden beds, P'etro saw Samuil, lying still and struggling to breathe. P'etro let go of the officer and limped

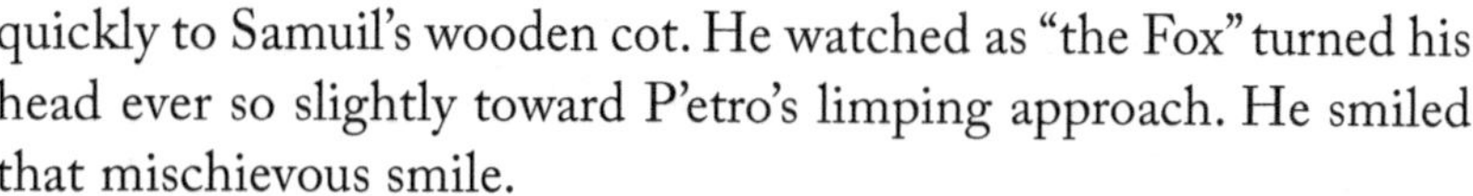

quickly to Samuil's wooden cot. He watched as "the Fox" turned his head ever so slightly toward P'etro's limping approach. He smiled that mischievous smile.

"Samuil," P'etro whispered softly.

"Hello, little friend."

"I'm so sorry!"

"No apologies, little friend."

"But—"

"Do not worry."

P'etro knelt next to Samuil's bed, but P'etro could not meet his gaze because of his feelings of helpless and guilty.

"This is all my fault Samuil."

"Shh, P'etro."

Samuil gazed at his little friend as heartfelt memories of a shared childhood filled his soul.

When P'etro looked at Samuil's he saw a gleam in his eyes and felt anew their binding friendship and camaraderie. Longing, hope, and desperation caught in P'etro's throat when their eyes met.

"No time for apologies little friend."

"But—"

"Listen. Be still and listen."

For a long moment, nothing but strong emotion filled the silence between them.

"P'etro, only you and Ivan are left."

Samuil winced and coughed and then continued. The Brotherhood is gone."

"No."

"It's gone, P'etro."

Samuil breathed deeply, his eyes closing momentarily.

"You were always a schemer. You keep us together…while we played and built. You plotted and planned our binding unity and future."

Samuil paused, grimacing in pain and P'etro laid a hand on his shoulder.

"You were the rock that kept us together."

Coughing and out of breath, Samuil stopped once more.

"Let me get you some water."

Samuil coughed again.

"No, listen. My last act is your new name. "The Bear" chose it before the war."

"Dimitri?"

"Yes. Today you're *the Rock*."

P'etro smiled.

"You're P'etro "the Rock"."

Samuil coughed and grimaced.

"You're strong, unmovable, and true."

"The Fox" coughed again, his strong shoulders shaking with the effort, and P'etro was unable to respond because of his grieving mind.

"P'etro, look after Ivan. He's a good man, but he needs guidance." Samuil coughed once again.

"Understand?"

Speechless, P'etro stared at "the Fox".

"Do you understand?" Samuil repeated.

"No! None of this is right. This shouldn't be happening. You're going to be all right."

Samuil looked into the eyes of P'etro and squeezed the hand of his longtime friend.

"I'm dying. Promise me so I can go in peace."

"Samuil, stay with me. Don't go. I don't want you to die. You are too young to die. We are all too young to die in this damn war!"

"P'etro … you're the Rock … be the Rock."

"No, Samuil, no! Only yesterday we were children playing in the dirt on the farm. Even now, with rifles and uniforms, we're still just children."

Samuil smiled at his young friend but moaned painfully. He gasped and clenched his eyes shut.

"Do not die, Samuil. Please!" P'etro begged.

"Fight, Samuil. You can't die. You can't. It's not right. I need you."

Samuil nodded.

"It's all right, P'etro."

After a long, choking moment, Samuil squeezed P'etro's arm.

"Be the Rock … promise me."

"I promise, Samuil. I promise," P'etro said with a heavy heart.

Samuil smiled and closed his eyes.

"Samuil! Samuil! No! Come back! Samuil!"

Heartbroken, his spirit crushed, and his body trembling, P'etro shouted, "No! No! No! Samuil! No! Fight, Samuil! Fight! Stay with me. Please. No, no. Come back, Samuil. Come back." He yelled and them sobbed.

With clenched fists, P'etro yelled and swore at Death.

"Let him go! Damn you, let him go! Let Samuil go!"

P'etro bowed his head and closed his eyes, chilled to the bone and jarred to the soul. Childhood memories flooded his mind. The precious thoughts made him weep.

The sounds of battle roared again in P'etro's ears. Closing his eyes, he saw ghostly images dancing in the dark corners of his mind, and he shook. Touching his forehead to Samuil's, his soul plummeted into darkness.

CHAPTER 4

Prince And Princess

While brushing her mouse-brown hair in front of a mirror, Ilia tried to put all the bad news about the Shadow War out of her mind. She closed her mocha-brown eyes and daydreamed of Moscow.

Ilia's royal buggy came to an abrupt stop in the middle of the admiring crowd. Unable to proceed because of the crowd, she waited impatiently. Another buggy pulled to a stop behind her. A noble prince from a faraway kingdom stepped out of his buggy and walked over to Ilia's.

"My fair lady," the prince said with a bow before continuing.

"Seeing that our transportation has failed us, might I be so bold as to invite you for a stroll through this great city?"

The prince extended his hand.

"Yes, my lord. Though I live here, I have never seen the sights." Stepping down from her buggy, Ilia thought about asking the prince the perplexing question that was troubling her and frowned.

"Do you know your way around the city? Your accent tells me that you are not from here."

"Oh, my lady, I have been coming to Moscow in the summers since I was a little boy. I know this city like the back of my hand."

"Oh?"

"Come, let me show you around."

"Yes, my lord," Ilia replied with a shy smile.

Ilia took his arm and thanked him for his courtesy. The prince escorted Ilia to all the finest places in the city. Store owners fussed and fought for her attention. Restaurants offered her tender cuts of meat and glasses of wine, delicious sweets, and tantalizing tidbits. Her head spun at the lavish compliments and admiration. Ilia curtsied and waved to her admiring crowd as they cheered and shouted. How she loved Moscow. The glory, the wonder, the intoxication, and the enchantment.

The prince was such a gentleman. He was polite, courteous, and witty. He quickly stole Ilia's heart.

"Would you like to tour the cathedral?"

"Oh yes, I have only seen it from afar."

"Very well then. I will send a messenger ahead to prepare for our arrival."

"Here we are, my lady. Saint Basil's Cathedral. The dignitaries eagerly await you. Lavish preparations have been made for you."

"Thank you, my prince, I am honored. But I have a request."

"Your request is my command," the prince promised with a deep bow.

"It would please me to stroll the courtyard and gaze upon the beautiful gardens. They are renowned, and I have always wanted to see them. I may never have another chance."

All around them, the elegant shrubs and flowers swayed in the breeze.

"Of course, my lady, whatever pleases you. Take my arm, and I will escort you there. I am sure the dignitaries will not mind the indulgences of the lovely princess's desires."

"Thank you, dear sir. You are so kind."

"My lady, it is my privilege to help and escort you."

"Thank you, kind sir …"

Ilia's daydream was shattered when her best friend Tatyana ran into Ilia's bedroom.

"Ilia! Ilia! The war is over! The soldiers are coming home!"

"When?"

"In a couple of days, they'll be in Moscow. There's going to be a parade!"

"A parade! In Moscow! We'll have to go!"

Both girls giggled, held hands, and excitedly danced in a circle around the room.

The two girls were inseparable. Tatyana was like Ilia's twin except that she had long black, curls. When together, they schemed, dreamed, and shared secrets.

"Ilia, you're such a naughty girl. You're thinking about boys again, aren't you?"

"You talk about boys all the time, Tatyana."

"Well, I'm older than you."

"Only by three months."

"That makes you the baby. Ilia's a baby. Ilia's a baby."

Ilia grabbed a pillow and smacked Tatyana. The pillow fight was on. Both girls screamed and giggled.

Ever since Ilia was thirteen, Momma Liliya and Papa Vitaik had talked to Ilia about marriage. Now that she was older, their fervor to get her married had reached new heights, and their tactics were sometimes embarrassing. Liliya was always talking about the neighborhood boys and how handsome they were. She even invited families who had handsome boys over for supper.

"If you meet the right man and agree to settle down with him, then perhaps he will take you to live in Moscow," her mother had teased.

"Mama, I don't want to get married. I want to go to university."

"Girls do not go to university, Ilia; they get married. As should you."

"Mama, stop."

Liliya tucked a fallen strand of her blonde hair behind her ear and stared at Ilia with her piercing blue eyes.

"I just want the best for you."

"Stop, Mama, I am not a baby anymore!"

"Of course not, dear."

"Mama!" Ilia screeched as she left the kitchen and ran to her room.

Disgusted, she slammed the door, ran across the bedroom, and fell onto her bed. Someone knocked on Ilia's door.

"Go away!"

"Ilia, it's me, Tatyana."

"Tatyana!"

Ilia ran to open the door. After giggling and discussing boys, they talked once again about leaving the farm for Moscow. Ever since her first visit to the breathtaking magical city, Ilia had dreamed of returning and living there. She begged her parents to move to the city, but her pleadings fell on deaf ears.

It was planting time, and families were busy preparing the fields. Her Papa asked Liliya and her aunt Olga to take Ilia and go to Moscow for supplies. Ilia wondered if her Papa secretly hoped she would meet a soldier on leave and fall in love. Another strong man on the farm would be more valuable than gold.

Ilia hated the long, rough ride to Moscow. Plus, it was embarrassing to arrive in an old wagon pulled by the family oxen. So, she envisioned something wonderful.

She saw herself riding into the city in a beautiful carriage pulled by spirited, shiny black stallions that pranced into Moscow behind the royal family. Down a narrow road that passed shops, and the shopkeepers rushed out to greet them with waves and invitations to sample their goods.

The crowd, horsemen, and buggies parted to make way for the royal procession where even the horses wore gold and jewels on their bridles.

From the edge of the street, shopkeepers scrambled for her attention.

"My lady, the finest cloths in Russia are here for your eyes only!"

"My lady, perfume from Paris! My lady, silk from the Far East!" "Your Royal Highness, the finest food from all over the world!" "My lady, books! Wonderful books all the way from London, volumes from all over the world!"

In her peripheral vision Ilia sees a bookstore and the vison fades away.

"Books, pictures, and stories," Ilia whispered, running toward the bookstore."

After only a few steps, Aunt Olga grabbed her by the collar and yanked her to a standstill.

"We don't have time for fairy tales or romances. Now, come on! We must catch up to your mama!" Olga barked.

As she rushed through the crowd, Ilia was pushed and shoved away from Aunt Olga's tight grip. Ilia hurried to catch up. She was amazed at how quickly Aunt Olga could move for a woman her size.

She was a short, stout, round lady with Liliya's hair and eyes. Yet she was surprisingly agile. She was also a stern woman who had a nasty temper when provoked.

Ilia giggled with excitement as she ran through streets packed with people wearing fancy clothes, elegant silks, and fine velvet. Well-groomed horses pulled shiny buggies and wagons. She knew she had to find a way to escape the farm and live in this glamorous city. She was enchanted with the lights, the smells, the music, and the handsome young men. She loved Moscow.

As they wound through the crowd, Ilia realized that she wasn't going to be able to enjoy Moscow with Aunt and Mama hovering. They were fixated on the task at hand and wanted nothing more than to hurry back home. Ilia wondered how she could get out from underfoot and enjoy this experience. She even considered getting lost in the crowd, exploring Moscow, and finding her way back home later.

"Parade! Parade! There's a parade for the heroic wounded soldiers at the square!" A gang of little boys yelled, running down the street.

Ilia grinned.

"A parade!" she squealed.

"Perfect."

For Ilia, the parade was the ideal opportunity for her to escape the clutches of her aunt and mother.

"Mama."

"Yes, dear."

"Did you hear? Wounded soldiers. If there is a soldier that isn't wounded badly, maybe he could help Papa with the crops. No other men in all of Moscow are free from the war, but they are."

Liliya looked at Aunt Olga and raised an eyebrow.

"What do you think, Olga?"

"It sounds like a good idea to me. We could use the help and a wounded soldier back from the war could use the money."

"Okay, then. It's settled. We'll load the wagon, take it to the stable, and go to the square," Liliya instructed.

Ilia beamed with excitement at the prospect of her plan coming together so smoothly.

When the ladies approached the square, crowds of people were milling around everywhere. There was no room in the street to walk. People were rambling around in every direction, and there were hundreds of them.

"Stay close, Ilia," Liliya whispered, pulling Ilia to her side.

"This is the last place you want to get lost. We may never find you in this crowd. And it is a long walk back home."

Ilia sighed in frustration as Mama held on to her arm. It was as if her mother could read her mind and knew of her plan to escape.

But it only took a few moments for Liliya to lose hold of Ilia's arm as she plowed ahead, trying to keep up with Olga. Aunt Olga weaved in and out of the traffic with near flawless agility and speed. Ilia watched the bustling crowd as it moved along like a meandering river, rhythmically changing directions as it flowed. She marveled as the gracefully flowing river of people swept Liliya and Olga away in its current.

Pushing their way through the busy streets, women rushed to shops like a hot wind on a stormy day. The crowding and shoving made it difficult for Ilia to maintain her bearings and keep her feet firmly planted on the ground. She watched her mama and aunt weave through the crowd, and as the distance between her and them grew, she smiled, realizing her opportunity to sneak away was nearby.

Olga pushed to the front of the crowd for a better view of the passing soldiers. With care, she stood watching the proceeding line of wounded men. The crowd cheered and the band played. Liliya caught up and stood by Olga's side. Both ladies waited impatiently, eyeballing every wounded soldier who passed. Ilia knew her aunt was in a hurry to find a soldier and get back to the farm. After all, there were chores to do. Ilia took her time weaving in and out of the crowd of dignitaries, soldiers, and locals as her mama and aunt faded into the distance. A second later, Ilia could no longer see them.

For as long as she could remember, Ilia had dreamed of running away to live in Moscow. As a little girl, she had envisioned numerous plans of escape to the big city. She had lived her entire life for this moment. Giddy with excitement and surrounded by a multitude of people, she hurried along.

Ilia moved through the streets with the rhythmic ebb and flow of the crowd. She had always dreamed of seeing the cathedral. She had often begged Aunt Olga and her mama to take her, but they always had a convenient excuse not to. Ilia had seen the cathedral from a distance as they passed near it on their town trips, but she had never seen it up close. She recalled overhearing the neighbor's elaborate description of the pristine cathedral when they visited late at night. Now, she stood staring at the majestic, holy structure, cradled in the arms of the clear blue sky.

Saint Basil's Cathedral sparkled and beckoned like a bright star on a dark Russian night. It was nothing like the grubby farm buildings she was used to seeing. It was a grand masterpiece, standing tall and proud for all to see. The magnificent building with its marble arches, golden domes, and spheres seemed to pierce the heavens. Stretching toward the sky, it kissed the sun. It was nothing short of mesmerizing—a beautiful, amazing structure made by the hand of man to the glory of God.

So far, her brief experience with the city had been extremely exciting but very exhausting. Determined, she pressed on through the swelling masses until the smell of roasting mutton and fried fish caused her to stop. Taking a deep breath, she opened her eyes and stared at beautiful palominos pulling fancy jeweled carriages up to golden-domed buildings. Then she heard the crowds cheering and the band playing for the war heroes. Ilia loved the chaos, the sensations, the crowd, and the spectacular sights. She couldn't wait to tell Tatyana all about this.

Ilia was unaware of anything around her except her own wonderful dream, which she was living out. Subsequently, she didn't detect the subtle shift of the crowd, nor did she sense the danger. Ilia was in her own world, a world beyond what was transpiring all around her. Absorbed in the moment, Ilia's spirit soared, and she didn't hear the screams of frightened people or the neighing of runaway horses.

P'etro's heart wasn't in the parade of heroes, yet he marched along with his comrades as best as he could. All he could think about was getting out of Moscow and going home.

As P'etro limped along, he noticed a change in the crowd and heard a ruckus. People began shouting and scrambling. Panic ensued, and frightened people were running, falling, and scrambling for safety.

He heard someone shout, "Stampede!"

Immediately after the warning, the spooked herd of horses stampeded down the street that the wounded soldiers were marching up. Everyone was in a panic, scrambling, pushing, and running in different directions. Ear-piercing screams filled the air as men, women, and children ran to get out of the way.

The herd raced toward the cathedral, where P'etro saw a beautiful young lady standing in harm's way. She stared up at the cathedral and seemed unaware of the danger. P'etro ran, limping, toward the young lady, stumbling over shoes and handbags abandoned by the panicked crowd.

P'etro was near enough to see a man shove the woman to the ground. When P'etro knelt beside her, she screamed. Looking up, he saw the hooves of a stallion as it reared above them. They were about to be trampled to death. Everything began to move in slow motion.

The stallion's hooves slowly descended toward the lady's small body. P'etro threw himself across her, and he felt something heavy smash into his back, crushing him onto the street. P'etro heard the call of the snow owl, and reality was blown away, like a feather in the wind. Then everything faded into the silent unknown.

Slowly, Ilia opened her eyes and saw a bright light. Blinking, she momentarily beheld angels. Then she heard Mama's voice.

"Olga, please move the lantern out of her face."

"Mama?" She whispered and then coughed.

"Yes, dear, it's me. I'm right here."

"Where am I?"

"You are in the health ward, dear."

"Oh. Why?"

"Here, the nurse brought you a cup of water."

Gently, Liliya lifted Ilia's head, and she sipped. The water was cool and delicious.

"What happened, Mama?"

"Do you not remember, dear?"

"I don't remember much."

"What do you remember?"

Ilia stared silently at the ceiling for a long time.

"I remember a parade…and horses. A stampede. But that's all."

"Do you remember the soldier?"

"No." Ilia grimaced as she sat up in the bed.

Around them, the ward buzzed with quiet voices and the snores of sleeping patients.

"A soldier saved your life, but he was pawed badly."

"Is he going to be alright?"

"Yes. The doctors say he will be.

Ilia sighted a breath of relief.

"Who is he, Mama? What's his name?

"His name is P'etro."

"P'etro. And he was in the war?"

"Yes, dear. He was a wounded soldier, returning home."

"And he saved my life?"

"Yes, P'etro saved your life, Ilia."

Ilia thought silently for a moment.

"P'etro's both a war hero and my hero."

"Yes, dear, he's a war hero and a hero for saving your life."

Her mother sat back and gave Ilia some space. Then she smiled. "He has agreed to come help at the farm while he heals."

CHAPTER 5

In Times Of Trouble

For his heroic effort in the Shadow War, P'etro received a land grant in Ukraine. He and Ilia married and immediately moved to a small farming community called Bakota. They instantly fell in love with their new independent life and freedom.

Sometime later, they sat on the porch and waited for the sunrise over the rolling hills of the river valley. P'etro closed his eyes and breathed in the rain-cleansed air, filled with the scent of evergreens.

"It's a beautiful day, P'etro."

"Do you think little Samuil will be born today?"

"Perhaps. I can tell it's going to be a boy, but babies have their own time."

"Well, the sooner the better. I could use a good plow hand."

P'etro smiled and leaned back in his rocking chair.

A breeze blew from the barn, and P'etro heard the snorts and bellows of the oxen.

"And if it's a girl?" Ilia asked.

"What? You said…"

Ilia rocked back in her chair laughing.

"I'm teasing. It's going to be a boy, and I'll be sure to tell baby Samuil to be ready for the plow."

P'etro grinned.

"What is that smell?"

"It's the smell of autumn in the air."

"No, it's the smell of the bacon you're cooking."

"Well, I best see to it before it burns."

"Please do."

From the comfort of his homemade chair, P'etro watched dawn's first light slowly wash through the awakening forest. As more and more shafts of sunlight flooded to life, he lit his handcrafted pipe, which his father had given to him. Smoking, rocking, and daydreaming, P'etro thanked the heavens for the dawn and its blessings as he watched his pipe smoke curl upward. The twirling shapes of the smoke looked like storm clouds struggling to form in an autumn sky.

"Ilia," he called out from the porch.

"I need to get to the field while it is still daylight."

"Listen to you. The sun is barely up, and you are complaining about being late."

"No. I'm complaining about being hungry."

"You are always hungry."

"Only and always for your magnificent cooking, dear."

"P'etro, you would say anything to anyone if you thought it would get you a plate of food."

P'etro chuckled quietly to himself, rose from his rocker, and walked into the kitchen. He watched Ilia flick her mouse-brown hair out of her eyes as she finished cooking breakfast. When he cleared his throat, Ilia turned to face him. Their eyes met, and they smiled. P'etro winked, and Ilia rolled her eyes.

P'etro had matured into a handsome man with a black beard. His gold-flaked hazel eyes danced with life and integrity. He was as strong as an ox, with broad shoulders, tree-trunk arms, and huge hands that made him appear to be as large as a black bear.

"I'm going to the barn to feed the oxen, maybe you will be finished cooking by the time I get back."

"P'etro! If you are within a broom's reach when I turn around, you will get smacked."

Chuckling, P'etro hurried out the door.

After feeding and watering the oxen, P'etro stepped out of the barn and shivered. Something didn't feel right. The forest was different. The air was strange. He closed his eyes and listened. Everything was stone still. All the creatures of the forest had gone silent, and the morning light flickered.

He looked into the forest and noticed the air ripple, wabble and changing. The snow-white clouds in the morning sky had turned black. The sun disappeared as a dark shadow cloud raced across the sky. Shadow strings dripped from trees, boiled into a charcoal fog that tumbled and knotted through the timberland. He noticed that everything was coming from the direction of the notorious Southern Forest, which was not far away. He had been told that nothing good ever came from the Southern Forest.

The fog twisted and rolled out of the forest and toward the barn. There was something different about this fog. He sensed it was just aggressive as the shadow fog in the war. P'etro took a nervous breath as the fog grew closer. He thought about running but froze in place.

If I run for the cabin, it might follow. I can't endanger Ilia and the baby she carries.

Looking down, he watched the fog slowly roll over his feet, making him feel strange, dizzy, and entrapped. Nervously, he backed up until he bumped against the barn wall. As he considered his precarious situation the fog thickened. P'etro trembled at the strange sensations he felt in his legs. The fog made one leg cold and the other hot. One boot turned molten red and smoked from the heat. The other turned white and smoked from the icy cold. As the fog rose to his waist, he frantically looked for an escape route.

"P'etro!"

Startled, P'etro looked toward the cabin where Ilia was standing. "Breakfast is ready!"

When he looked back to his feet, he gasped. The dark fog was receding. He watched the fog roll back into the forest and disappear. With the disappearance of the fog, the forest became a sunburst timberland once again.

"P'etro, come on before the food gets cold!"

He returned to the cabin, perplexed.

Hours later, at the end of a long day, P'etro walked from the field to the cabin. As the sun was sinking in the western sky, Ilia opened the cabin door and greeted him with a kiss.

"Ilia, supper smells wonderful. You must have been slaving in the kitchen all day."

"No, it is just bits and scraps that I threw together at the last minute."

"Well, then, lead me to the trough."

When Ilia entered the kitchen, she flinched. An unsettling frown spread across her beautiful face, and she grimaced. Concerned, P'etro opened his mouth to speak.

"I'm all right, honey."

"You don't look all right."

"It's time."

Startled, P'etro frowned at her, feeling confused.

"Time?"

"Yes, it's time, P'etro."

Wide-eyed, P'etro took a deep breath and froze. Looking as ghostly as if he'd been confronted by a bear in the forest.

"T-time?" He stammered.

"It's time for the baby, P'etro."

"Now?"

"Yes, dear. Now."

He sat down, then rose, then sat again.

"But—"

"It's time, honey."

P'etro stared at her.

With a reassuring wink from the mocha-brown eyes that had captured his soul in Moscow, Ilia smiled.

"It's time for our baby, P'etro."

"Oh."

"And it is time for the good doctor's help."

"Doctor?"

"Yes, Dr. Danil Mykhailo."

"Oh yes, time for Dr. Mykhailo. I'm on my way."

P'etro dashed toward the door. Giggling, Ilia called out to him to stop.

"Wait, dear. You need your jacket. It's cool out."

As she handed P'etro the jacket, Ilia squeezed his arm, looked deeply into his panicked eyes, and smiled again.

"Hurry to the Kostyk's. Tell Ivan "the Boar" to ride for the doctor. Then hurry back to me. I need you here."

P'etro gazed at her with concern.

"Very well. Will you be all right here alone?"

With a matter-of-fact expression, Ilia nodded and smiled.

"Yes, dear, I will be fine while you are gone. But hurry. It's time."

P'etro set his jaw, stuck his pistols in his belt, and grabbed his knife. In a sprint, he ran out the door and disappeared into the forest.

As he ran, P'etro felt his heart throb with excitement about the birth of their baby boy, already named Samuil, which was Ilia's idea. Papa P'etro didn't prefer that name—his best childhood friend was Samuil "the Fox", who was killed in the war, and the memory of "the Fox" still shook him with choking emotion—yet neither of them could come up with a name that he liked. Finally, P'etro agreed to Samuil.

The road to Ivan's was long and dangerous in the winter. However, P'etro's racing mind told him to run through the Southern Forest. It was much quicker that way, and he was in a hurry. He didn't know the Southern Forest well, and it had a bad reputation. Many a man had gone in and never come out. P'etro figured they'd sunk in the Bogs, but the townsfolk said the forest was haunted. They claimed it was filled with the spirits of evil men and witches. Others said it was the realm of demons and devils.

Rumors of malevolent spirits and disembodied evil kept most people out. P'etro had heard the tales about the Bogs' legendary snow owl, the blue glowing lights, and monstrous man-eating creatures. Neither he nor Ivan put any stock in those tales. But still, he was leery of venturing into the forest, especially after this morning and seeing the eerie fog. So P'etro decided it would be best and safest to stick to the road. If he ran, he could still make good time.

Within the hour, he arrived at Ivans cabin, and P'etro hurriedly explained the situation.

"I'm off," Ivan said.

Mounting his horse, Sergeant Major, he sunk his spurs into his flanks and thundered off to Bakota in a cloud of dust to get Dr. Mykhailo. P'etro smiled and watched him disappear.

P'etro quickly went to the stall and hitched Lady Girl to the buggy then he and Ivan's wife, Galina, loaded the buggy with her midwife necessities. She stepped up, slapped the reins, and they jerked down the road, rocks spewing behind them. It seemed to P'etro that every animal they owned was a speedster. He wondered if they would someday decide to own a slow horse.

At the cabin, P'etro helped Galina inside. Being an experienced midwife, Galina took matters in hand and quickly had Ilia comfortably in bed. As Galina busied herself in preparation for the coming event, P'etro stepped out to the porch and packed his pipe. While smoking, he heard a thundering rumble from the north. Looking up, he saw Ivan galloping down the road on Sergeant Major.

"Dr. Mykhailo is right behind me. He sent a rider to bring Nastasiya," Ivan explained.

"Good, another competent midwife will be helpful," P'etro replied in a shaky voice as he felt his pulse race with anticipation.

Sergey and Nastasiya Vitalik were their neighbors to the east, and P'etro was glad that she was coming to assist Galina with Ilia's care.

"Ivan, you can take Major to the barn; you know where the water and hay are."

Moments later, Dr. Mykhailo and Father Slavik rolled up in the doctor's medicine buggy, pulled by Old Betsy. Father Slavik, Bakota's priest and a family friend, stepped out of the buggy clothed in his customary Eastern Orthodox black robe. The stumpy parish priest with his long, unkempt beard came equipped with satchels full of sacred things. He had holy books and ornaments dating back to his days as a Catholic priest. And of course, he had plenty of holy water.

As the priest approached, P'etro noticed he had a nervous facial twitch. The priest blessed P'etro and Ivan, quickly crossed himself, and began sprinkling holy water while he chanted.

"Is the priest going to be all right, Dr. Mykhailo?"

"Yes, P'etro, he's fine."

"He seems awfully nervous to me," Ivan commented.

"Yes, maybe a bit."

"Why?"

"Because he knows about Ilia's trouble during her term. Once he has finished with his preparations, he will be all right," the doctor promised.

P'etro noticed that Dr. Mykhailo's dusty-blue eyes looked weary. His windblown gray hair was whiter than the last time he'd seen him. His tall, lean body was sprinkled with road dust, and he looked tired. P'etro hoped the dedicated, compassionate doctor was all right.

Father Slavik and P'etro stepped into the cabin. The priest blessed Galina and continued his preparations for childbirth. P'etro watched him set crosses, candles, oils, and incense throughout the cabin. Then he placed a cross and a small statue of Mother Mary holding the infant Jesus on the family hearth. Next, he lit the candles of birth rites, knelt, rubbed his fingers over the rosary, and prayed. As he did, P'etro saw a few thin threads, like shadows, twisting from the hearth and disappearing into cracks.

P'etro walked back outside to the porch, where he visited with Ivan. They were interrupted by a ruckus from the road as their neighbors to the east appeared in a cloud of dust. Sergey Vitalik, a tall, big-framed, rough-looking man, stepped down from the wagon and turned to help his hefty wife, Nastasiya, down. Then he extended his hand to their babysitter, Sofia, who was holding newborn Katya. Nastasiya flicked her red braid behind her shoulder and straightened up. P'etro remembered Sergey telling him she had a red-hot temper to go with her long red hair. He hoped to never see that.

Father Slavik walked onto porch and extended his hand to her. "Nastasiya, let me help you in the cabin. Dr. Mykhailo and Galina are with Ilia."

"Thank you, Father."

P'etro went inside too; Nastasiya and the priest entered the bedroom. The doctor stood at the foot of Ilia's bed, lost in thought. He ran a hand through his short salt-and-pepper hair and wrinkled his brow as if in deep contemplation. The room was quiet as the slender doctor deliberated.

"Sofia, come with me to the kitchen, and we will brew a fresh pot of tea. Perhaps the aroma will break up the medical intensity and give everyone a moment of peace."

Smiling, she followed P'etro to the kitchen.

The busy cabin finally began to calm down from the earlier hectic pace as Nastasiya walked into the kitchen.

"Do you have any more tea P'etro?" she asked.

"Yes, we do. It's just finished steeping."

"Well, let's have a taste of this wonderful brew," Nastasiya teased.

Grinning, P'etro handed Nastasiya a cup.

"P'etro, this is such a blissful brew. Where did it come from? Who made it?

"I did."

Nastasiya looked at him with a raised eyebrow. P'etro smiled and nodded politely.

"I experimented with my tea in the army."

Nastasiya stared at him with a look of disbelief and then frowned.

"The Russian tea was so bad, that when they threw it out, the dogs ran from it."

"Well, of course; it was hot."

"No, ma'am. The dogs howled because it smelled bad, and when the tea stood up and growled, the dogs ran."

"Really?"

P'etro was eager to tell the rest of his story.

"You see, Russian soldiers can't cook or think. They mindlessly take orders and fight. So, I learned to make good tea. And we used the Russian tea to poison the enemy."

"Oh my!"

Nastasiya's face turned faintly green.

"It's all in the fixings, ma'am. Good fixings make for good tea."

"Really? Let's have no more fanciful stories. Show me the ingredients of your soldier's tea."

"Very well, ma'am," P'etro said standing at attention and saluting like a soldier obeying a direct order.

"There, ma'am. On the counter, ma'am."

Nastasiya rolled her eyes and investigated.

Outside in the fresh air, P'etro rocked. Listening to the laughter, talk, and neighborly bantering that filled the air, P'etro smiled to himself. The men gathered on the porch to tell tall tales of the good old days. The enigmatic stories were more entertaining than belly dancers and a lot safer. Inside, the ladies continued their own chitchat while tending to Ilia's care and comfort.

The men's tall tells brought about hysterical laughter. Ivan fell out of his chair laughing. Red-faced and hooting, he rolled on the porch, clutching his sides and gasping for air.

Galina appeared in the cabin doorway, frowning, and shaking her head at the childish bunch of rowdy men.

"Now, now, gentlemen. I hate to break up your fun, but—"

"Oh, Galina, dear. We were just getting warmed up, dear," her husband, Ivan, argued lying red-faced on the porch.

"Well, Ivan honey you look more worn out than warmed up."

Galina, no longer amused, glowered at the teasing men and crossed her arms and tapping her foot.

"Gentlemen, we are serving up the food that Father Slavik's brought from the parish. Ivan, dear, you and P'etro can eat with the other animals in the barn."

"Well, then, it's time to separate the gentlemen from the animals," the doctor announced.

"Good luck with the hay, you two," Sergey whispered.

"God be with you, children," the priest said, blessing them with the sign of the cross.

P'etro helped Ivan to his feet. Looking at him, P'etro raised an eyebrow.

"Look at the mess you have gotten us into now." He teasingly scoffed.

"Well, you threw fuel on the fire."

Giggling, Ivan poked P'etro in the ribs.

"Come on, old man."

As evening approached Ivan and Sergey left to see to their daily chores. The women carried on in the kitchen, chatting away as they cleaned and made last-minute preparations for the new arrival. While they were busy, P'etro went to the barn to see to his own animals and chores.

After his chores, P'etro was sitting on the porch, watching the sun set, when a faint moan echoed from behind the closed door. Nervously, he held his breath and looked at Father Slavik, who calmly continued to move his lips in silent prayer. Before P'etro could say a word, a loud, painful moan shattered the silence. P'etro's heart filled with trepidation as he stepped into the cabin. Galina opened the bedroom door to reassure him that everything was just fine, and there was no need to worry. While P'etro relaxed in his rocker by the hearth, he dreamed of a baby boy growing up to be his helper on the family farm. A scream from behind the closed door jolted him back into reality. P'etro ran with his heart in his throat to the bedroom. He crashed open the door and ignored the complaints of the midwives as he moved to Ilia's bedside.

"Are you alright? What can I do? What do you need? How can I help?" He called out in a concerned voice.

Looking at P'etro, Dr. Mykhailo smiled.

"P'etro, we are not finished here just yet, but everything is going to be all right. Please go back and pray with Father Slavik. I promise you can see Ilia later."

"If you say so. But if you need me, or anything …"

"Of course, P'etro."

When P'etro reentered the parlor, Father Slavik, who was kneeling at the altar, motioned for him to come and pray. Moments later, Ilia screamed again, and P'etro jumped. Remembering the doctor's words, P'etro tried to concentrate on his praying. Father Slavik patted P'etro on the shoulder, and his mind settled.

The evening dragged on at a slow pace. Occasionally, the silence was interrupted by the sound of Ilia struggling to give birth. Late evening gradually turned to night. The howling winds of the forest settled into evening whispers. Slowly, everything stilled. Broken clouds swirled across the sky. Together, the moon and stars flashed their heavenly glory. The night air hung heavy and cool in the river valley. Fog rolled up from the river and tumbled across the tundra. Father Time tirelessly ticked on. The never-ending, stressful night slowly marched toward the awaiting embrace of morning.

Earlier, the men had left for their respective homes to see to their duties. Later, Dr. Mykhailo sent the midwives home to care for their families, and Father Slavik left to see to his duties at the church. The food was cold, the teapot was empty, and P'etro was asleep in the old rocker. Only the doctor remained, patiently awaiting the birth of the child.

"P'etro, P'etro," Dr. Mykhailo whispered, shaking his shoulder.

"Wake up, P'etro."

"Uh. Oh. What is it?"

"Shush, P'etro, Ilia is resting for the moment. She's having a difficult time, and I am afraid we will be here for a while."

"Oh?"

"Everything is in hand, P'etro. Ilia is fine. The baby's fine. It's just that babies have their own time and their own way in matters like these. With a guiding hand, a little assistance and prayer, we will have the baby here soon."

"All right. What can I do to help?"

"I need Galina's help. Hitch Betsy to the wagon, ride to Ivan's, and—"

"No, I will not take your wagon."

"But—"

"God forbid if something were to happen to the wagon, our good doctor would be on foot. That can't happen."

"Then ride Betsy—"

"No, same thing. Something could happen. Thanks, but no thanks, comrade. It will be safer on foot and almost as quick by cutting through the forest."

Pausing thoughtfully, Dr. Mykhailo finally agreed.

"P'etro, be careful in the Southern Forest, and do not get swallowed up in one of those devilish bogs."

"I'll be careful."

"When you get to Ivan's, have him ride like the wind to Bakota, and tell Father Slavik I need him. Have the priest come as quick as possible."

The doctor's words sent a chill through P'etro.

"All right."

"Now go and bring Galina back with you."

P'etro nodded.

"P'etro, be careful in the forest."

Dr. Mykhailo smiled and placed his hands on P'etro's broad shoulders.

"Everything is going to be all right, but I need a little help to make it so."

"Sure."

Without another word, P'etro ran to the kitchen. He stuffed his pistols in his belt, grabbed his hunting knife, and darted out the door.

Once away from the cabin and under the shimmering moonlight, P'etro's mind flooded with thoughts of his loving wife and unborn child. Struggling through the undergrowth, his pace slowed but his imagination ran wild with haunting scenarios. When he stopped for breath at the edge of the Haunted Southern Forest, his muscles screamed with pain and his body ached with wrenching emotion. A knot of anxiety twisted in his stomach as he gazed into the forest and saw a gray shadow fog moving through the trees. A hot breeze made the fog boil, twist, and knot. P'etro took a deep breath, exhaled, and ran into the forest.

Cresting a hill, he heard water singing, and he smiled. A gust of wind blew him into childhood memories. The memory magically transformed him, and he became a child running barefoot through the Russian woodland. With each step, the twilight exploded with wondrous emotions of the past.

Under the star-splashed sky, the Brotherhood ran into the forest. "The Bear", "the Fox", and "the Boar" ran with P'etro down narrow trails and across creeks at breakneck speed. Together, they raced to the swimming hole and jumped in.

P'etro was abruptly jolted back to the reality of the moment by the spine-chilling howl of a pack of wolves. Stopping, he listened as his mind vividly portrayed deadly scenes of the Southern Forest legends.

No time for demons and devils. If the Southern Forest wants a piece of me, it will have to catch me first. Bless me, Father. I must go!

As his body surged with adrenaline, P'etro ran on.

CHAPTER 6

Mysterious Borderlands

Splashing down a creek to throw the wolf pack off his scent, P'etro rounded a sharp bend. As he ducked under a limb that was hanging in the bend of the creek, he tripped, nearly falling into the muck at the water's edge. He steadied himself and resumed his sprint.

P'etro stopped and sat on large rock in the creek to catch his breath. While resting, he noticed that an eerie silence had fallen over the forest. The silence made his ears ring.

When the forest is quiet, danger is near. Something is out there.

P'etro looked around the moonlit forest, but he didn't see anything unusual or out of place. With his senses on high alert, P'etro tried to feel the pulse of the forest. When the hair on his neck stood up, P'etro decided the time to speculate was over. Splashing cool water on his face, he rose as the howls of the wolf pack pierced the silence again.

"Persistent little puppies," he whispered.

P'etro began jogging back down the shallow creek. When the pack howled again, he realized they were closing in. Somehow, they had picked up his scent. P'etro knew he would have to leave the creek and try to lose the wolves some other way.

Farther down the creek, he spotted a trail leading into the forest. The howling was growing louder and closer as he dashed out of the water and ran through the woods. Deep in the heart of the forest, he came to a larger creek. The water was swift but shallow. He splashed in and headed downstream, hoping to throw the pack off his scent. The farther he traveled down the creek, the steeper the creek banks became. Slowing his pace, he searched for a place in the steep bank to climb out.

P'etro tried to stop in the swift water, but he slipped on the uneven creek bottom, fell backward, and hit his head on a rock. He rolled over, moaned, and opened his eyes. Clusters of bright stars filled the sky. For what seemed like an eternity, he lay in the creek, trying to orient his brain to his surroundings. Finally, he struggled to a knee. Hot pain shot through his head and he felt a trickle of blood run down his neck. Dizzy, he fell back into the creek.

Moments later, he sat up and looked around. P'etro knew he was near the river and felt like he had been this way before. Everything felt so familiar. Yet he couldn't remember ever having been this far into the Southern Forest. Confused thoughts raced through his mind. Odd memories of a mangy old dog and a caveman flickered in his head. But he'd never met them. As soon as he tried to focus on them, they vanished. His mind brought up images of a crystal, a cloud, and a silver saber. When the wolves howled again—too close—the images vanished.

P'etro splashed water in his face to clear the fuzz from his mind. After several deep breaths, he looked for a way out of the creek. Both sides of the creek rose in steep banks that were impassable. As he surveyed the slopes, his eyes stopped on an unusual formation on one side of the creekbank. He frowned, rubbed his eyes into focus, and looked again.

What is *that?*

Walking down the creek, he stopped below the formation. He struggled to analyze what his eyes were seeing. A hole in the earth.

A cave?

P'etro gazed at the partially concealed large-mouthed cave.

That's impressive.

The cave was several feet above the water level. Climbing up the bank of the creek, he stepped inside the skylighted cave and gasped. There seemed to be no walls or ceiling. It was a massive cave, endless in every direction. In the cave, he saw a forest. He looked around in amazement. There was no visible cave end in sight.

Outside it was dark, but the inside of the cave was luminous. P'etro wondered where the light was coming from and how it got in.

Is this a dream? I'm bleeding from my fall, but I'm not dreaming.

Looking up, he gasped. He was staring into a starry sky with a harvest moon—but earlier there wasn't a harvest moon in the sky.

The moon had been full but not this bright.

What's happening here?

P'etro turned to step back outside, but the cave entrance had vanished. Puzzled, he looked around—the entrance was no longer there. It wasn't anywhere. He backtracked, but his tracks brought him back to where he started. But still no entry or exit. He was in a cave, with a starry sky, a harvest moon, and a forest. He was surrounded by trees, and the cave entrance was gone.

P'etro scratched his head and wondered. He took a deep breath and smelled the scent of pine in the air. He knelt, scooped up a handful of dirt, and smelled it. It smelled like dirt. Looking up, he saw the moon and stars but still didn't see an entrance. Then he noticed there were no forest sounds, and his worry grew. He took another deep breath and told himself not to panic. He even pinched himself to make sure he was awake.

How do I get to Ivan's from here?

Dr. Mykhailo needed him. Ilia needed him, and he didn't even know where he was. However, he knew he was trapped in a cave—if it really was a cave. He thought this must be another land, a different place, but he didn't understand what was happening. Taking a breath, P'etro decided to explore the forest. Perhaps he could find an exit somewhere.

Walking through the forest he noticed the eerie silence. There was the complete absence of animal, bird, and insect noises. He stepped into a plush meadow. He thought it odd that there wasn't a breeze in the meadow and that, like the forest, it was silent.

Coming to a trail, he decided army double-time was the quickest way to get to wherever he was going. So, he ran. As he ran, moonbeams danced on the leaves of trees. Their reflecting silhouettes formed various ghostly shapes of shadowy things that were keeping pace with him, yet they showed no aggression. He wondered where they came, what they were, and why they were following him.

Rounding a bend, P'etro stopped. The trail was blocked by ghostly figures, and they were speaking. At first, it sounded like gibberish to P'etro. As they continued, their speech became clearer. Though their lips hardly moved, P'etro heard them in his mind. Together, they spoke as one.

"We know who you are."

"How do you know me?"

"It matters not how we know. We know."

P'etro raised an eyebrow, cocked his head, and stared.

They suddenly vanished, and he wondered if they were enemies, spies, or friends.

Looking around, P'etro saw the shape of a shrouded structure illuminated by the silvery light of the harvest moon. He stopped, searched the area with his eyes, and silently moved closer.

It's a cabin.

P'etro's thoughts were suddenly interrupted by the sound of running water. Walking around the cabin, P'etro saw a stream running along one side. He bent and drank the cool water. Then he stepped into the stream and walked to the far bank. But when he reached the bank and tried to climb out of the stream, he couldn't. There was something invisible yet solid along the bank of the creek, and it impeded his way. Whatever it was, P'etro couldn't see it, but he could see through it.

Beyond the invisible barrier was a dimly lit colorless world. The stream was a border between the cave world and the dark world beyond. Squinting, he observed the foreboding land. An eerie feeling tingled down his spine as he watched shadowy shapes racing through the dark, charred forest.

P'etro turned and walked back to the cabin. On the ground around the cabin, lights began to quiver and flash. He froze and hypnotically watched the mysterious lights dance. As the lights flickered and swayed, he realized the ground around the cabin was littered with glass shards. Thousands of broken pieces of glass were everywhere. The dancing glass slivers were conducting a kaleidoscope show. After a distracted moment of enjoying the anomaly, P'etro raised his eyes and saw that all the cabin windows had been shattered; their glass was lying everywhere around the cabin. That meant something—or someone—had broken the windows from the inside.

But why?

P'etro continued his inspection of the cabin from a safe distance. He saw that the cabin door was partially open. When he stepped on the porch, he noticed a sign tacked to the door that read, Welcome to the Borderlands.

He creaked open the door, stepped inside the eerie cabin, and was met by a screaming raven that clawed at his eyes. Swatting with one hand and protecting his eyes with the other, he stumbled into the kitchen. The raven flew away.

The cabin looked empty, except for a table and chair in front of the hearth. In the kitchen was another table and chair. Beyond the kitchen table was a broom closet with the door ajar. A dim light flickered all around the door, illuminating black bird feathers. It wasn't a normal bright light from a candle or lantern. It was a dark light with a dim glow and a murky aura that made everything look odd.

Curiously, he watched the beaming light as it flowed out from under the closet and lit up the kitchen in a strange sort of way. It gave the room a dreamy, otherworldly look and feel.

A faint sound like the crackling of a fire came from the closet. P'etro gazed at it curiously and wondered what was going on. He didn't smell smoke, but he heard fire sizzling and burning. Pulling off his shirt to extinguish the fire, he ran to the broom closet and opened the door. He was startled to see that there was no fire. Instead, he saw the black light shining through cracks in the closet floor. The light was under the floor, and it was dancing and crackling like fire.

When he examined the floor, he discovered a trap door. He carefully began lifting the door. After raising it only a few inches, the door shot open like a spring-loaded trap. P'etro staggered, slipped, and plummeted into the closet hole, hitting his head as he fell. P'etro grabbed the edge of the closet floor with one hand to stop his fall.

Dangling in midair by one hand, he took a moment to allow his head to stop swimming. As his dizziness waned, he tried in vain to grab the floor with his other hand and pull himself up. One last time, he pulled upward with all his might and grabbed the floor with his other hand. Taking a breath, he tugged, struggled, and heaved his body upward. This time, he pulled himself up and out of the hole.

With his feet dangling in the hole, P'etro sat on the edge, allowing his aching body to recover. When he rubbed the back of his head, he felt blood run through his fingers and down his neck. He had reinjured his head wound. Then a strong, hot hand grabbed his ankle and pulled him down. P'etro plummeted into the hole.

Ilia screamed in pain, breathed, and screamed again.

"Where is P'etro? Where is Galina?"

"Ilia, everything is fine. I sent P'etro to get her," Dr. Mykhailo explained.

"Why aren't they back?"

"I'm positive they are on their way."

Pain shot through Ilia's body, and she screamed and closed her eyes.

"Samuil! My baby! Samuil!"

"Your baby is fine."

"But—"

"Everything is all right, Ilia."

"No, it's not. P'etro is in trouble. I know it. I feel it. We must help him!"

"He's fine, Ilia. And he'll be back soon with Galina."

At end of another long labor pain, Ilia shouted impatiently.

"No! The Borderlands are dangerous! The Shadow Lands terrifying!! And the Badlands are deadly!!"

"What?"

"They're dangerous. And vile. And filled with evil spirits and demons!" Ilia explained deliriously.

Another severe pain struck, and Ilia screamed.

"Breathe, Ilia. Breathe. That's it."

The doctor wiped her face with a cool, damp cloth.

"Oh, my baby! My baby!"

"Ilia, breathe … that's it. Breathe."

"P'etro's lost! He's gone! He needs our help! And we need his."

In pain, she paused and rolled her head from side to side.

"They're coming for Samuil."

"Who?"

"They're coming for us all."

"What?"

Ilia passed out.

As P'etro fell, he watched the black light disappear. Then he landed on something that stopped his fall, but he wasn't on solid ground. He was suspended in midair, and the air smelled strange. He had landed in a dark shadow cloud. Red lightning streaked through the cloud, knocking him down. Body sizzling, he tried to move but couldn't. He sensed a dark presence and knew something evil was nearby. From within the darkness, he heard something unnatural. It sounded like a growl, but it became a voice.

"Welcome to the world of shadows, P'etro."

"What?"

"You are in the Shadow Land."

"Who are you?"

"I am the Shadow Lord. Yes, I am the darkness. I am the shadow. I am the evil. I am the destroyer. I am he who will destroy Samuil."

"No! I won't let that happen."

"You can't stop it. I am he who will destroy everything and everyone you love. Then I'll destroy you."

"No! I won't allow it! I will fight you! I will destroy you! I will destroy the destroyer!"

"No, you won't. You can't. It's already beginning."

"No!" P'etro shouted.

With renewed strength, he struggled and stood, bouncing oddly in the cloud matter.

"I will fight you! I will beat you. I will—"

The darkness laughed menacingly.

"You and yours are mine, P'etro. It's only a matter of time until I'm strong enough."

Slowly, the cloud twisted and began to dissipate. P'etro fell. After splashing into a pond, he surfaced, swam to the shore, and crawled to the bank. Deep in the forest, a speck of dim gray light appeared like the black light in the cabin. It knotted, twisted, and swirled through the dark forest. Rolling into the shadow fog, it raced toward him. In the blink of an eye, it enveloped him.

I'm so cold. No, I'm hot. No, I'm both.

Within the fog, P'etro heard strange noises and saw ghostly figures. As he struggled to make sense of it, a sinister voice whispered, "I'm coming."

As the fog tumbled and coiled, P'etro closed his eyes and prayed for the return of reality. Opening his eyes, he looked up and saw a very large white bird fly across the sun and dive into the forest.

P'etro wanted to run, but he couldn't see a way out of the fog. Staring into the smoky vision of nothingness, he saw a blue light in the dark forest. It looked far away and dim, but it was pulsing and flickering. Slowly turning and gently rolling, the faint glimmer brightened. Suddenly, it flared into a blue mist. As it rolled to P'etro, silver streaks flashed within, and it grew into a blue cloud.

Swirling through the forest, the glowing blue cloud flashed with blue and silver lightning. It stopped, hovered, strengthened and suddenly, exploded tossing P'etro onto the ground and filling the forest with and the shadow fog with its silver-blue light.

P'etro watched as black and blue light flared and swirled together into the sky. Dark and silver vortexes crashed together as the encounter continued at a vicious pace. A blue fog spun-out of the fray and rolled toward him. He smiled as he felt its warm radiance pulsate all around him and then within him.

Lighting flashed and he looked to see the blue and gray clouds spiraling above the treetops. Entangled black and silver, red and blue lightning flashed as the clouds tumbled through the forest violently. Twisting, writhing, and shaking the ground the violent mass rolled away, as angels and demons, monsters and saints, heroes and dragons, all battling within it. Deep inside, he felt uneasy.

A huge wolfhound and a white-bearded old man with a silver sword step out of a low-hanging silver cloud. They seemed familiar.

P'etro rubbed his chin and tried to remember them.

"Do I know you, comrade?"

The old man spoke in a mesmerizing tone. "Oh yes, P'etro. Yes, yes. It's time to remember. He-he."

His memory clicked.

"Yes, I do remember! I know you. I was a boy. And you are the man in the cloud at the circus."

"Yes, P'etro. Yes, yes. You remembered. That's good. I am

Nikolai of the Caves, and this is Wolf Killer."

Wolf Killer barked.

"P'etro, you just watched something strange and unusual."

"Yes, but—"

"No buts, no buts. No, no, no. You saw what you saw."

"Yes, I did."

"Do you understand?"

"No."

"Soon you will. Yes, yes. One day soon it will begin. Soon, soon, soon. When it does, I will need your help. And Samuil will too. Yes indeed, yes indeed."

"Samuil?"

"Yes, Samuil."

"But—"

"I know, I know, he's not here yet, but he will be very soon."

Wolf Killer whined.

"I'll need your help too, old boy. Yes, yes."

The sky rumbled, and the trio ran for the safety of a small cave. Inside, they watched as black hail pounded the forest and dark rain soaked the ground. The forest was devastated. The landscape was brown and scarred.

"Is this the beginning?"

"No, no. Relax, relax. This is but one of many preludes. The shadows are just testing the waters. He-he-he. Watch, watch."

Slowly, Nikolai's silver cloud rose into the sky and transformed into a giant blue rain cloud. The blue cloud dripped rain from the heavens, and a magical transformation began. Gradually, a new forest, river, and valley began to appear.

"Come, P'etro. Come, come, come. You must go."

"Go where?"

"To the Borderland Ocean."

"Yes, but what—"

"I have sent someone there to meet you. And that is the beginning of where it begins. Yes. Indeed."

Nikolai took P'etro by the hand and led him to the silver cloud. P'etro stepped into the cloud and rose into the air. Suspended in the cloud, he began to drift. Like a feather in the breeze, he floated along. It felt strange to travel without walking or moving a muscle.

Though P'etro was adrift, he felt safe. No, he felt hopeful. Then he heard the melody of the singing water. His heart jumped with joy, and his spirit smiled. P'etro saw his familiar land, river, rolling valley, and forest. Blinking, he saw his cabin. But everything was blue.

Gradually, the cloud floated, flickered, and drifted through the sky, heading beyond the familiar into the unknown. P'etro fought to remain awake, but the last thing he remembered seeing was the blue forest that looked like his forest back home. The last thing he sensed was being afloat on the cloud.

Someone was singing, and it was a lovely voice. The sound was so graceful, enchanting, and familiar. He opened his eyes and saw a tiny angel fluttering beside him, singing softly. It was the most beautiful song P'etro had ever heard.

How?

For a while, P'etro felt at ease and rested. Then he was falling. Or was he flying? He couldn't tell. Out of the surrounding blue, he heard the rhythm notes of surging waves breaking on shore. As ocean spray soaked his beard, P'etro looked about more closely. He was standing on the shoreline of the Borderland Ocean.

Again, P'etro heard singing, making his spirit stir and his heart fill with joy. And he remembered. P'etro couldn't believe his ears.

It's Ilia? She is here. But how?

"Ilia."

"Yes, P'etro, I'm here."

"I've been waiting P'etro. I knew you would come. And now you're here."

"Ilia, how did you get to the Borderland Ocean?"

"I came in a blue cloud, like you."

"But your labor, the birth, the baby?" P'etro asked, touching her protruding belly.

"Yes, P'etro, it's not over yet. There's a battle coming. You will have to fight for all our lives. You must be strong, P'etro. You must fight. You must save us all."

P'etro was silently thinking.

Her lovely face, beautiful voice, and radiant spirit was worth fighting for.

Then he looked at her questioningly.

"But how?"

"You shall see. You shall learn."

"Now you sound like Nikolai of the Caves."

"Nikolai is the one who told me."

P'etro nodded and gazed at the ocean.

"Listen P'etro. The sea breeze, the ocean spray, the surf, and the sunset—it's all so wonderful, P'etro. I've never seen the sun dip into the ocean. Have you?"

P'etro frowned and drooped.

"A long time ago, Ilia. A long time ago."

"Oh, the war."

"Yes, the war."

"I'm sorry. I wasn't thinking. I didn't ..."

"It's all right, Ilia."

"No, it's not. You've just gotten here, and I've already ruined the moment. Oh P'etro, I'm so sorry."

"Ilia, kick off your shoes, take my hand, and we'll dance in the breaking waves along the seashore."

Tossing her head into the gentle wind, Ilia looked like a teenager. No, she looked like an angel. Her countenance glowed. Ilia smiled, and P'etro laughed as the sea breeze blew long strands of brown hair in her face. Beams of moonlight illuminated her beauty and took P'etro's breath away. Ilia took his hand, and together they sashayed through the Borderland Sea.

Sitting by the seaside, Ilia wiggled her feet into the sand and listened to waves break gently on the seashore. P'etro sat in the sand beside her and put his arm around her petite shoulders. Ilia looked up at the starry sky and began to hum. Quietly, P'etro listened.

"I love all of this, P'etro."

"Yes."

"Let's stay here forever. It's so beautiful, so peaceful. I could dance on the seashore under the twilight skies every night."

"Sure. I'll build our castle over there under the pines."

"Yes, it would be an ideal setting. Come dance with me under the stars."

P'etro took Ilia in his arms, and they waltzed barefoot in the sand by the seaside. Under the blushing moonlight, they lost themselves in the whimsical moment.

"You're the most beautiful ballerina I've ever seen on the salty sea."

Ilia blushed.

"I better be the only one."

"Of course, dear."

Ilia slapped him on the arm and then smiled. With a giggle and a kiss, they continued their seaside dancing. Abruptly, P'etro stopped dancing and stared out to sea. On the wings of the ocean breeze, he heard it.

The sound was faraway and barely audible but nonetheless, he recognized that wicked, hissing voice. The laugh made him remember; then it made him dread. P'etro knew what it was, and he didn't like what was coming. In his gut, he knew this was the beginning.

"P'etro, did you forget the steps?"

"No, my love," P'etro whispered, gazing into the sea.

"What is it?"

P'etro stepped away and stood quietly, staring into the night. Ilia walked up and took his hand. Both stared into the distant sea.

Then Ilia heard it too.

"They're coming, aren't they, P'etro?"

"Yes."

"I'm scared."

"Everything will work itself out, my love. But now I must go."

"I know. I love you. Be safe."

"Sorry I must leave you so soon after finding you. But for all our sakes, I must."

"I know, and I know you'll do right by us all. See you on the other side."

CHAPTER 7

Deadly Badlands

P'etro stood on the shore and prayed that Ilia would be safe during his absence. He was thankful that the Borderlands, in its strange way, had prepared him mentally for the upcoming struggle. Stepping into the moon-washed sea, P'etro watched and waited.

Slowly, a bright-blue bridge with shining silver railings and supports rose out of the misty sea. P'etro stepped onto the mysterious bridge and began walking across the ocean. A mile into his walk, he heard a voice from the ocean and stopped.

"P'etro, they said you would be coming this way."

P'etro turned and looked but saw nothing. Then—a flicker of movement from the water, and a creature appeared before him. Before P'etro's eyes she turned multiple shades of brown. She saw his puzzled look and explained.

"I turned the color of the ocean to hide from a leviathan."

"I have heard that seahorses can change colors, but I've never seen it until now."

Looking at P'etro, she blushed turning a bright red.

"I'm sorry if I misspoke." He apologized.

The giant seahorse nodded and turned green, her tiny wings flickering steadily.

"Do I know you?" He asked.

"Nikolai sent me to help you."

To his surprise, she leaped on the bridge beside P'etro and transformed into a wrinkled old witch with white hair and a wart on her crooked nose.

"My name is Kalypsis, the Wicked Witch of the Sea."

P'etro tried unsuccessfully not to stare, but her silver rings, bejeweled bracelets, shining diamonds, worn leather boots, and burlap dress were unusual. Kalypsis poked him with her magical walking stick and grinned a toothless smile.

"Walk with me, P'etro, and I'll tell you about the Badlands and the beginnings."

He nodded, feeling he could trust her. They began to amble along the seashore.

"As you know, the Borderland is a mysterious place. However, the Badlands are full of evil and danger. Monstrous shadow creatures and all sorts of demons roam the Badlands. You must always be aware."

"What about the beginnings?"

"The beginning begins in the Badlands."

"So that's it?"

"Yes, my friend."

"When will this end?"

"No one really knows. Perhaps never. Perhaps with Samuil's birth."

P'etro absorbed the knowledge of the Wicked Witch of the Sea as they walked together. Finally, they came to dry land and a forest. Kalypsis transformed into a beautiful palomino mare.

"Mount up, P'etro, and I'll take you through the forest."

A short distance into the forest, they came to a trail and followed it to the mouth of a great river.

"P'etro, beyond the river lies the burning Badlands." She said with a shaky voice full of emotional memories and stress.

P'etro smiled and patted her on the neck. Around them, P'etro saw fires raging in the forest, the meadows, and the hillsides. Sitting on the bank of a river, he rested and waited and shivered with a chill as he thought about what lay ahead.

Kalypsis transformed once more and splashed into the river. With his mind racing and heart pounding, he mounted the transparent blue seahorse and entered the river. The water rose and caressed them. With a thought, Kalypsis directed the water, and in a flash, they were on the shore of the Badlands.

The sky was dark and filled with soot. Thunder rumbled in the background, and dark shadows lurked in the forest, but far above, there were dim silver lights. A dark fog rolled through the land, reached into the sky, and ballooned into a cloud. The cloud smothered the dim lights.

Urgency choked P'etro's mind, and he clenched his fists. Everything about this place was unnatural. A huge flaming red eagle burst out of the sun, flew into the sky, and soared above the Badlands. Circling above gray clouds, it flew high and then plummeted toward P'etro. He watched anxiously as the magnificent bird approached him.

"It's beginning, P'etro. Surrender to the eagle," the seahorse instructed.

He took a deep breath and stood stone still.

The descending eagle extended its talons and grabbed P'etro. It soared high over burning mountains, and then dropped him. As he fell toward the earth, he saw his life flash before him. He closed his eyes, prepared for death, but he landed on the neck of a giant fire phoenix, and two silver swords magically appeared in his hands.

The golden green-eyed phoenix brandished black feathers from its fiery death, white feathers from it rebirth, and red feathers from a bloody battle that was about to begin. P'etro rode the giant phoenix high in the sky, with the wind in his face. Gliding over the Badlands, he saw shadow strings seep from the leaves of the forest and gather. Red lightning flashed in the sky, and evil dripped like rain.

P'etro saw something appear in the clouds. Crashing through the fire and smoke, a demon champion of darkness appeared on the back of a monstrous shadow dragon. Fire poured from the dragon as it opened its mouth to roar. Flames burned through the sky, and the demon rider laughed hideously.

P'etro and the fire phoenix circled high in the sky. Looping through the burning gray clouds, the phoenix turned to face the foe. In turn, the dragon twisted in the sky, preparing for battle. Through the darkness, the demon rider attacked with dragon fire. In return, P'etro and the phoenix attacked with Nikolia's silver lightning and blue wind.

The demon rode hard and fast as fire and smoke blazed from the mouth of the dragon. Atop his phoenix, P'etro flew straight and true. Bolts of lightning magically flashed from the phoenix's talons. The two fliers collided in the boiling sky and fought ferociously. Lightning flashed and thunder bellowed. The battling crusaders flew through the dark heavens, rolling, clawing, and burning.

Fire streaked the heavens, and smoke boiled from the shaking earth. Darkness and light collided like fire and ice. The dripping moon turned black, and the fading sun blushed to orange as the battle escalated. Light and dark struggled. Smoke and fire twisted together as the phoenix and the dragon fought.

The dragon tore into the mighty phoenix with molten teeth and fiery claws. Scorched feathers burned in the sky. The phoenix screeched a terrible scream of pain and fear. P'etro felt her wings falter but then steady. The mighty phoenix fought back with her razor-sharp spurs of fire and lightning. P'etro and the demon clashed swords. Hand to hand, they battled and bled.

Looping out of a smoky cloud, the dragon caught the phoenix off guard and smothered her with fire. The phoenix flamed red, her spirit blazed blue, and her soul burned white-hot. With sheer determination and the last of her strength, the phoenix flew fast and hard toward the dragon's side.

With his silver swords in hand, P'etro slashed at the demon rider but instead ripped open the dragon's throat. The wounded demon plummeted. Exhausted, P'etro and his bird fell. The burning phoenix and the bleeding dragon collided. They fought with the last of their strength. Together, they tumbled through a flaming cloud of burning feathers and bloody scales to certain death in the fiery mountains.

Exhaustion seized P'etro's mind. His muscles ached, his eyes burned, and his body smoked. As he fell, panic chilled his heart, his limbs tingled, and his consciousness slipped away. When he hit the water, he sank into the river's darkness.

"P'etro! P'etro!" Kalypsis yelled as she ran to the river and splashed in.

But P'etro couldn't hear her above the melody of a beautiful singing voice from the river bottom. Magically, the voice became voices, and the melody grew even more hypnotic. When P'etro's feet touched the floor, a sinister hiss bowled through the murky Badland River.

Kalypsis nudged P'etro with her nose.

"Climb on, and let's get out of here before it's too late."

"It's already too late."

"What do you mean?"

"My feet are stuck in the mud."

P'etro watched as a blue mist rose from the river mud. Then a silver light flicker in the water. When the light and mist met, they erupted and spun into a giant waterspout, sucking the river dry. Kalypsis shimmered, transformed once again and they walked out of the riverbed.

The Wicked Witch of the Sea smiled.

"P'etro, my friend, it's time for me to return to my home."

"Thank you for all you've done. I would have never made it this far without you."

"I didn't do much. We're alive because of the light and mist."

"Yeah, and I'm relieved it's over."

"P'etro, as I told you, the beginnings are not over. They are strangely intertwined with Samuil's birth and perhaps his life going forward."

"And the shadow world?"

"It's the lifeblood of the beginnings."

"How can that be?"

"My friend, that's a discussion for another time. It's time for you to go. Follow that trail through the Badland Forest. If you vary from the trail, the beginnings will never end. If you stay with the trail, you will find and battle the beginnings."

"How will I overcome them?"

"That's all I can tell you. My task is complete, and I must return to the sea."

She turned and walked away, bracelets clinking, her long skirts swirling about her feet. Her feet left footprints in the sand.

She must be real.

P'etro ran down the trail and through the dark forest until he came to a thick shadow fog. He took a step to walk around it but stopped when he recalled Kalypsis words. Taking a deep breath, he stepped into the fog.

The fog was thick, and the air was heavy and dank. P'etro looked around for the trail, but it had disappeared, and he was standing in muck. At first the dark fog was deadly silent, but farther into fog, he heard bloodcurdling screams and painful shrieks.

Finally, P'etro heard the familiar sounds of domesticated animals. With renewed courage, he pressed on, and when he heard an ox bellow, he knew there must be a homestead ahead. When P'etro arrived at the barn, he believed he was home. Looking in the stalls, he saw his own ox.

"Big Boy, I'm home. I don't know how but I'm home."

Big Boy bellowed. Thrilled he found his ox, P'etro struggled through the dark fog toward where the cabin should be. He tripped over a sandbox and fell.

This is Samuil's sandbox. How do I know that? Samuil is yet to be born. This place is a future reflection of home.

A beastly roar shocked P'etro back to the moment, and he stumbled toward the cabin. Peeking through a window, he saw his handmade double-rocker sitting in front of the hearth. His favorite teacup and handmade tobacco pipe were beside the rocker. The bear rug was on the floor.

Howling winds began to blow as a dark storm rumbled toward the cabin. As the tempest intensified, P'etro realized he should seek shelter inside the cabin. When he did, he stumbled into an entangled time with the beginnings. Confused, he closed his eyes and attempted to make sense out of this crazy situation.

Where is Ilia? Dr. Mykhailo? How is this happening?

P'etro saw shadow threads swirling through the cabin, seeking out dark corners to hide. Ghostly shapes lingered in the darkness, visible only in his peripheral vision. Hovering over the cold hearth, red eyes stared, and eerie shrieks erupted.

Outside, hurricane-force winds began to roar. Debris slammed into the cabin. Windows shattered. Blinding dust sent P'etro to his knees in the corner of the cabin. As quickly as it had all begun, it stopped, and out of the silence a hideous hiss arose. P'etro found a candle and lit it.

From the bedroom, a woman's voice painfully called out.

"P'etro!"

"Ilia? Is that you, Ilia?

Another plea rang out. "Help me! Hurry!"

P'etro burst through a door to see his beloved Ilia struggling to give birth. Father Slavik was still there, and Dr. Mykhailo called out, "The window, P'etro!"

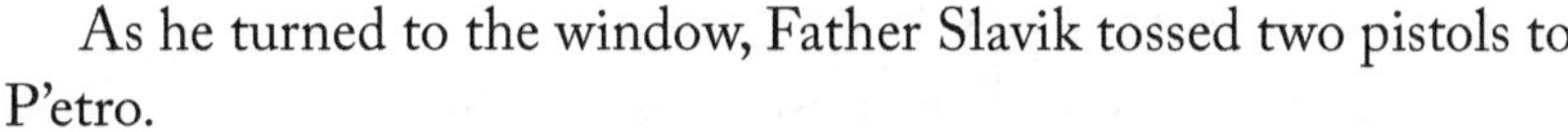

As he turned to the window, Father Slavik tossed two pistols to P'etro.

"Shoot quick, or we're all dead!" Father Slavic yelled.

P'etro fired. The priest sprinkled the bullet with holy water as it flew by. The window exploded, shards of glass sailed through the room, and a ghostly goulash shape lay dead on the floor.

Father Slavik gazed at the shape and gasped.

"P'etro, be careful and be aware, my son. Evil is present everywhere. Dark spirits are lurking."

Suddenly, Ilia screamed, "P'etro!"

Spinning, P'etro turned to face her.

"Kill the monster, P'etro! Kill it!" Ilia pleaded.

Adrenaline raced through P'etro's body, and he fired the second pistol. As the bullet flew from the barrel of the pistol, the priest sprinkled it. The bullet hit its mark. A stalking devil shrieked in pain and fell.

A multitude of sinister creatures began hissing in the night outside the cabin, where they circled and waited. The priest handed P'etro his reloaded pistols. P'etro noticed they were still dripping with holy water and hoped they would fire.

Dark figures raced through the cabin as smoke from the netherworld boiled out of the hearth. Choking on smoke and strangling on evil, P'etro blindly fired the pistol, killing the smoldering demon. P'etro tossed the empty pistol to Father Slavik for reloading and took aim at another evil spirit. P'etro fired, and the priest threw a bottle of holy water in the air. The bullet hit the priest's bottle, and holy water fell like rain, soaking all the inhabitants in the room. Hosts of evil spirits fell dead on the floor. Other demons screamed hideously and fled. Before long, the room began refilling with hordes from Hades.

With pistols blazing, P'etro fired as the priest reloaded. Again, dark spirits and ghostly shapes filled the room. Volley after volley of lead flew through the room. Sanctified gunpowder filled the air, and pistol fire lit up the night. But still the demons came.

"I'm sorry, my son, but there is no more ammunition," the priest said.

P'etro dropped the pistols.

"Take this, my son." The priest handed P'etro a saber.

"It is purified and has been blessed by the bishop."

P'etro yelled and charged into the darkness. While P'etro battled the malevolent presence, Ivan "the Boar" burst through the cabin door astride Major. Rearing and kicking, Major trampled demons while Ivan leaped through the air with swords slashing. P'etro fought his way to Ivan. Together, they fought the devils and forced them back to the hearth, where demons were descending in multitudes.

Fire blazed from the heavens. The cabin shook. A ball of fire hit the cabin. The foundation cracked, and the hearth exploded. Unholy muck burned. Smoke roiled through the busted windows. The night filled with the stench of demon flesh. The wind blew black ash across the moon. Stars disappeared in a blanket of fiery soot.

Ivan lit a lantern and set it on a table near Ilia, who was still panting, still deeply in labor. Even though he was wounded and bleeding, P'etro struggled to raise himself on a knee. A sinister voice began calling out to P'etro, but something from the beyond warned him to be very careful. P'etro struggled to stand. Wobbling and unsteady, he looked around the room.

As the voice faded, P'etro stared into the darkness. An unnatural presence hung in the cabin. An angry whisper slid from the silence. P'etro's ears rang, his mind raced, and his body ached. Falling to his knees, he doubled over in pain and collapsed on the floor. His head was foggy, he was exhausted, and his heart was heavy.

Out of the shadows, two red eyes stared menacingly. Something rubbed against P'etro's arm, sending a shock through his body. His mind engaged. Adrenaline surged. Just beyond his reach, P'etro felt something menacing.

A hot breath blew across his neck. There was a roar in the darkness, and something wet dripped on his cheek. Exhausted, he stepped back. A huge paw knocked him to the cabin floor. While lying there, he heard the howl of a hound, and everything turned blue.

Opening his eyes, P'etro tried to focus. He sat up and waited for his vision to clear. In front of him sat a large beast. P'etro wondered whether the beast was friend or foe. The beast took a step toward him. P'etro froze. The beast licked him and barked.

A dog?

By the flickering light of a candle, P'etro saw a scruffy old man standing beside the shabby dog. Both were watching him. The old man fidgeted, clearly unable to sit still, and the old dog scratched.

Neither pair of eyes left P'etro. Struggling, P'etro stood up.

"Oh. My, my, you've come back," a voice said.

P'etro flinched, rubbed his face, and tried to focus.

"Well, well. Welcome, welcome. You're back to the land of the living, my friend."

"Yes, yes. Welcome back, welcome, welcome." "Welcome back?" P'etro asked.

"Oh yes."

"Where have I been?"

"You have been here and there. Here and there."

P'etro rubbed the back of his head and realized he was bleeding.

"Easy my friend. You have a big knot and a gash in the back of your head."

"Where am I?"

"You are in a cave."

"A cave?"

"Yes. A cave. My cave. Yes, yes."

It was a large cathedral cave with a stream. The air was cool and brisk, and it was lit by sunshine slithering through cracks between boulders.

"Nikolai, what happened?"

"Oh, my, my. Do you remember anything? Anything at all?"

"Not much. It was a dream, wasn't it?"

"Oh no, no. But yes, yes. I think. Oh well, it was, and it wasn't." Nikolai cocked his head and considered P'etro.

"What?"

"How rude of me, oh my. Forgive me. You've been through a lot tonight."

"How did I get here? Did you find me?"

"Full of questions. Yes, yes, of course."

"You brought me here?"

"Yes, we did, we did. Wolf Killer found you passed out and bleeding in the forest. Or was it the barn?" Wolf Killer barked.

"Oh, yes, yes. Very well. I patched you up, best I could."

"Thank you."

"No need. No, no. It's my privilege—P'etro, the hero of the Allied Shadow War! The rock of the Brotherhood. My, my! The war hero in my cave!"

Nikolai began to sing and dance around in circles. Wolf Killer joined in, howling and chasing his tail. Amused, P'etro watched until they stopped.

"Nikolai, I remember floating and falling in the dark."

His voice steadied as his memories returned.

"There was a blue light. And there was blood, wind, storms, and demons."

"Easy now; you had a bad fall. Wolf Killer saw you and then he found you."

"Saw me?"

"Oh yes, yes, he has visions, you know. Bad dog. Naughty, naughty, naughty."

"Uh, you were there too. Weren't you?"

"Well."

"You brought me back here. You and the blue mist."

"Well, that's a crystal-blue story for another hazy time."

"Oh?"

"You were going somewhere in a hurry."

"Yes. I was. I am. I must get to Ivan's place, but I don't know where I am or how to get there."

"Oh my. Why hurry? Why, why? It's not often that Wolf Killer and I have company. And we never have heroes. Never, never."

P'etro glanced about the dim cave. Despite that it felt safe to him, he wanted to leave.

"I'm in a hurry. My wife's having a baby, and she's in trouble. I've got to get help."

"Oh, I see. What will you name the boy?"

"We don't know if it is a boy or not."

"I do."

Shocked, P'etro looked at the old man curiously.

"How do you know it is a boy?"

"Wolf Killer told me. And his name is Samuil, a sandy-haired blue-eyed baby boy."

"How…"

"Wolf Killer saw it in his vision."

P'etro stared in disbelief at the two.

"I see that I should reassure you, young P'etro. Ilia is fine. So is Samuil."

"How do you know?"

"Wolf Killer told me."

"Oh."

"Samuil is my friend. Yes, yes. He's a good boy. And he loves Wolf Killer. Indeed, indeed."

Wolf Killer barked.

"Nikolai…"

"I know, I know. You have questions, and you need to get to Ivan's cabin. Wolf Killer, take P'etro to the Southern Forest."

"But—"

"Don't worry. He knows the way. Goodbye, P'etro. Goodbye, goodbye."

P'etro rose and Wolf Killer strode to his side. They ran out of the cave and disappeared into the night as the crystal in Nikolai's hand turned blue.

Running through the Borderland Forest, P'etro caught glimpses of shadowy shapes pursuing them. Quivering silhouettes raced through the forest, always ahead and just out of reach. Partially hidden by the rolling fog, demons darted from tree to tree, stalking them. When P'etro rubbed his unfocused eyes, the things vanished as quickly as they appeared. If Wolf Killer saw or smelled them, he never shied away from his trail-blazing duty. With a steady pace, the two clawed their way swiftly through the woods.

Finally, P'etro tripped, fell, and came to a stop when he hit a boulder. When he turned over, Wolf Killer jumped in his lap, his huge body squashing him down. P'etro pulled himself to a sitting position, but the hound growled.

"Easy, boy, easy. What is it? What's out there?"

Wolf Killer flashed his canines and whined.

Something wasn't right. P'etro could feel it. He could sense a change in the air. Everything was deathly still. The hair on his neck and arms stood up. Wolf Killer bristled. Together, they listened to the silence. Keenly aware, they waited. With senses tingling on high alert, they peered into the smoky forest.

Overhead, thick clouds tumbled through the sky, racing toward the horizon. Black streaks of lightning flashed in the heavens. The night air shook with thunder. Melting starlight dripped like candle wax as light vanished and the darkness grew.

"Wolf Killer, I don't like the shadow world."

The hound growled again, as if in agreement.

Unnatural sounds crackled in the forest. The screeches were eerie and otherworldly. Something scaly brushed against P'etro's arm, paralyzing him. With a furious bark, Wolf Killer sprang into action. Unable to move or see, P'etro listened as the struggle raged. The sounds of battle faded into the forest.

Alone in the dark, he listened and waited. P'etro saw a shimmering light floating in the dark sky. It lit up the night like a harvest moon, but the soft light was a radiant blue. For some reason the light was comforting, and its glow was strangely warm, even at a distance. The distance began to slowly close as the blue light moved in his direction.

Ivan? Sergey? No, it's Nikolai. I know that light.

Slowly, the forest went black, and then P'etro's world did too.

CHAPTER 8

Bewitched Beginnings

Half conscious, exhausted, and bleeding, P'etro collapsed on Ivan's front porch. Ivan opened the door and stared at him.

"P'etro, what happened to you?"

"It's the baby, Ivan! Dr. Mykhailo needs Galina's help."

"Galina!" Ivan yelled.

He quickly repeated P'etro's words. Galina gathered her medical supplies as Ivan thundered off on Major.

P'etro stepped outside and walked to the road. A rustling at the edge of the forest made him limp faster down the dark road.

When the noise grew louder, P'etro reached for his pistols, but they were gone. He scanned the area and saw a tree limb at the edge of the road. He picked it up, took a deep breath, and readied himself to do battle with whatever was coming his way. At the very last moment, he recognized the rustling as that of a horse and buggy, with a bouncing lantern guiding the way. The buggy came to a stop in front of him. He reached out and rubbed Lady Girl's nose.

"Get in!" Galina yelled.

P'etro grinned, and quickly climbed in the buggy.

"Why didn't you wait for me?" Galina asked.

"I tried, but there was a voice in my head, calling me."

"Oh?" Galina responded, raising an eyebrow.

"Hold on, P'etro; here we go! Get up, Lady Girl!"

With a slap of the reins on Lady Girl's rump, they were off. The jolt sent P'etro slamming into the back of his seat.

In a flash, Lady Girl was at the cabin. P'etro helped Galina out of the buggy, and they rushed inside. They found Dr. Mykhailo continuing his struggle with Ilia and the baby. P'etro looked at the doctor.

"Everything going to be all right, P'etro."

P'etro knew that was his cue to exit the room.

"Galina, I'll see to Lady and the buggy."

"Thank you."

After bedding Lady down for the night, P'etro walked back to the cabin, brewed some tea, and took it to the caregivers. P'etro sat in a chair at Ilia's side. As he took Ilia's hand, she opened her eyes.

Seeing P'etro, she grinned.

"You're still here."

"Of course. I wouldn't be anywhere else."

Ilia touched his cheek with her palm.

"You are bleeding, P'etro."

"It's nothing. Galina will fix me up."

Ivan rode out of Bakota, with Father Slavik holding on for dear life. The priest prayed for Ilia, the baby, and Dr. Mykhailo, and he prayed he wouldn't fall off Major. In a cloud of dust, Ivan and Father Slavik arrived and rushed into the cabin. To P'etro's relief, they looked ready for whatever they might encounter. Weary and out of breath, they looked at Dr. Mykhailo with questions in their eyes. The doctor set down his cup of tea and nodded at his friends.

"Galina, we have unfinished business to attend to. Father, wash up, have a cup of tea, and join us, please. Ivan, go with him."

As they exited the room, the doctor looked at P'etro.

"You should go with them and have some tea."

As P'etro reached for the door, a pain-filled cry shattered the still night.

"P'etro! P'etro!" Ilia screamed.

P'etro rushed to her side. She lay in their bed, sweating and panting.

"P'etro! Hold my hand. Don't leave me. Don't leave me."

"Ilia, everything's fine. I'm here."

"I'm scared, P'etro. I need you. Don't leave me. Stay here with me."

Ilia winced and she squeezed P'etro's hand while the doctor calmly continued performing his medical magic.

Outside the bedroom door, Father Slavik relit candles and knelt to pray. While he prayed with his back to the hearth the Shadow Lord slid down the chimney and vanished into the candle smoke. From the smoke and grinned wickedly and stared with black eyes at Father Slavik.

"Priest, the time has come for me to claim what is mine. To take that which I have hidden in the womb of the chosen one."

"No! you have no right! Be gone beast!"

The Shadow Lord waved his hands, the candle lights blinked, and the priest flew out the door and rolled across the ground into a shadow fog where he lost all memory of the night's events. The shadow fog swirled to the Bakota church and dropped the priest on the floor of the church sanctuary. Everything went dark as time stopped and then wrinkled as the Shadow Lord smiled and left with what had been fated to him long ago.

When the dim light of morning kissed the eastern sky Ilia was holding a sandy-haired, blue-eyed baby boy.

After Dr. Mykhailo and Father Slavik left, P'etro sat on the porch. In the still of dawn's slowly gathering light, he sipped his tea. Though exhausted, his adrenaline-filled body couldn't relax, nor could his racing mind slow down. While watching the dim morning light dance above the trees, he was startled by the rustling in the woods.

A beast came charging out of the forest and right to the porch. With no sleep, no weapons, and no time, P'etro jumped to his feet and readied himself for the assault.

The beast leaped onto the porch, stopped, barked, and wagged his tail.

"A dog?" Woof!

"Where did …?

Woof, woof!

As P'etro stared at the mangy mutt, he noticed something tied around his neck. Taking the light-blue note from the hound, P'etro opened it and read:

> Hello, P'etro. Nikolai here. Congratulations on a new baby boy. Yes, yes, yes. Indeed, indeed. Sorry that I could not come, but I sent Wolf Killer instead. Yes, yes. Best regards to Ilia and Samuil. Regards, regards. Remember, P'etro, remember, remember. P'etro, it's time now to remember. Yes, yes indeed. Remember, remember, remember.
>
> Your comrade
> Nikolai

A trickle of memory flashed in P'etro's head.

Nikolai. Wolf Killer. The Badlands. The demons. The battle.

Woof!

"Oh. Wolf Killer, it's you. You gave me quite a scare, dog. You came to see Samuil?"

Woof!

"You did. Well, he's sleeping. Moaning won't help, and don't you dare howl. If you wake the baby, Ilia will whip you with her broom all the way back to the cave."

Woof!

"Shush, come on. I'll take you to see Samuil. You can see him through the window."

After seeing the sleeping child and mother, he and Wolf Killer sat enjoying the peaceful dawn. While sipping his tea, he noticed Wolf Killer bristle. Then he growled.

"Easy, boy, I heard it too. Something's in the forest."

P'etro petted the hound, calming him. Together, they stared through the hazy light into the forest. P'etro slowly rose to go into the cabin and fetch his pistols when Wolf Killer growled again. He petted the hound and focused on the edge of the forest.

A shuffling to his left caused P'etro to jerk and look.

Deer?

Wolf Killer bristled.

"Easy, boy."

Scanning the tree line, P'etro saw weasels, rabbits, squirrels, red foxes, and a polecat. As he puzzled over the unusual situation, the silent forest came alive. Every night creature he had ever heard simultaneously began its song. Frogs, lizards, and bugs of all sorts covered the yard. Fireflies lit up the dim dawn. P'etro sat, stared, and listened.

As first light flooded the eastern sky, morning sounds rustled through the forest. When the sun broke the horizon, color burst throughout the sky. The morning dew transformed the forest into a sparkling water-colored world as dawn's light danced atop the dewdrops.

Songbirds came to life as morning light spread. Soaring out of the forest, they circled the barn. Red, blue, purple—finches, sparrows, cardinals, and jays fluttered about joyfully. The morning flocks perched atop the cabin, landed on the fences, and filled the surrounding trees. Night songs quickly became day songs, and the new morning air teemed with joyful music.

P'etro and Wolf Killer watched and listened in amazement. He had never seen so many birds, nor had he ever seen them act like this. Their rapturous melody was pleasing to the mind and endearing to the soul. P'etro was grateful for their peaceful choruses after the night he had experienced.

He heard tapping on the windowsill.

"Ilia! My darling."

"Good morning, P'etro."

"Look, dear."

P'etro opened the bedroom window.

"Hear them? They are everywhere, Ilia."

"Yes, I heard them at first light, but I've never seen so many."

"Yes, there are thousands."

"Have you ever heard such a choir, P'etro?"

"No, never. And it's been like this all morning. They began before sunrise. The valley is different—strange. I thought it was just me because of the rough night and no sleep. I thought it was my fatigued mind playing tricks on me. But look at all the birds and all the animals."

"They're saying hello to Samuil, P'etro."

"What a hello."

"I must rest now. You should do the same."

"I will after I feed and water the oxen."

P'etro stepped back onto the porch, expecting to see Wolf Killer, but he was already gone. P'etro smiled. He was grateful for his visit and note. Carefully, so as not to step on any of the forest crawlers, P'etro made his way to the barn. As he walked into the barn, something caught his attention. In the diffused morning light, there was a glow coming from the forest. Curious, he stepped out of the barn, walked to the edge of the forest, and stared.

A flickering silver glowed in the forest air. P'etro's flesh tingled. He shook himself as a chill raced through his body. The cool morning breeze abruptly ceased, and he broke out in a sweat. A feeling of déjà vu washed over him.

Not again. Not now.

P'etro stepped into the forest and immediately sensed an obscure anomaly in the air. He stopped and quietly listened to the silent forest. In the distance, he saw a blue mist hovering and twisting above the forest floor. He watched as it cascaded along the creek and rolled to the porch. He looked down and saw that he was standing in the blue mist. He watched it spin and roll around his feet. Slowly, warmth spread through his body, and he felt peace flowing through his veins. Breathing deeply, P'etro looked up and saw a silver halo ringing the sun, which made the forest and vegetation take on a silvery glow.

The blue mist wove back through the trees, taking P'etro with it. As it slid into the Southern Forest, the ground abruptly buckled and cracked open. Black fire blazed, and shadow smoke collided with the blue mist. Light and darkness exploded through the sky, and P'etro fell into the creek. Blinking his weary eyes, he saw the entrance to a large half-hidden cave.

Then he heard the wicked voice.

"Beginning again may not come to the same end, but we will see when we meet again."

CHAPTER 9

Haunted Southern Forest

After struggling through a restless night, P'etro woke before dawn and thought about young Samuil. He couldn't believe how much Samuil had grown in just a few weeks. Sitting in front of the hearth with his cup of tea, P'etro watched the hearth flames dance on a cozy winter's night.

He sipped his tea and thought about his past blessing. It had all begun with meeting Ilia and when the tsar granted his land after the Allied Shadow War.

Many good men died in the Allied Shadow War, and their families never received any gift.

P'etro and Ilia were proud of their new homestead nestled in the Nieper River valley near the small village of Bakota. It was a good place to live and a great place to raise a family. He loved everything about his new life, family, and friends. Though it was a rugged lifestyle in a ruthless land, it was his longtime dream come true. P'etro took another sip of his tea and relaxed. It had been a good year—lots of rain and a bountiful crop.

He knelt to place another log on the fire, and his thoughts raced back to the indescribable horrors of the Allied Shadow War. The screams of dying men roared in his ears. The smell of gunpowder choked him. The image of streams running red with the blood of dead soldiers turned his stomach. As his mind raced with gory images of battle, something hot dripped on P'etro's hand, making him flinch.

"Ouch!"

"Oops, sorry."

"It's all right. You just startled me."

"Lost in thought?"

"Yes."

"The war?"

"Yes, sometimes it just comes. I don't know why."

"Here, tea and biscuits should help."

"It always does, dear; thank you."

Together they sat silently in the rocker watching the cozy fire crackle and send its comforting light and warmth through the cabin.

P'etro glanced outside and saw a winter storm rolling through the valley. The howling wind whistled through the frosted windows and swirled the landscape into portraits of icy beauty. The blizzard twisted snowdrifts into giant mountains of sculptured snow. Moonlight bathed the whitewashed land, making the snow crystals sparkle. The snowstorm was magically transforming the Nieper River valley into a winter wonderland.

An enticing aroma filled the cabin. Unable to resist, P'etro went into the kitchen for a peek. He had always savored the wonderful aroma of fresh-baked goodies.

"Oh my, blackberry pie," he whispered, drooling.

"Ilia, dear." "Yes, hon?"

"May I have another cup of that wonderful tea and a large slice of that pie?"

"Oh, husband, you ask so much of me," she teased.

"Please."

"Of course, dear. We can't have you starving now, can we?"

"You are such a wonderful cook, and you're so kind."

P'etro returned to the hearth to impatiently wait for the blackberry pie. Staring through the frosted window into the wintry night, P'etro lost himself in blustery reflections.

On his weathered face and tanned arms, P'etro bore with pride the unique scars of a hardworking man. Ivan called them battle scars. Sergey called them body scars. To P'etro, they were much more. In his mind, the scars were like military decorations acquired in the line of duty—a duty not for country, like in the war, but a duty to family.

Family duty…Love inspires duty; duty leads to labor; labor leaves its scars. Scars of loving labor. And all of that is driven by devotion. That fits. Yes, I like that. Medals of devotion for labors of family love.

Ilia called, breaking P'etro's concentration.

"Tea and pie await you on the kitchen table. Come and get it before I throw it out to the wolves."

P'etro jumped to his feet and hurried to the kitchen. After kissing and praising Ilia for her masterful skills in the kitchen, P'etro gobbled his goodies.

Later, he returned to his rocking chair by the hearth and his thoughts about family devotion.

Ivan talked about bravery—medals for bravery earned at the expense of bodily scars. Scars are body medals earned by sacrificial service. Life medals for sacrificial works of love borne on the flesh. It's not about bronze, silver, and gold. It's about heart, soul, and spirit. Yes, my scars are my heart medallions engraved on my body by the hand of nature. Applied with the needle of labor and the ink of sweat. My body scars are my heart medals, and I'll always wear them proudly.

Again, P'etro watched the blowing snow race across the whitewashed forest. It looked like an ivory river, endlessly meandering through the valley. To P'etro it was a masterful work of art, a tapestry on which the artist creatively captured the beauty and danger of the blustery winter wonderland. It reminded him of the thrilling winters of his childhood.

As a young boy, P'etro and his friends played in the mounds of drifted snow, dry enough to drift high yet wet enough to tunnel. As if it were yesterday, P'etro remembered climbing atop his parent's shanty as Samuil "the Fox" counted down for the dive into the snow. Eager and excited they awaited the countdown.

"All right. Ready. On the count of three!" "the Fox" instructed. "One … two!"

They never got to three. No one could wait that long. So instead of a synchronized swan dive, it was every man for himself falling through the air. Unceremoniously, bodies tumbled through the air. They yelled as they fell in a twisting bunch of wildly flailing body parts. Plummeting, they disappeared in a white cloudlike blanket of drifted snow. After digging out, they repeated the thrilling dive over and over.

P'etro smiled, remembering those moments, as the memories danced in the flickering firelight from the hearth.

<hr>

Ilia was sipping a hot cup of tea at the kitchen table when she heard the scream. In that terrifying moment, time froze, and panic gripped her heart. Stunned, she dropped her cup of tea on the kitchen floor.

Horror momentarily paralyzed her limbs as a knot of anxiety swelled in her stomach. She forced her body into motion, jumped out of the kitchen chair, and screamed, "P'etro!"

Panic-stricken, Ilia ran. Weak-kneed, she stumbled into the kitchen wall. For a moment, she struggled to think and fought to breath.

"P'etro!" She yelled again as he ran into the kitchen.

After a breathless second, they dashed through the cabin's flickering shadows to the baby's room.

As they entered the room, Ilia shivered from the cold and was shocked to see snow blowing through a broken window. Both moved quickly through the darkness. P'etro stuffed banks in the broken window and lit candles while Ilia rushed to the screams coming from the broken crib. In the flickering candlelight, she sobbed and picked up her screaming baby boy. She held and rocked her wounded child. He was covered with imbedded shards of glass and gashes on his head.

Shock and fear raced through her body as she looked helplessly at P'etro, who handed her a baby blanket.

"P'etro, he's bleeding, and he's blue from the cold," she sobbed.

"Come on, Ilia we have to get him warm and remove the shards. Take Samuil to the hearth. I'll get warm water and a cloth."

"Hurry, please! Samuil's still bleeding!"

P'etro shut the door behind them and then rushed to the kitchen and quickly gathered up as many emergency supplies as he could find. Grabbing the kettle of warm water still setting on the stove, he hurried to the hearth.

Ilia removed the shards in front of the fire and P'etro returned to the nursery. Pillows, glass, candles, and blankets were scattered everywhere. Plus, there was blood and snow on the floor. He removed the blankets from the window and saw more blood outside. He restuffed the window, went to the kitchen door, and hurried to the nursery where he found huge, strange, bloody footprints leading into the forest. He sighed and returned to Ilia.

"My baby, my poor baby." she sobbed.

She wept as she tended to Samuil's bleeding.

"Shh. Shh. Don't cry, Samuil. Now, now, Mama's here. It's all right, Samuil. Now, now, it's all right."

After some minutes, she calmed down.

"P'etro, what happened?"

"I am not sure, but this was not an accident. The bedroom is a wreck—the window, the snow, the blood and there are bloody footprints leading into the forest."

"P'etro, it looks like a battlefield in there. I told you they would come back."

"In a blizzard?"

"You know the cold doesn't slow the shadow creatures, and we're only a couple of minutes away from the Southern Forest."

"Then I'm to blame."

Terrified, Ilia shuddered and sobbed as she soothed her baby.

"P'etro, no one is to blame you must go to Ivan and have him bring the doctor."

"I will."

He bent and kissed them both.

"Will you two be all right while I'm gone?"

"Yes. Go now. Please hurry!"

"I'll be back in a flash."

<hr>

Like a soldier on a life-or-death mission, P'etro rushed for the door. He grabbed his coat, holstered his pistol, sheathed his knives, and attached his snowshoes. Asking for help from above, he opened the cabin door and shuffled into the arctic night.

With a knot gnawing in his gut, he wrestled with the decision of which path to take. He knew the road to Ivan's was safe but farther. He also knew that cutting through the Southern Forest was shorter but more treacherous. He set his jaw and stepped into the howling wind of the Southern Forest.

With the aid of broken moonlight, P'etro dashed through the snow-covered night, dodging trees and low hanging limbs. Thanks to his snowshoes, he stayed atop the soft snow and made good time. Coming to a frozen creek, he stopped and gazed into the Southern Forest. The splintered moonlight cast eerie shadows through broken snow clouds. He ignored them and stepped onto the ice of the border creek to cross over. As he crossed, his feet began to tingle. Kneeling, he brushed the snow away and noticed shadow strings floating like driftwood under the ice.

That's trouble.

As he entered the Southern Forest, he slipped on a rock, fell, and broke a snowshoe. He discarded the snowshoes and plowed on through the haunted woodland at a much slower pace. Without his snowshoes, he soon found himself knee-deep in frigid layers of snow. His journey quickly became slower and tougher. With each step he took, he moved deeper into the snow-blown forest.

Inch by inch, he struggled through the massive drifts. Tree by tree, he felt his way forward. Driven by paternal instinct and adrenaline, he slowly plowed onward, like his yoked oxen breaking hardened soil.

The wind suddenly howled back to blizzard force. He leaned into the wind and stubbornly fought the blizzard. In his mind, he could still hear the screaming. Blinking away the images of smeared blood and broken glass, he pressed on through the whiteout.

As he slowly chiseled his way through the blizzard, he was stopped in his tracks by a bone-chilling cry. He frowned, puzzled and worried.

It's too cold for a wildcat. Exhausted, he listened as the wind died down and the snowstorm ceased. Searching the forest with military precision, he saw a gray fog rolling toward him. From within the fog, he heard the ear-piercing cry again.

A snow leopard? Here? That's unusual.

P'etro quickly buried himself in the snow and watched as the fog moved closer. Momentarily terrified by the thought of being stalked by a shadow beast, he shivered. He slowed his breathing and listened for more predatory sounds. Squinting into the forest, he pulled out his pistol just as the cat sprang from the fog. He fired, the cat fell, and the shadow fog began rolling toward him.

Again, P'etro struggled through the snow. He saw a small cave at the bottom of a hill and climbed inside for safety. He rested and thought as the fog lingered just outside. As he watched the fog, he saw a glaring red eye appear, search the forest, disappear, and reappear.

When the fog rolled away, he stepped out of the cave. Looking around, he tried to determine how far he had come into the Southern Forest, but the blinding blizzard made it impossible to tell. Taking a breath of resolve, he stepped back into the arctic night.

After hours of battling the elements, P'etro stumbled to the ground and closed his eyes. A moment later, he opened them and stared down at the snow. He shook when he saw the leopard tracks.

He shook again when he heard the animal scream.

It's stalking me.

He heard sinister voices racing on the wings of the blizzard wind, and he reached for his pistol. Without warning, an avalanche fell from the trees, burying P'etro. After digging out, he rubbed the snow from his face and tried to clear his mind.

Slowly, the forest began to swivel. Broken snow clouds raced across the sky, casting eerie shadows. A corona of black and gray light fizzled and danced above treetops. Silhouetting figures darted between trees.

The shadow creatures.

In the broken sky, stars exploded like cannonballs. Shards of flashing light fell all around him, and the moon spun in the sky. The smell of gun smoke filled the air. P'etro rubbed his face and frowned.

The demons of the Southern Forest are playing with my mind.

"Soldier!" A commanding voice yelled from the forest.

P'etro looked in the direction of the voice and saw a large man in a ragged uniform marching through the snowy forest toward him. P'etro put his hand on his pistol.

"Soldier!" The man repeated.

P'etro's mind raced as he struggled to recognize the tall, husky, black-bearded ghostly officer.

"Friend or foe?" The stranger asked as he aimed his rifle at P'etro.

"Who are you?" P'etro asked.

The soldier stopped a rifle barrel away.

"General Kovalski, commanding officer of the Russian Forces in the Allied Shadow War."

"But you were killed."

"That was the first time, but it hasn't been the last." The man pointed the rifle to the ground.

"And who are you?"

P'etro snapped to attention and saluted.

"P'etro Fedorchak, sir."

"Ah, the hero of the dawn battle."

Their conversation was abruptly interrupted as a roaring bear lumbered out of the shadow fog into the snowy tree line.

The general let go a thunderous whistle and a small army of twelve ghostly soldiers emerged from the forest behind them. They were armed and dressed in ragged, soiled winter fatigues, and they wore snowshoes. Their images were gray against the white snow, and they wavered, as if in a breeze. But the night was still.

"That's your army, General? Ghost soldiers?"

The general leaned forward until he was nose to nose with P'etro. Staring into P'etro's eyes, he grinned a toothless grin.

"Give me twelve good dead men, and I'll conquer the world."

Staring into the general's eyes, P'etro noticed one was blue and the other silver.

"Yes, sir!" P'etro shouted and then saluted.

The general addressed his battle-hardened soldiers.

"To arms, men! To arms! Into the eye of the storm, we go!" He shouted into the wind.

The soldiers attached bayonets and readied their loaded rifles. P'etro pulled his pistol and nodded at the general. At the general's signal, the soldiers yelled and charged through the snow.

P'etro yelled from the depth of his being as he ran. He yelled at the elements that buffeted him. He yelled at the demons that attacked him. He yelled at fate that betrayed him. He yelled at the circumstances that trapped him. He yelled and yelled and yelled until his voice cracked and his throat closed, and he could yell no more.

Ahead of them, a bear trudged through the deep snow. P'etro was alone following the bear on the ground, and two of the soldiers quickly floated into action ahead of him. Before they reached the bear, ten more bears emerged from the shadow fog. The army stopped and fired. Bears fell, but others emerged to take their place. Half the army charged to fight in hand-to-hand combat while the rest reloaded and fired.

"Retreat!" the general shouted.

"No!" P'etro yelled, grabbing the general's arm.

"We must stand and fight!"

"P'etro, we're overwhelmingly outnumbered."

"So, your twelve good men can't conquer the world?"

"Yes, we can, but not like this."

"Do you have a plan?"

"Yes. Trust me."

"Yes, sir," P'etro said, stepping back and saluting.

"Infantry, fall back to the cave with me! Artillery, blast those snowy shadow creatures back to Hades."

As they retreated, the multiplying shadow creatures chased them into a cave. The general pulled a crystal from his pocket. It was glowing red, but as he gently caressed it, the crystal turned blue and sealed off the cave entrance.

The shadow fog thickened at the mouth of the cave, and demonic creatures screeched and clawed at the cave entrance.

"General, we're trapped," P'etro said with disappointment in his voice.

"So it seems my son, but not for long."

"What?"

"I have just begun to fight, P'etro. Watch and see. Watch and see."

He placed his crystal in the center of the cave, and the army kneeled around it and began to hum. The air in the cave swiveled, the ground buckled, and the rocks twisted. P'etro gasped and looked at the general. He looked up, smiled, and spoke to P'etro's mind.

"Twelve good men, P'etro. Twelve good men."

Outside the cave, P'etro heard cannonballs exploding. The barrage went on continually for several minutes, and then there was silence.

The general took his sword, rubbed the crystal across the blade, and tossed the blade to P'etro. He caught it, and it gleamed bright silver in his hand.

"Attention Men!"

The ghostly solders stood.

"P'etro told me he must make it safely through the forest to save his baby boy, Samuil, who was attacked by the shadow creatures and barely escaped with his life. So, this is for Samuil!"

Together, the soldiers began yelling, "Samuil! Samuil! Samuil!"

"It's time to seize the day! It's time to beat the shadows back into the darkness!"

"Samuil! Samuil! Samuil!" the infantry shouted as they prepared to rush from the mouth of the cave.

The general caressed his crystal, and the cave's protective entrance vanished. P'etro and the infantry charged with the willful determination of battle-hardened warriors while the artillery continued their bombardment.

As giant deformed shadow creatures attacked them, P'etro drew his sword. Yelling and swinging his sword beasts fell staining the silken snow crimson. When the cannons ceased, he looked up and saw the artillery men besieged by shadow demons. They fought bravely with knife and sword. Demons littered the ground around them, but there were just too many. Overwhelmed, he watched as they began to fall. He knew they had all died in battle several times before, and he knew they would continue to die fighting for what was right and good. And this time, they were fighting for Samuil.

As the battle continued, P'etro slew shadow beasts as the hilt of the silver sword smoke in his hand. The blade burned fiery hot. Gradually, one of P'etro's hazel eyes turned red and the other silver. P'etro yelled and charged to the rescue of his doomed new friends.

Crashing into the demon horde, P'etro fought like a man possessed. Wielding the sword, demons fell all around him as he slashed his way to the soldiers.

"P'etro!" the general yelled as his cavalry charged to the rescue, their horses leaping through the snow.

Battling his way to P'etro, the general dismounted, and as the war raged around them, he grabbed P'etro by the shoulders and stared into his eyes.

"Time for you to go, comrade."

"What? The battle—"

"P'etro, Nikolai is my grandfather, several generations removed."

"What?"

"Listen, P'etro, he told me time is crucial, and you must go now, or you will not make it to Ivan's cabin."

"But what about you and your men?"

"We stay. We fight. You go."

Choking back the tears, P'etro nodded.

"You're the best man and soldier I've ever known, and your soldiers are the bravest I've ever fought with."

The general snapped to attention and saluted P'etro. P'etro saluted back.

"God bless you and your men, sir," P'etro said.

The general threw back his head and laughed robustly.

"We've been dead and doomed for years. There's no blessing to be had here, comrade. Now, we stay—for Samuil; you go—for Samuil."

With a sad heart and a sinking soul, P'etro turned and ran.

CHAPTER 10

Whispering Blizzard Winds

While Ivan rode to Bakota for the doctor, P'etro helped Galina harness Lady to the sleigh. They raced into the night. The snow-covered road that bordered the edge of the Southern Forest was narrow and winding. On a blizzard night it was even more difficult to navigate, but Galina was in a hurry to help Ilia.

"Slow down, Galina. I can't see anything."

"No need, old friend. Lady Girl is sure-footed and knows the way."

With the words barely out of her mouth, the sleigh hit a sheet of ice in a lazy bend of the road and turned sideways. As the sleigh skidded along the edge of the slick road, it hit a boulder. The sound of shattering wood filled his ears. The sleigh broke away from Lady, jumped the ditch, and flew into the Southern Forest. As it bounced along, it tossed Galina into the frozen night. Speeding through the forest, the sleigh hit a fallen tree and threw P'etro into the winter-wrapped woodland.

The snow rolled away as he rose from under the drift where he had been roughly tossed. He opened his eyes, and all he could see was white. Then he saw red.

Drops of blood were sprinkled in the snow. He rubbed the stinging on his brow and saw blood on his hand.

What happened? Where am I?

P'etro tried to concentrate, but his thoughts were still jumbled and confused. Unable to make sense of his situation, he breathed deeply and tried to calm himself. His incoherent thoughts were interrupted by a noise in the forest.

Observing the forest, he saw nothing out of place, but he sensed something abnormal. When the wind died down, he saw shadow strings moving in the forest. With a shiver, he wondered if they would gather and roll into a shadow fog. Slowly, they moved toward him. He held his breath, sat statue-still, and watched as the strings slithered across the snow with ease. Some wound around trees, snaked to the top, and twisted into shadow fogs. The blizzard wind roared back through the forest, blowing the fog back to strings. They slid down the trees and disappeared into the forest.

The wind stilled, but the snow kept falling, making it difficult to see. He heard an undistinguishable screech that made him jump. He looked in the direction of the screech and wondered what was out there. His thoughts were interrupted when he heard it again. He wrinkled his cut brow and strained to hear. He heard only silence.

P'etro rubbed his temples tried desperately to relax and concentrate. Staring into the whiteout, he searched for a clue as to where he was. On a low-hanging snow-covered branch, he saw two golden eyes. He stared at the eyes; they blinked and then disappeared.

Am I imagining things? Well, I am in the Haunted Forest.

P'etro's thoughts were interrupted by a faint whisper on a frosty breeze, calling his name. He couldn't determine what the ghostly voice was. Again, P'etro heard the whisper resound from somewhere within the icy forest as the blizzard renewed. Now it echoed in the storm like the rustling voice of blowing leaves.

A whisper in a tempest? How is that possible?

Through the crackling pines, the breath softly called again as it danced on falling snow.

"P'etro…"

He flinched, closed his eyes, and wrestled to understand. Again, the whisper faintly called out.

"Hurry…"

The sounds melted back into the dark night.

"Who's there? Who are you?"

P'etro listened, but all he heard was the wailing of the wind.

Abruptly, the howling wind whipped the sound around the forest with such violence that the call appeared to be coming from every direction.

"Find them."

"What? Who?"

"Leave…"

"Who are you? Where are you?"

As suddenly as the wispy plea began, it oscillated and faded away on the wind. P'etro walked through the forest, trying to see something familiar. All he saw were white mounds of drifting snow, blowing in the wind. As he focused on a snow-covered tree swaying in the wind, a clump of snow fell, swirled in the wind, and blew away. P'etro stared at the tree. Two huge golden eyes stared back.

He scrutinized the pine. The golden-eyed snow owl blinked at him from the snow-covered branch. He looked again and realized a bird was either hidden in the tree, or it was white as snow. The large golden-eyed bird cocked its head, ruffled its feathers, and spoke to P'etro's mind.

"They're coming. You must leave. I cannot protect you now. Be vigilant. Protect the family. In thirteen years, he will come."

Mysteriously, the bird disappeared in a puff of windblown snow. As soon as it vanished into the night, the breathy rasp reappeared.

Frantically, Petro searched the trees and snowdrifts again. There was nothing. Spinning around, he looked for the golden eyes snow owl but something else had taken it place. A raven perched where the snow owl was a moment ago. The raven stared at him with cold, dead eyes fluttered down and walked toward him, climbing awkwardly over the snowdrifts. He shivered as the raven came closer. A gust of wind-driven snow blinded him, and he heard the raven cry and fly away.

Floating on the tips of snowflakes and echoing in the thundering squall, the whisper called out, "P'etro…"

Through the forest, it hissed and beckoned from every direction.

Bewildered, P'etro struggled to his feet and turned in a circle, looking for the voice.

"Galina! Where are you?"

"P'etro…"

Again, He looked in the direction of the wispy voice and saw nothing. Weak and weary, He fell to his knees.

Still the voice called again.

"P'etro."

He struggled to his feet, listening for the mysterious sound, but there was silence. In the forest, the shadows strings reappeared and knotted into a shadow fog. In his peripheral vision, he saw dark shapes lurking behind snowdrifts. P'etro reached for his pistol; it was gone. He felt for his knife; it too was gone. Realizing he was unable to defend himself, he squatted and eased away.

"Soldier!"

Startled, P'etro jumped and turned around. To his surprise, the general stood before him, grinning a toothless smile. P'etro couldn't hold back a relieved grin.

"You survived, sir."

"Of course. That's what I do."

"Sir," P'etro said, snapping to attention and saluting.

"P'etro, we need a plan."

"We?"

"Me and my twelve good men."

"They also survived?"

"Of course. Did you expect anything less?"

"Well, they were getting…"

"But here we are again in the midst of trouble."

"So it seems, sir."

P'etro scratched his head and thought.

But how?

"Nikolai sent us to help you, so you can help Samuil."

"You've seen Nikolai?"

"Of course; we are in his service. We've fought for him for years."

Their conversation was interrupted by gunfire. Ducking, P'etro looked in the direction of the gunfire. Six ghost soldiers were retreating out of the forest, shooting at creatures emerging from a shadow cloud. Two groups of three men were manning the cannons. They were alternatively firing and retreating.

"P'etro, find your friend and go. We will keep the beasts at bay."

"No. I'll stay and fight."

"P'etro, we must help Samuil, so he can save us."

"I don't understand."

"Then simply believe."

P'etro snapped to attention, saluted, and ran until a movement in the forest made him stop.

Galina's horse, Lady Girl, trudged through the forest, dragging part of the broken sleigh behind her. Momentarily, she stopped, pawed the ground, nickered and walked away. He whistled, she stopped, and he walked up to her and untangled the broken bits of the sleigh from the mare. Together, they searched the forest, looking for Galina. When he spotted a lump in a snowdrift with an arm exposed, he approached to investigate.

It was Galina. She looked frozen and lifeless. As he leaned over for a closer look, Galina moved ever so slightly.

"Galina, you're alive. I've been looking everywhere for you."

"Help me out of here." Her voice croaked.

P'etro helped her to her knees. Taking a breath, she rose to her feet.

"Are you all right, Galina?"

"Just cold and bruised."

"Do you still have your medicine bag."

"I grabbed it while we were flying through the forest."

Lady Girl walked up and nudged Galina. She turned and kissed her on the nose.

"Hello, Lady Girl," she said, hugging her neck and looking around.

"P'etro, all I can see in every direction is snow howling in the wind."

"Galina, we've got to get out of the Southern Forest. It's not safe."

The two jumped on Lady and arranged Galina's bag between them. P'etro looked over his shoulder, hoping to catch another glimpse of the legendary snow owl. He swore to return in search of it. Before turning around, he saw a blue light fading into the night.

"Nikolai?" He whispered.

At P'etro's cabin, Galina reigned Lady to a stop, and both raced to the door and anxiously entered. Galina quickly readied her supplies while P'etro knelt by Ilia and Samuil.

"Ilia, let me take baby Samuil. I'll examine him while you change your bloodstained clothes."

"Thank you, Galina."

As Ilia handed Samuil over, he stopped crying, opened his eyes, and looked at P'etro. The wounded baby boy's dark eyes suddenly changed. His right turned silver and the left blue.

Stunned, P'etro called out, "Ilia!"

When Ilia saw her baby's eyes, she fainted and P'etro caught her as she fell.

"P'etro! I've never…" Galina gasped.

"It's all right, Galina. You continue seeing to Samuil, and I'll take care of Ilia."

Galina tended Samuil's many wounds while P'etro stroked Ilia's brown hair. When she opened her mocha-brown eyes, he smiled, and she blinked.

"Are you alright?"

"What happened?" She asked in a shaky voice.

"You fainted."

"Samuil?"

P'etro smiled and nodded.

"Samuil's all right. Galina stopped the bleeding, and he's sleeping."

"Dr. Mykhailo?"

"He hasn't arrived yet."

"His eyes, P'etro? Samuil's eyes?"

"They're back to normal."

"How?"

"I don't know?"

Ilia turned away, and except for Galina's soft humming, there was silence for several minutes.

"P'etro, will they ever leave us alone?"

"Who?"

"The shadow creatures."

"Ilia, I promise I'll always be here for you and Samuil. I'll double my vigilance. I won't let them hurt us again."

A chill raced through P'etro's body making him shiver.

"Ilia, would you like me to make some tea while you hold Samuil?" Gaina asked.

"Yes, thank you."

After tea, Ilia and P'etro sat in the oversized family rocker, holding each other and slowly rocking Samuil. After all that had happened since Samuil's birth, P'etro was anxious about the safety of his family. His bright dreams of a happy future were shoved to the back of his mind. His envisioned life of sunshine, children, and good fortune was rapidly disappearing. Now, heartache, anxiety, and worry filled his thoughts.

Ilia looked at P'etro with sad eyes.

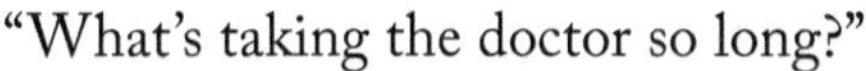

"What's taking the doctor so long?"

"It's a long way to Bakota and the weather is the worst I've ever seen. It'll be tough traveling for them."

"I know, it's just—"

"Ilia, I'm sure they'll be walking through the door any moment now."

P'etro's heart ached, both for his baby boy and for Ilia—he felt she was wounded almost as badly as Samuil. The sturdy old rocker, crafted by the skillful hands of Papa P'etro, squeaked as they rocked and hummed to Samuil.

"Why is this happening? It's not supposed to be like this," Ilia whispered in a broken voice.

Seeing his beloved wife in such agony crushed his heart. The battle-scared soldier shook his head. He looked tearfully into the dancing flames of the hearth and thought. For a long time, they sat in silence, rocking Samuil and staring into the flickering flames. P'etro battled the monsters that hid in the dark corners of his mind and wrestled with the condemning thoughts of his heart.

Why? Why us?

He knew something wasn't right. But he didn't know how to fix it. Ilia had told him about the constant crying, the fits, and the terror she saw in Samuil's eyes. P'etro understood because he had been just like that as a baby. He had felt things, sensed strange things, and had dreams like his mother, Liliya. He had also been afraid as he and the Brotherhood battled the shadow creatures.

Ilia looked into P'etro frightened eyes, sighed and bit her bottom lip. He saw the fear and guilt in her eyes before he spoke.

"Everything is going to be all right, Ilia. The doctor will be here soon. He will see to Samuil and perhaps uncover the root of his troubling symptoms. We going to make it through this, Ilia, and Samuil will be all right. You'll see."

"Why, P'etro? Why are the monsters after our baby?"

"I don't know, dear."

"They broke into our cabin tonight and tried to take Samuil. Or maybe they tried to kill him. Why Samuil, my baby? He's just a helpless little baby."

"I know."

"How could this happen to my little baby?"

P'etro slowly shook his head and sighed. He knew she had been very watchful, vigilant, careful, and prayerful.

"Ilia, sometimes things just happen. Crazy things. Bad things. Things that come out of nowhere and knock you down, whether you are watching out for them or not. Sometimes things just catch you unaware while you're going about life."

"But P'etro…"

"Ilia, you are a wonderful and caring mother. No baby could ever hope for a better mama than you."

With a lump growing in his throat, P'etro paused to take a breath. Then he forced himself to continue.

"Samuil loves you very much. He's been his mother's boy from the day he came into this world."

"Thank you, P'etro. That's so sweet, and you do make me feel better."

"Ilia, I need to tell you something."

"Yes?"

"I've dreamed things also."

"Oh?"

"Yes, things that are all jumbled up in my head, and I don't know if I can explain them to you."

He grasped her hand tightly.

"Please try."

"All right. They're things about us that I don't understand. Things about Samuil. Crazy things. Disturbing things about my childhood. Unnatural things about Samuil's birth. Things that happen in the Southern Forest. Things that frighten me. A ghost in the forest told me that we had to help Samuil, so he can—"

"Stew's ready!" Galina called from the kitchen.

CHAPTER 11

Medicine Man

Abruptly, the cabin door flew open, filling the kitchen with freezing air and a dusting of snow. Ilia jumped and turned around to see what she thought was a snow-covered monster from the Southern Forest step out of the blizzard and into the cabin.

Before Ilia could scream or P'etro advance, a tall, slender figure tipped his hat in the broken moonlight and spoke in a deep yet familiar voice.

"I came as quickly as I could."

"Dr. Mykhailo! You're here!" Ilia said with relief.

"Come in out of the cold and warm yourself," P'etro said.

"Thank you, P'etro."

Ilia smiled at the salt-and-pepper-haired doctor standing inside the kitchen door. Behind him, broken clouds raced through the sky. It was indeed a strange sight to behold. Yet for Ilia, it was a welcome and comforting sight as well.

The well-groomed doctor removed his coat and looked around the room with his dusty-blue eyes and warm smile.

He was known as a dedicated man with a tender heart and a jolly spirit. He was also known for his compassion. Everyone loved and trusted Dr. Mykhailo.

"It's good to see you, Ilia, and I'm sorry if I frightened you by bursting in like that."

"We were expecting you at any time," Ilia reassured him.

"P'etro, I came as soon as I received the news," the doctor said, as Galina entered the kitchen with Samuil.

"Thank you, Dr. Mykhailo."

"Galina, bring Samuil over here." The doctor motioned Galina to the table.

"Ilia, Ivan told me Samuil fell and hit his head on the floor?"

Ilia looked at P'etro, who nodded.

"Yes," Ilia answered, feeling guilty.

Weary and trembling from her fitful night with Samuil, Ilia sat down beside the doctor, who had already begun his examination.

"Tell me what happened, Ilia."

"I scooted our bed against the wall and put pillows on the other side to keep Samuil from falling. But he fell and hit his head."

Though trying desperately to be strong, Ilia choked to a stop.

"Samuil has more than one head wound. Was there anything on the floor he could have hit his head on?"

"Yes."

Clearing her throat, she regained her composure and forced herself to continue.

"I am sorry, Dr. Mykhailo."

"It is quite all right, Ilia; please go on."

"When I saw Samuil lying on the floor, bleeding … well …"

Ilia stopped; her stomach knotted as she remembered the horrible scene. Samuil began crying, and Galina handed him to Ilia. P'etro gave Samuil his grandmother's handmade stuffed bear named Teddy, and he stopped crying. The doctor slid his chair closer to Ilia.

"Now, now, this is not the first time something like this has happened. You have to expect accidents with children."

Ilia struggled to calm herself, as Samuil twitched fitfully in her arms.

"Let me have another look at Samuil and see what I can do to make things better."

With a smile, the doctor continued his examination.

"Has he been bleeding?"

"Yes, but Galina was able to stop the bleeding and clean him up."

"Hmm," Dr. Mykhailo grunted.

"Galina, you did an excellent job at removing all these deep shards and dressing the wounds. Ilia was the glass from the window?"

"Yes. The blizzard winds blew a limb into the window."

"There, there, Samuil. Everything is going to be fine. I will fix you right up. You'll be better in no time at all."

Concentrating, he mumbled, "Uh-huh … uh-huh."

Ilia watched the subtle change in Dr. Mykhailo as he slipped into the world of scientific medicine. She had observed him navigating this complex medical world with grace, charm, and complete confidence. She wondered if he was aware of anyone or anything else in the room.

"Hmm. Ilia, all his cuts are superficial, except these two on his neck. There seem to be deep claw punctures."

She gasped.

"How could that have happened?"

"I was about to ask you that."

"I have no Idea."

"Look here, Ilia. There's another one that just missed his heart."

Hearing those words, Ilia fainted again. P'etro caught her before she fell out of the chair and carried her to the big rocker. Galina stayed with Ilia while P'etro and the doctor continued Samuil's examination. When Ilia regained consciousness, she hurried back to the kitchen.

"Will Samuil be alright? How long will it take him to recover?"

"His superficial wounds will mend in no time at all."

The doctor rubbed his chin and took a breath.

"Babies heal quickly. But the deep punctures and the head wounds will take longer."

Ilia grimaced at his words and asked the question that was burning in her heart.

"I know his wounds are serious. Will he completely recover?"

"Only God knows, and time will tell."

"Oh." She whimpered.

Devastated, tears filled Ilia's eyes; she stared at the floor to hide them. The doctor reached into his medical bag and handed Ilia some valerian root and alfalfa.

"Ilia, this is what I gave Samuil to soothe him before I began my examination. Steep these together with this powder. After it cools, add a bit of honey, and have Samuil drink it all. It will help him to sleep while it works its magic within."

"Thank you."

"I'll be back early in the morning to check on him."

"Thank you for coming," P'etro said gratefully.

"Yes, thank you so much for tending to Samuil. We are very grateful," Ilia added.

She turned to Galina.

"Thanks again for your help, Galina."

"Ilia, no thanks needed. I was happy to come and help."

Ilia smiled and hugged Galina as a tear ran down her cheek.

"Galina, I will take you home," the doctor offered.

"Ivan can fix your sleigh tomorrow, and I am sure P'etro will take good care of Lady until you return."

"Of course."

"I'll come by in the morning."

"Till morning, then, Doctor." P'etro said.

Ilia held Samuil tenderly as she and P'etro watched the doctor disappear down the Bakota road.

"P'etro, the shadow creatures tried to kill our baby."

"Yes, I think so."

She was right, of course, but hearing it aloud sent a chill down his spine.

Ilia shook with indignation. She walked to the door and picked up a pistol.

"Never again, P'etro."

"Everything will be all right, Ilia. Come on; you need to rest. It sounds like Samuil is going to have a long recovery. And he needs rest too. Come now; let's all get some rest."

***

P'etro rose before the sun to tend to his morning chores; he wanted to be finished before Dr. Mykhailo returned.

Sprinkled with snow from the trip, Dr. Mykhailo—a smile on his face, a worn medicine bag under his arm, and a fresh batch of medicine in hand—walked to the Fedorchak's door and knocked.

"Greetings, comrade," the doctor said with a smile.

"Good morning." P'etro answered with a nod.

"Yes, it is. A cold and brisk morning."

"It's definitely cold. I had to break ice for the oxen this morning. Why are you up with the chickens, Doctor."

"I have a lot to do before I sleep."

"Yeah, me too." P'etro sighed.

"P'etro, something strange happened this morning."

"What?"

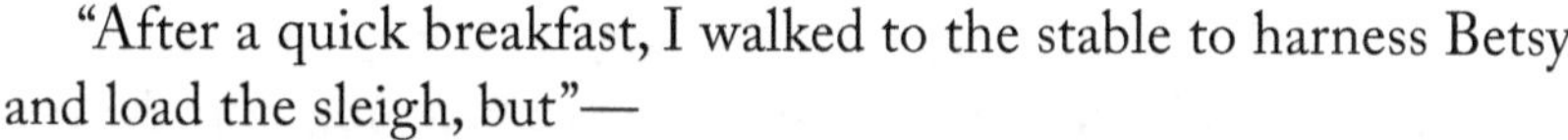

"After a quick breakfast, I walked to the stable to harness Betsy and load the sleigh, but"—

The doctor took a deep breath—

"It felt as if something was stalking me. There was something menacing at the edge of the forest. I picked up a twisted branch and walked toward it. Then something in the brush moved. I saw a shadowy fog. Then I heard an eerie sound. The unnerving sound grew into a whisper that came from the shadows. I jumped back and stared at the bushes. A smoky shadow rolled across the ground. When Betsy nickered, the shadows slinked away into the forest, but there was a chill that lingered in the air."

Ilia entered the kitchen, and the two men abruptly ended their conversation.

"Good morning, Dr. Mykhailo," Ilia greeted him, handing both men a cup of tea.

"Thank you, Ilia. Just what I needed. Did you have a rough night?"

"Yes, both of us."

"I'm sorry to hear that."

"Samuil rested well, but we did not." Ilia sighed.

"How is Samuil this morning?"

"Still asleep," Ilia replied with a tinge of anxiety.

"The medicine you left helped Samuil to sleep through most of the night. I'll go get him."

While the doctor sat quietly sipping his tea, P'etro walked across the kitchen to Ilia. The wood floor creaked under his feet, reminding him of another repair he had not yet done.

"Ilia, I'll take Samuil to the doctor."

"All right." She handed the baby to him.

Samuil's eyes were barely open as he yawned and stretched, dropping Teddy on the kitchen floor.

"Well, well, now. How are we doing this morning, Samuil?" Dr. Mykhailo asked.

Samuil groaned and wriggled. Squealing, kicking, and crying, he protested as the doctor tried to examine him. Quickly, P'etro grabbed Teddy, from the kitchen floor, handed him to Samuil, and the world was at peace again.

"Now, now, Samuil. Be a good boy and hug Teddy tight. Everything is going to be all right. The doctor's going to make you better. This won't hurt a bit," Ilia promised.

"Ilia, did the bleeding reoccur at any time last night?"

"No."

"Good. Good."

"What do you think, Dr. Mykhailo?"

"Well, his wounds are alright. No infections."

Pausing, the doctor rubbed his chin.

"You said he slept through the night?"

"Most of the night."

"I see."

He turned his attention back to Samuil.

"Now, now. Let me have one more look at you, big boy…there, there…almost finished."

After completing his examination, the doctor sat back and appeared lost in thought. Ilia lay Samuil near the hearth and covered him with a homespun blanket and returning to the kitchen. She looked at the doctor inquisitively.

"Ilia, take this valerian root and alfalfa, and do as I instructed yesterday. Do it morning and night for the next three days."

"All right."

"And take these herbs, blind them in warm water, and dab them on the deep wounds."

"All right."

"I will check on him again in a few days.

"Thank you, Dr. Mykhailo," Ilia said with a smile.

"I have to go now. The widow Marta isn't well, and I need to check on her."

"Oh, tell Marta we will pray for her."

"I will, Ilia."

"Godspeed, Doctor."

"Thank you, P'etro. I will see you soon."

With the tip of his hat, the good doctor turned to leave.

"Oh…"

Dr. Mykhailo hesitated in the doorway.

"I almost forgot. Father Jakiv and Father Slavik send their regards, they were going to come with me, but were summoned by the bishop for an urgent task."

"Thank Father them for us," Ilia said.

"I will and I believe there is a miracle to come for Samuil."

"Thank you."

"I pray you find peace and comfort. If you need me, just send word."

"We will."

The doctor waved and disappeared down the road.

Samuil squirmed atop the bearskin rug. Ilia smiled as she remembered the day Papa had gone hunting and brought the bear home from the forest. Samuil squeezed Teddy, curled up beneath his blanket, and fell asleep. Over the howling wind, P'etro heard the faint cry of a wildcat.

P'etro frowned.

I'll have to get that cat.

CHAPTER 12

Alarming Encounters

As Samuil ran giggling across the kitchen floor, Ilia looked up and smiled.

Samuil has grown up so fast. I can't believe he's already eight years old.

"Good morning, Mama."

"Good morning, Samuil. Breakfast is on the table."

"Thank you, Mama." Samuil ran to the table and grabbed a biscuit in each hand.

"Samuil, sit at the table and eat."

"No time, Mama. Me and Teddy got things to do at the barn."

"Samuil today is the wedding. When I whistle, you come running to help me with all we must do in preparation for the wedding."

"Okay, Mama." Samuil said as he dashed out the door.

As Ilia prepared things for Lena's wedding, images of Samuil's strange behavior flooded her mind. Yesterday when she checked on Samuil, she found him in his room, silently staring into the sky with a distant look in his eyes. When she called him, he didn't respond. He sat in the window for hours, motionless and expressionless.

That afternoon she watched him hug his knees to his chest and stare off into space. She cringed when his azure-blue eyes danced, as if he was somewhere else, observing something in motion.

My poor baby.

Some nights, Samuil hid under the bed and refused to come out. Some days, he squeezed himself into a corner and buried his head in pillows. A chill ran down her spine when she remembered the first time she saw him listless and withdrawn. Often, she found him curled up in fetal position, eyes closed and grimacing. Then there were his yelling fits, temper tantrums, sudden outbursts, and other disturbing episodes. She frowned when she remembered how extreme some of Samuil's conduct had been. The worst was when he screamed and fought her embrace. She desperately prayed that Samuil would grow out of all this strange behavior.

If I can't even help my baby. How can I forgive myself?

With time, Ilia's guilt eased somewhat, but her despair continued to plague her. She was happy when Samuil appeared normal and behaved like other children. However, she feared that Samuil would never really be normal. Whatever was going on with Samuil, she felt that it was her fault. Whether it was the demons at birth, the shadow creature attack, or a family curse, she felt that the guilt was hers to bear. She trembled and prayed that Samuil wouldn't get worse. Fueled by frightening thoughts, her mind raced. She sought desperately for any kind of rationale that would reassure her that Samuil was normal.

Samuil is fine. He's a normal boy. His speech has improved. All this is behind us now.

"Ilia! Are you ready?" P'etro yelled.

"Yes."

"We need to hurry!"

"Is the wagon ready?"

"Yes. Ready and waiting at the door."

"If you load the wagon, I'll get Samuil."

"On my way."

In the barn breezeway, Samuil sat down, propped Teddy up, and stared into the forest. Samuil and Teddy had always been friends. They had battled through everything imaginable; they faced life's struggles joined at the hip. From crazy escapades to miserable misfortune, they courageously stumbled and fumbled through life. Afraid yet resilient, bewildered but determined, they were inseparable. They ran, laughed, played, and bounced happily along the road of life.

They fussed, fought, and reconciled like best friends do. As blood brothers, they took an oath to never reveal a secret, even if tortured or threatened by death. Through it all, they possessed a lifetime of adventures that they swore on the Bible never to tell. For as long as Samuil could remember, the worn, torn, one-eyed bear his grandma had made for him had always been by his side.

Though Teddy was smaller than Samuil's hand, he was always near and ready at Samuil's side in all situations. He was a mysterious soul mate that magically spoke to Samui's mind.

"*I love Saturdays, Teddy.*"

"*Me too. That's when Mama makes blueberry pie.*"

"*Well, yes. But even better, there is no school on Saturday.*"

"*Oh yes, that's right next to blueberry pie, Sammy.*"

Samuil heard a noise.

"*Birds, Teddy.*"

"*Yes, I hear them too.*"

"*Come on. Let's go see.*"

"*Adventure time?*"

"*Nothing like an adventure.*"

Samuil grabbed Teddy, stuffed him in his pocket, and ran out of the barn. He stopped by the water trough and listened for the birds. Hearing nothing, he took Teddy out of his pocket and looked around.

"*Where'd the birds go?*"

"*I don't know.*"

"*Well? What now?*"

"*Time to search. Come on.*"

Walking to the stalls, Samuil peeked through a knothole and saw Blackie, one of the family's oxen. With their minds, they had an interesting conversation about the best-tasting grasses to eat. Samuil smiled and scratched Blackie behind the ears.

He hated leaving Teddy out of their conversation, but he couldn't hear a thing they were discussing.

Poor Teddy! He has no clue what we're talking about. He doesn't even know we are talking.

Samuil fondly remembered his introduction to the great outdoors in his Papa's loving arms. He instantly fell in love with all the sights, sounds, and smells of the river valley. Before he could walk or talk, Mama bundled him up late one evening, and Papa took him to the barn to feed the oxen. From that moment, Samuil was determined to go with his Papa to feed the oxen every evening.

To ensure his chances of always going with Papa, Samuil devised a plan. As soon as Mama started clearing the table, he made a beeline to the back door and sat on Papa boots. When Papa sat down to put his boots on, he'd smile and ask Samuil for a boot. One at a time, Samuil handed Papa his boots. Slowly standing, Papa looked at Samuil's pleading face. He swooped him up and threw him high in the air. Samuil screamed with excitement. Laughing and giggling, the two headed off to the barn.

On this cheerful Saturday morning sitting outside the stalls, Samuil and Teddy drew circles in the dirt. Sensing something move, Samuil jumped and looked around. He watched as something quickly scampered under a large pile of hay. Samuil shuffled over, sat down by the hay, and sniffed.

"Smells good Teddy."

"Like weeds?"

"No."

"Well, wet grass?"

"No."

"What then?"

"Well, it smells good, like hay."

"Does the bug like it?"

"I don't know if it was a bug or not."

"Well, did it like the smell of hay?"

"I don't know; he didn't say."

"Well, ask him."

"All right, I will."

"What did he say?"

"He said he likes the smell of hay, and it is good for hiding in too."

Samuil was always happy to make a new friend. Now it was time to play. The bug, however, was a bit shy so Samuil tried everything he could think of to coax the bug out of his hiding place in the hay.

Samuil was distracted by a cool breeze, heavy with the scent of pine. He closed his eyes and breathed in the evergreen fragrance.

Lately, Samuil had been discovering the pleasant-smelling aromas of the valley. The various scents were soothing and irresistible. There were the sweet perfumes of flowers, the spicy smell of green grass, the earthy aroma of plants, and the piney essence of the forest. He loved the briskness of the new morning air and the cool, moist scent of water. Finally, there was the smell of fresh-cut hay and the musky odor of the barn. Samuil cherished all the exotic forest fragrances that lingered in the valley air. It helped him to forget all about the shadow monsters and dark creatures.

Samuil's brow wrinkled inquisitively for a moment as he pondered a new idea.

"Teddy, I wonder what it smells like."

"Dirt."

"No, I don't think so."

"Sammy, bugs and things crawl in dirt. They live in the dirt. They even eat dirt."

Samuil frowned.

"No, Teddy, it doesn't smell like dirt."

"How do you know?"

"I just know. Okay?"

"And what if you're wrong?"

"And what if I'm not?"

"Only one way to find out."

"Yes, I know."

"Smelling time!"

He turned his attention to the hay, peered closely at the spot where the bug had disappeared, and quietly lowered himself to the ground. Crawling to the spot where he'd seen the bug dart under the hay, he prepared for the smelling.

"Shh, Teddy, don't scare him."

"You'll scare him if you keep talking."

"Teddy, be quiet."

"Like a mouse?"

"Yes. Quiet like a mouse."

Samuil lowered his head and slowly exhaled. Then he quickly and strongly inhaled. Hay dust thick with pollen, exploded in his nose, scratched down his throat, and burned his lungs. Overwhelmed, he rolled on the ground, gagging, spitting, and gasping for air. Between bouts of coughing and choking, Samuil took deep breaths of clean, fresh air. He sat up and calmed himself. Filling his lungs with fresh air, he savored every breath.

"Did it smell that bad?"

"No."

He coughed again.

"Did it smell like death?"

"No, Teddy, it didn't."

"A polecat?"

"No."

"But it must have smelled really bad."

Samuil frowned.

"Why do you say that?"

"You choked up."

"I know."

"So, the stinky death thing choked you up."

"No. That isn't what choked me."

"All right, if it didn't choke you up, what made you choke?"

"It was the dusty hay."

Teddy thought for a long moment before speaking again.

"So, what did it smell like?"

"I don't know."

"Why not?"

"Because. I couldn't smell it because of the hay scent."

Both sat silently, lost in thought. Around them, the sounds of the barn soothed Samuil. Blackie walked around his stall chewing on hay, a barn owl rustled in the rafters, and a breeze blew through the stalls.

"So, will it come out to play?"

"I don't know."

"Well, why don't you ask it?"

"All right, be quiet and let me think about how best to ask it."

Samuil sat silently, thinking about how to coax it into coming out to play.

"I can give him an invitation. What do you think?"

"That's a good idea."

"All right."

Having decided on a course of action, Samuil directed his attention to the creepy-crawly. Reaching out with his mind, he spoke to it.

"Mr. Crawler, come on out and play with me and Teddy. It'll be fun."

Samuil watched quietly as the creature inched its way out from under the hay.

"Teddy, it's a cliff lizard."

Flicking its tongue, the lizard tasted the air. Samuil thought that was amazing, so frowning like a lizard, he flicked his tongue. He slowly knelt and scooted his fingers closer to his newfound friend. Then he waited. The lizard slowly crawled up his fingers and onto his hand. With a smile as big as the Nieper River, Samuil watched as the lizard crawled up his arm.

Out of the forest came a rustling that disturbed Samuil's concentration. He jerked and looked in the direction of the noise. The frightened lizard jumped and fled.

Excited by the prospects of a new adventure, Samuil shouted at Teddy. "Come on!"

"Wait."

"No time to wait; it's a chase! Come on quick before he gets away!"

"But—"

"No buts! If we don't hurry, we will lose the lizard."

<hr>

Ilia stepped into the backyard and whistled for Samuil. When he didn't respond, she called. After a second call with no response, Ilia ran to the barn. After searching the barn, Ilia sighed and shook her head. Samuil and Teddy were nowhere in sight. First, she was angry. Then her boiling emotions quickly swelled into a tidal wave of motherly concern. Anxiety surged through her body, and she shivered as dreadful images raced through her mind. A knot of panic formed in her throat. Covering her mouth with shaking hands, she closed her eyes and said a quick prayed.

"P'etro!" She yelled.

"What is it?"

"Come quick!"

"Coming!"

P'etro ran out of the cabin to where Ilia stood at the barn.

"What, Ilia? What is it?"

"It's Samuil."

"What?"

"He isn't here. He asked to play at the barn and was to return to clean up when I called. He did not come when I whistled. He's gone. He and Teddy are gone."

"Come on; we will look in the barn."

"I already have."

"Let's look again."

Hand in hand, they ran into the barn.

"Ilia, you search the barn again, and I will look in the stalls."

"All right. But hurry."

"I will meet you back here shortly."

Moments later, they gathered.

"He's not here. P'etro" She said sensing something very wrong.

"Did you see him?"

"No."

"Where could he have gone?"

"He's probably in the forest. Come on, Ilia; we will look behind the barn first. Maybe we can find his tracks."

"Why would Samuil and Teddy disappear like that? Today of all days. Why? Where could they have gone?"

P'etro chuckled.

"They are probably playing some silly game or exploring."

"Oh, they should not be far, then. Hurry, P'etro. We have to find them before they wander off deep in the forest."

"I'll go have a look, Ilia. Samuil's probably not too far off." "No," Ilia disagreed in a stern voice.

"We will both go."

They walked out of the barn to look for clues.

"Ilia, you look here. I'm going to look on the other side. Call me if you find anything."

"Yes, I will."

P'etro disappeared around the corner of the barn to look for tracks. Ilia frantically searched the surrounding area for signs. She scanned the undergrowth for impressions and the brush for broken stems. She looked for anything that hinted at Samuil's whereabouts or the direction of his disappearance. While desperately praying for help, Ilia heard leaves rustle at the edge of the forest.

Quietly, she looked around. The forest was slowly changing. Green leaves were falling off trees. Twigs bounced around on the forest floor, and the air became stale. Suddenly, everything became surreal. Quietly, she breathed and stared into the forest. A shadowy fog roiled through the forest, blanketing trees. When Ilia heard a monstrous growl, she jumped.

Shadow creatures.

"P'etro!"

P'etro ran around the corner of the barn and almost ran into Ilia.

"Are you alright?"

"Yes, I was just startled by a noise in the forest."

"What was it?"

"I don't know."

"Did you see something?"

"A shadow fog."

She trembled and tears formed in her eyes. Her body flooded with cold apprehension, and a chill ran down her spine. Danger screamed in her head, and fear squeezed her heart.

P'etro doubled up his fists.

"Come on. I found Samuil's footprints leading away from the barn."

Ilia squealed with joy when she saw them. Then her mood changed as her eyes followed the footprints into the forest.

"Hurry, P'etro, let's follow them."

"You stay here, Ilia. I will be right back."

"But where are you going?"

"Back to the cabin to fetch the rifles. Don't move a muscle till I get back."

"All right but hurry."

With single-minded purpose, Samuil and Teddy pursued the frightened lizard through the forest. Without a care in the world or a concern for danger, they scampered along, looking for the following reptile.

"Aren't lizards wet and slimy?"

"No, not unless it's raining. Now come on; we can't let him escape. Teddy, flick your tongue like a lizard. Maybe it will help us smell him."

"What?"

"That's what lizards do. If you want to find a lizard, you have to be like a lizard."

"Who told you that?"

"Never mind. I have another idea. I'll reach out with my mind to find him."

After Samuil reached out, there was silence. When Samuil started to moved, Teddy stopped him.

"Wait—I heard something, Sammy."

"Yes, I heard it too ... There it is again. It's a bird."

"Why did a bird answer?"

"I don't know. I was talking lizard-talk. Maybe it overheard. Teddy, there it is again. It's a bird like the one we heard at the barn. Come on, let's follow it.

Together, they scampered off through the timber in pursuit of the bird with the lovely song. They moved through ferns and bushes, flowers and damp earth. Farther into the forest, Samuil stopped abruptly.

"Why are we stopping?"

"I heard something."

"What?"

"There it is again."

The forest grew dark as a low rumble whispered above the trees.

"Did you hear that?"

"Yes, sounds like a thunderstorm."

"It's more than that. Look," Samuil whispered, *pointing at the changing air.*

Fog crept through the wood, lending a gray cast to the air around them.

"It's just fog."

"No. The fog is more than a fog, and the cloud is more than a cloud."

"What? Why are you speaking in riddles?"

"I'm not. The dark ground fog rising into the sky is a shadow fog. And that dark cloud is a shadow cloud."

"How do you know that?"

"I overheard Papa talking about them."

"Where did they come from?"

"They come out of the haunted Southern Forest and the Bog."

"Are we close to the forest? Surely, we're not in it, are we?"

"No, but it looks like the Southern Forest is coming to us."

Both watched as string shadows menacingly twisted out of the forest. The fog whirled, looped, and boiled into the air. The blue sky began churning and changing. They watched as a shadow cloud kneaded, bubbled, swirled, and grew darker. Spinning upward, it mushroomed through the sky and dropped a dark funnel that began sucking the forest floor clean of debris.

"Teddy, hold on!"

"To what?"

"To me! Quick—before you're sucked into the shadows!"

Samuil grabbed a tree and held on. With his arms and legs locked around the tree, he watched. The spinning funnel sucked small animals into the shadow cloud and spit them back into the forest as giant monsters.

"Come on. We have to get out of here, the shadow cloud is feeding!"

"What?"

"You want to get eaten?"

"No."

"Then run!"

Running through the forest, they came to a big tree with a hollow base. They quickly crawled in and hid. Once safely inside

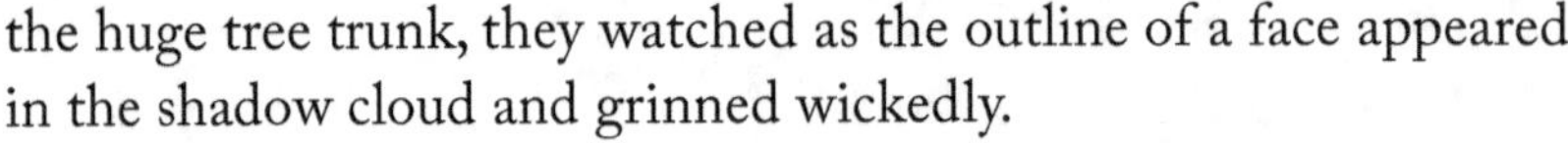

the huge tree trunk, they watched as the outline of a face appeared in the shadow cloud and grinned wickedly.

"Did you see it?"

"See what?"

"The shadow. The shadow has a face. That means that the shadow cloud is more than a cloud."

"Okay, what is it?"

Samuil thought for a moment and looked at looked at Teddy.

"I don't know. But it's more than a cloud. It's alive."

"Then it's a monster."

"Yes, and that isn't good."

"Did you hear that, Sammy?"

"What was it?"

"I don't know, but it made the shadows disappear."

"It's Mama's whistle. And Papa's yell."

"The wedding!"

——♦——

An hour later, the entire family was reunited and on their way to Bakota and the wedding. P'etro had mixed filling about it all. He had made a promise to Dimitri "the Bear", and he intended to see it through to the end. However, remembering the dreadful day of his death was killing P'etro inside. He frowned and tapped the reins of the cart with a somber expression.

"Are you all right, dear?" Ilia asked.

"Yes, I suppose."

"You seem distant."

"Yes, well, it's been a long time coming. But I knew Lena would find someone one day. Do you think Marina will ever remarry?" With a smirk and a raised eyebrow, Ilia answered.

"No. She's a one-man woman like me."

"Oh, you are?"

"You know I am."

Nearing Bakota, Ilia laid her head on P'etro's shoulder.

"Dimitri was your best friend, and I'm so thankful that he saved your life."

P'etro nodded.

"You are keeping your oath to Dimitri. That is an honorable thing in everyone's eyes." She kissed him on the cheek.

P'etro rode the rest of the way to Bakota in silence, recalling the bittersweet memories of "the Bear."

When they arrived at the church, they were met by a swarming mob of church ladies. Everyone in the community was busy getting everything just so for the wedding. After what seemed like hundreds of trips, toting everything from corn cobs to kitchen tables, P'etro heard his name called. Looking up, he saw Father Slavik motioning for him.

"Thank the good Lord," P'etro mumbled.

I'll have to give an extra tithing in appreciation for his timely appearance.

P'etro rushed over and shook the priest's hand.

"Greetings, P'etro," Father Slavik said with a grin.

"Hello, Father, and thank you for rescuing me."

"Whatever do you mean?"

With a tilt of his head and a raised eyebrow, P'etro gestured in the direction of the busy-bee housewives. All were swarming around frantically with their last-minute preparations.

"Oh, I see. No thanks necessary, my son."

"What can I do for you, Father?"

"There is something at the Chapel of Saint Priscilla you need to see."

"All right. Thank you, Father."

As P'etro made his way to the chapel, he thought about Ilia's parents farm in Moscow and wished he was back there. As he dreamed about how to make that happen something in the forest moved. He watched as three ghostly, glowing, hooded figures with red-black swirling eyes mysteriously weaved their way through the eerie dawn forests without their feet touching the ground. They glided out of the forest; their cloaks blowing in the breeze; and reminded P'etro of the promises he has made to Samuil "the Fox" and Dimitri "the Bear".

CHAPTER 13

Enchanted Chapel

Butterflies swarmed in P'etro's stomach as he made his way to the chapel. He hadn't seen Marina Popovitch, Dimitri's widow, in years. Yet as promised, he had kept in touch regularly by letter. P'etro fought back the torrent of feelings surging through him and opened the chapel door.

"Marina!"

She turned and stared in silence. P'etro stepped inside the chapel.

"Marina, you are a sight for sore eyes."

Marina rose and smiled. P'etro stared. He always thought she and Dimitri had been an odd couple. Marina was petite and short, but "the Bear" had been tall and huge. Marina had long, straight blonde hair; "the Bear" had short, curly red hair. Dimitri had glacier-blue eyes; she had green eyes. They were the most compassionate people he had ever met.

Marina ran to P'etro, threw her arms around him, and hugged him like a long-lost sibling.

"P'etro, is it really you? After all this time. Oh, my."

"Yes, Marina, it is me."

"P'etro, it's so good to see you."

"It's good to see you too, Marina. You're as beautiful as ever." P'etro turned to Lena and smiled.

"And who is this beautiful princess you have with you, Marina?"

"This is Lena. You remember little Lena."

"Yes, but this can't be your daughter, Lena Popovitch."

Giggling with embarrassment and smiling shyly, the girl looked at P'etro.

"It's me," she announced.

"No. How can this be?"

"I'm grown up now, P'etro."

"Yes, I see. Why, you were not any bigger than a mouse the last time I saw you. The little Lena I remember was a skinny tomboy running through the woods, chasing frogs."

"That was me, P'etro. But I stopped chasing frogs when I met Misha."

Lena blushed and covered her face. Her dress swirled around her ankles as she moved shyly. P'etro rubbed his brow.

"Let me look at you, Lena. My, my, you have grown into a beautiful woman. Your father would be so proud. You have your father's glacier-blue eyes and your mother's blonde hair."

Through the window, P'etro saw Ilia running to the chapel, and he smiled. Seconds later, she burst through the door and squealed, "Marina!"

"Oh, Ilia!"

The two embraced.

"It has been so long, Marina."

"Too long."

"Oh, I know. I have missed you."

"And I have missed you too."

All three ladies began talking and giggling and the room filled with joy. P'etro heard a knock at the door and opened it. He froze and couldn't believe his eyes. His brother Fadir stood there smiling. P'etro threw his arms around Fedir and lifted him off the ground in a bear hug. Nervously, Ilia hurried to the open door. Seeing Fedir, she scowled at P'etro.

"Where are your manners, P'etro? Fedir, Valya, come in." Ilia invited.

"Thank you, Ilia."

"Fedir, Valya, what a surprise. It is so good to see you. Moscow is so far away we did not know if you would come." P'etro said.

"Little brother, we wouldn't miss this for the world."

"Fedir, this is Lena, Dimitri's daughter."

Fedir bowed graciously.

"Pleased to meet you, Lena," he said with a big smile.

"Marina, Lena, this is Valya, Fedir's wife."

Valya curtsied. Mother and daughter politely returned the curtsey.

Fedir, like P'etro, had fiery hazel eyes and a black beard. Fedir was a little taller than P'etro, with broad shoulders and bulging biceps. His skin had a leathery look from years of metal work in a Moscow furnace, which made him appear much older. Before the war, he was shy and gruff, but now he was a likeable enough gentleman.

Valya was beautiful. Her olive complexion, dancing hazel eyes, and long, flowing black hair made her look more like a princess than a seamstress. P'etro had always thought that she was spoiled by her well-to-do parents.

"Fedir, remember Marina?" Ilia said politely.

"I have known Marina longer than P'etro has," Fedir said.

"I always said Dimitri was a lucky man to have found such a pretty woman for his bride. And Lena, you're just as beautiful as your mother. If Dimitri could see you now."

"Do you remember your Papa before those dreadful days?" Valya inquired.

"Not really," Lena replied.

"I was quite young when he left for the war. But I feel like I do. Mama and P'etro have told me so much about him and about all of you growing up together. I feel like I know you all."

"Come; we should not keep the groom waiting any longer. We must not allow Lena's enchanting spell over Misha to be broken," Fedir teased.

As they walked from the chapel, Ilia took P'etro's hand and gave him a kiss.

"I'm so happy, P'etro. We are all together today, and Fedir has come. It is so wonderful. Marina's heart is filled with joy, and Lena's getting married."

"I know. It has been so long."

"Yes, it been too long."

The church bells rang out all around.

⋯⟡⋯

Outside the church, P'etro sat on a bench as nostalgia flooded his mind. Once again, his heart was flooded with bittersweet childhood memories of Fedir, Dimitri "the Bear", Ivan "the Boar", and Samuil "the Fox". Reflecting on the memories, his heart grew heavy, and his mind filled with the devastating nightmare of Dimitri's heroic death.

The cries of dying soldiers screamed in P'etro's ears. The distant blasts of cannon fire, screaming bullets, and the clashing of swords thundered in his head. He saw innocent men falling in battle. He felt hot led strike his body. Again, he was trapped and feared for his life. Then, suddenly, he was kneeling beside his dying friend. With a shaking hand, he gently closed his friend's eyes and yelled at the gods of war who had brought this calamity upon them. Then he heard the echo of his vow.

I promise, Dimitri. I will care for your family. I will see to Lena's upbringing. Rest in peace, my friend.

A hand on his shoulder shocked him back to reality. P'etro looked up into the eyes of Father Slavik.

"Are you all right, P'etro?"

"Yes, Father. I feel fine."

"Father Jakiv has arrived, and it is time for the wedding to begin, my son."

"All right, Father. I am ready."

P'etro forced his mind back to the present. Glancing around, he saw Misha, the groom, standing and waiting.

Misha was an ambitious young man. As a carpenter by trade, he worked long hours but always made time for his Lena. He was devoted to her but scared to death of P'etro, whom he knew was a war hero and had been best friends with "the Bear". Plus, he had sworn to care for Dimitri's family. All the letters Marina had shared with him were intimidating. At the wedding, Misha avoided P'etro at all costs.

Once again, P'etro's thoughts slipped into the past. Marina had been exceptional with her correspondence over the years. Moscow was a long way from Bakota. There was no railroad, and it was too great a distance to travel any other way. If it hadn't been for faithful Marina, P'etro didn't know how he ever could have kept his word to Dimitri. He still had all the letters the two of them had written back and forth concerning Lena. The correspondence had always made him feel as though Lena had grown up before his very eyes. Often, and in detail, Marina had corresponded with P'etro concerning Lena's eventful life in Moscow. In return, P'etro had answered every letter with as much insightful wisdom as he possessed.

In the letters, Marina had also gone to great lengths to inform P'etro about Misha. He was the strong, handsome, ambitious carpenter who had stolen Lena's heart. P'etro never asked but always wondered if Marina, as instructed, had given his letters to Misha. They were filled with a godfather's advice and stern warnings. The way Misha acted around P'etro at the wedding made him think that the younger man had read every word.

A familiar voice startled P'etro out of his daydreams.

"Come now, my son," Father Slavik said.

"Take Lena's arm and walk her down the aisle. It's time to give her into Misha's loving arms and fulfill your promise to your old friend."

P'etro sighed. "Yes, Father. Thank you."

Finally, after all these years of fatherly correspondence and instruction, the time had come. He nodded his head at the priest, smiled at Marina, and took Lena in arm. Together, they walked down the aisle.

P'etro walked up to Ilia and took hold of her hand.

She turned and gazed into his eyes.

"The music is calling us, Ilia dear. Ready to dance?"

"Yes, handsome."

"Come with me, my love."

On the dance floor, they twirled and swayed to the music. Together with the other guests, they whimsically sashayed the afternoon away.

When the music stopped, P'etro sat to rest while Ilia went to help the ladies clean up.

Dr. Mykhailo walked over with an engaging nod.

"How is the family, P'etro?"

"We're doing very well."

"Good, good."

"How is the good doctor these days?"

"I'm fine, P'etro. Just fine."

"Glad to hear it."

"How is little Samuil?"

P'etro looked at the doctor and sighed.

"He seems to be doing well some of the time. But Ilia tells me that he still has bad moments, but not often."

"What kind of bad moments?"

"His anger. And other times it's like he's there, but not there. But not very often."

"I will drop by on Wednesday and check on Samuil."

"That will be fine. Ilia will have tea and biscuits awaiting your arrival."

"That sounds wonderful."

"We will see you then, Dr. Mykhailo."

"Yes, very well. Oh, by the way, my colleague Father Jakiv inquired about Samuil. He would very much like to see him before leaving for his parish. Over the years we have often talked and prayed about Samuil. He has been on his mind and in his prayers almost as much as mine."

"Very well," P'etro responded, but he felt a bit puzzled.

With that, the doctor was off.

P'etro thought it strange that Father Jakiv had been concerned about Samuil all these years, yet he had never visited him. He realized the priest was a very busy man with lots of responsibilities.

Plus, the doctor said he had tried to visit on many occasions.

But it's been eight years.

P'etro spotted Ilia with her busy friends and walked over.

"Where is Samuil?"

"I'm sure he around somewhere."

"I need to find him. Father Jakiv has asked to see him."

"Oh?"

"Yes, the doctor informed me."

"He's been playing with Katya."

P'etro found Katya and told her about Father Jakiv's request to see Samuil.

"I will get Samuil for you and bring him to the kitchen. I am supposed to be hiding, and Samuil's supposed to find me. It's a fun game we play. I will go find him."

"Thank you, Katya. Hurry now; we don't want to keep Father Jakiv waiting."

P'etro walked back to the kitchen, where Ilia was helping to tidy up. P'etro heard someone calling his name. When he turned around, he saw Katya crying and running toward him. She was shaking and as pale as a ghost. With tears running down her cheeks, she sobbed, "Samuil's gone!"

Ilia was so shocked she dropped the plate she was holding and gasped.

"Oh no!"

"I'm sorry, Mrs. Ilia. I promised you I would take care of Samuil while you helped the ladies with all the preparations," Katya sobbed.

"Now, now, child. Stop crying and tell me what happened."

"We were playing hide-and-seek and after I found him, I was hurrying to hide when you saw me. He was supposed to come find me."

Katya dried her eyes and took a deep breath.

"I promised to look after him …"

"Katya, it's not your fault Samuil ran into the forest this morning, got lost and luckily, we found him. He does this all the time. Now I need your help."

"All right, Mrs. Ilia. What can I do?"

"Dry your face. Don't say anything to anyone about Samuil disappearing. We don't want to ruin Lena's beautiful wedding."

As Ilia spoke, a fearful chill raced through Katya's body, causing her to shiver.

"All right, Mrs. Ilia."

"Remember—not a word to anyone."

"Yes, ma'am." The girl wiped her face.

Ilia turned to P'etro.

"What are we going to do?"

P'etro knelt to speak to Katya.

"Go find Dr. Mykhailo. Explain to him that Samuil has fallen ill, and we have taken him home and if he doesn't recover quickly, we will call for him. And ask him to please inform Father Jakiv."

"All right."

Sniffing and trembling, Katya turned and apologized again.

"Oh, Katya, dear," Ilia said.

"It's not your fault. Samuil sneaks off all the time. Sometimes, he even gets lost in the forest. He's probably out there now."

Ilia hugged Katya and gazed at her compassionately.

"P'etro and I will find him, Katya, but we need your help."

"All right, Mrs. Ilia."

"I am counting on you to relay the message and save the wedding."

"Yes, ma'am."

"Now dry your tears. I know you can do this Katya. Father Jakiv is expecting to see Samuil and will be looking for us very soon. Go now, quickly."

"Yes, ma'am."

Ilia found Fedir, explained the situation, and asked Fedir to take their wagon home.

"P'etro and I will find Samuil and walk home through the forest. It may take a while, but we should be home before nightfall. Fedir, I can't spoil this day for Lena. P'etro made a promise, Fedir."

"Don't worry. Everything will be fine. I promise."

He met her gaze and smiled.

"The Bear" would be proud, and I am honored to assist."

"Thank you, Fedir."

Ilia rushed back to P'etro.

"We have to find him."

"It shouldn't be too difficult to find Samuil. He's either at the Bakota Cave Monastery, or in the forest, or headed to the river."

Ilia suddenly felt her heart race with alarm.

"Why would he leave Katya like that?"

"Well, it has something to do with the magical allure of the forest and the mysterious songs of the river."

"Men."

P'etro smiled and snickered but didn't say anything.

"Come on, P'etro. Samuil's probably not very far away." "There's a stream nearby. He may be there."

Searching for tracks, they walked into the forest.

Samuil was determined to have a closer look at the songbird, so he and Teddy followed it into the forest. He stumbled and tripped through grass and weeds, following the musical calling of the songbird then abruptly, the song stopped and Samuil stopped too. Puzzled by the silence, he stood, listened, and then spoke to Teddy.

"Where did it go?"

"I don't know. Did it get lost?"

"No, birds don't get lost."

"Well then we're lost."

"No, we're not lost either. We just lost sight of the bird."

"Oh, it's just gone. Not lost."

"Yes, it's gone. Come on; we have to find her."

"Where do we start?"

"Come on this way."

The two friends ran out of the forest onto a grassy knoll. Coming upon a soft clump of grass, they sat and rested. Samuil took in their new surroundings. Sniffing the various fragrances in the forest air, he smiled. The scent of the timberland was so different from that of the town. Everything smelled so crisp and distinct. The forest air smelled new, clean, and fresh. After sitting, smelling, and committing the fragrance to memory, Samuil sighed.

"He's gone; we lost him."

"Where did it go?"

"I don't know where it went."

"And you don't know where we are either. Do you?"

"Yes, we are lost too. I've never been this far in the Northern Forest before."

"Are we really lost?"

Samuil sat on a stump and looked Teddy in the eyes.

"Uh-huh. We're really lost."

"Are we going to die in the forest?"

"No, we'll be fine. The forest is our friend."

"Will we die in the river!"

"No, we are not going to die in the river. The river, the forest, and the creatures of the forest are all our friends. Friends do not kill friends."

"I still don't trust the forest or the river. The shadows live in both."

"Well, if you don't trust the forest or the river, can you trust me?"

For a moment there was silence as Teddy considered the question.

"I can. You won't trick me, will you?"

Samuil smiled.

"I'll take care of you."

"Promise?"

"Sure, we're best friends.

"Then why did you steal my mittens?"

"I didn't you lost them."

"So, they're lost like the bird and us."

"Yes, I suppose so. Sorry, Teddy."

From the corner of his eye, Samuil saw something move in the brush. Forgetting everything else, he stared into the undergrowth.

"Teddy, we're not alone."

"What is it?"

"Something in the brushes moved."

"Is Papa P'etro here?"

"No. Shh."

"Mama Ilia?"

"No. Be quiet. It's something else."

"What?"

For a long time they listened

"It's something that's not supposed to be here. Something dangerous."

"How do you know? I don't see anything."

"I feel it, and I've felt it before. Come on; quiet like a mouse."
"Invisible like a ghost."

Slowly and quietly, they moved closer to get a better look. Samuil suddenly stopped and stared at the ground.

"Look."

"What?"

"They're three different-sized white feathers on the ground."

"Why three?"

"I don't know. But look at that one; it's huge."

Samuil picked up the smallest feather and examined it.

"What kind of bird has white feathers?"

"I don't know."

A rustling in the forest caused Samuil to flinch and put the feather in his pocket.

"Teddy, look."

Samuil pointed to a grove of pines where shadowy and unsettling shapes moved in the trees.

"Is that what I think it is, Sammy?"

"Yeah, the shadows have come into the Northern Forest."

"They can come this far?"

"Look, shadow strings are dripping from the trees and wiggling through the forest. They must be hunting."

"Yeah, for us?"

"I don't want to wait and see."

"So, let's go Sammy."

"Quiet…"

"Yeah, yeah, and invisible."

After quietly sneaking far away from the shadows, they stopped to rest, and Samuil saw something fluttering in the forest. Startled, he quickly and quietly began moving toward the noise.

"Stop, Sammy! It might be more shadows."

"No, this is different. Come on."

They moved closer for a better look until a noise startled them. Samuil turned and saw the songbird.

"Teddy, it's back!"

"What?"

"The songbird."

"You sure?"

"Yes, I'm sure. Let's follow it."

"All right."

"Come on, quiet like a mouse, invisible like a ghost."

Slowly, carefully, and quietly, so as not to frighten the songbird, Samuil got to his feet.

"Slow as she goes, like the ship captain says."

"But I want to be a pirate."

"You can be a pirate. Pirates have captains too."

"How did a captain get on a pirate ship without getting killed?"

"It's not like that, Teddy. Pirate ships have pirate captains."

"Oh."

Sneaking through the forest, the two adventurers followed the songbird.

"Slow down, Teddy. We must be quiet and careful. We do not want to scare it."

"Are you going to talk bird-talk to it, Sammy?"

"Bird-talk won't work, Teddy."

"Why?"

"Because it's a songbird, and I don't sing."

"All birds sing, Sammy, so all birds are songbirds. So, talk to it in bird-talk."

"It's not that simple. They are special birds that sing special songs in a special way. They are songbirds and they don't speak bird-talk."

"Are you sure about that?"

"Yes. Sit down and be quiet."

Sitting quietly on the grass, Samuil marveled at the wonderful plants around him. The colorful flora mesmerized him. Everything looked so lively and smelled so fresh. Curious, he observed the plants. To him, all the vegetation was beautiful. There were large pines and hardwoods. Beneath them saplings struggling and stretching to catch sunlight and grow. The grass and the wildflowers smelled sweet. The bushes, thickets, and undergrowth were bright green.

"Look at the colors, Teddy."

"Which ones?"

"The flowers."

"Oh, I see them. There are star flowers and sky flowers by that rock."

"Yes, and red flowers over there."

"They're all pretty."

Quietly, Samuil sat listening to the forest noises and the distant sound of the singing river. Though he recognized lots of the river valley sounds, he didn't know all the creature calls. Some calls, like the song he was following, were new. Still, he marveled at all the new sounds. A song called out directly above him. Looking up, Samuil saw a beautiful bird perched on a tree limb, singing. It was blue. As the bird sang, the sun dimmed.

"Teddy, something is wrong."

"What?"

"I don't know, but there's something there." He pointed.

"What is that?"

"It's the shadow fog, like we saw before. And this one might grow into a shadow cloud."

"Why is it here? Why did it come all this way? What does it want?" Samuil thought for a moment before speaking.

"I don't know, but it's here. It might have followed us."

"What are we going to do, Sammy?"

"We'll hide and watch."

"No, let's run."

"If we run, it will catch us."

"Not if we run as fast as the wind, Sammy."

"We can't run that fast. Now come on—quiet like a mouse…

"Invisible like a ghost," Teddy finished.

They watched as a dark fog rose, fell, knotted, and twisted. Then it rose above the treetops blotting out the sun. Rolling, it dived earthward and splashed into the river. The water bubbled, boiled, and spun into an angry whirlpool before the fog rolled away.

"We're lucky it didn't see us, Teddy. Come on."

***

Even though P'etro was a veteran tracker, Samuil's trail was hard to follow. Plus, Samuil wasn't heavy enough to leave much of an impression on the forest floor. So P'etro had to search for broken twigs, imprints in the mud, and places where Samuil had doodled in the dirt with his fingers.

"Samuil! Samuil!" P'etro called out.

Then he listened quietly, hoping for a reply, a sound, something to indicate where Samuil might be. Yet the only sounds were those of the woodland creatures.

His anxious mind swarmed with horrible images as they slowly trudged through the forest. When Ilia stumbled, P'etro reached out and caught her before she hit the ground.

Tears ran down her cheeks, and it broke his heart when she whispered in a shaky voice, "Samuil, our dear boy."

"Ilia, dear. Don't cry. We will find Samuil. I promise. Everything is going to be all right."

Nodding her head, she tried to make the tears stop, but they continued to flood her eyes and run down her face. It was heartbreaking, and P'etro leaned in and held her tight. For a long time, they sat together silently in the cool river valley grass and held each other.

"Everything will be fine. We'll find Samuil, I promise. And when we do, you can spank him all the way home."

"I do not want to punish him, P'etro. I just want to find him and go home."

"Okay, come on. Samuil's probably around the next bend, playing in the dirt. Let's go find him. I'm hungry, and don't want to be late for supper."

"Of course, you are always hungry."

Ilia looked into P'etro's endearing hazel eyes, and for the first time since leaving the church kitchen, she smiled. With a rekindled spark of hope, P'etro took Ilia's hand, and together they continued their search through the forest. With his renewed sense of determination and a keen eye for strategic observation, they moved quickly. Around every bend and crook, he could feel an air of expectation. His optimism swelled in the air like an exploding cumulus cloud in the eastern sky.

They walked to an overhanging cliff with a cascading waterfall that rushed toward the Nieper River. P'etro stopped, wiped his brow, and looked for tracks. He knew how Samuil loved the singing waters, and he felt Samuil must be somewhere close.

Ilia stumbled when she slipped on a rock. P'etro reached to grab her, but she fell, hit her head, and passed out. P'etro took her in his arms and ran to the river. Lying her next to the waterfall, he tore his shirt, wet it, and dabbed her face.

P'etro glimpsed an unusual shape in the water. As he turned, he saw shadows strings cascade over the waterfall. He watches as they bubbled and grew into a gray fog that floated atop the water; then the shadow fog rolled, expanded, and rose above the trees, becoming a smoky cloud. P'etro stared at it and saw undefined objects moving in the shadow cloud. Unnatural things were rising, falling and forming.

This is bad. There's something in the shadows. Something menacing. No—evil.

P'etro froze as a red-eyed demon from within the dark cloud growled and stared at him. Snarling hideously, it beckoned him to the cloud with a wicked crooked claw. He picked Ilia up and ran. Jumping over a creek, he ran far enough into the forest to feel safe. He stopped at a grassy knoll, gently laid Ilia on the grass, and dabbed her face with his wet cloth.

Moaning, she woke.

"P'etro?"

"Yes, Ilia. You hit your head, but you'll be fine in a minute."

"Samuil?"

"We're still looking."

"P'etro."

"What?"

"Splashing? It's the sound of a child playing, P'etro. Maybe it's Samuil."

"Come on; let's go see."

As they walked along a path leading to the river, the noise grew louder. P'etro heard birds singing, frogs crocking, crickets chirping and beavers slapping their tail as an eagle cried above the forest canopy. Quietly walking closer, they saw Samuil sitting by the river with his feet in the water with all kinds of critters surrounding him. The trees were full of singing birds and the forest was alive with the sounds of all kinds of music.

P'etro grabbed Ilia, pulled and her to the ground, and pointed.

"Look at the river."

"A blue mist? What does it mean?"

"Maybe it's Nikolai. Perhaps he's protecting Samuil."

They squatted and watched Samuil as a blue mist swirled just above the river while forest creatures interacted with Samuil.

Samuil and Teddy were surrounded by birds, butterflies, frogs, spiders, and all kinds of bugs. P'etro saw a beaver in the water, playing with Samuil's feet. Lizards crawled on his arms, birds perched on his head, and a snake coiled around his leg. From the edge of the thick tree line, P'etro watched a deer walk out of the forest and up to Samuil. Badgers, lizards, butterflies, rabbits, and all kinds of other creatures emerged from the forest to gather around Samuil and gaze at him intently. It was as if they were communicating.

"Ilia, I think he's talking to the animals, and they're responding."

Not far from Samuil lay an old mangy dog, hidden in the tall grass. The dog was camouflaged and nearly invisible, except to P'etro's keen eye.

"Wolf Killer?" P'etro whispered in disbelief.

At the sound of P'etro's whisper, Wolf Killer disappeared into the forest before Ilia saw him.

Nikolai, are you here too? He must be. That would explain the blue haze.

The parents continued to watch the unbelievable scene until P'etro saw a large shadow race across the ground. He looked up and saw the tail feathers of a large white bird.

Could that be…

P'etro's thoughts were interrupted by a shout.

"Mama! Papa!"

P'etro saw Ilia's expression suddenly change from a smile to a scowl.

"P'etro, his new clothes are ruined! His shirt's torn, he's covered in mud, and his new shoes are missing!"

"But Ilia, we found him."

"I know, but look at him, Papa."

P'etro took Ilia's hand, and they walked up to Samuil.

"Young man!"

At the sound of her voice, the birds flew, and the animals instinctively ran away. Beavers squealed and splashed to their home, the deer dashed away, and the snake slithered back into the tall grass, leaving Samuil alone to face the wrath of his angry mama. Samuil reached out gently and offered her the butterfly that had been sitting on his arm.

"You like my new friends, Mama? This one is yours."

CHAPTER 14

Here Comes TROUBLE

On the evening of Samuil's twelfth birthday, P'etro was feeding the oxen and reflecting on the day's events when he heard a disturbance coming from the road. He immediately recognized the racket as that of a horse and wagon. The screaming and laughter had to be coming from the Vitalik children. Thinking of supper, P'etro's mouth watered, and his stomach growled. He walked to the cabin arriving about the same time as his visiting neighbors.

Sergey, a big lumberjack-looking man with a thick brow that reminded P'etro of a Neanderthal, shouted in his deep raspy voice,

"Hello, friend!"

"Greetings, comrade. Hope you're hungry."

Thinking of food put a smile on Sergey's weathered face. P'etro knew that behind that smile, which stretched from one gnarled ear to the other, hid a mischievous mind. Snapping to attention, Sergey saluted. P'etro saluted back. Both laughed.

"It smells divine, P'etro. I could smell it all the way to my cabin," Nastasiya said.

P'etro smiled at the plump woman with fiery-red hair and pale completion. As far back as he could remember, Nastasiya had been a cheerful soul and the boss of the henhouse.

Sergey hopped down from the wagon and helped his wife down. All four of their children bailed out of the wagon. Running, shoving, and yelling, they made their way to the cabin. Inside, Katya rushed to the kitchen to help Ilia with last-minute preparations for the feast. The two boys, Borysko, the elder brother, and Lauro, raced to Samuil's room.

Outside, Sergey's mules began to fidget. Nervous and agitated, they lay their ears back and pawed the ground.

P'etro felt something in the forest move.

<hr>

"Hello, Ilia," Katya said as she entered the kitchen.

Her little sister Alonya was holding her hand. Alonya's golden tresses bounced, and her amber eyes smiled when she saw Ilia.

"Hello, Katya, you look so pretty in that skirt."

"Thank you.

"And you look lovely also, Alonya."

Alonya smiled shyly.

"What can we do to help?"

"Can you stir the poultry stew?"

"All right."

"You are good helpers, girls. Your mama is fortunate to have such good help with all the kitchen chores."

"Yes, but it's more fun helping you cook, Mrs. Ilia, especially today with Samuil turning twelve," Katya replied with a smile.

"Well, thank you, Katya. If I knew you girls liked birthday baking so much, I would have invited you earlier."

"I like cooking with you any time. You bake with a smile, and all the things you make are new and different."

Ilia smiled and gave Katya a hug.

"You girls can come over any time, and we'll have lots of fun cooking."

"Really?"

"Yes."

After supper, the children gathered around Sergey, begging to go outside and play.

"Sure. Why not? But if you get into mischief, I will tan your backsides good."

"We won't, Papa," Katya promised.

"Boys don't play rough or mean, or you will answer to me when we get home. And you know what that means. Right?"

"Yes, Papa. We'll be good," Borysko promised, and his younger siblings agreed.

Katya took Alonya by the hand and winked at Samuil, who took Alonya's other hand. Together, they hurried to the door. Alonya held their hands tightly, and the trio made their way off the porch. Alonya beamed from all the attention she was getting from Samuil and her sister. She looked at her sister and then at Samuil as they made their way to the dirt pile.

"Samuil, tell me about the warrior's pledge."

"You know about the warrior's pledge?"

"Yes."

"How?"

"I just do."

Samuil's mind raced uneasily.

How could she know? Only Teddy and I know about that.

"Tell me, please."

Samuil took a deep breath.

"Well, it's a solemn oath between people."

"And?"

"All involved swear to secrecy."

"How?"

"They spit on the ground, stomp it, cross their arms, and bump elbows."

"What does all that mean?"

"It's a covenant of sworn silence; plus, it sends the oath to our ancestors, who bear witness to it. And whoever breaks it is haunted forever."

"Forever?"

"Yes, forever and ever."

Katya smiled.

"Samuil, I want us to take a warrior's pledge," Katya said with a spark in her eyes.

"Me too! Me too!" Alonya shouted with excitement.

"You do?"

"Yes, we do."

"Okay, what kind of pledge do you have in mind?"

"Best friends."

Samuil rubbed his brow.

"We already are."

"But I want us to be warrior-pledged best friends."

"Okay, me too."

After they took the pledge, Katya looked into the forest and saw a thin silver-blue mist slowly swirling.

Samuil had always known how Katya felt about him. He could see it in her eyes, her smile, and her attitude, and she told him in his dreams. The two of them had a connection that bound them like glue. Samuil didn't care that she was a month or two older. Being older made her more sophisticated, and that was a good thing. Samuil thought she was the most beautiful girl in the whole world. Plus, he knew she would never harm a living creature unless provoked.

At school, Katya tried to keep Samuil out of trouble as he broke rule after rule and never did his homework. At recess, older boys picked on him. He fought back, and once he bloodied a big boy's nose. After that, they would sneak up on him, push him down, and run away.

Samuil and Katya had always walked to and from school together. One day while walking home, they came upon Krasnoff, the school bully. He was fourteen, tall, burley, and mean. Everyone feared Krasnoff but Samuil.

"Hey, worm, why are you with the pretty girl?" Krasnoff snarled.

Samuil reached out and pulled Katya behind him. Katya stiffened.

"I know you," Krasnoff spat.

"You're the weird kid, Samuil, who does strange stuff."

"And you're the bully who picks on everyone," Katya snapped, stepping out from behind Samuil.

Krasnoff stepped up, Katya stepped back behind Samuil, and Krasnoff threw a punch at Samuil.

"Duck!" Katya yelled.

Samuil ducked, and a rock busted open Krasnoff's left eyebrow.

He cried out and stumbled backward, his hand covering the wound.

"Samuil, catch," Katya shouted.

He turned around just in time to catch a rock Katya tossed him. He spun around and threw it at Krasnoff, and it smashed into Krasnoff's other eyebrow. The bully drooled and yelled in pain as blood ran between his fingers.

"Time to go, Katya!"

Samuil and Katya ran through the forest, knowing Krasnoff couldn't track them. They stopped by a stream to catch their breath, looked at each other, and started laughing.

"You don't throw like a girl."

"And you're not scared of anybody, no matter how big they are."

"We make a pretty good team, Katya."

"Yes, we do."

"We'll have to be careful. Krasnoff will be looking for revenge."

"Right now, he can't see for the blood in his eyes."

They giggled.

Samuil felt thrilled and excited over the warrior's pledge with Katya and Alonya. While they sat in the dirt pile with Alonya, the brothers ran past them, laughing and yelling.

Samuil heard Teddy whisper.

"Sammy."

"What?"

"I do not like Borysko. He's a big, mean bully. And as fat as a pig. Lauro's just a smaller version of his big brother and a copycat. I don't know why they have to visit. Their Papa should tie them to a tree and leave them at home."

"Yeah, I wish he would."

"Dirt, Samuil!" Alonya squealed interrupting his conversation.

"Play with me Samuil."

Samuil sat Teddy alongside them in the corner of the dirt pile. Then he and Katya played with Alonya. Borysko ran over to where they were playing and kicked dirt in Samuil's face which got into his eyes. Then he laughed and kicked dirt in the girls' faces. Lauro was quick to join in, and together they continued kicking dirt in the children's faces.

"Worm!" Borysko yelled to Samuil.

"Sissy girls!" Lauro taunted.

"Stop!" Samuil yelled, coughing, choking and blind.

"Quit!" Katya screamed.

Blindly, Samuil reached out for Alonya. He pulled her into his lap for protection.

"Worms and sissies!" They continued yelling.

Rolling over on the ground, Samuil covered Alonya's face as the dirt assault continued. When Katya saw her younger sister in Samuil's protective arms, she jumped up and ran.

Around and around, the brothers circled, taunting and kicking dirt in Samuil's face while he shielded Alonya with his body. Screaming at her brothers and shaking with anger, Katya pelted them with rocks. As they ran away, she rushed over to check on Alonya and Samuil. Both were covered in dirt. Alonya smiled when she saw Katya.

"Sissy got them. Got them good."

"Yes, she did, Lonya," Samuil agreed.

"Are you hurt, Samuil?" Katya asked.

"No."

"Oh, good."

"You throw pretty good for a girl." Katya giggled and slapped him on the arm.

"That was brave of you to help Alonya."

Katya smiled and kissed Samuil on the cheek. Samuil smiled and blushed. Ducking his head, he spoke to Teddy.

"If you breathe a word of this, I will poke your one good eye out and call the ancestors!"

Teddy turned a ghastly shade and shivered at the thought.

The brothers didn't stop running until they reached the barn. At the barn, Borysko picked up a rock and hurled it at Big Boy. In the distance, Samuil heard the big ox bellow as the rock hit him in the head. That made him angry. Borysko picked another rock and threw it, hitting the ox in the head again. When Samuil heard the ox bellow the second time, he grabbed Teddy and ran to the barn. As he ran, he heard Borysko yell, "Prepare to die! The champion of Mother Russia is here. Borysko the Brute is going to slay you."

Running past the water trough, Samuil noticed a blue mist rolling over the edge of it and pooling on the ground. Then he saw Lauro pick up a large stick, throw it like a spear.

"Die at the hand of the tsar's brave champion, Lauro the Lordly! Die, you old fat cow!"

With that, the air was filled with big sticks of death that flew like spears from the mighty hands of the Brothers of Wrath. Together, they shouted and pumped their fists in the air.

"Die in the name of the tsar! Die in the name of the tsar!"

Big Boy began to bellow, and Samuil felt his pain. Kicking, bucking, and snorting he rattled the whole barn to the point of spooking Blackie. Blackie began to bellow and buck. Samuil felt his fear. Smelling the scent of blood, the Brothers of Wrath began throwing more rocks and sticks. Chanting, they yelled for the demise of the two beasts.

Anger boiled inside Samuil, and he ran to the rescue like a soldier on a mission.

"No!" he yelled. As he neared the barn.

Samuil's mind filled with images of carnage and destruction. Tears filled his eyes.

They're Katya's brothers and our neighbors, but I've got to do something for Big Boy, for Blackie.

Samuil stopped and slipped into the forest. With red-faced indignation, he began to formulate a plan. In the moon-streaked night, he searched the ground.

"I have to find a stick, Teddy."

"Here's one."

"No. A big stick, like a log."

"Take that tree."

"Don't be silly. A tree is too big."

"I think it's just the right size."

"Fine. You pull it down, and I'll use it."

"Uh."

"I thought so."

As darker shades of night quickly descended, they continued their search until Samuil uncovered a big, solid branch.

"Here, Teddy. This is it. Help me."

With Teddy's help, they dragged it to the barn. Together, they prepared for their assault.

Back at the barn, Samuil saw Borysko pick up a snake and throw it at Big Boy. The frightened ox bellowed in fear. He bucked, kicked the stall door open, and ran for his life into the woods.

The brothers doubled over; they fell on the ground and rolled with laughter. Clutching their sides, they gasped for air.

When Samuil heard a lull in the wild laughing, he whispered to Teddy.

"Watch this and pay attention to what I'm going to do."

In the quietness of the moment, Samuil picked up his tree branch and dragged it across the barn wall; it made a scratching, clawing noise. He waited a tense couple of seconds and did it again. In the dark barn, the siblings momentarily froze. They looked at each other in wide-eyed terror.

"What was that?" Borysko whispered.

Lauro, pale with fear and frozen in silence, shrugged and closed his eyes.

In the silence of the terrifying moment, Samuil knew he had their absolute attention.

"We've got them now."

"Time for step two, Sammy."

Winking at Teddy, Samuil closed his eyes and quietly whispered, "The dark is good. The night is good."

He took a deep breath.

"Darkness is good. Darkness makes them all go away. Dark is quiet. Dark inside me."

He waited a moment for effect.

"Dark too dark."

From the great beyond, the unharnessed might of the universe screamed into Samuil's body. In the core of his being, a firestorm of indignation began to burn. Ignited by the fuel of passion, rage blazed through his veins. The deep-rooted, emotional intensity knotted in his chest. A guttural force reverberated in his throat, and Samuil growled, huffed and snarled as he slammed the tree branch into the side of the barn. The clawing and grunting sounds of an angry bear filled the barn. Again and again, with strength from somewhere outside of himself, Samuil banged the barn and grunted like a furious bear.

Suddenly, from somewhere in the forest, a bear roared as if on cue. As the bone-chilling roar resounded, the boys cringed.

"Bear!" Lauro shouted.

"Run!" Borysko yelled.

Screaming like little girls, the boys ran for the safety of the cabin. In their dark flight, they tripped and fell; they prayed the ravenous bear wouldn't kill and eat them on the spot. They jumped up, ran around the water trough—and stumbled into Katya.

"Borysko! Look where you're going! You tore my dress!" she shouted.

"A bear!" Borysko yelled.

"It's coming to get us!" Lauro screeched in fear.

The children continued running back toward the house.

Samuil looked at Teddy, and both slowly turned around. Expecting the worst, all they saw was a giant bear disappearing into a blue mist in the forest. Teddy looked silently at Samuil. Samuil shrugged and winked.

"That'll teach them, Teddy. I don't think they'll mistreat the oxen ever again."

"They'll remember this for a long time."

"We did good, Teddy. Thanks for your help."

"All that night training in the forest paid off tonight."

"Yes, it did, Teddy. Yes, it did."

⌁

P'etro was the first to hear the ruckus approaching the cabin, and he felt something was very wrong. For a moment, he puzzled over the noise. Realizing it was the sound of screaming children, he rose and started toward the door. Before he reached it, the door burst open. Wide-eyed pale-faced children ran into the cabin, stammering, stuttering, and shaking in fear. Breathlessly, they stared at one another. The startled adults waited impatiently for an explanation, but none came. Not willing to wait any longer, Sergey glared at the children with a look they had come to understand as meaning, *I'm going to get the leather strap.*

"Boys, what happened?"

"The…the…ba…barn," Borysko stammered, out of breath.

"A bear!" Lauro shouted.

With a look of horror on her face, Mama Ilia looked at Katya.

"Where is Samuil?"

"I don't know."

"Where is Alonya?" Nastasiya asked.

"In the barn!" Lauro huffed.

"With the bear!" Borysko yelled.

Nastasiya turned ghostly white, gasped for air, and fainted.

Samuil and Teddy stood proudly in the breezeway of the barn as the glimmering harvest moon sprayed silver light across the river valley. In the moonlight, Samuil saw the silhouetted figure of a frightened little girl at the edge of the forest. Alonya lay curled up on the ground near the edge of the forest, crying and shaking. Seeing her that way crushed Samuil's heart. He walked over and knelt beside her.

"Hey, Lonya, it's me. Samuil. Everything is all right. Don't be scared."

Alonya sat up and smiled. Samuil wiped a tear from her eye.

"I'll protect you, Lonya."

"Thank you, Samuil."

"Would you like to play in the dirt?"

"Uh-huh."

"Come on, Lonya, the good dirt is over there in the forest. I'll show you."

Alonya hesitated. She still seemed scared of the bear in the forest.

Guilt-ridden for having frightened her, Samuil confessed.

"Lonya, the bear is gone. It came on a blue forest light, roared for me, and then left on the blue light. Sorry if it scared you."

Alonya smiled shyly.

"Me and Teddy had to scare off your brothers. They were hurting the oxen."

"Oh."

"Over here is some good dirt, Lonya. Good for playing in. Come on."

Together they walked into forest until Samuil found the dirt pile. They played there and lost themselves in the joy of childish fun.

"Samuil, I like drawing circles in the dirt."

"Me too, Alonya."

As they continued playing in the soil, Alonya touched Samuil's hand.

"Not scared of blue bear," she said quietly.

Samuil winked and smiled.

"The blue bear is a good bear. It won't hurt you." Samuil explained.

They looked at each other with a glimmer of friendship in their eyes, and they smiled their childhood smiles of understanding. In that quiet moment in time, fear faded, and friendship deepened. Together, under the flickering star-splashed sky, they played together like good friends do.

After some time, Samuil pointed to the cabin light.

"There, Lonya. Your mama is over there. She's in the cabin where the dim light is flickers through the trees."

"Alright, thanks Samuil."

Alonya continued playing in the dirt and when she turned around to say thank you to Samuil, he had already vanished into the night on another adventure.

Deeper into the forest with Teddy in his pocket, Samuil glimpsed a spider's web shimmering in the silvery moonlight. Fascinated, he walked over to the web, being very careful not to disturb the craftsman. He sat Teddy down and began an intense inspection of the spider's amazing work. He admired the well-designed symmetry and marveled at the wonder of it. Kneeling, he leaned in for a closer look and spotted the spider in a dark corner of its home.

Samuil froze, slowed his breathing, and gazed at the creature. The creature looked back. The two studied one another, eyeball to eyeball. Not wanting to frighten his potential friend, Samuil slowly and carefully stretched out his hand. Inching closer to the web, Samuil abruptly stopped when he heard the words of his mama echo in his mind.

"Samuil, you must always be careful around spiders, snakes, and such. They are easily frightened by strange things and people. To them, people are trespassers. When alarmed or frightened, they'll bite you. Some can hurt you, and others can make you very sick."

For a moment, Samuil considered her words of warning and the situation at hand and then redirected his focus. The web's craftsman was still sitting off to one side of the web, waiting. Quietly, so as not to startle this magnificent creature, Samuil spoke to the spider with his mind.

"Hello, Mrs. Spider, don't be scared."

"Are you going to hurt me?"

"No, Mrs. Spider. I will not do anything to hurt you or your web. My name is Samuil. And that's Teddy over there."

For a long moment there was silence.

"My name is Mrs. Webber."

"Oh, hello, Mrs. Webber. Nice to meet you. Let's be friends."

"Your kind do not like my kind."

"Teddy and I like all the forest creatures and haven't I seen you in Big Boy's stall.

"Yes, my cousin lives there. A friend of Big Boy is a friend of mine."

With formal introductions over, Samuil felt much better about the situation. He smiled and moved his fingers toward the cautious spider. He stopped his hand next to the spider and waited. Remaining as motionless as a breezeless night in the forest, he studied his new friend. Samuil prayed that the long introduction had sealed their friendship. The last thing he wanted to do was scare the spider into a frenzy of biting. That wouldn't be good for anyone.

Samuil marveled at the distinct features of his new friend. Her body was small, much like Samuil's. Her dusty hair was short and scruffy like his. Samuil wondered if the spider's mother also fussed at her for not properly washing and grooming her hair. Her spindly legs, much like Samuil's small bony ones, moved slightly.

Samuil frowned, wondering why she was still sizing him up. Calculating the situation, he readied himself to jump and flee for safety if attacked. Her tiny eyes never left Samuil. Samuil's eyes never left hers. He waited motionless for the spider to accept his outstretched arm.

Having discovered so much in common, plus having a lengthy conversation, Samuil thought the spider should be ready to play. To his sheer delight, the spider moved. Slowly, she reached out with a leg and touched Samuil's hand. He was excited but remained motionless. Even though he wanted to jump and shout, he stayed very still. Whether realizing their friendship or just sensing no danger, Mrs. Webber walked onto his hand.

Carefully, so as not to startle his friend, Samuil sat upright, and the spider walked from his hand to his arm. When he placed his right hand on his arm near the spider, she crossed over to his other hand. Lost in the ecstasy of the moment Samuil and the spider played until out of the corner of his eye, he saw something move in the straw.

"Teddy, look."

"What?"

"A leaf monster. Over there. Quiet—don't move."

Quickly, Samuil explained to Mrs. Webber that there was an intruder in their midst, and he had to look into it. Mrs. Webber walked back to the safety of her spun home.

Samuil slowly turned his head and focused on the spot. Suddenly, it shot out from the leaf and darted to toward a tree and wiggled into a hollow log. Samuil jumped to his feet, walked to the log and curiously peeked into the dark log where he saw movement.

The leaf monster was preparing for his next daring move. In a flash, it raced out of the stall and rushed for the safe cover of the forest. Samuil grabbed Teddy and followed.

"Did you see that?"

"Yes. What was it?"

"A leaf monster, and it went that way. Come on, before it gets away."

"But—"

"You're scared."

"No, I'm not."

"Then stop shaking, and let's go find it."

"Well."

"We have to hurry, or it will get away."

"All right."

"Quiet like a mouse. Invisible like a ghost."

Samuil, unafraid of the dark or the creatures of the forest hurried quietly into the woodland. Being accustomed to nightly romps in the forest, he maneuvered swiftly in the moonlight as he followed the unknown creature.

"What kind of creature is it, Sammy?"

"I'm not sure."

"If it's big and mean, it could turn on us."

"It's small."

"Small monsters can be very dangerous, especially if it's a shadow monster."

"Shadow monsters don't run; they attack."

The small, swift, mysterious creature stopped at the base of an old tree. Samuil stopped also. He stared at the forest floor in the moonlight, searching for the creature. Finally, Samuil caught a glimpse of the monster trying to conceal itself in the fallen leaves. As the sly leaf ogre moved, Samuil turned. Moving his eyes in the murky stillness, he tried to focus and identify the leaf ogre. Two yellow eyes stared up at him from under the pile of leaves. The hiding creature widened it eyes in the dark.

Samuil readied himself for a defiant standoff. Having made eye contact, they exchanged icy stares. In the eternal moment of that hypnotic eye lock, they connected. In their linking, the creature's eyes narrowed into a squint, his pupils into slits.

A screech owl cried in the night, startling Samuil. He jumped, dropped Teddy, and fell. The creature seized that opportunity to escape. Quickly, it dashed into the dark depths of the forest. Not to be outdone, Samuil grabbed Teddy by his one good ear, and they ran.

"I think I know what it is! He's a runner! Come on!"

Samuil raced through the forest, chasing the woodland beast.

"Wait, stop, Sammy."

"What?" Samuil asked as they slowed.

"You said you knew what it was. Does it bite?"

"I don't know."

"I'm not going any further till I know if it bites."

"Oh, come on, Teddy. I won't let it bite you."

"Promise?"

"Yes, I promise."

"You go on. I'll stay here."

"I'm not coming back for you."

"Oh?"

"Come on—before we lose it."

Again, in pursuit, Samuil explained his plan to Teddy.

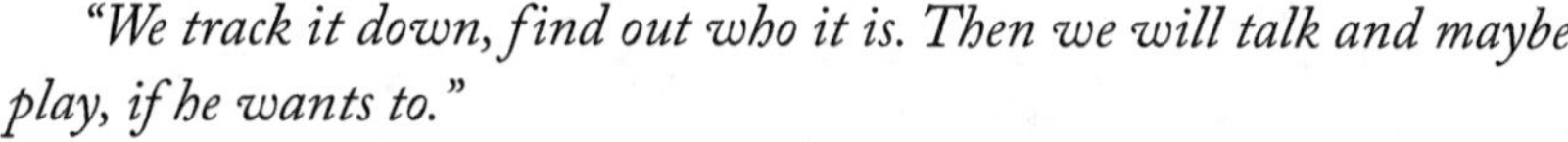

"*We track it down, find out who it is. Then we will talk and maybe play, if he wants to.*"

"*And if it's a she?*"

"*All right, if she wants to. Then if you still want to go home, we will.*"

"*Promise?*"

"*Yes, I promise.*"

They rushed deeper and deeper into the forest in pursuit of the woodland rogue.

CHAPTER 15

Run For Your Life

Suppressing his anger, Sergey spoke in a deep voice.

"Stay with your mama, Katya, and keep this wet cloth on her head."

"Yes, sir."

Then he spoke to his boys sternly.

"Stay here and help tend to your mama."

With a frown, he spoke to them all.

"I will deal with you children when I get back."

Frightened by the bear and their Papa, all three siblings looked at one another and shivered. As Katya tended to their mother, the boys silently stared at Katya.

With a knot of anxiety growing in his stomach, P'etro grabbed Ilia's loaded rifle and tossed it to her. Then he grabbed his own loaded rifle and pistols, as well as hunting knives. Ilia stuck two loaded pistols and a hunting knife in her belt. As they stepped out the door, Ilia grabbed a lantern.

Running into the moonlit night, P'etro lead the gallant group to Sergey's buggy where he grabbed a long rifle, and knives and pistols. With weapons raised, senses heightened, and every muscle tensed, they continued to the barn and stopped at the barn entrance. Quietly, they listened for sounds of the children or the bear. In the chilled stillness of the night, they heard nothing. In the empty silence, P'etro signaled the troop to gather.

"Let's search for tracks. Sergey, search the barn and stalls with the lantern. We will go around back and look around. We'll meet up back in the barn."

"All right."

Defiantly, Sergey looked into the sky and angrily mumbled under his breath.

"I will kill the bear. I will kill it with my own two hands!"

P'etro saw the veins on Sergey's neck swell and every muscle in his body rippled. With a look of deadly intention, Sergey turned and disappeared into the night.

After a thorough search around the barn and stalls, the adults met in the middle of the barn.

"Any sign of the bear, Sergey?" P'etro asked.

"No. Did you see anything?" "No."

"Big Boy broke out of his stall, and he's gone," Ilia reported.

"And Blackie?"

"He's fine and still in his stall."

The brush behind them rustled, disturbing the still of the night and startling everyone. P'etro and Sergey raised their rifles and were ready to fire when Nastasiya stumbled and fell out of the edge of the forest, wide-eyed, with her pistol drawn and ready for blood.

"Nastasiya?"

"Sergey! Help me out of these bushes."

"Nastasiya, are you alright?" Ilia asked.

"Yes."

"What are you doing?" Her concerned husband asked.

"I left you in the care of the children. You had a fright. You should be resting."

"I'm fine—thank you very much, husband. I knew I would find you here. And I am here to help find the children."

With a sigh, Sergey gave in.

"There's no signs of Samuil or Alonya." Ilia explained as her eyes filled with tears.

"There are no signs of the bear either," Sergey added.

"Ilia, you and Nastasiya take the lantern, hang it in the barn, and wait there for the children to return."

"Will they be able to see it?" Nastasiya asked as Ilia held the lantern with shaking hands.

"Yes," P'etro replied.

"Ilia, turn the lantern light up as high as it will go. Even if they only see a dim glow, they'll follow the light."

"Alright."

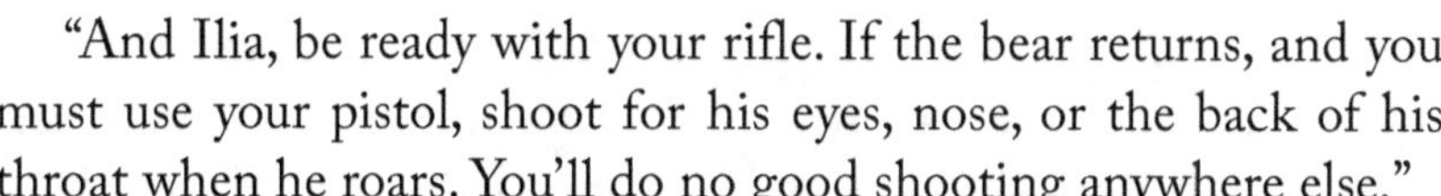

"And Ilia, be ready with your rifle. If the bear returns, and you must use your pistol, shoot for his eyes, nose, or the back of his throat when he roars. You'll do no good shooting anywhere else."

Ilia bit her bottom lip and stared blankly at P'etro, as if her mind had locked down.

"Do you understand?"

"Yes."

"Sergey and I will track the bear down and kill it."

"And we will find the children too," Sergey promised.

By the beaming light of the moon, P'etro saw something out of place and motioned to Sergey.

"What, P'etro?"

"There, at the back of the barn. Come on."

"It's a tree branch, P'etro. The wind must have broken it off."

"No, there are footprints. Someone was here. And there is another print leading to the tree line. Come on. We will follow them."

The two tracked the small footprints to the edge of the tree line. There, the footprints vanished. They walked into the forest and searched but found nothing. Finding no bear tracks or signs, they looked at each other and shrugged.

"Nothing here, Sergey. Nothing but a footprint leading nowhere."

"Let's go back to the barn and check with Nastasiya and Ilia. Maybe the children saw the lantern light and came to the barn."

"Good idea."

They returned to the barn, only to learn that neither Alonya nor Samuil had returned. P'etro looked at the women and sighed, wishing he had better news for them. He told them about the tracks and cold trail.

"There are no marks, no scratching, no sign of a bear anywhere. Sergey and I searched carefully."

"Oh, Samuil. Oh Alonya." Ilia squeezed P'etro's hand and gazed into his hazel eyes.

"Where could they be, Papa?"

"I don't know, Mama. I don't know."

"Maybe they went back to the cabin, Ilia." Nastasiya said, her voice shaking.

"We should go back to the cabin and check, Nastasiya," Ilia said. "If Samuil and Alonya are not there, maybe there is something the children can remember that will help us decide what to do next."

"Good idea, Ilia. And if need be, we can regroup and start again," Sergey added.

Earlier in the evening, Samuil had directed Alonya to his cabin, where her parents were. As she walked toward the cabin, he stepped into the forest. When Alonya turned around to speak to him, he was nowhere to be seen; he had disappeared into the night.

Disappointed, Alonya plopped down on the ground, where she picked up a bug. Holding it in her hand, she examined it.

"Did you see where Samuil went?"

When the bug didn't answer, she looked away.

"Me either. I need to find him."

She paused and looked back at the bug.

"I was on my way to his cabin but changed my mind. I want to play with Samuil. I don't want to be in the cabin with my mean brothers. I don't want to be alone in the night. I want to draw lines in the dirt with Samuil."

She smiled at the bug and continued.

"Samuil's my only friend. He doesn't pick on me like my brothers. He's not bossy like Katya. Sometimes he's sad. Sometimes he's pouty, but still, it makes me happy to play in the dirt with Samuil."

A distant clap of thunder caused Alonya to look in the direction of the noise. Then she looked back at the bug.

"Samuil likes Lonya. Lonya likes Samuil. Samuil likes dirt, me too. Samuil likes to play; me too. I will find Samuil so we can play."

Lightning flashed in the dark sky and fingered out like elongated tree branches. The flash flared through the heavens, lighting up the night and startling Alonya. She jumped, grabbed the bug, and ran to where she had last seen Samuil disappear into the woodland. As she ran to the cabin light, she saw another light flickering in the night. The little light was just above her. She stopped and puzzled over the appearance of this little light so soon after the big flash of lightning. Wide-eyed and with her mind racing, she gasped and searched for answers as the lightning continued to dance in the sky. Startled by another flash, she jumped.

"Wow, Mr. Bug, big light and little light. Little light little … big light big. Big light boomed. Little light flashed. Big light way up. Little light just here."

She squatted on the ground, tilted her head, and spoke to the bug again.

"Little light fell from the big sky light. The big skylight flashed. The little light flickered. Little light dropped from big light."

As she puzzled over what she'd seen, the little light flickered again, shocking Alonya back into the moment.

A flickering firefly slowly maneuvered overhead. Alonya put the bug on the ground and followed the firefly. She was captivated, and as the little light blinked away, Alonya hypnotically followed. Unaware of anything but the blinking light, she walked toward the nocturnal world of the Southern Forest.

Samuil continued the pursuit of the night monster, with Teddy in his pocket. Deep in the woods, the monster darted into a clump of grass.

"He's hiding, Teddy."

"Yeah, but he might run again."

The creature knew it was cornered by the relentless pursuer and hugged the ground. Samuil watched as the mystery monster turned to face him. Instinctively, the woodland ogre made a move that gave it away. Samuil watched as the leviathan coiled and flicked its forked tongue in the glistening moonlight. He recognized the maneuver and knew the leviathan was tasting the air around it in search of his adversary's scent.

Samuil poked Teddy.

"I knew it! Just as I thought! A snake."

"I knew it too."

"No, you didn't, you said it was a dragon."

"Well, dragons and snakes are cousins. So that's the same thing."

"No, it's not Teddy, and you know it. This could be the snake Borysko threw into Big Boy's stall?"

"Maybe."

As if unraveling a great mystery, Samuil bit his bottom lip and thought about the various possibilities. He stuffed Teddy in his pocket and carefully crawled toward the snake. In his mind, Samuil thought about being a snake, so he stayed as close to the ground as possible and tried to slither. Slowly wiggling and barely breathing, he carefully inched closer to the snake. The snake flicked its tongue, trying to identify its pursuer. Samuil sensed the snake's uneasiness.

The snake either tasted me in the air or felt my movement through the ground or maybe both.

Not wanting to spook the snake, he stopped and watched for a long time. He desperately tried to remember the words of wisdom his Papa had drilled into him. Samuil racked his brain.

How did Papa explain it? Is this a common viper or a forest- steppe? Maybe it's a grass snake or a water snake. Is it poisonous or not?

Samuil couldn't recall the exact warning. Slowly, he backed away from the snake. Wrinkling his brow, he tried to evoke the memory. *How did Papa explain it?*

"I can't remember Teddy."

"I do."

"Oh, you remember?"

"Yes, I do."

"Fine, tell me."

"That's the poisonous viper that Papa described."

"No, it's a grass snake."

"It's not green. It's a man-killer."

"Some grass snakes are brown."

"Are you sure?"

"No, but if it bites you and you die, then we'll know."

Samuil shook his head and frowned at Teddy.

"Come on, let's go talk to the snake."

"No, I don't want to."

"Why not? Are you scared?"

"No."

"Then come on."

"It might be venomous."

"Teddy, I won't let it bite you."

Seeing Teddy's hesitation, Samuil tried to reassure him.

"Teddy, I'll put you in my pocket. You will be safe there."

"All right."

"Okay. Quiet like a mouse…"

"Invisible like a ghost," Teddy concluded.

Samuil knelt and slowly slithered to the snake. When the snake flicked its tongue, tasting the air, Samuil stopped.

"Why did we stop?"

"The snake doesn't know us, and I don't want to scare it off."

Slowly, Samuil backed away and took Teddy out of his pocket.

Talk to him first Sammy. Make sure he's not angry or upset. And tell him we're friendly."

"He's not upset, Teddy.

"Well, he might think we have weapons."

"Okay, Teddy. If I tell him that we are unarmed, can we go back in?"

"Yes but tell him not to bite. I don't want to die."

Samuil rolled his eyes and began forming snake words and placing them in the snake's mind. As he spoke to the snake, the snake answered. For several minutes, they communicated and got acquainted.

"Okay, Teddy. He wants to play."

"Did it identify itself?"

"Yes, it's a poisonous forest viper, and it wants to play."

"Not with me, he isn't. I'll have my fun from right here. I call it fun from a distance."

"All right."

Again, Samuil approached the snake. Nose to nose with it, he stopped. The boy and the snake looked at each other for a long time. Each time the snake flicked his tongue, Samuil flicked his. When the snake moved its head, Samuil moved his. As the snake became more comfortable with the situation, he uncoiled, and Samuil relaxed.

Samuil gently scooted his hand toward the snake and told the snake to crawl aboard. The snake flicked his tongue. Samuil remained very still. Slowly, the snake slinked toward Samuil's outstretched hand. The snake stopped, looked around, tasted the air, and laid his head in Samuil's palm. A second later, the snake slid up his arm. Teddy shook and grimaced as he watched.

Samuil wanted to shout for joy, but instead he bit his tongue and relaxed. He carefully took hold of the snake and put it around his neck. Teddy shut his eyes and held his breath as the snake slithered all over Samuil.

The snake slinked down his neck and into his shirt. Samuil chuckled, trying not to shiver or flinch. Reaching Samuil's chest, the snake stopped. He slid his head through a gap in Samuil's shirt, looked at him, and flicked his tongue. Samuil giggled, flicked his tongue in response, and pulled the snake out of his shirt. For a long time, they played their silly game. Finally, the snake slithered to the ground and crawled away. As Samuil watched, the snake stopped, coiled, looked at Samuil, flicked his tongue, and waited.

"Come on, Teddy. Mr. Snake wants us to follow!"

"You go on. I'm fine right here."

"Oh, come on, Teddy."

"No. I don't want to go."

"Are you afraid?"

"No, Sammy. It's just that we're going in the direction of the Southern Forest. I can hear the stream where the forest begins."

"So, you're scared."

"No, I'm not. I just don't want to go into the Southern Forest."

Before Teddy could answer, Samuil grabbed him and stuffed him in his pocket. Quickly, Samuil followed the snake deep into the forest. Totally oblivious to everything else in the universe, Samuil played his game of following Mr. Snake.

When Ilia arrived at the cabin to talk to the children, she opened the door and called out for Samuil. All she heard was silence. Nastasiya called out for Katya, but her daughter didn't answer. She called for the boys and was greeted by silence and a chilling absence. Earlier in the evening, the cabin had been alive with laughter and joy. Now, there was only the heavy breathing of winded parents.

Inside, the parents looked around the empty cabin until Sergey growled, breaking the eerie stillness.

"Where are the children?"

"They were here when I left, and I strictly told them to stay in the cabin till we returned," Nastasiya explained.

Grumbling, Sergey answered, "But they're not here now."

"Why would they leave?" Ilia asked.

"I don't know," Nastasiya said anxiously.

"We have to find them."

"We will, Nastasiya. Maybe they went looking for Alonya. If so, they shouldn't be far." Ilia said.

Nastasiya broke the tense silence with a question.

"Maybe we scared them, Sergey."

"What?" Sergey grunted and wiped sweat from his brow.

"We both threatened them with a whipping. Maybe they ran away."

"Maybe they just went home. There's a full moon tonight, so we should be able to find them," P'etro reminded everyone.

"They haven't had time to get home yet. They must be still in the forest. Maybe we can find their tracks," Sergey suggested.

P'etro thought for a minute before explaining his plan of action. Sergey and Nastasiya traveled east toward their cabin skirting the timberland and then circle north through the pasture that lead to their cabin hoping to find the children already home. Ilia and P'etro went west through the dense woods and circle north where they would all meet up in the north corner of the pasture.

"Sergey if you find them before we meet up, fire off two shots. We will do the same. Go now. Be quick and be careful," P'etro said.

CHAPTER 16

Deadly Forest Night

After hours of trudging through the moonlit forest, Katya knew they were lost and walking in circles. Frustrated, she yelled at her brother.

"Borysko, stop! We're lost."

"No, we're not."

"Yes, we are. This isn't the Northern Forest. Nothing here is familiar."

"What do you know about the forest?"

"I know that stream we crossed way back there is the stream that leads into the Southern Forest."

"No, you don't."

As they quarreled, the bone-chilling scream of a wildcat echoed through the river valley. Everyone froze. Katya shook when the cat cried again. In the silence that prevailed, she noticed that her brothers were quiet. She sensed terror in the air, and she squeezed Borysko's arm and shivered. Her mind filled with fearful thoughts of a slow, painful death in the jaws of a ferocious beast. The possibility of her death sent more fear coursing through her veins.

The siblings huddled together and stared into the forest. In her confusion and fright, Katya wondered what she should do. Long, dark shadows, as thin as threads, dropped from the trees. Some slithered through the forest and disappeared into the moonlit night. Others gathered, tumbled, intensified, and rolled into a shadow fog.

"Borysko, there's a dark fog building in the forest," Katya warned.

"There's always fog in the forest."

"Yes, but it looks like more than fog."

"What do you mean?" He asked sounding puzzled.

Katya looked at the fog and then looked back to Borysko before answering.

"I don't know. Something is inside it and its moving. That is not a normal fog."

"Where did it come from?"

"The trees."

"We should go?"

"There's nowhere to go. The fog is everywhere."

"Then we should run."

"There's nowhere to run." Katya insisted.

"If you're trying to scare me, sister, it's working."

Katya shivered as the shadow fog rolled closer. The fog twisted, looped, knotted, and rolled into the meadow from every direction. From deep within the fog, a wildcat screamed. Terrified, Katya tried to think as shadow strings swirled around the sibling's ankles. The hot and cold strings entrapped them, and they gasp in fear as the dark fog rose to their knees and then to their waist. Sinister sounds rose from the fog hissing and growling. Slowly, the fog engulfed them.

Inside the fog, Katya squinted to see. Slimy things were scurrying around her feet. Scaly things were rubbing against her calves. She shivered as a huge long-legged spider walked her way.

"Don't move, Lauro. Don't breathe, Borysko." She warned.

"Why?" the boys asked in unison.

"There's a huge wolf."

"What wolf? I'm looking into the eyes of a giant saber-toothed cat," Borysko said with a quiver in his voice.

"A two-headed fire-breathing dragon is glaring at me," Lauro explained.

As the wolf flashed its teeth and snarled, Katya froze. Out of nowhere, a giant snake slithered through the fog and chased the giant spider. Her mind quickly filled with horrifying illusions of terrible things. Then a gust of wind blew the fog back into the forest.

Katya drew her knife from its sheath under her skirt and looked around the foggy forest.

I will not go quietly into the arms of darkness. I will fight you, and I will slay you.

Borysko set his jaw, picked up a branch, and began whittling it into a spear point. A beast cried in the night, and all the children shivered.

When she heard the cry of the angry cat, Katya scanned the foggy tree line and glimpsed a saber-toothed cat.

"Over there, Borysko. It came from the fog."

She watched in shock as Borysko waved his spear in the air, yelled, and charged into battle. Sadness and terror filled her soul as her fearless brother rushed into the teeth of death. She gasped as he plowed into the shadow fog.

The forest echoed with piercing screams from the shadow beast and the blood-crazed battle cry of a resolute warrior. The night filled with the fierce sounds of battle. Beasts roared, Borysko yelled, and Katya prayed.

Then there was silence. Anxiously, she waited and listened, hoping against hope that her brother had prevailed.

"It's dead! It's dead! I've beat the beast!" Borysko yelled, running out of the fog bruised and bleeding but alive. Exhausted, he fell to his knees.

"Are you sure it's dead?" Katya asked.

"No animal could live after being speared and stabbed dozens of times."

"Look Borysko It's still alive." Katya whispered.

"How?"

To her dismay, Lauro yelled and raced into the fog. Inside the fog, he ran through the meadow, as a two-headed monster pursued breathing fire. Katya fell to the ground as the fire blew over her. She wondered how a boy with a knife could defeat a two-headed fire-breathing shadow dragon. Again, she heard the yells and screams and noise of a fierce battle.

When Lauro emerged from the fog, his shirt was burned off, and his arms were blistered from the monster's fiery breath. She knew he wanted to run, but he stood bravely, stilled his racing heart, took a deep breath, and ground his teeth. As the head of the dragon emerged from the fog, Lauro grabbed a jagged rock and hurled it at the monster. The deadly projectile pelted the angry monster with a precise, slicing blow. With all his might, Lauro threw another and another.

As the crazed monster charged out of the fog, all three children joined the battle. Katya and Lauro bombarded the dragon with rocks as Borysko charged with his spear. Jagged rocks struck home, tearing flesh and drawing blood. The wounded monster turned and disappeared again into the fog.

A giant wolf ran out of the fog. Then the dragon reappeared, followed by the saber-toothed tiger. Borysko and Lauro froze. Katya shivered. She couldn't believe her eyes. She clenched her fists, screamed at her brothers, and started throwing rocks. Her scream broke their trance, and they also began throwing rocks. In her terror- filled mind, Katya felt the wolf's burning eyes on her. When it howled, she cringed, realizing the overwhelming power of the fiery monster.

"Run!" she yelled.

She ran through the forest with the wolf chasing her. The monster leaped from a rock and pounced on Katya's back. When she fell, she grabbed a handful of dirt and threw it in its eyes. It's howling cry thundered through the forest. Again, she ran staring into the forest and trying to still her racing heart. Katya knew that it would come for her again.

"Katya, over here," Borysko whispered.

"Borysko, Lauro, how did you get here?" Katya asked.

"Same as you—we were running for our lives," Lauro explained.

"We have to hide. It will be back." Borysko said in a shaky voice.

Katya stared into the night as the receding shadow fog twisted angrily through the eerie forest. The wild cat screamed again, and its terrifying echo filled the valley. Fear gripped Katya's heart and she yelled. "Run."

Deep in the Southern Forest, Samuil and Teddy continued their games with the snake. Samuil watched the snake slide over a stump and disappear in a hole under a rocky overhang. Weary from the night's adventure, Samuil sat down, propped Teddy up, and yawned. Moments later, he and Teddy fell asleep and dreamed of snakes— snakes in the barn, moccasins in the water, vipers in the trees, adders on the rocks, sidewinders in the dirt, serpents in the bed, snakes on the ground, snakes all around.

In the middle of Samuil's nightmares, he jerked himself awake. He rubbed the fading dream from his eyes and struggled to orient himself. String shadows coiled and dripped from the trees. They gathered, twisting into a dark fog, and rolled over Samuil and Teddy. Engulfed, he searched for Teddy. He found Teddy wiggling in the fog. Then he realized Teddy wasn't wiggling at all. He was sitting still, and balls of smoking shadow snakes were slithering all over him.

Samuil felt something at his feet. He saw that he was also being covered with jumbled wads of twisting shadow snakes from the waist down. He jumped to his feet and began kicking and slapping the snakes off him. The angry snakes glowed red, and smoke poured from their scales. When Samuil swatted them, they burst into red flames, burning his flesh. The flames of the fiery snakes flashed through the fog like lightning.

When the fog rose and rolled over him, more smoking and agitated shadow snakes slithered around Samuil. Samuil picked up a stick and began thrashing them. Again, the fire snakes exploded, filling the air with fire and smoke. Samuil burst out of the fog, ran to the river, and jumped in. The river water cooled his burned skin, and he sighed in relief.

Now he had to free Teddy from the demon horde. He stepped out of the river, took a deep breath of courage, and walked back toward Teddy and the fog. Fiery snakes slithered out of the fog, coiling and spitting fire at Samuil. When he swatted the snakes, they exploded, whistled back into the fog, regenerated, and came back in a fiery blaze.

Against all odds, Samuil fought on. Fire blistered his arms, smoke burned his eyes, and snakes crawling all over him. As the battle raged, a giant python wrapped itself around Teddy and opened its mouth. It sank its teeth into Teddy and then disappeared in the fog.

Taking a deep breath, Samuil raced through the fog, and when he saw the tail of the snake wiggling, he charged forward, determined to rescue Teddy at all costs. He grabbed the snake by the tail and tugged. To his surprise, a giant shadow dragon turned to face him with Teddy in its teeth. Samuil grabbed a rock and threw it. The rock flew true smacking the dragon in the eye. The dragon threw back its massive head, roared, and tossed Teddy high in the air.

As Samuil ran out of the fog to catch his best friend, the dragon spit fire. When he reached the edge of a cliff, Samuil leaped in the air to retrieve Teddy, just as the dragon's fire struck. Teddy vanished in a puff of fiery smoke, his fur crackling, his eyes wide.

Samuil fell as the fog grew into a shadow cloud. Samuil fell into the dark cloud and saw all kinds of terrible monsters thrashing around on the fringes. As he fell through the cloud, beasts reached out with claws and beaks, ripping at him. He splashed into the singing river and heard its melody and relaxed.

Samuil swam out of the river and decided to head back to the cabin. As he walked, he thought of Teddy.

Poor Teddy.

Samuil dropped to the leaf-covered forest floor and looked up at the moon.

The dark is good. The night is good.

Darkness is good. Darkness makes them all go away.

Dark is quiet. Dark inside me. Dark too dark.

As Samuil began walking again, he heard a noise. Startled, he instantly stopped, squatted, and looked around. Thinking it was the dragon, he listened. Again, he heard the noise. This time it was a quiet sound, soft and non-threatening. It was almost like a whisper. It didn't belong to the forest; it was out of place. It didn't feel right, but he did not know why. What he did know was that the noise was coming from the direction of the rocky, snake-infested overhang. When it stopped, it was replaced by a heavy silence. Softly, like a leaf in the wind, he heard it again as moonbeams danced off the forest floor.

It's a giggle. No. A snicker. A chuckle. It's a person.

Samuil quietly hurried in the direction of the sound. He heard a faint shuffling and slowly crept forward. Now near enough to see, Samuil wiggled into position and peeked out from an entangled mesh of twisted vines. He saw Alonya chasing a firefly. Alonya spotted Samuil as he stepped out from behind the mingled vines.

"Samuil!"

"Are you lost?"

"No, I'm playing with the little lightning. See?"

"I see a firefly."

"Oh. That's what it is."

"Do you know how to get home?"

"No."

"It's all right, Alonya. I know where we are."

"Samuil, let's play with the firefly."

Forgetting about Teddy, Samuil and Alonya played with the elusive fireflies. They skipped and laughed and ran through the forest after their firefly friend. After a while, Alonya stopped and sat on the ground. She called for Samuil, and he sat beside her. Alonya held Samuil's hand, and together they gazed into the moon-washed forest. Suddenly, a rabbit hopped into their peaceful moment. Lonya giggled and whispered in Samuil's ear.

"Bunny." She pointed.

"Oh."

"Bunny, Samuil."

"Shh, Lonya. Be still and watch."

Samuil slowly rose to a squat. As he prepared to dart out and catch the fidgety rabbit, a coyote howled, spooking both the bunny and Alonya. Alonya screamed, grabbed Samuil, closed her eyes, and prayed for deliverance from the monster of the night. The bunny ran.

"Come on, Lonya. Follow me."

The two brave souls trotted off through the shadowy forest, jumping logs and dodging branches.

"There, Lonya, over there. The bunny. See him?"

"Yes."

"Come on."

Carefully, they sneaked closer. Samuil stepped on a dead limb, and it snapped. Alonya squealed, and the frightened bunny hopped away. Hand in hand, they ran in hot pursuit of the bunny. They clamored through the woods, splashed across streams, climbed over cliffs, and jumped over boulders after the rabbit. As Samuil ran, he tripped over something large and solid. It let out a low, unintelligible beastly growl. Samuil froze.

"Alonya, it's a shadow monster!"

"Run, Samuil!"

Samuil rose, took a step, and fell over another large clump of twigs and leaves. It rose to all fours like a wild hog, and Alonya screamed.

"A monster!"

Samuil crawled backward, never taking his eyes off the monster. Alonya screamed again. "Another monster!"

Samuil looked over his shoulder to see another beast make a wolflike shuffle, rise, and growl. All three creatures of the night grunted and moaned. Samuil scrambled backward into a boulder. Lonya ran to his side.

As he struggled, one of the monsters slowly rose from the forest floor. Leaves, sticks, and branches rolled off the monster as it gruffly groaned like a wounded animal, stumbled, and fell. For a moment, everything in the moonlit forest fell silent. Samuil tried to speak with the monster, mind to mind, but there was nothing to connect to, so he and Lonya crawled away.

Shaking and grunting, the leaf ogre stood.

"Samuil!" Alonya squealed, squeezing his arm.

As fear raced through his veins, he wondered if this might be his last breath. Alonya covered her eyes. The tree monster groaned. The leaf beast menacingly stared at the two rabbit hunters. A new voice startled them.

"Alonya? Oh, Alonya!"

"Katya! Katya!"

Samuil sighed in happy disbelief as Katya ran up to them and swooped up Alonya. Squeezing her tight, Katya smothered Alonya with hugs and kisses.

"I'm so glad we found each other."

Together they spun in a circle, laughing and singing.

"The trees in the forest grow up, up, up. Up, up, up. Up, up, up. Straight to the sky."

Borysko and Lauro appeared, looking disheveled and panting heavily. The brothers looked at one another and wrinkled their noses at the silly, girlish play.

"Why did you bury yourself with brush?" Samuil asked.

"We were hiding so we could ambush the shadow monsters." Borysko explained, glaring at Samuil.

"More like you were scared and hiding from the shadow creatures." Samuil said with a smerk.

"Shut up, worm, before I break your nose."

Samuil called to the girls breaking up the merriment.

"Katya! The monsters are still out there. We need to go."

Alonya turned and saw Borysko. She rubbed her eyes in disbelief and cried out. "Borysko!"

"Singing and dancing are for sissies," Lauro scoffed.

"Lauro!" Alonya called.

Ignoring their brothers, the girls' revelry continued until a high, shrill scream rang out through the forest. It echoed through the river valley in every direction. Katya dropped Alonya. Alonya shuddered and grabbed her sister.

"A wildcat," Samuil said.

"He's back; do not move," Borysko commanded.

"Look." Lauro pointed, tilting his head.

Samuil looked into the forest. First, he felt the wildcat's piercing red eyes glaring from a dark, rolling fog. Then he saw it. Their gazes locked menacingly. Neither blinked. Their silent staring filled the air with hostility. Giving the wildcat his meanest look ever, Samuil wrinkled his brow in defiance. With his mind, he told the cat to leave. The shadow cat growled, slinked back into the darkness, roared, and raced toward them.

P'etro looked at Ilia, and he could see both fear and fatigue in his beloved's eyes.

"Papa, we should have found them by now," she said wearily.

"It's a big forest, Ilia."

"But not even a trace. A track. A sound."

"Shh. Did you hear that?"

"All I hear are frogs."

"It came from over there. It sounded like distant screams."

"A wildcat?"

"I don't know. But that is the direction of the Southern Forest."

"If they're lost in the Southern Forest, they're in trouble. Come on."

He hefted his rifle, and they hurried onward.

They ran through the shimmering forest in the direction of the sound. They entered the Southern Forest and moved ahead, slowly and quietly, listening and searching for clues to the identity of the sound. Ilia stumbled and fell. P'etro helped her to her feet.

"Are you alright?"

"Yes," she answered and gathered herself to continue.

"Listen, Ilia. I think I heard it again."

"I don't hear anything."

"Maybe it was only my imagination. The forest has grown quiet again."

"P'etro, I need to rest. I need to catch my breath."

"All right, but this eerie silence bothers me."

While Ilia rested, P'etro stared warily into the misty forest. They sat on a fallen tree with only the faint sound of their labored breathing between them. Ilia sighed and looked at P'etro.

"Where could they be?"

"There."

"They're here? Where?"

Ilia jumped up and looked around with excitement.

"No. No, it's another sound. I keep hearing something."

"I know. Now the forest is alive with all kinds of sounds."

"Yes, but this is different."

P'etro stilled his breathing and listened. In the distance, he heard a muffled, shuffling noise.

"Ilia, do you hear that?" "What?"

"I'm not sure."

"Does it sound like a predator?"

"No, it's a different sound. It doesn't sound like a predator. Come on. We have to get closer and see what it is."

P'etro eased his way carefully through the thicketed forest and stepped behind a large oak. Squinting, he saw the moon-swept silhouette of something large. Before he could determine what it was, it moved out of sight, around the bank of a stream. He followed quietly and caught a glimpse of the bulky contour as it disappeared into the misty forest.

"Over here. Come on, Ilia. This way."

"But that is in the opposite direction from—"

I know this stream and I know where we are. This is the stream that separates the Forest's and circles back into itself just beyond those boulders. We can follow this water and come out ahead of the beast on higher ground and get a safe look at it."

Holding hands, they rushed downstream, scaled a slippery cliff, and circled behind a boulder. Winded, P'etro stopped and leaned on the rock.

"Ilia, see that thicket?" P'etro asked, pointing.

"Come on—we will be out of sight there and can watch the stream."

<hr>

The terrified children stood motionless and wide-eyed with hearts throbbing as Samuil stared at the stalking cat. Menacingly, he watched the wildcat, never taking his eyes off the beast. Breathlessly, the children waited as the cat growled and moved slowly into the moonlit night.

"Is it gone? Are we safe?" Katya asked Samuil.

"No. It will leave eventually but probably come back enraged.

It's a monster and will stalk us, separate us and pick us off one at a time. It gone for now, but it'll come back. It wants to kill us."

"Let's all run out of here together!" Katya said with pale with fear.

"No!" Samuil demanded.

"There is a cave over there." He pointed.

"What cave?" Lauro grunted.

"The cave beside the stream under the tree. Over there. Come on; I'll show you."

Overgrown with brush, vines, and grass, the hole in the side of the cliff was half blocked by a fallen tree. Samuil realized the tree would hinder the cat and other monsters from entering. He knew it would be a good place to hide.

"We can hide here."

The brothers looked at each other and rolled their eyes. Samuil wondered why they weren't all running for their lives to the cave. Frowning, Samuil crossed his arms in frustration and wondered.

What's Borysko thinking? Lauro is waiting on Borysko to decide. Katya is scared, and so is Alonya.

"Hurry!" Samuil snapped.

Exploding in the moment of tension came a chilling cry from the big cat. The bloodthirsty beast filled the forest with repeated screams. The wildcat's roar scared the children into motion. The brothers ran for their lives to the dark hole in the cliff. Katya instinctively grabbed Alonya's hand, and Samuil grabbed her other hand, and they ran, with the cat in hot pursuit.

Borysko and Lauro stumbled over tree branches and fell into a bed of dried reeds. Together, the two brothers picked up an armload of reeds and dashed for the confines of the cave. They tossed their dried reeds into the cave and dived in headfirst. Inside, Borysko sat on a rock, opened his pocketknife, and whittled reeds into sharp points.

"Nice knife," Samuil said.

"You know what Mama told you," Katya scolded.

"Mama's not here. If you tell her, I'll cut your tongue out."

"Here," Borysko said, handing Katya a sharp stick and then resuming his carving.

"What am I supposed to do with this?" Katya demanded.

"When the wildcat comes, jab him. If you can, jab him in the eyes.

Now take my blade that I'm not supposed to have and carve some more."

The wildcat screamed again, and a dark fog seeped into the cave, forcing them to scramble backward. Samuil looked around the large cave and saw moonlight flicker in a side tunnel. Excited, he decided to follow the light into the tunnel. He knew the children would be safe, and maybe he could find a safe way out of the Southern Forest through these tunnels.

"Katya, see that light."

"Yes."

"That means there's a back way out of here, and I'm going to find it."

"Okay, I'll tell the others."

"No. The moonlight could be shining through a hole too far or small for us to climb through. If I can climb into the forest, I'll be back with help. If I can't, I'll return to help in the fight. You'll be safe here with your brothers."

"You be safe too, Samuil." Katya kissed him on the cheek and ran back to the mouth of the cave.

Samuil crawled along the tunnel until he came to large cavern. Moonbeams washed through an opening, flooding the cave with dancing light.

Look at that! A castle underground, and it is lit with moonbeams.

Excited, he followed the dancing light out of the cavern and crawled through several other tunnels.

P'etro and Ilia hid in a thicket, nervously watching the stream. He knew the mystery creature would arrive any time, and he was waiting expectantly. The night was alive with forest sounds that comforted him. A singing forest meant that there were no predators lurking. Abruptly, a bloodcurdling scream erupted in the still night, shocking them both.

"Is it a wildcat?" Ilia asked.

"It could be a snow leopard."

"This far south?"

"It could be extending his territory. It's happened before. Come on; it could be stalking the children."

"Wait—it's time to fire the shots."

"But we've not found the children."

"Maybe we have. Regardless, we'll need help with that big cat."

"You're right."

Pulling both pistols from his belt, P'etro fired two shots. The shots echoed through the valley and went silent. Reloading, the worried parents walked into the star-flooded canopy sky of the Nieper River valley toward the echoing cry of the big cat.

"I heard gunfire. It's Papa! We're saved!" Katya squealed.

She was excited at the thought of being rescued and eager to be reunited with her parents.

"Come on. Everyone outside. We'll make lots of noise so they can find us," Katya directed.

"But what about the wildcat? What if the gunshots didn't scare him off?" Lauro asked in a shaky voice.

"If the gunshot didn't scare him, then we will," Katya swore.

"Are you crazy?" Borysko yelled.

"Everyone takes a spear and charge with me, yelling into the night." Katya handed everyone a spear. She wasn't thrilled at the idea of screaming and rushing into the night, but she couldn't think of any other way to keep them all alive and signal her parents their location.

At Katya's command, they all charged from the mouth of the cave into the forest, stumbling and yelling at the tops of their voices. With spears in hand, they formed a circle. Dancing and chanting, they readied themselves to fight and kill the stalking beast. In the chaotic commotion of the moment, Katya prayed Samuil would find help and return to rescue them.

⸻ ◆ ⸻

Hearing the rifle fire Samuil smiled.

"Papa is coming!"

Quickly, Samuil followed the silver moonlight through the cave, taking mental notes of the caverns and tunnels along the way. Entering a large cavern, Samuil looked around. Above him, he saw the night sky and the silvery moon.

Studying the cavern walls, he realized it wouldn't be a difficult climb. There were boulders and small saplings on the cavern walls, and it doesn't look too steep. He noticed the soil was loose and knew he would have to be surefooted to get out of the cave.

Samuil began to climb. To his surprise, he was able to find lots of handholds. As he pulled himself up behind a boulder, he saw something protruding from the soft dirt.

A bone. I wonder what kind of animal this is.

Excited by the discovery, Samuil began digging. When he uncovered a boney finger, he jerked to a stop.

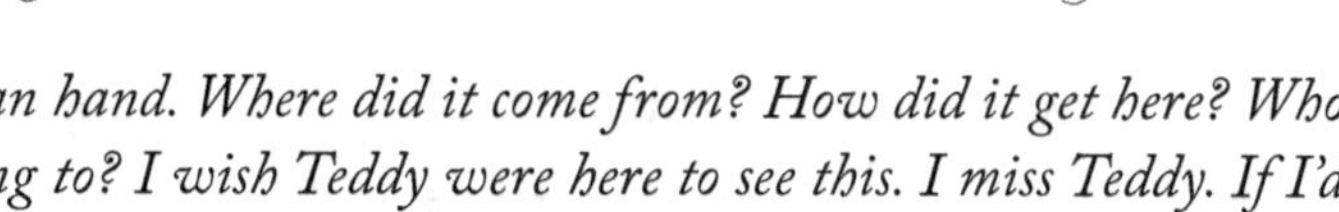

A human hand. Where did it come from? How did it get here? Who did it belong to? I wish Teddy were here to see this. I miss Teddy. If I'd been a little quicker, I could have grabbed Teddy and saved him from the dragon fire. What am I going to do without him?

With a sad heart, he continued his climb out of the cave. Once outside, he looked around for something familiar, but Nothing was. Then he heard the singing water and ran toward it. He thought it was the stream at the mouth of the cave—but it wasn't.

I am upstream. I must have traveled a long way through the winding caves. I must get help. I'll have to go downstream to find Papa.

With the pistol shots still ringing in his ears, Samuil moved through the trees with heightened awareness. The leaves on the forest floor suddenly started to rustle. He stopped, squatting behind a bush and stilled himself. All his senses flared. Something wasn't right. There was something in the forest that didn't belong.

He heard twigs snap and leaves rustle. Samuil dropped to all fours and crawled out of sight. With keenly intense senses, he listened. A crackling movement shuffled toward him. Samuil realized it was a heavy-footed sound like that of an elk or bear. Carefully, he slipped from behind his cover and crawled closer to the creature. Samuil was determined to discover the identity of this mysterious animal.

With a deep bellowing grunt, the beast stepped into the open and glared at Samuil. Startled, Samuil froze, hoping to blend in with forest foliage and be overlooked. However, the creature wasn't fooled. Breaking the suspenseful silence of the moment, it bellowed.

Moooooooo!

"Big Boy! It's Big Boy! Big Boy, it's me, Samuil. Found you, Big Boy! Or maybe you found me."

Chattering away to his long-lost gentle giant, Samuil slowly moved toward him, talking all the way. Speaking softly in a reassuring voice, Samuil walked up to Big Boy. Taking hold of his halter, he scratched him behind the ear and began singing a soothing melody.

"Samuil!" a voice called out from the forest.

When Samuil heard his name, he froze.

"Samuil!" The voice called again.

Ilia came running through the moonlit canopy. Reaching Samuil, she grabbed him in a bear hug.

"Are you hurt, Samuil? Where have you been? Why did you run off? We've been so worried. Where are the other children?"

"Ilia, dear, slow down," P'etro said, jogging up to them.

"Take a breath. Give Samuil a chance to answer."

As Samuil began telling his parents about the night's events, he was interrupted. Blowing in the wind were broken crying noises. The fragmented sound rose into something that resembled a ruckus. The ruckus from deep in the forest echoed through the rolling hills, escalating in intensity. Samuil instantly recognized the voices.

"That's the children, Papa." He tugged on his father's arm. Come on!"

"The children?"

"Yes, Papa. They're over there."

"And the big cat, Samuil?"

"He's there too, Papa."

"Come on; we have to hurry."

As they rushed through the forest, the sounds changed. To Samuil it sounded like a battle cry of crazed warriors engaged in combat.

"That way, Papa. They're over there." Samuil pointed.

The children were overjoyed to see P'etro and Ilia. Ilia checked the children to make sure there were not any wounds; then she pulled her pistols from her belt and fired two shots in the air, signaling their position to the Vitalik's.

"Perhaps the shots will keep the cat away too," Ilia boasted with a grin.

"Perhaps they will," P'etro said, grinning back.

"Children," Ilia said in a matter-of-fact tone.

"You shouldn't have run away. You know the Southern Forest is dangerous. Look what almost happened. That cat could have mauled you. I'm relieved that we found you. I'm happy that you are safe. But you had us scared out of our minds."

Katya walked over to Ilia and spoke softly as the boys hung their heads.

"Thank you for finding us, Mrs. Ilia. I'm sorry we ran away and got lost."

Ilia knelt and hugged her.

"We are in big trouble, Borysko," Lauro whispered to his brother.

"I know, and Papa's strap awaits us," Borysko answered.

"Children, form a line and follow Mr. P'etro," Ilia instructed.

"What are we going to do, Mrs. Ilia?" Katya asked.

"We're going to meet up with your parents."

CHAPTER 17

Shadow Dreams

Once he was back at their cabin, Samuil went straight to sleep, still fully dressed, but he tossed and turned fitfully and drifted into vivid and frightening dreams.

Piercing screams ripped through the night air. Fear and adrenaline rushed through Samuil's body. With his heart in his throat, Samuil ran toward the scream. He stopped, out of breath, and looked up at the broken rainclouds racing across the moon. A shadow fog as tall as the trees rolled menacingly through the Southern Forest. The scent of blood lingered in the air, and Samuil felt the presence of the shadow creatures.

In the distance, the crying of the big cats had stopped, and the stillness of the woodland became eerie. Silence blanketed the forest. Nothing moved or called. Abruptly, a sinister cry filled the night. As Samuil ran, he stumbled though the undergrowth and fell. He watched the shadow fog buck and roll and knot as he lay on the ground, and he listened, breathing quietly. Whispers emanated from the fog, and the air was dripping with malice. Evil hissed ominously, soaring on the wings of the wind. Shadow crawlers seeped out of the fog and transformed into monstrous wildcats. The sights and sounds of the eerie forest made a shiver race through his body.

A frantic plea interrupted Samuil's thoughts startling him and making him jump.

"Help!"

I know that voice.

"Help!

"Katya! Where are you?"

"Over here! By the waterfall!"

Samuil's heart pounded as he ran through the moon-washed forest toward the sounds of falling water. He found Katya sitting on the bank of the stream, leaning against a boulder. With concern in his eyes, he knelt and took her hand.

"Katya, are you hurt?"

"No, but I am bruised and frightened."

"Why are you shaking?"

"I'm afraid."

"Katya, everything will be fine.

"Hold me, Samuil."

Samuil wrapped his arms around Katya, and she laid her head on his shoulder. He held Katya in the shimmering moonlight until she stopped shaking. Then he saw the blood.

"You're bleeding. What happened?"

"It was awful. The attack…the fighting…the screaming. The wildcats were monsters. I have never seen anything like them. They were everywhere."

"It's all right now. I'm here. I need to wrap your wounds."

Samuil tore off a piece of his shirt, wet it in the stream, and cleaned the blood from Katya's shoulder. He was surprised when she didn't even grimace.

"I was lucky to escape with only a clawing."

"Yes, you were."

Samuil winked at her, tore off another portion of his shirt and carefully wrapped more wounds. His reward was a warm, beautiful smile.

"Samuil, have you seen the waterfall?"

"Yes, it's raging, and the stream is as big as a river. Everything will flood soon."

"Something strange is going on."

"What?"

"It must have something to do with the shadows. They seem to be everywhere."

From a tree hanging over the flooding stream, Samuil saw a shadow string stretch from a branch and slowly worm its way toward the water. Halfway down, it dropped into the stream, slithered into the waterfall, and tumbled over.

"Samuil, what's happened to the stream?"

"The shadows are in it."

"How?"

"I don't know, but the creeks are raging out of control. And there's a giant dark wave."

Samuil and Katya stood and ran up the hill, dodging trees and jumping over brush. Behind them, they could hear the torrent of water and feel the ground shake from its power. They didn't stop until they reached the top of the hill. Feeling safe, they surveyed the moonlit forest. Moonbeams bounced off the floodwater. There was water everywhere they looked, and it was littered with uprooted trees, drowned animals, and forest debris.

"Where did all the water come from?"

"I don't know, Katya."

"I'm so tired. I wish this was over."

"Me too."

They sat in the grass on the hilltop, and Katya laid her head on his shoulder. The two sat quietly, gazing into the starry night, each with their own thoughts. Samuil was the first to break the silence.

"Have you seen my Papa? He should be here."

"Samuil…"

"What is it?"

"Your Papa…he's…"

"No! That can't be."

"I'm sorry."

"And Mama?"

Katya shook her head. Tears rolled down Samuil's cheek, and she wiped them away.

"The wildcats came out of the shadow fog. First there were two monstrous wildcats—at least that's all the big ones I saw. And then more and more came—more than I could count— They were strange and ghostly, and they shimmered in the dark and they attacked your parents."

Samuil shook his head, moaned and looked away. Katya took his Hand. When she squeezed, he looked at her.

"Samuil your Papa saved my life."

For long, lonely moments, they sat holding hands in silence.

"What about your parents, Katya? What happened to them?"

"They're gone too."

"Wildcats?"

"Yes."

"Alonya?"

"Borysko ran away with her, but I don't know if they escaped."

"Where are the beasts now?"

"They're here hiding and waiting."

"Why are they still here?"

"They're not through killing."

With a sad heart, Samuil thought about his parents. He knew they would have fought to the end. He wished he had been there to help.

Katya nudged him.

"There's blood here. They can smell blood. They'll be back.

"They'll—"

"Come on," Samuil said.

"We need to go."

The night shivered around them.

"Where?"

"To the cave."

"No, Samuil, the wildcats know about the cave. They trapped us there."

"All right. Take my hand. We have to run."

"Where?"

"To the cabin."

Together they ran through the wood, staying on high ground to avoid the floodwater, the fog, and the cats. They were stopped in their tracks when they heard the roar of cats.

"Samuil!"

"Yes, I heard them too. They're between us and the cabin."

"What now?"

"It's not safe here. Come on—this way."

They decided to take a longer indirect route to the cabin in order to avoid the shadow cats. They saw cats by a roaring stream near the cabin but avoided them by altering their rout.

"There should be food in the cabin," Katya said.

"Yeah, but we'll have to sneak around those cats. Ready?"

Stealthily, they began maneuvering through the muddy flood waters and around the cats. When they came to a rushing stream, they had to figure out a way to cross it.

"Look at the water, Samuil; it's like the other creek. We can't swim in that. It's too swift."

"Right."

"What are we going to do?"

"You sit here and rest. I'll find a place to cross."

"No, I want to go with you."

"You're safe here. You can watch me as I walk up the creek to find a crossing. And I'll be back as quickly as I can."

Samuil ran upstream. When he came across a broken beaver dam, he stopped and reached out with his mind to the beavers.

A large beaver paddled closer and looked at Samuil.

"What can I do for you, friend?" The beaver asked.

"Did the floodwater crash your dam?"

"Yes, evil is abreast, and we have suffered."

"Let me help you repair it so my friend and I can cross."

"All right. What do you propose?"

"I'll get my friend. We'll gather branches and logs and bring them to the water's edge. Then your clan can repair the dam."

"That's a good plan."

"We'll meet you back here shortly."

Samuil ran back for Katya, and they returned and began the project with Samuil and Katya gathering armloads of various sized logs and stacking them on the bank. The beavers grabbed them and disappeared beneath the water's surface to repair their dam. In only a few minutes, Samuil and Katya were able to hop onto the beavers' home and cross over the water.

"Samuil, I'm bleeding again," Katya said when they reached the other side.

"Here, let me take care of your arm. I'll rewrap it; that should stop the bleeding."

"If you keep tearing your shirt, you will end up without one."

"Never mind that."

They moved on through the forest, trying to stay on higher ground to get to the cabin. They stopped and Samuil pointed.

"That stream over there will lead us to the rapids."

"I've never seen the rapids. Is the water there as fast as this?"

"It's faster, and they are protruding boulders as well. We'll climb that bank and go through the forest. The moonlight will help to keep us on track."

The journey through the shadowy forest was frightening. The shadow creatures were everywhere. Red-eyed demons rode on giant fire-breathing bulls. Others rode on red flaming beetles that spit molten lava, setting the forest ablaze. Samuil and Katya dodged forest fires as they ran from monsters and snaked their way to the cabin.

When they finally were inside, They collapsed.

"Can we rest now? Is it safe?" Katya asked.

"Yes, the cabin is safe. You rest in Papa's old rocker while I look for weapons and food."

"Oh, good. I'm starving."

"Be back before you miss me."

Samuil searched the cabin and found very little. It was a wreck. Shattered glass and broken furniture were everywhere. Dust covered everything and he found verry little food and no weapons. Disappointed, he returned with a bowl of beans.

"What did you find?" Katya asked.

"Not much."

He handed her the bowl.

"Beans?"

"Better than nothing."

"Nothing and a pinch of salt might taste better."

"Well, there is no salt. Just beans and nothing."

"Pass the beans, please."

The meal was interrupted by the screams of wildcats. Samuil peeked out the window and saw that the animals were all around the cabin.

"Katya, we're trapped."

They quietly made their way to a closet in Samuil's room, where they huddled together in a corner and waited.

Samuil heard cats prowling through the house and others scratching across the roof. Katya heard them too and trembled in Samuil's arms. However, they never came into Samuil's room.

"Katya, everything will be all right." He whispered.

"Listen. They must have grown tired of the hunt. They're leaving. In a few minutes, we can escape."

"All right."

"They're gone, Katya. We can go now, but we have to move fast and quietly."

"I'll be right behind you, Samuil. Invisible as a ghost and quiet as a mouse."

"Good. That's what it will take to get out of here."

They ran from the cabin and sprinted into the forest, trying to put some distance between them and the shadow beasts. Katya, gasping for air, slowed to a stop and pointed.

"Samuil! That's Lauro."

"Katya, he's gone. We can't…help him."

"No!" She cried.

Samuil drew her to him and hugged her. When she stopped weeping, Samuil looked into her eyes.

"We have to go."

Katya took his hand, and together they ran. When they heard a wildcat scream, they stopped on top of a hill and climbed a tree to be less visible. Even though they had run downstream, doubled back, and swept away their tracks, they knew the cats were still coming. Samuil knew, down deep, that it was only a matter of time before they would have a confrontation. He also knew they couldn't stay here with all the cats much longer. They were too exposed.

"Katya the river is over that slope."

"We need to get to the river. It'll be a good place to make a stand. If we have to, we can retreat into the river. Cats hate water."

"All right. We need rocks and sharp sticks."

"What?"

"Weapons, Katya. We need to gather weapons…but be careful not to reopen your wound."

They gathered weapons and then hurried toward the river.

"Samuil! The cats!" Katya screamed.

Samuil spun around to see a cat running out of the forest. It leaped through the air, landing on Katya. Samuil jumped and tackled the cat on top of her. Rolling on the forest floor, they fought. Samuil kicked the cat off, but another immediately attacked him. Katya screamed.

As Katya was screaming, Samuil woke from the nightmare, still kicking and jabbing the wildcats on top of him.

He rubbed his eyes and rolled over. Squinting, he looked around his room for Teddy. Then he remembered the shadows, the snakes, the dragon, and Teddy on fire; Teddy wrapped up in snakes and burned up by a fiery dragon. He tried to put it out of his mind and go back to sleep. Then he heard something at the window. Astonished, he gasped when he saw the legendary giant snow owl outside the window. It stared at Samuil with its golden eyes and blinked.

"Soon, Samuil. Soon."

CHAPTER 18

The Morning After

P'etro tossed and turned all night. He finally got out of bed early in the morning, while it was still dark. His heart was heavy, and his mind was still spinning after his talk with Ilia. He knew how important Teddy was to Samuil, and he assumed that Samuil's heart must be heavy after losing the bear. He was determined to do something about it. P'etro lit a lantern and stepped into the night.

In the forest, he eventually found what he was looking for and returned to the porch. By the time the sun rose, he had finished the small carving of Teddy, threaded a leather cord through it, and placed it on the kitchen table for Ilia to see. Then he left for the barn.

P'etro busied himself preparing Blackie for a long day's work. The late-night antics were weighing on every muscle in his body. Yawning, he yoked the ox and led him from the barn, around the edge of the woods, and to the field. He hitched him to the plow and began walking behind his ox. Smiling as he walked, P'etro tilled the ground for planting as the sun rose higher in the sky.

Blackie labored dutifully in the gently rolling hills of Bakota. As P'etro walked behind him on this lazy spring morning, his mind drifted to daydreams of bounty. Together with his ox, he proudly toiled under the sun. The tilling of the family fields made P'etro happy, so he whistled while he walked.

As a devoted family man in love with the land, he didn't mind the work. He enjoyed the crisp morning air, the solitude, and the birds who gathered to sing for him. With pride, P'etro plowed behind his faithful ox in anticipation of the fruitful days that he hoped lay ahead.

Samuil woke up to the enticing aroma of breakfast and ran downstairs. After breakfast, Samuil remembered they were going to the field to have lunch with Papa. While Mama Ilia prepared food for the trip, Samuil continually interrupted her with questions.

"What time are we going? When can we leave?"

Ilia finally banished him from the cabin. Samuil went straight to the barn.

I can't wait to see Papa. It will be exciting to go through the forest. I wish Teddy were here.

A crackling sound startled Samuil but he didn't see anything unusual. Suddenly, the air became thick and stale. Looking around, he saw shadows leaking from dark corners of the barn. Tumbling, they raced across the ground. Samuil ran to Big Boy's stall and squeezed into the far corner to hide. Big Boy came over and lay down in front of Samuil. Samuil peeked over him and scanned the barn. His eyes stopped on the fog. As he watched, the fog thickened. From its bowels, monsters hissed and squirmed. Claws reached out and grabbed for Samuil.

Samuil hugged his knees to his chest and rolled up in a ball. He closed his eyes and fought in his mind to keep the beast at bay. Deep within him, the battle began, and it was brutal, painful, and exhausting. In the deep, dark recesses of his mind, Samuil built walls, but the monsters tore through them. He stabbed them with spears, but they rose again to fight. He pelted them with rocks, but they continued to charge. Big Boy gored them, and they woke from death to fight again. Hordes charged, and Samuil braced himself for the assault.

"Samuil! I need your help!" Mama Ilia shouted.

A moment later, she whistled. At the sound of Mama's voice and whistle, the monsters slithered away. Samuil smiled.

Mama just beat the all the monsters into submission with her words.

He ran back to the cabin, where Mama met him at the steps with a big smile.

"It's time to go the field and eat lunch with Papa, but before we go, I have something for you. Papa stayed up all night carving this for you. Now close your eyes and open your hand."

Samuil felt Mama place something in his hand.

"Open your eyes."

Samuil gasped and then smiled.

"Teddy! Papa brought Teddy back!"

Mama placed Teddy around Samuil's neck.

"Mama, I must show Big Boy. I'll be right back. Promise."

"All right, but don't take long. Papa's probably hungry by now."

Samuil raced to the barn. He nervously took Teddy from around his neck and held him in his palm. He took a deep breath of hope and palming Teddy, he closed his eyes and said a little prayer.

"Teddy, are you in there?"

Teddy didn't speak.

"Wake up, Teddy. Wake up. It's me, Samuil. Teddy, are you in there?"

"What? Where am I? How did I get here? I feel different. What happened? Where have I been?"

"Teddy?"

"Sammy?"

"Your back."

"Back where?"

"Home Teddy! Your home!"

"It's me. You're here, Teddy. You're back."

"Where have you been Sammy? Back from where?"

Samuil told Teddy about what had happened to them in the Southern Forest.

"Wow. I was roasted by a dragon."

"You were fire and smoke falling through the sky, Teddy."

"I feel stiff."

"Well, you're kind of wooden."

"Oh. Like a tree?"

"Yes, like a tree."

"Am I sappy or splintery?"

"You're fine, Teddy. You're my golden, shiny, wooden Teddy, hanging close to my heart. Now come on; Mama's taking us to eat lunch with Papa."

"Good. I'm hungry."

Joyously, mother and son walked out the door and ran past the barn on their way to the field where Papa plowed. Samuil glanced at the barn and saw a shadow. He stopped and stared, fearing that the shadows might ruin the day. Big Boy bellowed and kicked the stall wall, and the shadow slithered back into the forest. Samuil smiled.

As he strolled through the forest with Mama, Samuil listened to the wind whistle through the trees and watched birds soar through the midday sky.

"Having fun?"

"Yes, Mama. We should do this every day."

"But what about school?"

"Mama, I hate school."

"Samuil, you know you must go to school and learn."

"No. I would rather walk in the forest with you. Or plow with Papa. Or play with the oxen. Or chase bugs."

"Oh Samuil, whatever will I do with you?"

Running ahead, Samuil stumbled, fell, and rolled down a slope. He came to a stop at the edge of a rocky overhang and moaned from the pain of the fall. He was dizzy as he staggered to his feet and looked down at Teddy.

"Are you alright?"

"Yes, but you should watch where you are going. I don't want to die again."

"Samuil!" Mama called.

"I'm all right."

"Papa's waiting. Climb back up, and let's go."

When they arrived at the field, Mama set the lunch basket in the shade of a tree, and they stepped onto the plowed ground.

"There's Papa!" Samuil said.

"Blackie too! Come on, Mama!"

Samuil let go of Ilia's hand and ran stumbling across the clods of dirt in Papa's freshly plowed field.

"Come on, Mama!"

"Slow down, Samuil."

"Papa! It's time to eat."

While struggling to keep up with Samuil, Mama tripped on a clod of dirt and fell in the freshly plowed field. Samuil ran ahead. Papa saw Samuil lurching awkwardly toward him, and he slowed Blackie to a halt. Without warning, vipers slithered out from under a plowed-up clump of grass that had been their nest and angrily struck at Blackie.

Blackie spooked, kicked and ran bucking in a blind panic. P'etro was tangled in the reins, and Blackie dragged him through the plowed dirt. Seeing the ox stampeding toward him, Samuil frantically fled from the terrifying rampage. He tripped and fell headfirst into the path of the terrorized ox.

In desperation, Samuil reached out for his Papa as the ox dragged P'etro past. Their fingers touched as the panicked beast continued his flight trampling Samuil underfoot.

Ilia opened her mouth to scream, but nothing came out. A paralyzing shock washed over her, reality ceased, and reason blurred. In agony, all she could do was watch helplessly as the horrific scene unfolded in slow motion. She couldn't believe the ongoing nightmare she was seeing. Time seemed to stand still, and she was trapped in the moment. Slow motion wound to a stop as the air was filled with clods of dirt and drops of blood. With a sprained ankle and a terrified heart, Ilia crawled her way toward the mayhem.

"Samuil!" She crocked.

Hoping against hope, she rose and limped through the field toward her wounded boy. Her mind spun and her heart throbbed, as she realized she would see the tragic events of that day replay in her mind for the rest of her life.

She helplessly watched as the spooked ox kicked, bucked, and ran wildly. Tears ran down her face as she saw Samuil lying in the field, seemingly lifeless. She died inside when she saw P'etro entangled in the reins, disappear in a stampede cloud of beast, leather, blood, and dust.

"Oh, merciful Mother Mary! No! Please, God! Please! Let them be alright! Please! Mother Mary, full of grace, help them!" Ilia screamed. "Samuil! Papa! This can't be! Samuil's gone! Papas gone! No! Why! This isn't real…I'm dreaming."

Before Ilia could clear her foggy mind or come to her senses, she saw something. A figure appeared in the whirling dust. She closed her eyes, shook her head, and tried to focus. Opening her eyes, she saw P'etro walking out of the dust cloud. He was carrying the limp body of Samuil in his bloodied arms, and Teddy dangled from his fingers.

Bruised, bleeding, and limping, he approached Ilia and knelt beside her. When he looked into his beloved's tear-filled eyes, his heart broke.

'It's all right, Mama. It's all right."

"Samuil?" Ilia choked.

"I have him."

"Oh…oh. My baby," she whimpered.

"Papa, let me hold him."

Gently P'etro placed Samuil in her lap. Her gaze raced over Samuil's body, searching for information. He was unconscious and pale. He was bleeding from cuts and scratches all over his body. He had multiple large bruises and a gash on the back of his head.

"Will my baby be alright P'etro?"

"Yes, Samuil will be alright."

"Are you going to be alright?"

"Yes, Mama, I'll be fine. Everything is going to be fine. Come, now. We need to get Samuil home. Hand Samuil to me, and I'll help you up. We have to get to the house and send for the doctor."

Ilia sniffed. "Oh, Papa. Oh, Samuil."

With P'etro's help, Ilia painfully stood and steadied herself,

❦

P'etro stoically gazed toward the heavens, listening for the whisper of God on the wings of the wind. Unable to hear anything but silence, P'etro forced himself to walk. Ilia followed, holding Teddy.

In the shade of a grove of trees, the ox stood panting. He was trapped, held in place by the broken plow wedged between two trees. Ilia let go of P'etro's waist and slid to the ground. P'etro gently placed Samuil in her lap. Then he walked to the ox and unhitched the exhausted beast from the broken plow. P'etro helped Ilia onto Blackie and handed Samuil up to her. With a lead rope tied to Blackie, he led his wounded family home through the forest.

Once P'etro had helped his family inside the cabin, Ilia boiled water in preparation for mending her two men. There was a scratching at the cabin door. Thinking it was a critter, P'etro grabbed his pistol and went to the door. When he opened it, he saw an old mangy dog.

"Wolf Killer?"

P'etro stepped outside and scratched the hound's head.

Ruff! Wolf Killer barked his reply and wagged his tail.

P'etro rubbed his chin and puzzled.

"Are you lost? Hurt? What?" *Ruff, ruff!* Wolf Killer barked.

Wolf Killer howled and began chasing his tail.

"Easy boy. What's wrong?"

Wolf Killer stopped, howled, and shook his head. P'etro saw a folded piece of paper fall to the ground; it had been neatly tucked in the hound's collar. P'etro saw his name on the paper. He unfolded the note and read.

> P'etro,
>
> Sorry to hear about your mishap today. Yes, yes, sorry, sorry, indeed, indeed. However, I've sent Wolf Killer to fetch the doctor and then to you. Yes, I did. Yes, yes indeed. If you're reading this note, then the good doctor should be arriving soon. Yes, soon. Indeed, indeed. I've seen that everything will be all right. Yes, everything, everything. With the help of the good doctor and time, everything will be fine. Indeed, indeed. Yes, yes.
>
> Your friend, Nikolai
> And oh yes, Wolf Killer too.

When P'etro finished reading the note, Wolf Killer wagged his tail, barked, and ran for the forest. P'etro watched him disappear into the woods.

Thank you, old friend.

He smiled and walked back to the cabin. As he stepped on the porch, he heard the doctor's wagon rattling down the bumpy road. He stopped and waited for the doctor's arrival.

⁂

Several weeks later, Samuil's physical wounds had healed nicely, thanks to the doctor's skill and medications. His cuts and bruises left no marks or scars, but P'etro perceived that his son's demons within were growing darker and getting stronger.

Some days, Samuil fought the demons, and other days, he retreated within himself. P'etro had seen him frightened, confused, withdrawn, and helpless. Once he overheard Samuil directing Teddy on how they could build, fortify, and hide in a castle constructed in his mind. P'etro watched helplessly as his son's behavior became more erratic and his mood swings unpredictable. He and Ilia tried to talk to him, but he shut them out. They didn't understand, and it broke their hearts. When Samuil wasn't sulking in his room or fighting with his mama, he was somewhere in the forest with Teddy.

P'etro followed Samuil and Teddy into the forest one Sunday and discovered that he was a happy, normal boy, at peace there. He also watched him for a couple of nights in the forest, where he was happy and unafraid. Yet when Samuil slept, nightmares haunted him. P'etro figured that Samuil somehow found his peace and courage in the forest.

One evening after a hard day's work in the field, P'etro sat on the porch smoking his pipe. Ilia walked out with a cup of tea in each hand. She handed P'etro a cup, sat beside him, and asked the question that apparently had plagued her all day.

"Has Dr. Mykhailo said why Samuil isn't getting any better?"

"No. He's as puzzled as we are."

"Why are all these terrible things happening to our family?"

P'etro shook his head.

"Why Samuil? What's wrong?"

Ilia's painful questions crushed P'etro heart. She stood to go back inside, and P'etro quickly stood and embraced her. Together, they swayed and cried. The things they knew were confusing, and the things they didn't understand were frightening. Their future hung over them like the Sword of Damocles.

It hurt P'etro to see Samuil's condition escalate. His son's unreasonable and defiant attitude appeared more frequently. Normal, happy days became fewer and fewer. He could be an angel one moment and in the next moment, at the drop of a hat, rave out of control. Sometimes he was nowhere to be found, but P'etro figured at those times, he was in the forest by the singing water.

Six months later, little had changed. While plowing in the field, P'etro pondered the family's trouble.

Mama said I was a lot like Samuil as a child, but I don't remember much about my early childhood. Perhaps what's happening to Samuil is something else. Something different. Bizarre and mysterious. Mysterious like Nikolai's world. Dr. Mykhailo thinks it's physical. Father Slavik thinks it's shadowy, otherworldly, and unnatural. Oh, Mother Mary, not unnatural. What's happening? Destiny? Twisted fate? A family curse passed on generation after generation.

Finding no reason, no answers, and no sense in any of it, P'etro decided to hold the line.

If fate wants a fight, it's come to the right man. By all the gods, I'll give fate a fight!

P'etro raising his fists to the heavens and yelled.

"No! Not while I live! Not my son! I'll fight you! I'll beat you! Man, devil, beasts, or gods! I'll battle you to the death!"

As P'etro caught his breath, he realized that he had allies he could count on for assistance.

Dr. Mykhailo is relentless and will never stop pursuing all the medical possibilities. And the priests, Father Slavik and Father Jakiv, will never stop praying. And then there's Ivan, Sergey, and Nikolai, and even old Wolf Killer. Just thinking about it made P'etro feel better.

"It's good to have friends, Blackie, come to think of it, I didn't realize I had so many."

Samuil's voice rang out from the edge of the woods, and P'etro looked to see him running across the field, waving his arms.

"Papa lunchtime! Mama brought food! Teddy is hungry! Me too!"

P'etro smiled.

It's a good day. Things are going to be fine. I know it. Like a ship on stormy seas, everything will right itself.

CHAPTER 19

Cross My Heart

Ilia stepped outside the cabin and felt a chill in the air. She quickly found Samuil and told him to go inside.

"But I promised Teddy to take him somewhere special tonight."

"Samuil, it's getting dark, and a storm is brewing."

"I promised."

"Samuil, we need to go inside. Storms can be dangerous."

"It only rain, Mama." Samuil scowled, gripping Teddy in his hand.

Ilia sighed.

"Samuil, look at me."

Reluctantly, Samuil slowly raised his head and looked at her.

"It's time to go inside."

"I promised Teddy! It's something special!"

"Samuil!"

"A promise is a promise!" Samuil said and ran into the forest.

"Samuil!"

Sad and angry, Ilia went to the barn to get P'etro. As she neared the stall, she stopped, lost in thought. A flood of memories rushed through her mind. For her, life with Samuil had become a daily battle at a blistering pace and an all but impossible task. Even though he was thirteen, he sometimes acted like he was six. Ever since the trampling almost a year ago, his demeanor and behavior had gotten worse. Every day was a new and different kind of challenge. Even in her dreams, she heard Samuil scream.

Ilia had watched Samuil fortify himself in his room and retreat into his own little world. Sometimes he sat in the corner, withdrawn for hours, holding his knees to his chest and rocking. Other times, Samuil silently stared off into space and refused to acknowledge anyone or anything. Then there were those days when Samuil was stubbornly fitful. Those were the worst days for Ilia because they were filled with screaming, fussing, and temper tantrums. On such days, P'etro had to be called in from the fields to help deal with him. The saddest times were the days when Samuil was rolled up in a ball in the corner of his room, limp and listless.

But there were other times when Samuil was a normal boy, running through the forest, playing in the dirt, and throwing rocks. Most days, Samuil wandered into the timberland to play with the forest creatures until long after dark. Recently, however, the bad days far outnumbered the good ones.

Ilia knew that P'etro fought back his worry and fears, but her broken heart and exhausted spirit caused her to cry herself to sleep, night after night.

Samuil ran far enough into the forest to feel safe from his parents; then he stopped and stared into the night sky. On the horizon, lightning slapped the sky and thunder whispered a warning.

"Look, Teddy. There's a light show on the horizon. Ready for the adventure?"

"I'm always ready."

As they walked into the forest, Teddy asked Samuil to stop.

"What? Did you change your mind?"

"No, Sammy. I'm wondering how much trouble we're in with Mama."

"Don't worry."

"We could go back and not be in much trouble."

"No. I'm keeping my promise."

"Okay, but we'll be in big trouble when we get back."

"I know, but I promised."

Samuil ran through the forest with the wind in his face and felt free. The air rushing over his sweaty skin was cool and refreshing. With the breeze ruffling his hair, it seemed as though he was flying. Spreading his arms, he imagined being a bird, soaring in the sky.

Samuil liked birds; he thought they were magnificent creatures. Out of breath they stopped.

"Are we close to the Bogs?" Teddy asked.

"We still have a way to go before we get to the Bogs, but the Southern Forest is across that creek." Samuil pointed toward it.

Teddy smiled, and then they ran.

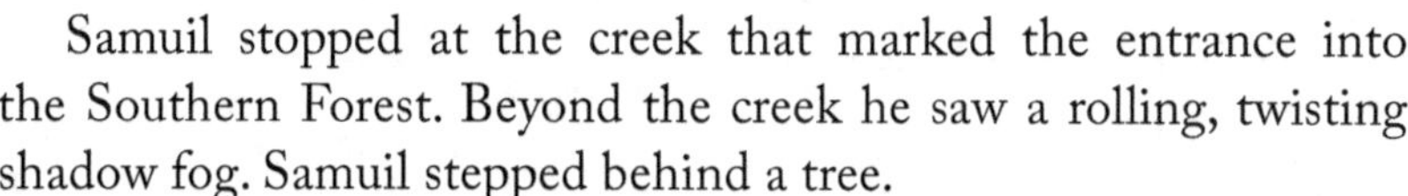

Samuil stopped at the creek that marked the entrance into the Southern Forest. Beyond the creek he saw a rolling, twisting shadow fog. Samuil stepped behind a tree.

"Here we are." He whispered to Teddy.

"I had forgotten that the Southern Forest was so close to the cabin and the Bogs are just up ahead, deeper into the forest."

"I haven't forgotten Sammy."

Before they continued, Samuil explained that the Southern Forest was between them and Ivan's cabin, and the Bogs were east, toward the river. He also told Teddy that Papa had occasionally gone through the Southern Forest because it was shorter than taking the road to Ivan's.

"I overheard heard Papa telling Ivan that when he went that way, he saw the bubbling mud bogs, the dark fog, and huge shadow creatures. The bears are big as trees, and wildcats are bigger than the bears. He saw spirits, demons, ghosts, and strange lights. He heard growls, screams, voices, and whispers."

"Oh?"

"I think the shadow creatures and the demons and monsters come from beneath the Bogs."

"And Papa also saw the legendary snow owl."

"Wow!"

Samuil went on to explain everything he had overheard about the golden-eyed snow owl, who some knew about but very few had ever lived to see. The legendary Snow Owls originated from the family of owls who lived at the top of the world, where it's so cold, your breath freezes. They now live in the beyond and only came to the Southern Forest to keep the shadow creatures in check. A legend that few know says, that once there was a great battle between the hordes of dark shadows and the legions of snow owls. Only one giant snow owl survived, and now all the creatures of the forest rely on its protection. Everything in the Southern Forest belonged to the snow owl, and it takes care of the spirits and souls of the forest world. The snow owl is regarded as the watcher and guardian of everything good in the Southern Forest.

"And I saw it, Teddy."

"The snow owl?"

"Yes, outside my window."

"When?"

"A few days ago."

Abruptly, Samuil stopped and slowly look around.

"Teddy, something moved. Let's go."

Cautiously they stepped into the Southern Forest. Samuil heard leaves rustling and followed the noise, which leads them deeper into the forest. When the noise stopped, so did he.

"Where did it go, Sammy?"

"It stopped just ahead."

"What is it?"

"I don't know."

"Reach out with your mind and talk to it."

"No, this is the Southern Forest. The evil in here is always waiting, listening, and watching."

Out of nowhere, hundreds of fireflies flashed into sight. Samuil and Teddy watched the blinking creatures hover and swirl in a synchronized light show. When the fireflies began moving away, Samuil and Teddy followed.

"Why do we always follow fireflies when they appear?"

"Because they are light, and we follow light."

"Now you sound like Father Slavik."

They walked quickly through the forest, following the light show until Samuil smelled sulfur. Cautiously, they looked for the source and saw a smoking bush, but there was no fire. Samuil realized that it wasn't smoke; it was a shadow fog, and the fireflies were flying straight for it. They watched as more and more of the fog spewed out of the bush. The shadow fog began to twist, knot, roll, and spread as it transformed the forest in front of them into an eerie, shimmering woodland.

Samuil wanted to rescue the fireflies before it was too late. The only thing he had time to do was warn them. He reached out with his mind. When nothing happened, he tried again. He shook his head and looked at Teddy.

"Sammy we have to warn them before it's too late."

"I tried. Something's wrong."

"What do you mean?"

"They didn't hear me."

Samuil's mind began to formulate a plan of rescue. Before he had time to blink, however, the fireflies flew into the shadow fog and disappeared. He rubbed his chin, wondering why the fireflies didn't hear his warning and why they flew into the fog.

As Samuil turned to leave and realized the shadow fog had moved to cut them off. It had maneuvered around behind them and was between them and the stream. As Samuil looked at the shadow fog, it erupted. Samuil dived behind a bush and watched as the shadow fog soared upward, splashing into the heavens, and growing into a dark, spinning cloud.

"Come on; it's time to hide."

"I'm not scared of a little rain."

"Me either, but I am scared of demons and dragons. Start gathering limbs and brush. We'll make a lean-to over there."

When they finished their lean-to, they crawled inside, and Samuil closed the opening with brush. Secured and hidden, they waited. Within seconds they heard a ruckus. Samuil pulled a leafy limb to one side and looked out.

"See anything, Sammy?"

"Yes, bad magic."

"Bad magic?"

"Yes, shadow magic."

"That is really bad magic."

The two watched as the shadow cloud twisted, bucked, and spun back down to the forest floor, becoming a fog. Samuil saw something move inside the fog but couldn't tell what it was. He watched as things began to move more rapidly within the fog. He bit his bottom lip and stared as the fog bubbled. A strange creature began to emerge, slowly appearing and continuing to take shape.

Samuil had never seen a winged creature this large and deformed. It was wormlike, with dark wings that slowly unfolded, and it had a strange, dark, blinking light on its tail. Other creatures that had been floating in the fog began dropping out and untangling. Suddenly, hundreds of them gathered and hovered just outside the fog.

"What are those things? They're big as a dog and shiny black, and look at those fangs, Sammy."

"I think they're dark fireflies. The dark magic must have changed them and made them larger and stronger."

"Are they dangerous?"

"Everything in here is dangerous."

"Then let's go while we still can."

When the two explorers snuck out of their shelter, a monster firefly with red eyes and glistening fangs split off and fluttered toward them. The dark monster slowly circled overhead. Samuil ran and stumbled awkwardly through the moonlit forest. The relentless chase took the two friends deeper into the mysterious Southern Forest. They stopped running when a sudden gust of wind surprised them.

Cutting through the forest, the wind twirled into a growing eddy. The moonlight disappeared behind a blue storm cloud. On the wings of the wind, Samuil smelled rain, just as lightning flashed brightly overhead. In the silent darkness, thunder abruptly exploded, shaking the ground beneath his feet. Undeterred, they dashed headlong into the blustery wind until the threatening thunderstorm erupted in a torrent of windblown rain. The rain washed the shadow fog and its monsters away.

Soaked to the bone and blinded by rain, Samuil slipped and fell in the mud. He stood, struggling to keep his balance. Stumbling over a broken tree branch, he fell face-first in the mud. He struggled to his feet again and fought the howling wind, but after only a couple of steps, he slipped again and tumbled down a steep, muddy slope, bloodying his nose as he did.

In the thundering loneliness of the dark woodlands, the rain finally stopped, as the blue cloud dissipated, and a wolf howled. Samuil's heart skipped a beat. An answering wolf cried out from the night, chilling Samuil's soul even more. Samuil felt surrounded by danger. Behind him, a limb snapped.

⸺⟨◇⟩⸺

At the barn, P'etro heard a noise. He turned and saw Ilia looking distraught. He realized she was weeping, and he reached out to touch her arm.

"What's wrong, Ilia?"

"Oh, P'etro! It's Samuil. He's having one of his bad days. And I can't do anything to help."

"What happened?"

Ilia took a deep breath, and a tear ran down her cheek. In a shaky voice, she explained the gut-wrenching events of the day.

"This afternoon Samuil came in the cabin with that faraway look in his eyes. I tried to talk to him, but he shut me out. It was as if I wasn't there. And neither was Samuil."

"I'm sorry, dear."

Sadly, she continued.

"He wouldn't respond to me except to argue. He pushed me away when I tried to hold him. He flinched and withdrew when I tried to touch him. You know how he gets when he's in one of his moods."

"I know, and I'm sorry for what he's putting you through, Ilia."

"He is defiant now. He won't mind me. I can't do anything with him."

Lightning streaked across the sky and thunder rumbled, interrupting the conversation. Ilia jumped, but then sighed.

"I don't know what to do."

"It will be all right, Ilia dear."

"No, it won't. I can't handle him any longer. Nothing I do seems to work anymore."

Her face crumpled again.

"And now he ran into the forest with Teddy."

"I'll talk to Dr. Mykhailo tomorrow about a visit. Samuil always seems better after he visits."

"Perhaps that will help."

"Sure, it will dear. It will all be better in no time at all."

Overhead, lightning exploded and again lit up the night sky. Ilia shrieked and covered her eyes, shielding them from the blinding flash. The lightning struck a tree at the back of the barn and blew off a limb. Bellowing thunder echoed through the valley.

"Come on! Let's get to the cabin before we get soaked!" P'etro shouted into the howling wind.

He took Ilia's hand, and they ran for the shelter of the cabin. Inside, they looked for Samuil, hoping he had decided to heed Ilia's warning.

The two began a strategic search of the premises with no success.

"He and Teddy must have continued into the forest. P'etro, the storm."

"Stay here, Ilia. I'll find him."

Grabbing his rifle, pistol, and knife, P'etro kissed Ilia on the cheek and raced out the door into the raging storm. Ilia stood in the doorway and watched as P'etro disappeared into the forest. Then she grabbed her weapons and stepped out into the storm.

In the Southern Forest, thunder roared, and wolves howled, filling the night with waves of trepidation. Samuil began to worry. He took Teddy from around his neck and stuffed him in his pocket. As the fury of the storm rolled away, the furious cries of the wolves got closer. Broken moonbeams transformed the forest into a silvery, surreal no-man's-land. Samuil's mind raced, and his imagination ran wild.

The strange forest flickered with ghostly silhouettes that lurked and vanished. The moonlight cast shadowy shapes of eerie images. The foggy bottom twisted into distorted, spine-chilling contours.

Mist swirled, casting sinister shadows of lurking monsters. Behind every bush he saw lurking things prowling in the night.

When thunder cracked and lightning popped, Samuil covered his head with his shirt. Peeking into the forest, he sensed nocturnal creatures on the move and angry shadows stalking. Looking around, Samuil heard the wind rustle bushes and rattle branches as it hissed through the trees. Again, lightning streaked the sky. The exploding light illuminated eerie, red-eyed goblins that prowled and demons that hid behind every tree. Samuil decided the best thing to do was run.

He ran until he found a large hollow log. Crawling inside, he felt safe. He listened as the thunder rumbled and the lightning flashed at a distance. At long last, the storm moved away.

Samuil had not been so lost and alone in all his life. In the stillness of the Southern Forest, the wolf cries constantly echoed. Their howling made the hair on the back of his neck stand up.

Snug in the hollow log, he rolled up in a ball and tried to shut out the forest sounds. Try as he might, he couldn't stop the pounding of his heart or the echoing of the wolf cries. He was lost in the Southern Forest, surrounded by apparitions and shadowy images. He wished he was home with his family, where it was dry, warm, and safe. Soaked to the bone, he shook from the cold. He closed his eyes and pulled his knees tightly to his chest and whispered to the darkness.

"The dark is good. The night is good. Darkness is good. Darkness makes them all go away. Dark is quiet. Dark inside me. Dark too dark."

Samuil took Teddy out of his pocket, placed him around his neck, and took a deep breath. With fearless determination, Samuil set his jaw and crawled from the safety of the hollow log. The forest was filled with fresh, clean air. Samuil looked up, smiled at the new sky filled with stars, and greeted the beaming moon.

"Look at the sky, Teddy."

"The rain has washed it clean. Now it can show us the way home."

"We're not going home. We're going to the Bogs."

"We're not going anywhere if we don't get out of this mud hole."

Struggling, Samuil attempted several times to climb the muddy slope, but each time he slipped, fell, and slid back to the bottom. Exhausted, he tried one more time and finally made it out. Atop a little tree-filled hill, he sat down on a stump to rest.

A limb snapped, startling Samuil. When he heard a sudden movement in the brush, he looked up and saw a fox. Quietly, they pursued it until it stopped. Holding his breath and unsure of the slippery footing, he carefully inched as close as he dared.

In the dancing light of broken clouds, he saw a sable lump on the ground. Wet moonbeams flickered through the dark forest. The light was bright enough to cast shadows in every corner of the dripping woodland. Samuil was sure the lump was the fox. It was just out of reach, lying on a wet clump of grass. He got closer still and saw its glossy red fur and cheerful fox face. He reached out with his thoughts, but like the fireflies, the fox ignored him and trotted off.

With renewed zeal, they followed the fox as it scampered through the forest, paying little attention to where they were.

Captivated by the pursuit, the duo was unaware that the fox was slowly leading them deeper into the Bogs.

"Where is it going, Sammy?"

"I don't know, but we'd better keep up."

"What if we get more lost?"

"Don't worry. I can get us out of here. But not now. Come on, or we'll lose the fox."

In the middle of the hot pursuit, Samuil abruptly stopped. He quietly listened for the song of a bird or the chirping of a frog, but the forest was eerily and completely silent. The only sound was raindrops dripping off trees.

"Why is it so quiet Sammy?"

"Strange, huh?"

"Yes."

"After a rain, the forest should be booming with songs of thanksgiving."

"This is spooky!"

Samuil scratched his head. Times like these were odd and disturbing. The only thing moving in the forest was the fox. At the thought of the fox, he looked up, but it was gone.

Where did it go? How could it move that fast? And why haven't we seen more animals?

"Are we in the Bogs, Sammy? You said it would be spooky in the Bogs."

"We've been in the Bogs for a long time."

"Why didn't you tell me?"

Their discussion was cut short when Samuil saw the fox hopping through the tall grass. The two quietly followed the fox and as they did, Samuil felt the silence following—it was a chilling feeling. The fox disappeared in a grass-covered hole. With the fox gone, it was even quieter. Samuil sat on a stump and tried to figure out exactly what was happening in the forest.

A sudden chill ran down Samuil's spine. He felt as if he was being watched by something evil. Samuil shivered as he felt sinister eyes fixed on him. He shook from the intensity of his feelings. Something with ill intentions for him and Teddy was nearby. He knew it; he sensed it.

It had been too quiet for too long, and they hadn't seen a living thing besides the fox for some time. Samuil continued puzzling over the absence of the forest creatures and the silence of the forest and couldn't decide if they were hiding or dead.

In the silence of the night, Samuil pondered the mystery until he was abruptly interrupted by a deep, guttural snarl—both he and Teddy heard it. Samuil slowly looked around but saw nothing.

"The wolf pack has found us, Sammy."

"Sounds like it."

"Do they like to eat people?"

"Sometimes."

"Time to go home."

"Not yet. Come on."

When Teddy shook his head, Samuil knew he would have to come up with a secure plan. So, he promised Teddy that they would run quietly and stay ahead of the pack. Teddy shook his head again. Samuil swore that they would climb a tree if the wolves posed a threat. Teddy said they might be flying shadow wolves. Samuil promised they would fly higher and faster. When Teddy protested, Samuil stuffed him in his pocket.

Samuil walked slowly and quietly between the increasing number of bogs. The deeper into the Bogs they went, the more sinister growling, snarling, and whispering sounds he heard. He took Teddy out of his pocket and placed him around his neck. Together, they quietly listened to the uncanny noises until they heard a splash. Samuil pointed and they moved toward the noise.

"It's coming from over there."

"From that bog?"

"Yes, let's go see. Quiet like a mouse; invisible like a ghost."

Samuil and Teddy moved toward the unknown noise until they came to a stream. They observed that the stream wasn't singing.

"Sammy, why isn't it singing? I thought all water sang."

"The dark water of the Bogs doesn't sing."

"Why not?"

"Because it is dark and mysterious. Plus, it has great potential for evil."

"Evil water? Come on, Sammy. Stop trying to scare me."

"Water in the Southern Forest and the Bogs draws evil like the ground draws lightning."

As they spoke, the stream began to change It turned dark, and shadow strings rose to the surface. On the bank, a shadow fog began forming. Something rustled in the brush, and Samuil turned to see the fox again. Both he and Teddy watched silently as the fox disappeared into the fog and splashed into the dark water. Behind them, they heard rippling water and heavy breathing. They turned to see a red-eyed demon surface from a bog.

CHAPTER 20

Ghostly Bogs Of The Southern Forest

Ilia stumbled through the wet, cold, windy, forest following P'etro's trail as quickly as she could. She was soon soaked and freezing by a torrent of cold rain and wind under a dark stormy sky. When she lost P'etro's trail she sighted and realized there was no way to follow his trail in the relentless storm even though time was of the essence.

Lightning filled the sky lighting up the mouth of a cave and she quickly slashed through the slush and into the safety of the dry cavern. Trembling, she sat and hugged her knees to her chest as she impatiently waited out the monstrous storm.

As she lingered in the shelter of the cave, she thought about Samuil, lost or hurt in the Southern Forest. The thought filled her heart with aching anxiety, but her prayers to Mother Mary eased her mind. Please let Samuil be safe was the theme of her forest prayers on this stormy night.

When the storm ceased, Ilia stepped back into the forest. Frightened but resilient, she pressed on with resolve into the now moonlit night. It was not difficult to see the signs by the light of the moon. Plus, the muddy prints in the storm-soaked forest floor were easy to follow. She noticed that the prints left in the mud were large like P'etro's boot prints. Relieved that she was on the right trail, Ilia—her spirit renewed—bravely trudged on in the mud.

A cold shiver shot through her body when she thought about Samuil being in the forest alone. She shivered even more as she watched the broken moonlight cast eerie shadows in the forest. Silently, she chastised herself for not bringing the lantern. She really needed it in this unfamiliar and notorious part of the forest bog. She had already lost the trail twice, and at this pace, it would be sunrise before she found Samuil or P'etro.

Startled by a distant yelp, Ilia stopped and listened. The bone chilling cries of a wolf pack on the hunt rang out somewhere deep in the forest. Fear shot through her limbs, and she inhaled sharply. Shaking away the fear, she quickly hurried on. Ilia prayed to find

P'etro and Samuil before the wolves found her. Again, the spine-chilling howls erupted in the darkness, and they were closer this time. Quickly, she rushed on, heart pounding and hands shaking. She stopped when she was out of breath, and when she did, she heard the pack draw nearer.

Are they on my scent? Have they found me?

She thought of her son again, alone in the forest. Slowly, she drew her pistol and readied herself for a life-or-death struggle.

***

When the big muddy shadow demon stepped out of the bog, Samuil hid in the undergrowth. Praying the demon didn't see him, he held his breath, hoping it wouldn't hear him. He hugged the ground, lying as flat as he could. He even sucked in his breath, hoping to get closer to the ground. The demon walked past him, so close that Samuil thought it was going to step on him. He watched the demon walk away until it disappeared into the fog.

Samuil walked upstream in the opposite direction of the demon. He wanted to put a good deal of distance between him and it. Feeling safe, he stopped and sat on the edge of the stream. Slowly, a shadow fog rolled to the bank opposite him.

"Look at the stream, Sammy. Dark, ghostly shapes are swirling in the water."

"It's something from the shadow fog. Probably a variation of the shadow strings."

As they watched, the fog rolled down to the water but not into it. The dark shapes in the stream began to drive fish toward the fog. Other dark shapes touched the fish, causing them to jump into the fog. Inside Samuil could see them thrashing about for air. In a couple of seconds, the fish jumped back into the water, but they were enormous and different. They were too big for the shallow stream, and they had legs and a scorpion tail.

"Time to go, Teddy. Come on."

Once they were safely away from the pond, they ran deeper into the Bogs, but Samuil was forced to slow down and step more carefully when the bogs became more numerous and closer together.

"Why are we slowing down?"

"We must be very careful. If we step into a bog—"

"Yes, I know; we're demon meat."

Samuil stopped, breathed deeply and didn't move for a moment. His heightened sixth sense had kicked in again, and he felt something. The feeling wasn't malevolent or threatening. It was familiar but somehow different. It was a feeling of entrapment and fear. Closing his eyes, he reached out with his mind, but the intense fear was so strong that it blocked all scenery perceptions and foresight.

"Teddy, something's wrong. I can feel it."

"What?"

"Trouble."

"Sammy, I'm ready to get out of here. I've had enough adventure and excitement for one night. Let's go home and eat supper."

The noise of a struggle and the slurping of mud made Samuil think that a creature was stuck in a bog. He ran in the direction of the sound.

As he got closer to the sound, he heard more thrashing and splashing and knew something was in trouble. Slowly, he crept through weeds and tall grass for a closer look. When he was close, he carefully rose and stared over the tall grass, trying to focus on the creature that was stuck in a bog. The brush and trees hindered his sight, but he could see well enough to tell the creature was as big as a bear. Yet it wasn't acting like one. Samuil closed his eyes and though.

It might be a shadow monster, but why would it be stuck in a bog? It must be something else. But what?

As Samuil maneuvered for a better look, he was startled by the distressed bellow of a bull. He wondered why a bull would be in the forest, much less in the Bogs. The creature cried out again, and Samuil strained to see. Climbing a tree for a better view, he was shocked by what he saw, Blackie was stuck in a bog.

Samuil climbed down and ran to his entrapped ox as fast as he could, fearing the animal would sink all the way to Hades before he got there. He reached out with his mind, hoping to calm and reassure the ox.

"Hold on Blackie, hold on I'm coming!"
When he arrived, he questioned the ox.
"How did you get here? How did you get stuck?"
"Mooo."
"Easy, Blackie. Easy. It's all right. I'm here. Teddy and I will get you out."

Samuil glanced around for something in the Bogs he could use to get Blackie out of the bog, but he didn't see anything helpful. He didn't have a rope to pull him out and besides, the ox was too big. So, he sat on the edge of the bog scratching the ox neck and talking to him. That worked until wolves howled and Blackie panicked.

The only other thing Samuil could think to do was sing. Blackie had always liked that, and it calmed him when Samuil sang. So, Samuil sang Blackie a melody. It was one that Ilia had sung to Samuil when he was upset or afraid. As soon as he started singing, Blackie stopped thrashing and struggling.

Teddy joined in, and together, under the star-splashed sky, the duo sang their off-key melody to Blackie. Strangely enough, as the duet continued, Samuil was pleased to hear the forest creatures join the chorus. Together, the squeaky voices of the duo and the melodic songs of the forest creatures blended, and the mingled composition filled the forest, becoming a symphony.

⊱ ·❖· ⊰

Struggling through the mud, P'etro had a difficult time staying on his feet, much less following Samuil's trail. He often lost his footing on slick slopes and hills. Several times the trail disappeared, as Samuil's muddy tracks mingled with animal tracks. Above, broken clouds swept across the sky, often impeding the bright light of the harvest moon that lit his way.

He knelt on the bank of the river and washed muddy blood from his arms, hands, and face. When the sand began to shift, he stood. When the ground shook, he stumbled and fell to his knees and struggled to rise as the ground shook harder. The river sand rose and rolled like a wave toward him. He tried to run inland, but the sand wave rolled him into the river, where he sank.

Shadow strings fell from the trees into the river and threaded their way toward him. He tried to swim, but some force was pulling him down. When he reached the river bottom, it began to shift, wobble, and roll. A fire-breathing leviathan circled him roared and spewed flames. Hot bubbling water bubbled and boiled as P'etro swam frantically.

A red demon with fiery eyes appeared, mounted the sea beast, and pursued P'etro. Fire shot past him, and the water sizzled burning P'etro as he swam into a large underwater cavern. The force of the steaming water from the monster shot P'etro deeper into the cavern and upward. Fire, water, and P'etro all broke the surface of the river and gasping for air, he opened his eyes.

The first thing P'etro saw were silver moonbeams in the night sky, and then a giant dark shadow blotted out the light. Out of the night, talons extended and soared toward him. He gasped in horror, closed his eyes, and wondered if this was his end.

Instead, a soft, familiar hoot instantly relieved his fears. He knew this was the legendary golden-eyed Snow Owl, coming to rescue him. The snow owl pulled P'etro from the demon river and flew away as the heavens filled with shadow clouds and red lightning. The kaleidoscopic sky rolled and twisted. Abruptly, it erupted. Shadow beasts dripped like rain from the sky, and in his mind, P'etro heard the Shadow Lord shout angerly.

I'm coming for the boy but first I will take care of Ilia, then you, then the bird, then I'll take the boy.

⟨═◦◇◦═⟩

As they sang their melody to Blackie, Teddy interrupted in a whisper.

"Sammy."

"Don't interrupt the singing. That's rude."

"We're not alone."

"What?"

"Listen."

Samuil listened quietly but heard nothing out of place. The only sound he heard was the symphony, and it was so loud there wasn't a prayer of hearing anything else. He decided Teddy was hearing things that weren't there. Before he could rejoin the harmony, Teddy poked him.

"There it is again."

"No, Teddy, that is only a forest creature adding his voice to our music."

"Sammy, I'm telling you something else is here, and it's making noise."

"Like what."

"It's stomping through the forest snapping limbs and breaking trees. Something is happening in the forest and it's coming our way."

"Nonsense. Be quiet and stop interrupting the—"

Samuil stopped midsentence when he felt the earth shake. When he heard a bog erupt, he knew trouble was coming. Quickly, he began formulating a plan. He knew they had to protect Blackie, but he also knew they couldn't get him out without help. Samuil put Teddy around his neck and ran toward the spewing bog, where he watched a six-foot slimy-looking lizard emerge, with daggerlike claws and a razor-sharp spear of a tail. When it stared at him its black eyes were full of evil intent. Samuil reached out to the beast with his mind and was met with a dark wall. Seeping through the beast's wall were feelings of confusion, pain, and hunger.

The monster screamed in Samuil's mind. He grabbed his head and fell to his knees in pain. The lizard flicked his red-hot tongue, and wrapped it around Samuil's ankle, burning his skin. The creature began dragging Samuil rapidly through the dirt. Samuil grabbed a broken stick and jabbed it through the creature's tongue and into the ground. The beast shrieked and shook with pain. Samuil jerked his foot free and limped toward the river, leading the beast away from Blackie.

Samuil noticed the river water wasn't clear, the sand wasn't clean or smooth, and trees had toppled. Broken limbs littered the ground.

Samuil wondered what had happened here. It looked like a battle zone.

"Was this what you heard, Teddy?"

"Yes. I tried to tell you, but you wouldn't listen. Something has happened here. Something bad."

At that moment, the shadow of a huge bird fluttered across the ground. Samuil saw the giant snow owl and heard her speak to his mind.

"I am currently engaged with the Shadow Lord and trying to stop him from wreaking havoc on nature. Now you must deal with the shadow creatures. I'm unable to assist you with that just now."

Samuil heard more thrashing sounds in the forest and knew it was time to go. The trees in the forest drooped, sagged and creaked as rotten leaves fell and were replaced with new rotten leaves. Hurrying through the Southern Forest, Samuil led the shadow monster away from Blackie, but he could tell that he was quickly losing ground. Then, strangely, the beast was all but on top of them. Samuil saw a bowed tree halfway up the cliff. He pointed it out to Teddy, knowing it was their only route of escape.

"That tree, Teddy! Come on!"

"Lizards can climb too."

"Not monster lizards; they're too big and fat to climb."

The lizard whipped his spear-like tail at Samuil. As it slashed through the air, Samuil ducked. Zing zagging ahead he ran as the beast slashed its tail braking branches and suddenly imbedded its tail in a tree. Samuil darted from a stump and scampered up a tree. The lizard freed itself and continued its pursuit. At the tree, it stopped and hurled its tail at Samuil. As the spear-like tail whistled through the air, Samuil knew he wasn't out of range.

<hr>

After the demon hissed threatening words, P'etro felt anger stir deep within him. It was an old but familiar feeling. When he breathed it away in a sigh, a sense of peace returned to his troubled mind. As he made his way away from the river and the Bogs, the snow owl landed on a hill in the forest and spoke to P'etro's mind.

"You are safe here and now, but Samuil is in grave danger."

"The shadow creatures?"

"Yes, you will have to go back into the Bogs to help him. I have done all that I can do for now."

"Thank you," P'etro said as he tilted his head.

"What is your name?"

"You are incapable of hearing or speaking it. So, you may call me the Great Snow Owl."

The bird ruffled its feathers, as if annoyed, and looked at P'etro.

"It was you I saw in the blizzard. Thank you for all your help, Great Snow Owl."

The snow owl blinked, flapped its giant wings, and flew away. The wind from its wings blew his hair.

P'etro rushed back through the forest, tracking Samuil. He heard a strange sound when he entered the Bogs. It was a faint noise, unrecognizable. He knew it wasn't the sounds of a shadow creature; neither was it the sound of large predators. He also ruled out the sounds of warbling birds, croaking frogs, and chirping crickets. It was softer than the sounds of forest creatures. However, it was familiar. Carefully listening, he moved forward, following the noise. P'etro stopped again and listened.

That could be Samuil.

He decided to get closer for a look. Tiptoeing through the Bogs, he followed until he slipped and fell on a slick rock. To his surprise, the noise didn't stop, rather, it increased in frequency and grew closer. Before P'etro could rise, a creature popped out of the underbrush and stared into his eyes. P'etro gasped and then smiled.

It was a white rabbit.

The rabbit spoke to P'etro's mind.

"Quickly, quickly! You must hurry! You must come! There is trouble!"

"What kind of trouble?"

"Shh. There is a monster."

"A monster?"

"Yes, a monster, a tree, and a boy."

"It's Samuil. Take me there."

P'etro followed the white rabbit through the forest and deeper into the Bogs, where the rotting forest was silent, but the air was thick with evil. Shadow strings hung low in the trees, and fog lingered just out of sight. Rushing through the Bogs, they raced to Samuil's aid.

By the time P'etro arrived, the lizard had left. Samuil yelled for his Papa to stop and climbed down from the tree. He threw his arms around P'etro's neck.

"You're here, Papa! You found me! I knew you would come!" Samuil squealed.

"Are you all right, Samuil?"

"I'm fine. Teddy too, but not Blackie."

Samuil explained the situation in detail to his Papa.

"We've got to get him out, Papa. There are hungry wolves and monsters on the prowl in the Bogs."

P'etro sensed the danger and felt the lurking evil.

"Take me to Blackie."

"This way, Papa.

Blackie groaned from the bog, thrashing and splashing as they approached.

"He's scared of the wolves, Papa!"

"Yes, I heard them in the forest."

P'etro began analyzing the situation and it worried him. Out of the silent darkness came a soft and familiar voice.

"P'etro?"

"Ilia? Ilia, is that you?"

"Yes! Yes! It's me!"

"We're over here, Ilia!"

When Ilia appeared out of the dark forest, Samuil jumped to his feet and ran to her.

"Mama! Mama! You're here! You came for me and Blackie!"

"Yes, Samuil. I'm here."

"Ilia, how did you find us?" P'etro asked.

"P'etro, you ask an old tracker like me a question like that?"

Ilia smiled, P'etro frowned, and Samuil giggled.

"Ilia, we'll need Big Boy's help to get Blackie out of the bog.

Will you and Samuil be able to bring him here?"

"You know I can't handle that big old ox. He doesn't mind me like he does you."

"All right. Take my pistols and hunting knife; you may need them more than I will. And here—I'll only need one rifle."

With a resolute expression, she smiled.

"All right, but you keep your rifle. I'll be fine with pistols and knives."

"You know I should be the one staying, in case of danger and—"

"We'll be fine, dear. Now go."

P'etro handed her his weapons. She quickly tucked them in her skirt along with her own. Ilia straightened herself and stood tall; she winked at P'etro.

P'etro frowned, even though he believed she was ready to battle anything that came her way.

Samuil took Mama Ilia's hand, Ilia smiled and then looked at P'etro.

"See you back here at the bog, Papa." Samuil said with a smile.

Ilia winked again, blew her beloved a kiss, and wrinkled her nose. Hand in hand, Ilia and Samuil walked over to Blackie.

P'etro shook his head in dismay and mumbled under his breath. "And I had to marry a Russian woman!"

Grabbing the rifles, P'etro took off at a trot to the cabin, planning to return as quickly as possible to rescue his family and resolve the night's challenges.

While Samuil sang his melody to Blackie, Ilia thought about their situation. The forest was illuminated by the light of the full moon, which made it easy to see any creatures that might approach.

But she knew they had almost no defenses.

"Samuil."

"Yes, Mama?"

"Come help me find some dry wood to build a fire. It will be our lighthouse in the forest to guide Papa back to us. Plus, it will keep any creatures at bay."

As the fire blazed Ilia pulled out several strips of dried meat from a pouch in her pocket.

"You brought supper, Mama?"

"Yes, I did. I know you and Teddy are always hungry."

"Thanks, Mama. You're always prepared."

They stared into the fire and ate their jerky, and then they sang to Blackie again. As the night choir of humans and critters sang their melody, Ilia stoked the fire.

Moments later, Blackie became agitated and began thrashing about in the muddy bog. Abruptly, the accompanying forest melody ceased, and for a moment, everything became very still. Samuil looked at Blackie and thought.

I wonder if the music has lost its magic and why the creatures have stopped singing.

Moooo! Moooo! Blackie bellowed, startling everyone.

Again, Blackie cried out in fright.

With a brave look and a worried heart, Ilia surveyed their surroundings but saw nothing.

"Samuil, the forest creatures have gone silent. Something's here. We are not alone anymore."

In the forest, a twig snapped. Ilia grabbed Samuil and gave him a little shake, getting his attention.

"Be quiet Samuil." Ilia whispered with a finger to her lips.

"Look at me and listen."

She took a deep breath, trying to hide her trembling. Her whisper was soft.

"Samuil, Blackie and the forest are telling us something is out there."

Blackie cried out again and frantically began to thrash and toss about in the mud.

"Listen to Blackie, Samuil; he smells something. He's telling us there is danger. I need you and Teddy to help me protect Blackie from what is approaching through the forest."

"All right, Mama. What do you want us to do?"

"You and Teddy are going be my spotters. I want you to run as fast as you can and climb up that tree by the bog. Up there, you and Teddy can be Mama's eyes in the sky. My sky scouts."

"That sounds exciting."

"That's my scouts."

"What do you want us watching for Mama?"

"Wolves."

As Samuil climbed the tree, the night became even more eerie.

CHAPTER 21

Eyes Of Death

In the silence of the spooky bog, Ilia's concentration was interrupted by the cry of a raven. Then the forest filled with ferocious growling, further unsettling the night. The growls were followed by an angry bark and hair on the nape of Ilia's neck stood on end. Within seconds, another fierce growl sounded, scaring a *moo* out of Blackie.

The frightened ox began struggling to get free.

"Samuil, what do you see?"

"A wolf by the fallen tree! And another one to the left of him!"

In a flash, a red wolf darted toward Ilia with its white fangs flashing and black eyes shining in the pale moonlight. It stopped on the other side of the blazing campfire and snarled. Ilia noticed something odd about the wolf as she stared at it in the flickering light of the campfire—it had cold, dead eyes, as black as onyx. She could see the reflection of the flickering fire in those eyes, and the wolf's body shimmered like smoke. Out of the darkness, another wolf leaped through the air as Ilia pulled her pistol. With no time to aim, she remembered her mother's words.

Point at what you intend to hit, and hit what you point at, little girl.

Ilia pulled the trigger.

Running through the moon-washed forest, P'etro looked up and saw candlelight emanating from the cabin. The flickering light brought back precious childhood memories that warmed his heart. The glow reminded him of the lights alone the shore of the Moscow River that filled him with the hope of a promising tomorrow.

Although not bright enough to light his way through the woods, the candle also reminded him of the dimly lit backstreets of Moscow that had walked as a wounded warrior. The memory made him shudder as a chill raced up his spine. Wincing, P'etro returned his attention to the dimly lit trail that led him back to the family cabin.

P'etro went to the barn and gathered the needed gear for the rescue. When he walked past Blackie's stall to tether Big Boy, he noticed Blackie's stall gate was unhooked and standing wide open. Puzzled, he shook his head and scratched his wet black beard. As he searched his mind for a rational explanation his thoughts were abruptly interrupted.

Kapow!

The echoing gunshot shattered the stillness of the night. P'etro gasped, and his heart skipped a beat. Momentarily frozen in place, his mind raced with gut-wrenching thoughts of horror. An icy fear gripped his body. Petrified by the shocking reality of his loved ones in imminent peril, he shook as a chill raced through his body.

Adrenaline surged through P'etro's body, he gasped and raced to the cabin for weapons.

No. Oh God, no!

He grabbed two pistols, ran out of the cabin, into the moonlight at a blistering pace and disappeared into the forest. When the second gunshot sounded, echoing off the hills, it momentarily shocked P'etro to a stop. He crossed himself, gritting his teeth, and raced on through the forest at breakneck speed. He splashed across creeks and clawed up slippery slopes. He had to get to them. He had to rescue his family.

Ilia's pistol shot screamed into the night. Now empty, it smoked in her hand. Through the pistol flash, she had seen the dark wolf fall. It lay lifeless at her feet.

From the tree, Samuil yelled another warning.

"Another one, Mama! Behind you!"

Before Samuil finished speaking, Ilia was already in motion. In a dreamy state of reality, she dropped the smoking pistol and pulled another from her skirt. Like a pirouetting ballerina she spun, pointed, and fired.

Hot lead roared through the night, striking the red wolf with the flaming eyes. Now, two wolves lay lifeless in the mud at Ilia's feet. For the moment, there was a lull in the deadly action, and everything was quiet. Ilia walked toward Samuil, hoping the pack had fled back to the safety of the dark forest.

From the corner of her eye, Ilia saw movement. Turning to look, she saw the two dead wolves disappear into the forest. She leaned against a tree, her shocked mind spinning with inexplicable questions.

"She did it, Teddy. Two shots, two dead wolves,"

"Yeah, but they're gone. They jumped up and ran into the forest."

"They have to be shadow wolves."

"We're in trouble now, Sammy."

"Yes, we are."

"Sure wished Papa would hurry."

Before Ilia could regain her senses, the night erupted with Samuil's scream.

"Mama, help! Help!"

Ilia whirled around and saw two wolves jumping, climbing, and biting at Samuil.

"Climb, Samuil! Climb!" Ilia screamed.

"Higher, Samuil! Higher!"

Samuil scrambled up the tree. He stopped, looked down, and yelled.

"Behind you, Mama."

Snarling wolves' had flanked Ilia while she instructed Samuil. She now looked into the hungry eyes of the once-dead red shadow wolf. The wolf leaped through the air, and Ilia was met with flying teeth and sharp claws. Both fell and rolled on the ground. As she fell, Ilia felt something distant but near, strange yet familiar, tender but very strong. It engulfed her like a mist, infusing her with confidence and focus.

<hr>

She was just a little girl, younger than Samuil, when Papa Vitaik took her into the forest. They walked deep into the spooky timber of the frightening night. Ilia jumped at every crackling leaf and snapping twig, but on the outside, she never flinched. Unbeknownst to her, Papa Vitaik was determined to teach her to conquer her fears and believe in herself.

Vitaik was a big man with tanned skin and a leathery face baked by the Russian wind and sun during long, hard days of work. His eyes were kind and bright blue, like the sky. They reminded Ilia of deep-blue river water. His brown hair reminded her of bison fur and his huge hands of bear paws. His arms hung like huge tree limbs at his side. When he stood, he towered into the sky like a tall oak. When he spoke, his loud army drill sergeant voice rumbled like thunder echoing through the valley.

"The horrible monsters you fear in the night are never what your frightened mind envisions them to be. Your monsters are only what you conjure up inside yourself from the fearful imaginings of your heart. No fears, no monsters."

He waved his arms as if shooing them all away.

"You must conquer your fear, baby girl!" He spoke with a growl.

Ilia listened to every word but didn't understand what her Papa was saying.

"First and foremost, you must learn control. You must control your feelings, your thoughts, and your mind. To do that, you have to think. You must use your mind."

Again, she listened but didn't know how anyone could have that kind of control.

"You must learn to concentrate. To master your thoughts. To focus."

"Yes, Papa."

"You control your fear by reigning in your imagination. You conquer your imagination with your mind. Make it work for you, not against you. Understand?"

"Yes, Papa."

Even though she agreed, she didn't understand. Not truly.

"You must believe, baby girl. Always believe. And you must fight. Sometimes you pick your fights, and sometimes they pick you. Sometimes you win, and sometimes you don't. When you don't, you live to fight another day."

"Yes, Papa."

"Always remember, baby girl, to never give up. When all else fails, pull up your socks and battle on. You never lose until you give up. Never give up. If you never give up, you'll never lose. Never forget."

These words Ilia did understand, and she swore that day she would never give up.

Vitaik paused to allow Ilia time to absorb and process his words of wisdom; then he continued her enlightenment.

"Life isn't always easy. Sometimes it doesn't turn out the way you want. So, rejoice in the good, and make the best you can of the bad, baby girl."

As he spoke, tears welled up in his eyes.

"The forest is your friend. A tree limb can become a warrior's spear. A branch can be your defense, a rock your bullet, a pile of logs your castle. When all else fails, baby girl, you must battle on. Make the best of whatever the situation is."

"Yes, Papa."

"Now sit, close your eyes, and be still. Listen to the silence. Feel the earth. Touch the wind. Smell the air. Let the forest touch you as you become one with your surroundings. Now, look with your mind. See into the darkness of the night. Befriend your surroundings and become one with everything. As one, you're now in harmony. Fear has no place to reside. If monsters come, slay them with the power of the one—the one you have just become."

⸎

With fear knotted in his stomach, Samuil watched the airborne wolf strike Ilia. The initial force of the wolf's attack was enough for her to kick him off in a backward roll and end up on her feet again. In the blink of an eye, the red wolf was up. The wolf growled, flashed his fangs, and charged in for the kill. Ilia pulled her third pistol and fired. The red wolf dropped.

"Mama, your left!"

Ilia pulled her last pistol, turned, and shot the gray wolf.

"The tree line, Mama! There are more coming!"

From his treetop, Samuil watched as Ilia grabbed a tree limb, lite them from the fire, steadied herself, and pulled her hunting knife from her belt. When the wolves attacked, Ilia fought them with only her burning stick and knife.

Samuil jumped from his tree onto Blackie's back. Kicking and screaming, he tried to scare Blackie out of the bog. The wide-eyed ox was terrified by the wolves and the wild child on his back, and he struggled to get free.

The two wolves at the trunk of Samuil's tree turned and charged. With fangs shining, the brown wolf leaped through the air for Samuil and knocked him off Blackie when they collided. Both fell into the muddy bog. A spotted wolf leaped on Blackie, clawing and biting.

Hearing the commotion, Ilia turned and shouted at the top of her voice.

"Fight, Samuil! Fight, and don't give up!"

Blackie intensified his struggle to get out of the bog, and when he finally broke free, Samuil grabbed him by the tail. Blackie emerged from the bog, exhausted and panting for air. Samuil let go of his tail and wiped the mud from his face.

Samuil jumped to his feet and looked around. The first thing he saw were the empty pistols on the ground. He looked over his shoulder and saw the two wolves struggling in the muddy bog. Two more wolves emerged from the dark forest and joined the all-out attack on Ilia. Bravely, she fought them off with her flaming tree branch and her knife.

Danger hung in the air like smoke. Old Blackie pawed the ground, and Samuil reached out with his mind.

"Blackie, Mama's in trouble. There are too many wolves. We've got to ride into action now."

Samuil looked deeply into Blackie's dark eyes; he was certain that Blackie winked at him. Samuil filled his pocket with rocks, grabbed a sharp branch, hopped onto Blackie's back and Yelled at the top of his voice—"Charge, Blackie! Charge! To the rescue! Save Mama! Go, Blackie! Go!"

He kicked Blackie, and they thundered into the night. Whether Blackie understood Samuil's words or just sensed the urgency, he stampeded toward the battle. A wild child and thundering ox stormed headlong into the fight. Slinging his head, Blackie filled the air with snorts, snot, and saliva as Samuil hung on for dear life. His black bulk forced the wolves off course. Like a charging general, Samuil shouted his battle cry. Heroically, the ox and child, united in spirit and purpose, charged into the fight, attacking the attackers.

Nearing Mama Ilia, Samuil saw that three wolves had her backed up against a tree. Bravely, she fought for her life with her fire stick and the hunting knife. As courageous as she was, the brawl was not going her way. Samuil saw her weaken in the desperate life-or-death struggle, and he kicked Blackie again to get closer.

"Bleed and die, you devil!" He yelled.

Like crazed warriors, the one-ox/one-man cavalry splashed through the mud and brush. In a blind rage, they crashed into the teeth of the struggle. Bellowing, Blackie bolted into the wolf pack, spearing, trampling, and scattering the wolves. Wounded, bleeding, and yelping, two wolves retreated into the safety of the forest. Both stepped into the shadow fog. Moments later, they walked out, unharmed, and returned to the pack.

Bellowing as he thrashed his massive head, Blackie hooked another wolf and tossed it like a rag doll into the night. Atop the buckling, snorting ox, a crazed, wide-eyed wild child sat yelling. Both proved to be enough to send the pack running, tails tucked. Frightened and defeated, they ran into the forest where the shadow fog hung. One last strong thrust of Blackie's head caught Samuil off guard and tossed him to the ground beside his mother.

"Samuil!" his mama gasped breathlessly.

"Are you all right, Mama?"

"Yes. Thanks for the rescue, son."

"It was fun, Mama! Did you see me and Blackie? Did you see us?"

"Yes, Samuil. You are my hero."

"Blackie too, Mama."

"Yes, Blackie too, Samuil. Now quickly—we need to get up. The pack will be back soon. Grab some wood and help me build up the campfire."

While working on the fire, Samuil thought about the wolves.

These wolves are different. Any other pack would have left long before now. All the dead wolves are gone, and they didn't stay dead very long. Wolves that come back to life? And their eyes…

"Samuil, if the pack returns, set these branches afire and fight them. They are afraid of fire. So, they might not return, but if they do, swinging the fire branches at them will keep them away."

"All right, Mama."

"When they charge, poke them with the fire stick. Burn them, if you can."

Samuil nodded.

"Stay on your feet, Samuil! Stand like a man and fight beside your mama. Be brave. Yell, and show no fear! We won't be beaten unless we quit."

Looking deep into Samuil's eyes, she spoke with conviction and intensity.

"Do not quit, Samuil. Do not give up! Papa's coming! We must be brave and fight!"

"I will, Mama."

Ilia smiled at Samuil and patted his cheek.

"I love you, Samuil."

"I love you too, Mama."

In a matter of minutes, the wolves returned for the final assault. Smelling blood and sensing fear, the crazed pack gathered for the attack. Ilia and Samuil, with adrenaline surging through their bodies, stood ready for the beasts' assault.

The wolves charged, hungry for the kill, but mother and child stood defiantly, back-to-back, as the beasts rushed. Yelling at the top of their lungs, they swung their flaming sticks. Together, as trapped warriors, a petite woman and a scrawny boy fought like battle-hardened soldiers. Against all odds, mother and son raged against the death-filled night.

They were flanked and outnumbered by the monstrous shadow wolves, but Ilia and Samuil fought. For a moment, they kept the crazed animals at bay with their fire sticks. The wolves retreated, regrouped, circled, and then charged in another all-out attack. With flaming eyes, flashing fangs, and foaming mouths, the carnivores came at their prey. Again and again, they came in a ruthless onslaught. Each time they came crashing through the night with death on their breath, the duo fought them back with sticks of fire and hearts of hope.

An enraged wolf knocked Ilia off her feet. She grabbed for Samuil, and the two brave troupers fell to the forest floor in the furious assault. When she hit the ground, Ilia rolled and reached out with her blade, slashing the throat of the wolf that was on top of Samuil. Samuil lay on the bloody ground, trapped beneath the dead wolf. Mama Ilia lay beside him, fighting for her own life. Without taking her eyes off her assailants, she called out to Samuil.

"Hold … the dead one … on top of you! He'll be … your shield!"

Samuil held on to the dead wolf, even as the others bit his arms and legs. Three wolves jumped Blackie, growling and biting. He fought back kicking, bucking, and thrusting his huge horns at the blood-crazed assailants.

Erupting through the battle sounds in the bog came a deepthroated howl from the forest. A lanky hound snarled and leaped into the middle of the fight, knocking down wolves. Growling and biting, the old hound tore into the pack, drawing blood and ripping off hunks of wolf flesh. The wolves momentarily retreated.

"It's the hero hound! He found us! He has come to help!"

Samuil had barely gotten the words out of his mouth when the pack attacked again.

Fighting the pack, Ilia fell to the ground again.

"Mama!" Samuil cried.

The hound heard Samuil's sad plea and turned on the wolf's atop Ilia. Samuil pushed the dead wolf off him and grabbed a fire stick. He freed Ilia, and all three fought in a tangled web of blood and chaos. Two wolves tore at Ilia, one had hold of Samuil, several were embroiled with Blackie, and the hound was battling three. Try as they might, they were exhausted, bleeding, and outnumbered; things were quickly becoming bleak. Ilia fell once again, and the wolves quickly jumped on her.

Erupting through the forest came an earth-shattering explosion. The blast of a rifle screamed through the foggy bog air. Samuil jerked at the deafening discharge that broke up the desperate life-or-death struggle. The singing bullet hit the wolf atop Samuil, and it dropped to the ground. Samuil jumped to his feet, smiling.

"Teddy, we're saved."

"Finally."

Quickly, another lifesaving rifle blast roared out of the night and The wolf atop Ilia dropped.

"Good shot." Samuil shouted.

"Yes, do it again. Shoot them all." Teddy added.

Close to the dying echoes of the last shot, the forest was suddenly filled with the noise of breaking limbs and the shouts of the shooter as he closed in for a pistol shot. Samuil could see the moonlight silhouette of the brave hero charging through the night. As the madman of the Bogs burst into pistol range, he fired again.

Now three wolves lay dead on the bloodstained battlefield, but still the shooter tore through the timberland, yelling as the pack regrouped. With his hair blowing in the wind and mud flying from his boots, the crazed beast of a man ran like the wind.

Samuil watched as his Papa crashed out of the woods with nothing but a knife in hand. Shouting, he charged the pack. As he did, the hound joined the charge and then Blackie. What was left of the pack scattered and ran into the safety of the forest. With tails tucked between their legs, they surrendered the battle to the crazed wild man of the bog.

With victory secured, P'etro turned to his family, human and beast. "Is anyone hurt?"

"We're all right, Papa. Just a few scratches, bites, and blood."

For the first time since pulling the trigger, P'etro breathed easy.

Ilia was bloody and shaking and her clothes were torn from fighting off the demon wolves.

"Samuil, where did that old hound come from?" Ilia asked.

"Out of the forest, Mama."

"A hound who lives in the forest?"

"Yes, Mama. I'm sure glad he came to help."

The hound limped over and gave Ilia a hello lick on the mouth.

"I'll explain on the way home, Ilia," P'etro said.

"Yes, you will." When she raised an eyebrow, the hound took the hint and disappeared into the forest.

Two arms wrapped around P'etro's neck.

"You saved us, Papa! You saved us all!"

"I love you, Samuil. And I'm proud of you for being so brave."

"P'etro, help me find your pistols. Samuil, you go get Blackie, and we will all go home."

"Ilia, where are the dead wolves?"

"I'll explain on the way home."

"Oh, all right."

As Samuil approached Blackie, the ox snorted and dropped something on the ground. Samuil stepped up and saw that it was Teddy. Samuil took Teddy, put him around his neck, and threw his arms around Blackie.

"Thanks for saving, Teddy, Blackie. You're a hero, like Papa."

CHAPTER 22

Capricious Sunday

Two days later, Samuil was still having nightmares about the Bogs. When Sunday's sun broke the horizon, he was tossing fitfully in bed. As his frightening dream faded, he rubbed his sleepy eyes and stretched. Rolling over, he heard the forest's joyful melodies afloat on the morning's sunbeams. He ran to the window and looked out. Outside the cabin window, the trees were filled with birds that were greeted the dawning of a new day with their gift of song that filled the crisp morning air.

"Songbirds, Teddy! It's morning!"

Teddy groaned.

"Wake up—it's Sunday!"

"No."

Samuil grabbed Teddy and shook him into sleepy awareness. Wrapping him around his neck, Samuil ran through the cabin. He saw Papa in the sitting room.

"Morning, Papa! The birds are singing."

"Morning, Samuil; yes, they are."

Entering the kitchen, he found his mama happily laboring over breakfast while she hummed and sang.

"Morning, Mama. Hear the birds?" Samuil asked.

"Yes, I do, Samuil."

Samuil had observed his mama's Sunday routine for the past few weeks and had noticed that it was a chore for her. Samuil knew that every day was busy for his mama, but Sunday seemed to be doubly so. He could tell by watching her that it was nerve-racking to get everything and everyone fed and ready for mass. By the time she finished, she looked exhausted. However, he also knew that she looked forward to being with all her lady friends who gathered every Sunday after mass for lots of juicy gossip. This, in turn, gave him time to explore the large parish garden.

"Breakfast, Papa!" Ilia called.

At the sound of his mama's breakfast call, Samuil jumped up from the kitchen floor and sat at the table. The aromas in the kitchen were delicious.

"Come and get it, Papa, before I throw it out to the birds!" Mama shouted.

"Hurry, Papa, the birds are at the window," Samuil added.

"Well, they can't have my breakfast," P'etro answered, entering the kitchen.

He took in a deep breath of the delicious breakfast aroma permeating the kitchen and smiled in anticipation of a great breakfast feast. Hungry, he sat beside Ilia smiling and savoring the intoxicating waves of the morning's feast.

"We're ready, Mama! And we're starving!" Hungry Samuil announced.

"Well, well, my Sunday sleepers have woken hungry."

"Yes, and your exquisite kitchen magic is wonderful," Papa announced, and Samuil giggled.

"Yes Mama, it smells wonderful." Samuil added.

Everyone laughed. Papa blessed the meal, and they ate.

Afterwards Samuil walked with Papa to the front porch. P'etro lit his pipe, and Samuil listened to the singing birds.

"I like Sunday morning, Papa. It's so peaceful."

"Yes, it is. It's peaceful and relaxing," he answered, breathing in the crisp morning air filled with the scent of pine.

"Sundays are special, Papa."

"How's that?"

"Mama's meals are special, and the mornings are filled with music from Mama and the birds. Only on a Sunday do you have the time to relax on the porch and smoke your pipe. The air is fresh with morning dew and filled with all the fragrances of the forest. And I'm glad we don't have to worry about the shadow creatures attacking on Sunday. Does Father Slavik keep them away, or is it just because it's Sunday?

P'etro took his pipe out of his mouth and looked at Samuil. "That's very perceptive of you. I know this week in the Bogs must have been upsetting to you."

"Oh no, Papa. It was an adventure. It was exciting. It—"

"Slow down, slow down. It didn't scare you?"

"Well, maybe a little. But we won, and that was exciting."

"Son, the shadows have been here as long as the Southern Forest and the Bogs have. It's something we must live with and always beware of. And yes, the priests do help keep them away, but they are only able to do so much. You must always be careful when you are away from the cabin. They can be anywhere at any time."

"Thanks, Papa, I will be careful, but now I have to get dressed up in those itchy clothes and tight shoes for Sunday mass."

"Me too." Papa giggled.

During mass, Samuil and Teddy looked at one another, rolled their eyes, and giggled. They agreed that mass was boring and that the fires of Hades couldn't be any worse than sitting quietly and still for hours. The best part of mass was when it was over. That's when Samuil and Teddy ran for the parish garden to enjoy and explore its mysteries.

The magical garden was filled with numerous secrets that screamed for their attention and begged to be explored. Samuil's curiosity was more than willing to oblige. So, after the last amen, Samuil and Teddy were off like an arrow, running for the garden with adventures dancing in their heads.

On this Sunday's dash after mass, Samuil stopped short of the garden's waterfalls when he heard a faint noise. It wasn't a bird in a bush or a passing bee. It was more like another presence. Maybe the shuffling of feet. But was it human or animal? Whatever it was, he hadn't heard it here before. Darting behind a tree, he squatted and listened. Quietly, he peeked out. Seeing the cause of the sound, he ducked down for cover.

"Teddy, did you see that?"

"What?"

"Shh."

"Okay, okay, I'll be quiet. What did you see?"

"It's him."

"Who?"

"The new kid. Vladimir."

At the mention of that name, Teddy shook.

"He wasn't at mass."

"I know he wasn't at mass. But he's here now."

"Where?"

"Over there." Samuil gestured with his chin.

"But don't look! He might see you."

Samuil hadn't met Vladimir and didn't want to. He'd heard that Vladimir was big, strong, and mean. Carefully peeking from behind the tree, Samuil saw that Vladimir had a nasty scar from his nose to his right earlobe. It made him appear menacing. Samuil thought he looked mean and tough enough to whip a brown bear. Vladimir was new to Bakota, and no one knew very much about him or his background. Most didn't care, and others didn't want to know. It didn't take long for children to discover he was trouble.

Vladimir had been alone in Bakota for a short time, and he kept to himself. As far as Samuil knew, he didn't have any friends. Samuil heard that Vladimir didn't have a family, and that made Samuil sad. He couldn't imagine anyone not having a family. Even someone as big and mean as Vladimir should at least have family. Samuil frowned, wondering what must have happened to Vladimir's family. Then he remembered Papa telling Father Slavik that Vladimir was raised with chickens. Samuil wondered why.

Anyone who likes animals can't be all bad.

"Teddy, why do you think he's here?"

"I don't know, but he never comes to mass."

"Everybody likes the parish garden. Maybe he's here to see the garden."

"I don't think so."

"Me either. But it is beautiful here. You think Vladimir likes beautiful things?"

"No."

Samuil figured that there was no God in Vladimir's heart; therefore, his heart was a place of scars, brokenness, and darkness. In that barren land, the only resident was evil, and that was why he was always looking for trouble and up to no good.

Peeking out again, Samuil gasped and jerked his head back quickly.

"He's looking our way, Teddy."

"Did he see you?"

"No, I don't think he saw me."

Samuil's mind flooded with scary thoughts, all of which ended badly for him and Teddy.

"Is he looking for us, Sammy?"

"No, I don't think so."

Samuil considered every imaginable set of horrible circumstances. Then he considered every possibly getaway. All he could come up with was to run. But where to and how far? He didn't know. He didn't know if they could get away without being seen.

"Is it time to run?"

"No, not yet. When the time is right, we'll run and duck."

"Okay, I can run like a duck."

"No, we're not running like a duck."

"We're waddling?"

"No."

"Quacking?"

"No."

"I'm not laying eggs, Sammy."

Samuil shook his head in disgust and rolled his eyes.

"Teddy, listen, we will run through the garden, ducking behind bushes and trees. Understand?"

Teddy rolled his eyes in disgust.

"Why didn't you say that in the first place?"

"I did. Why do I always have to explain everything to you a hundred times?"

"You stutter."

"I don't stutter, Teddy."

"Yes. You do. You stuttered last month when you saw Katya in that pretty dress."

Samuil sighed and frowned at Teddy.

"That was different. We were in the ballroom, and Katya was wearing that pink dress—well, she was so pretty and smelled so good. And then she winked and waved. That would make anyone stutter. And it was just one time."

"I never stutter."

"That's because you are not smart enough to stutter."

"Yes, I am."

"No, you're not."

"You're mean. I'm leaving. I hope Vladimir breaks your nose."

"Teddy, I'm sorry. Don't leave."

"All right. Let's duck walk."

Samuil stuck Teddy in his back pocket and set his feet firmly in the dirt. Taking a deep breath, he ran the short distance to the next tree. He was relieved not to have been seen. Energy filled his veins, and he ran again. Now proud of himself and intrigued by the game, he darted to the next tree. Samuil inched his way deeper into the refuge of the garden with each burst of speed. He stopped one last time to catch his breath. When Teddy complained about missing all the action, Samuil took him out of his pocket and placed him around his neck.

"One more run, and we will be deep in the garden. Ready?"

"Let's go, captain. Running time."

One final time, he darted down a short path leading to the crystal stream of the garden. After only a couple of steps, he ran into something solid. Stumbling, he fell and tumbled to a stop in some prickly bushes. Samuil glanced at the monsters that had tackled him, but he was unable to comprehend the reality of the situation. He had fear in his eyes and terror in his heart. He blinked, and with heart racing and adrenaline pumping, he jumped to his feet, ready to escape. Then he heard a sound that stopped him in his tracks. Someone was speaking and it wasn't monsters after all.

Who could this be? It's Vladimir, and he's worse than monsters.

Samuil looked and was alarmed; he didn't see Vladimir, instead, he was looking at the red faces of Borysko and Lauro. The brothers shook their heads and climbed out of the bushes. Borysko growled irritably.

"Look where you are going, worm."

"Yeah, worm!" Lauro mimicked.

The two brothers glared angrily at Samuil.

"Sorry."

Borysko brushed the dirt from his clothes and swore.

"You tore my good shirt!"

He stepped toward Samuil.

"I'm going beat you to a pulp, you little worm."

With a doubled-up fist, Borysko swung hard at Samuil's chin. Samuil dodged the fist and rolled to the right, but he'd misjudged the incline. Samuil rolled downhill, coming to an abrupt halt when he hit a tree and Teddy slid from around his neck. Head spinning Samuil put Teddy in his pocket and sat up. He looked up with dizzy eyes and saw a red-faced Borysko racing toward him, with Lauro close behind. Samuil felt unsteady but trying to get to his feet; he stumbled and fell. Though his ribs ached, he gradually made it to his knees and then finally stood. He wobbled, tripped, and fell headlong into the bushes. Unable to run or even stand, he lay there, awaiting his slaughter at the hands of the two irate brothers.

When nothing happened, Samuil stared at the clear blue sky and wondered at the puzzling silence. An eerie quiet had suddenly fallen over the parish garden. There were no thundering footsteps or angry voices. Samuil was alone in the bushes and surrounded by silence. For a moment, he lay there confused but pleased.

It's a miracle in the garden of God. I have been miraculously delivered. I'll never skip mass again. I'll turn over a new leaf. I'll be a good son. I'll stop skipping school. No more trouble.

Samuil's mental promises were abruptly interrupted by a grunt and a groan. He pushed to an elbow and peered out of the bushes. He rubbed his eyes to make sure he was really seeing what he thought he was seeing. Vladimir was standing with his huge foot on Lauro's neck and his bear-sized hand clutching Borysko's throat. Vladimir held Borysko several inches off the ground and was staring into his eyes.

"Teddy! Where did Vladimir come from?"

"I don't know."

"How did he get here so fast?"

"I don't know."

Though Samuil despised the brothers, he was afraid that Vladimir might kill them. He wanted to run and thought he had a good chance of escaping. If he could get to the church, he could find help, but if Vladimir killed the brothers before he got back, there would be big trouble. With a racing heart, Samuil rose and walked over to the entangled trio.

"Are you Vladimir?"

"Who's asking, and why do you want to know?"

"I'm Samuil. These boys are my neighbors, and you should let them go."

"You going to make me?"

"Teddy will."

"Teddy? Where is he? I don't see him."

Reaching in his pocket, Samuil pulled Teddy out and placed him around his neck.

"This is Teddy. Teddy says let them go."

After a robust belly laugh, Vladimir stared at Samuil.

"I'm going to kill your friends." He shouted.

"Then I'll burn Teddy. Then I'll kill you. Think you can stop me worm?"

Samuil looked at Vladimir. He smiled, raised an eyebrow, and kicked him hard on the shin of the leg that held Lauro down. With a yelp of pain, Vladimir lifted his leg, and Lauro escaped. Now free, Lauro kicked Vladimir between the legs. Doubling over, Vladimir dropped Borysko. Together, the brothers took off running. After only a short distance, they suddenly stopped and stood at attention.

Vladimir glared at Samuil, who had been knocked down in the ruckus. He took a menacing step toward him, but he abruptly stopped dead in his tracks. Confused, Samuil got to his feet and heard a thundering voice calling from the heavens. The commanding voice roared and echoed through the garden, making Samuil's ears ring. Later, Teddy told Samuil it was the voice of an angel, maybe even an archangel. Both agreed it sounded angry.

"Boys!" The voice called.

Samuil started to run, but Vladimir tripped him. When he fell, he knew he was trapped. He slowly got up to face the music, along with the rest of the gang. Then Samuil heard the voice again.

"Come here, boys."

Samuil looked at Teddy and took a deep breath. He recognized the voice as that of Father Slavik. Exhaling, he hoped to breathe away both his fear and bad luck, but he knew they were in deep trouble. The priest was a strict man of God who believed that mercy came at an exacting price, and he was about to exact some.

"Is it an angel, Sammy?"

"No, if it were an angel, he might have mercy on us. It's the priest."

"The priest won't…?"

"The priest is probably going to rain down holy hell on us all."

"Boys, is everything all right here?"

No one answered.

"What's going on?"

Again, there was no answer.

The stumpy, black-bearded priest walked up to the guilty parties with an "angel of death" scowl on his face.

Samuil swallowed hard and prepared himself for judgment day.

"Been nice knowing you, Teddy. See you on the other side."

"Other side? What? Why?"

"Because Father Slavik is going to call on God to smite us down and throw us into purgatory."

"What? Why?"

"Shh."

"My, my, boys. If someone were missing an ear, one would think us to be in the garden of Gethsemane."

Teddy looked at Samuil for an explanation; Samuil shrugged. He had been daydreaming in mass and didn't have a clue what the priest was talking about. Plus, he'd seen the brothers snoozing in Mass too, so they didn't know either. Samuil wondered if Father Slavik recognized the conflict.

"Is anyone injured?"

When no one answered, the priest walked closer. Fearful, the boys stood reverentially stiff. Samuil expected immediate punishment, and his imagination ran wild. He remembered the story of Sodom and Gomorrah and expected hail and brimstone to start falling from the sky at any moment. He even glanced up to see if the sky had changed.

"All right. If everyone is fine, who wants to tell me what happened here?"

All the boys stood stone still and silent.

"How did you manage to tear your shirt, Borysko?"

Borysko cowered and looked at the ground.

"I take the silence to mean that the cat has gotten everyone's tongue."

At that moment, a butterfly landed on the priest's head. Samuil watched in amazement as another fluttered and danced around the priest's head. Instantly, Samuil's mind drifted away with fanciful thoughts of butterflies, saints, and angels.

"Well now, no one wants to talk. What shall we do about that?"

For an eternal second, the only sound was that of rustling tree leaves as the wind softly wove through the summer leaves of the parish garden.

"Borysko," the priest called sternly.

Borysko jumped, inhaled deeply, and looked at the priest.

"Tell me what happened here, my son."

"Uh…well…uh, nothing, Father. Really. Uh…we were… uh…playing."

"Just playing."

The priest looked at Lauro.

"Lauro, what happened here?"

"Uh…we were…just playing."

Finally, Father Slavik looked at Samuil. Samuil smiled and continued staring at the butterfly ballet performed atop the priest's head.

"Boys, you must be more careful in your play. We do not want anyone getting hurt."

"And you, son," he said, pointing at Vladimir.

"Come over here so we can talk."

At that Borysko, Lauro, and Samuil rushed off, leaving Vladimir and Father Slavik to their own private discussion.

Samuil was out of breath when he arrived at the wagon. He was surprised to find Mama and Papa still visiting with the church folk.

"We made it, Teddy. They'll never know."

Samuil jumped in the wagon without a word. As the family rolled down the dirt road toward home, Samuil looked at Teddy.

"I wonder if Vladimir killed Father Slavik."

"He's mean enough to do that."

"Yes, mean and scary too. We don't want him to ever find us. He will kill us like he might be killing the priest."

After a meal of fresh baked bread and wild boar, Samuil and Teddy were off running through the woods. Together, they observed forest creatures, soaked up the sun, and listened to birds sing. Running through the eastern woods, Samuil stumbled into Papa's tilled field. As he walked, he kicked up clods of dirt and then stopped and stared at the ground.

"Look, Teddy, worms in the moist dirt. It's time to fish."

Grabbing a handful of worms, Samuil yelled a thank-you to the heavens and ran to their favorite spot of the river where they kept their fishing poles hidden.

"Now let's catch some fish for supper."

"Do we have to clean them?"

"Yes. I catch them, you clean them, Mama will cook them, and Papa brags on us."

"Why do I have to do the cleaning?"

"Because I'm doing the fishing."

Samuil had no luck fishing that day so, he sat back on the cool bank of the stream and watched squirrels play in the trees. Samuil spotted a turtle on a log and jumped up.

"Come on Teddy! Let's catch her before she swims away."

Samuil stepped into the river and casually and skillfully walked up to the turtle without making waves. Clutching it to his chest, Samuil made his way back to shore. Sitting her down, he and Teddy began their examination.

"Is she dead?"

"No, she's nervous.

Teddy frowned and looked at Samuil.

"I thought you said she wanted to play."

"She did, but her family is expecting her, and something evil is coming."

"How do you know evil is coming?"

"She told me."

Samuil and Teddy escorted her back into the river and set her free. The moment the turtle swam away, Samuil stiffened. Something menacing was in the forest. The hair on the back of his neck stood on end. He listened intently but heard nothing. There wasn't a sound in the forest. Even the bugs were silent.

"Teddy, the birds are gone. Something's wrong."

"What scared them?"

"I don't know, Teddy. The crickets and frogs have stopped singing too." Samuil's skin began to tingle. He looked at Teddy and put his finger to his lips.

"Quiet, Teddy. Listen."

Samuil turned slowly in a circle, staring into the forest for any movement or anything out of the ordinary. He saw nothing but felt something that made the hair on his arms stand up. He carefully took Teddy from around his neck and stuffed him securely in his pocket.

Unnerved and with all his senses on high alert, Samuil stood still and listened. He was barely breathing as he tried to feel the thing that was out there. All he could feel was that something was watching. He stuck out his tongue like a snake and attempted to taste the air to identify the stalking creature. He tasted nothing but still sensed something. He sniffed the air like his deer friends but smelled nothing out of the ordinary.

He quietly knelt and called on all his senses. Reaching out with his mind, he tried to identify and talk to the stalking thing.

Nothing worked.

"Teddy, I think something is going on, but I don't know what."

"What are we going do? Run? Climb a tree? I don't want to jump in the river and drown."

"I don't know what we're going to do, but we need to get ready."

"Ready for what, Sammy?"

"For battle."

"How do we do that?"

"Fill your pockets with rocks."

"I don't have pockets. Besides, I'm in your pocket. Let me out."

He took Teddy out of his pocket, put him around his neck, and filled his pockets with rocks.

An eddy of leaves and dirt swirled through the bushes. It knotted and twisted and spun into a vortex that rose above the trees, surged, and dropped to the ground, where it expanded into a shadowy fog.

He ran into a thicket to hide and sensing something sinister, he peeked out. Shocked and confused, he watched as a shadow fog slid along the forest floor.

"Teddy, they have never come on a Sunday before."

"Why?"

"I think Father Jakiv and Father Slavik has been keeping the shadows away on Sundays?"

"Really."

Samuil was quietly lost in thought for a moment before he answered Teddy question.

"Well, I don't know for sure, but I know Father Jakiv has been spending more time in Bakota and they have been seen spending a lot of time in the Cave Monastery."

"Maybe we should start paying more attention in mass."

"Maybe we should, Teddy. The shadows used to not come to the river. Now they do. They used to not come on Sunday. Now they have."

"Maybe Papa should increase his tithes. That'll make the priests work harder. Right?"

"Maybe. I don't know."

Silently they watched the shadow fog as it spread across the forest. Red lightning streaked through the fog as it intensified and spread. It pulsated and swirled above the treetops. Looping and knotting it condensed back to the forest floor. Within it, black fire danced. Then a giant crawler slowly began to emerge.

The dark scaled beast with red eyes searched the forest floor. Sniffing the air, it caught Samuil's scent. Samuil darted from the thicket to the nearest pine tree and climbed it. Once he was high in the pine, he stopped, sat on a branch, and watched the crawler as it searched the forest. Growling and foaming from its mouth, the huge insect-like monster stopped at the pine, sniffed, and looked up. Samuil froze, hoping he was camouflaged in the tree. The massive scaly beast reared on its hind legs and placed its front claws on the pine bark.

⋘⊱◈⊰⋙

Katya rolled her eyes when her brothers begged her to ask Papa if they could go to the pond for a swim. Though annoyed she agreed, and in no time at all, the boys were off running to the swimming hole. As her brothers raced through the forest, Katya and Alonya casually walked hand in hand, picking flowers, watching butterflies, and giggling.

Katya enjoyed being with her little sister. In her mind, she wasn't babysitting; they were playing and having fun. When they went swimming, Alonya never ventured from the knee-deep stream, and Katya didn't mind. She shuddered at the thought of going near the big fallen tree that separated the pond from the river. Besides, she didn't want to roughhouse with her brothers. Two against one wasn't her idea of fun.

While walking, Katya sensed a subtle change in the forest. The air was different. It was becoming crisp and fresh, and it smelled like it was saturated with hundreds of wonderful fragrances. She looked at Alonya, but she was busy watching butterflies. The volume of sound from the crickets, frogs, birds, and other forest creatures increased. Katya closed her eyes, listened to the harmonious sounds, and smiled.

When Katya opened her eyes, everything in the forest had a blue tinge. She stared in amazement, wondering what was happening. When a blue mist appeared between them and the pond, however, she became a bit concerned.

"Katya, look—blue air. Let's run into it."

Quickly, Katya grabbed her sister's hand.

"No, let's watch it for a moment and see what happens."

Together they watched as the mist rolled and thickened into a blue fog. The fog encircled them, and all Katya could see was blue. The next thing she knew, they were inside it. The blue fog was refreshing and calming, and it almost tickled when it settled on her skin. Alonya giggled. Katya told herself to be calm. So far, there wasn't anything ominous about her situation.

Then she heard the voice—a faint whisper called her name. She turned in circles, looking for the source of the voice, but it was coming from everywhere and nowhere.

"Katya, this is fun. We have to tell Samuil."

"We will, but right now we must be still and quiet."

"Okay."

Again, it called Katya's name.

"Alonya, did you hear that?"

"I only hear butterflies, and they are telling me bedtime stories."

"Bedtime stories?"

"Yes, and now I'm sleepy."

"Alonya, stay awake."

Katya felt herself beginning to float. She was only a few inches off the ground, but it was unnerving. Alonya was floating and sleeping beside her. The voice began to softly whisper but was suddenly interrupted by a blood-curdling yell.

CHAPTER 23

Forest Adventures

Feeling safe in the tall pine, Samuil poked Teddy and pointed.
"See the crawler?"

"He's a monster."

"Yes, the biggest one I've ever seen. As big as he is, he's probably hungry all the time."

"Hungry and mean too. That's a frightening combination."

The stalking shadow crawler glared at Samuil with evil, menacing eyes. It squealed in a high-pitched voice, and Samuil saw rows and rows of large sharp teeth. He shuddered when the beast dug its sharp front claws into the bark of the tree. Samuil decided to teach it a lesson. Reaching in his pocket, he pulled out a rock and winked at Teddy.

"Watch this."

Samuil gripped the rock tightly and threw it. The rock boomed as it bounced off the beast's scaly head. Snarling, the shadow creature wailed and tried unsuccessfully to climb.

"Sammy, all you did was make it angry."

Taking another rock in hand, Samuil took aim and threw again.

The rock hit the beast on its soft snout.

The creature shrieked and ran into the forest.

"That was too easy, Teddy."

"I know; he must have been a sissy crawler."

Another crawler leaped out of the fog and ran to the tree. Approaching the pine, it wailed, circled, and leaped onto the trunk. With a high-pitched squeal, the monster dug its long, sharp claws into the bark and slowly climbed. Snarling, it eyed the trapped prey.

Samuil yelled in his best pirate voice and threw another rock. It cracked onto the scaly head of the big crawler and bounced away.

"You missed, Sammy!"

"No, I didn't miss. I just didn't hit him on the nose."

"That's a miss because the nose was the target."

"I know the nose is the target."

"So, if you don't hit the nose, it's a miss. Hit the nose, Sammy."

"Okay, okay, I'll hit his nose this time!"

The rock hit its target and busted open the crawler's nose. Blood spurted into the air, and the crawler screamed, fell, and ran back into the fog. Moments later, the healed creature returned, screamed, and attacked. It leaped through the air, landed on the tree trunk, and scampered up the tree after its two-legged meal.

Samuil climbed higher up the pine but stopped to pelt the creature with rocks again. This time, the creature kept coming.

"Here we go, Teddy! Climbing time! Climb to the clouds! Reach for the stars!"

"I really don't like heights, Sammy."

"What?"

"Let's just sit here and throw rocks."

"We have to climb. If he slobbers on you, you will die slowly, like a madman. If he catches you, you are lunch."

"Okay, let's climb."

Samuil climbed until he ran out of tree. At the top, he stopped and palmed Teddy.

"Hang on; we're going to jump."

"To the ground?

"No."

"Were going to die! Leave me in the tree. Hang me on a branch. You can come back for me later."

"We're not going to die. Just hold on."

Planting his feet firmly, Samuil yelled like a madman and jumped. He grabbed an adjoining tree branch and it instantly snapped under his weight, and Samuil tumbled, breaking tree limbs as he fell. He stopped with a thud, just short of the forest floor. Samuil gathered himself and dropped the short distance to the ground, where he rolled in pain. His legs ached, his back felt broken, and his head hurt. He sat up and breathed deeply. Slowly, he got up. He knew he needed to scamper for cover before the creature arrived.

"Are you all right, Sammy?"

"No, I'm not all right! Every bone in my body hurts, even my teeth."

"My teeth don't hurt."

"Be quiet. I have to think."

When Samuil heard the crawler hit the ground, he froze. Slowly turning, he locked eyes with the monster. Samuil stared at the crawler. The shadow creature stared hungrily at Samuil. In that pivotal moment of indecision, Samuil sighed, and Teddy flinched.

"I didn't see this coming Teddy."

Time stopped as the monster and Samuil glared at each other. Samuil struggled to force his panicked mind to focus. Snarling, he tried to look as menacing as possible. When that didn't work, he tried to reach out with his mind and talk to the monster. Entangled with the mind of the beast, a brain-scrambling shriek of anger and pain exploded through Samuil's body. His head flooded with screaming-hot colors of angry red, sickly vermillion, and desperate orange—shades of emotion he couldn't fathom.

Quickly recovering, Samuil decided to concentrate on being a tree. *"Don't move, Teddy. Don't even breathe."*

"Okay."

"Look like a tree."

"What?"

"Look like a tree. Be quiet like a mouse and invisible like a ghost and look loke a tree. Maybe we'll vanish."

The crawler growled, took a step closer, and maneuvered to pounce on its prey. Samuil wished he had Papa's rifle, pistol, or even his knife. But all he had was one last rock. And it wasn't very big. The crawler growled and showed its teeth. Samuil steadied himself, squeezed the rock in his hand, and got ready for the final battle.

Suddenly, there was movement in the forest. He spun around, searching for another monster. Steadying himself, he looked at the source of the movement and readied himself to throw his last rock at the new intruder. A bellowing blur of fur raced past Samuil.

He watched in amazement as the blur plowed into the shadow crawler, and they tumbled in a cloud of dust and leaves. The forest exploded with the sounds of battle. Hissing and screaming, the crawler backed away. The hound gnashed his teeth, barked, and howled. The beast vanished into the woods, and the forest returned to normal. The scuffle was over almost as quickly as it had begun.

At first Samuil was puzzled. Then he remembered the hound in the Bogs. When everything fell silent, he decided the beast chose to seek a less-challenging lunch elsewhere.

"Where did the hound go Sammy?"

"He chased the shadow creature into the forest, and he's making sure it doesn't come back."

Samuil thought about the hound again. If it was the same hound, he had saved their lives once again. Regardless, Samuil wished he would come back so he could thank him. If not for him, they would not have won the day.

"We have foiled the monster! Victory is ours! We're the champions of the forest!" Samuil yelled.

"Only with a little help from a friend."

As Samuil was shouting and dancing, something touched his leg. Startled, he jumped and saw the hero hound. He had returned from the forest to check on Samuil and Teddy. The hound barked and sat.

"Hey, boy. Thanks for saving us. That was brave."

Samuil scratched him behind his ears, and the old hound thumped the ground with a rear foot. Samuil checked the dog over for wounds or cuts.

"Can you stay and play?"

The dog barked loudly and then began to bay. Startled, Samuil watched as the panting hound licked his lips, turned, and disappeared into the forest as mysteriously as he'd appeared.

As Samuil continued through the forest, he heard another noise. Still uneasy from the earlier encounter, he stopped and listened, hoping there weren't any more shadow creatures around. This noise was different. It was like chirping. Though he hadn't heard this noise before, it felt like it belonged in the forest.

Quietly, Samuil followed the sound to a stream. As he drew near, he stopped and listened. The chirpers had moved farther downstream. He headed off slowly in the direction of the unknown sound. With the anticipation of a new discovery teasing his imagination, he silently stalked through the forest. Nervous and excited, he didn't know what to expect as he crept closer to the mysterious noise.

"We're close, Teddy."

"Let's crawl."

"Good idea. I'm going to put you in my pocket for just a minute."

Sneaking down to the creek, Samuil stopped beside a large log, placed Teddy around his neck, and peeked over the log. He couldn't believe what he saw. Before him stood a colony of beavers. Curious, he crawled toward them. He and Teddy stayed well hidden, and they watched inquisitively as the beavers waddled around, going about their daily activities. Today was home repair for the beaver colony. They gathered wood, took it to their dam, and scurried about, placing each stick in its new position.

The two friends were excited as they quietly moved closer for a better view of the clan's activities. As they watched, Samuil leaned on a branch. When it snapped, it sounded like a cannon blast in the quietness of the forest. Samuil and Teddy ducked out of sight. The beavers stopped what they were doing and stared in the direction of the noise.

Samuil feared their discovery was imminent. He stared at Teddy. Thinking he was in trouble, Teddy grimaced.

"I didn't do anything, Sammy."

"Well, if you don't be still and quiet, you will spook them and ruin everything."

Teddy shrugged. For a long time, neither Teddy nor Samuil moved a muscle. They held their breath and moved only their eyes.

Samuil peeked cautiously over the log they were hiding behind. He prayed the beavers had not run away. To his surprise, they were still busy with their repairs.

"Teddy, see the big one?"

"Yes."

"Let's name him Mr. Beaver."

"No, that's not a good beaver name."

"How about Boss Beaver."

"Oh, I like it. Boss Beaver. Now that's a good name."

Samuil raised his head above the log and looked at the big beaver. Boss Beaver's eyes met Samuil's, and they stared at each other. Boss Beaver sniffed the air. Samuil smiled, and Teddy grimaced. All the beavers watched the standoff in quiet anticipation.

Samuil thought he saw Boss Beaver smile. Encouraged, Samuil slowly tilted his head to one side. Boss Beaver moved his head to one side. Samuil slowly tilted his head to the other side. The big beaver did the same. Samuil crawled slowly out from behind the log. All the beavers watched, motionless. Samuil carefully pulled Teddy from the inside of his shirt so he could see what was happening.

Boss Beaver squeaked but remained still. Samuil played the head game again, and Boss Beaver mimicked his every move. After a few more head moves, Samuil stuck out his tongue and made a silly face at Boss Beaver. The big beaver turned and waddled back to his clan. All the beavers relaxed. Sensing no threat from the strange visitors, the beavers returned to their home repairs. Samuil decided to push the envelope and get closer.

"Teddy, it will be easier for me to get closer if I leave you here for the moment."

"Don't leave me here alone. Those beavers eat wood, Sammy. And I'm wood.

Remember?"

"All right, but if you make any noise, I will tie you to a tree and leave you for the beavers to eat."

With Teddy around his neck but inside his shirt, Samuil crawled slowly and carefully to the beaver dam. When Boss Beaver noticed the approach, Samuil stopped. He pulled Teddy out of his shirt and whispered,

"What do beavers eat, Teddy?"

"Trees."

"No, they don't eat trees. They chew trees to cut them down and make their homes."

"What do they do with the tree bark?"

"I guess they spit it out."

"They don't eat it."

"No."

"Why not?"

"Splinters."

Teddy rolled his eyes, made a face, and mumbled to himself. Hearing the racket, Boss Beaver perked up and looked their way. Meeting his eyes, Samuil tilted his head, and Boss Beaver tilted his. For the next minute, they played the head game again. When he tired of the game, Boss Beaver waddled back to work. Samuil took this as an invitation to get closer.

Boss Beaver and some of the colony went back to gnawing down saplings and moving wood to the water's edge. The rest of the clan joined in. At the edge of the creek, Boss Beaver stopped and stood up. He looked at Samuil, looked at the dam, and then looked back at Samuil. Suddenly, he called out. All the beavers stopped and swiveled their heads in quiet anticipation.

Boss Beaver called out again, and all the beavers dived into the creek. Samuil sighed and watched them disappear under the water. Smiling a sad smile, he and Teddy waved goodbye to their friends. Samuil silently said thank you to the clan for all they had taught him in the brief encounter.

Samuil walked to the beaver dam and noticed something odd. A rope was on the dam, coiled around a limb. Samuil inspected it, and he saw that the rope was fairly new and in good shape. Scratching his head, he looked for clues as to its origin.

"Teddy, does that rope remind you of anything?"

"Nothing."

"Have you ever seen it before?"

"Never."

"Well, it looks familiar."

"Oh, that's Sergey's rope."

"You're right. It is Sergey's rope. He left it in the barn when he went to the field with Papa."

Untangling the rope, Samuil and Teddy ran through the forest, laughing and roping everything in their path. They roped boulders, bushes, and tree limbs. Finding a spider, Samuil laid the noose around it. He sat and watched as the spider tried to find a way out. Having circled about half of the inside of the rope, the spider just climbed over. Samuil was disappointed.

After coming across several other bugs who did as the spider had, the duo came to a broken fence, and Samuil roped a post. Tugging and pulling, he wrestled the imaginary bull on the end of his noose.

"Got him, Teddy! Grab hold!"

"I'm grabbing."
"We will eat good tonight!"
"Yes, steaks for supper!"
"Pull, Teddy!"

As they were hog-tying their lassoed bull, the quiet forest erupted into yells.

Samuil jumped in shock and then listened.

"Did you hear that?"

"What was it?"

"I'm not sure. But I think someone is in trouble.

Again, desperate yells echoed in the valley. Samuil realized someone needed help. He shook the rope loose from the post and coiled it. He stuck Teddy inside his shirt and, like a soldier charging into battle, he ran.

With his mind spinning and his body tingling with adrenaline, he hurried through the forest. As he raced toward the desperate cries for help, his stomach knotted, his lungs burned, and his muscles ached. Through brush, over rocks, and up embankments, Samuil ran, following the continual screams of someone in trouble.

Samuil crashed out of the forest and onto the banks of a pond. He bent over, out of breath and gasping for air. He gazed at the surroundings as his mind wrestled to analyze the situation. He heard a frightened cry for help and knew someone was in a desperate life-or-death struggle.

Then there was only silence.

CHAPTER 24

Running From Trouble

In the eerie silence, a gentle breeze rustled through the forest. Samuil heard a soft, serene whisper riding atop the forest breeze. Then he saw a familiar silvery light and felt the breeze. The breeze absorbed the whisper and began to hum. When it consumed the light, it flickered, blazed, and vibrated. He watched the breeze twist, change, and transform. Something within was rolling and forming. Slowly, it moved through the forest. And Samuil followed, as if hypnotized. When it came to the pond, it stopped and hovered.

Samuil heard a rustling noise, and a familiar blue mist slowly rolled through the trees toward the pond. He stared at the mist and noticed it was also different. It was darker blue but light enough that he could see something moving inside it.

Lightning flashed through the heavens as the blue mist rolled over the pond. Samuil watched it hover and spin. Silver light dripped from the mist like rain. Then the mist rose and engulfed the breeze. Together they rippled and twisted across the pond, escalating into a blue cloud with flashing silver lightning. Whitecaps rose and splashed in pond, and the water spun into a giant whirlpool. The cloud spun the whirlpool into a giant waterspout that sucked trees into it and ruffled Samuil's hair.

The phenomenon mushroomed into the heavens, roiled, and tumbled back into the forest. Mud and water splashed high, mingled together, and then stopped. The cloud hung in the air, motionless, as time stood still, and the forest petrified. Breathless, Samuil stared in disbelief at the time-frozen world that surrounded him.

As the cloud rotated above the treetops, bits of the pond dripped back to the forest floor. A funnel dropped from the cloud, and water splashed back into the pond, forming another whirlpool. When the whirlpool slowed, the water stilled, gathered, and gently cascaded.

The cloud intensified, and Samuil saw lights and motion within it.

"What is that?"

"I don't know, but it is incredible.

"Sammy, ever since we arrived at the pond, everything has been incredible."

"Yes, and the incredible is getting bigger."

"It's time to run Sammy!"

"No, Teddy, keep watching."

"Put me inside your shirt. I don't want to see any more."

Whatever was inside the mist continued to take shape—and the shape was human. Elements appeared and disappeared, and lights flashed. Mysterious shapes formed, reformed, and magically rearranged themselves. A silhouette flickered, and he watched as a mysterious glittering figure took shape.

Vapor swirled within the churning cloud, and a radiant essence slowly shifted. He watched in awe as the figure elegantly, rose and stood upright.

"Look, Teddy, it's a woman."

"I don't care. I'm not looking."

"I think it's an angel."

"I still don't want to look."

"Teddy, her eyes are changing. They were blue as the sky, and now they are a bright, glowing silver."

As the water in the pond churned, she looked at Samuil with her crystalline eyes and smiled. Samuil's eyes got big, his mouth dropped open, and he stared in shock. The translucent woman in the hovering cloud above them was beyond beautiful. Slowly, she spread out her magnificent silver wings. Their glistening brightness was blinding as they shimmered and turned the forest into a dazzling kaleidoscope of colors. Streaks of radiant silver-blue lights twisted around her, and flashes of rainbow colors pulsated through her wings and body.

"Wow, Teddy, you have to see this. Look at her."

Peeking, Teddy grimaced.

Is she a ghost?"

"No."

"Is she an angel?"

"Maybe."

"She's beautiful."

"Yes, she is."

Samuil couldn't take his eyes off the creature. He knew it was rude to stare, but he couldn't stop himself. He and Teddy watched as she slowly swayed. At one moment her body was softly silhouetted then it glowed brilliantly in the cloudy mist. She hovered, motionless. When she blinked, the water rose and began swirling around her, from her sparkling-blue slippers to her emerald-studded silver crown. Inches off the forest floor, she was locked in timelessness. As she slowly and gracefully swayed, her movement cast golden flakes from the pond into the whirling cloud. As the flakes spun, they gathered and formed a flowing molten halo above her head. The halo crystallized and glistened and melded into a crown. When she smiled and curtsied, Samuil bowed, but kept his eyes on the angelic creature.

Her eyes flamed brightly, and she looked at Samuil. Locked in her gaze, he was stunned and paralyzed until he heard her voice inside his head, even though her lips never moved. Teddy heard it too.

"Come closer, my child."

"No. Don't do it, Sammy. Please. I don't want to die," Teddy pleaded in fright.

"Be quiet or pass out!"

When she held out her soft, glowing, gloved hand Samuil took a step closer then hesitated, not knowing what he should do. Taking a deep breath, he reached out and took hold of her hand. With a welcoming smile, she helped him inside the billowing cloud.

Samuil was afloat in mist with an angel in suspended time. He looked around and everything seemed so surreal. For a long moment she was silent, allowing him to take in his new and unusual surroundings. Patiently, she smiled, waited, and then spoke to him again with her mind.

"Samuil, I always knew you could hear me. And I knew you would come."

"Hear you?"

"Yes, you have been following my whisperings for some time now." She smiled gently and waited for his response.

"Whisperings?"

"Yes. The ones you hear within."

"Oh those. Who are you?"

"I am your ancestor."

Samuil tilted his head and silently thought about what the angelic lady had said. He wondered how she could be his ancestor. Papa had never mentioned her.

"Ancestor?"

"Yes, and I am called the Keeper."

"The Keeper?"

"Yes, I am the Keeper of the Southern Forest. I keep balance."

"I'm sorry, Keeper, but you need help. The balance is off."

"I am here to restore it, with your help."

"Me?"

Samuil's mind raced. He thought about her words for several minutes while she waited patiently. He couldn't imagine how he could be of any assistance to her in restoring balance in the Southern Forest. He and Teddy were barely able to stay one step ahead of the shadows. They had the skills to sneak, run, and hide but not to stand up to them. That was dangerously crazy.

"Yes, you, Samuil. You are in my care. I have chosen someone to guide and watch over you."

"Who?"

"The Guardian."

"Is he here too?"

"No, but you will meet him when you meet him. And you will know him when you know him. He will help you and teach you. He has been helping you all along."

"He has?"

"Yes, he was helping you even before you were born."

Confused, Samuil ran his fingers through his hair, wondering who this could be.

"Before I was born?"

"Yes, before you were born, he helped you, and he also helped your father. Helping your father was helping you also."

"Oh. What's his name?"

"Samuil, you will know him when you know him. Afterward, you won't know him until you need to know him."

"Oh?"

"And you'll forget him until you remember him. He will be a friend and your mentor."

Samuil thought about her puzzling words, but he couldn't sort it all out in his head. While he struggled to put it together in a way that made sense, she patiently waited. Finally, he gave up.

"What about you, Keeper?"

"I am here and there. I come and I go. So, you will see me when you see me. And I will be there when I get there."

"Oh?"

Again, Samuil struggled to understand the majestic creature's cryptic language. As he concentrated, his mind filled with fanciful thoughts of amazing things, and his soul filled with sensations of magical wonder.

She is my ancestor and keeper. Plus, I have a chosen watcher and guide who is my teacher and helper. I can't wait to meet him. And I will not forget. Teddy won't let me.

His thoughts were interrupted when Katya stepped into view. She looked at him, smiling. Samuil gasped. Her gray eyes were gone. Now her left eye was a bright, glowing silver, and her right a bright, glowing blue. Samuil stared in amazement. Before he could say a word, Alonya walked out from behind her sister. Her amber eyes were as blue as the sky, and she was grinning from ear to ear. Samuil blinked.

Katya reached out with her mind and said hello. Samuil's eyes widened. Alonya reached out and giggled.

"Alonya? Katya? How?"

Katya explained, mind to mind, how they met the Keeper in the forest on the way to the pond. She also explained how the Keeper changed their eyes and opened their minds.

"Wow," Samuil whispered.

"Samuil," his ancestor called.

"I am Katya's and Alonya's ancestor also. Plus, the Guardian will teach and guide them as well. You must prepare; the shadows have powerful evil allies. They have human allies as well. This will not be easy, but together, we will fight the shadows and their evil allies. Together, we will return harmony to the forest."

Samuil wondered how they would be able to do that and if it was even possible. After all, Papa told him that the shadows were stronger than they had ever been. He wondered about the evil human help until the Keeper called to him.

"Samuil, come now."

The Keeper stepped up to Samuil and told him to open his eyes wide. He did as told and she reached out and pulled a silver strand from the cloud with her right hand. With her left hand, she pulled a blue strand. She gently rolled each between the finger and thumb of both hands creating a tiny ball. Stepping up to Samuil, she placed the silver ball in his right eye and the blue in his left. Samuil blinked.

"Look, Samuil." She pointed to the spinning center of the cloud.

Samuil looked and saw his new bright, shining eyes. They were like Katya's, but just opposite. Now your heart and mind are open and ready to learn magic from your guardian teacher.

"It's time, Samuil," she said.

"Time?"

"Yes, time for my assistance to stop. Now you must take your rope, save the brothers, and kiss the girl. Here, take my hand, and I will help you down."

When Samuil's feet touched the ground, timelessness began to wane. He felt a breeze ruffle his hair. He watched as the mist slowly dissipated, and the pond began to ripple. He heard birds sing as time slowly rolled back into motion.

"I must go, Samuil. Always beware of the shadow creatures. Stay away from them for now."

Before Samuil could answer, the cloud flashed and thundered. Like a mirage in the heat of summer, it spun into the ripple and vanished.

As the memory of the vision melted away, the mist in Samuil's head thickened.

At the edge of the pond, Samuil saw another foggy figure appear.

Those eyes. I have seen those eyes before. I know those eyes. Those eyes? Is that Katya?

Katya ran to Samuil, grabbed his arms, and shook him from his stupor.

"Katya, your eyes are gray."

"Of course they are. They always have been."

Samuil stared at her and tried to remember. Something in the back of his mind was trying to tell him that things weren't as they appeared to be. However, that strand of thought was just out of reach.

Alonya screamed and ran toward them. As she neared, Samuil saw tears. Sobbing, she pointed at the tree in the pond.

"My brothers are drowning!" She screamed.

Samuil looked at Katya, confused. His brain was still fuzzy, and his head was still spinning from whatever he experienced a moment ago.

Was Katya the angel in the cloud? Or was—

"Samuil, help them!" Katya pleaded.

Samuil looked toward the river and saw Borysko and Lauro beating the water, trying to get back to the tree to no avail. Though they were near the tree, they didn't know how to swim to it. Splashing and gasping for air, Borysko lurched forward on top of Lauro. Lauro disappeared under the water.

Katya screamed and looked at Samuil.

"Samuil, they can't swim. You have to help them."

Samuil looked toward the deep side of the pond where they were beating the water frantically. He realized they were panicking.

Tears ran down Katya's face. She kissed Samuil and whispered pleadingly, "Hurry!"

His heart was broken by her fear and his soul dizzied by her kiss. When Alonya screamed again, he darted into action. Samuil slung his coiled rope over his shoulder and ran to the deep end of the pond. Stepping on the old tree, he looked for the brothers. All he saw was water.

Walking carefully along the tree trunk, Samuil saw two heads bob up from under the water and he called out, "Borysko! Lauro! I'm coming!"

The brothers went under again and didn't reemerge. Samuil stared at the water.

They drowned. I'm too late. Too slow. Everyone will say it was my fault. Thinking about all the bad things he had wished on the brothers, he sighed.

Sorry, Borysko. Sorry, Lauro.

With Alonya sobbing in the background, Samuil remembered just how mean the brothers had always been. But still, he didn't want them to die like this. He wished he could have gotten there sooner to help them.

If only Ivan had been here or Papa or Sergey. They would have known what to do. They could have helped. If only they'd been here, they could have saved the boys.

Suddenly, there were noises from the water. Breaking the surface, the brothers fought the water, gulped air to fill their lungs, and begged for help. Samuil saw Borysko grab a tree branch. Then Lauro grabbed Borysko, and the branch snapped, plunging them both back into the murky deep.

Knowing the brothers were alive and fighting, Samuil's spirit was renewed. He picked up the rope and rushed into action. Gripping the rope in his hands, he enlarged the loop, secured his footing, and walked out onto the big tree. Balancing himself, he twirled the rope above his head and waited for the brothers to resurface.

Just like Papa does it. Now it's time to rope them.

He didn't have to wait long. Borysko surfaced for air first. Samuil twirled the rope above his head and lassoed Borysko around the neck. Quickly wrapping the rope around the tree trunk, he tossed the other end to Lauro. Both boys pulled themselves to safety.

The brothers sat on the tree, spitting water, coughing, and gasping for air.

Glaring angrily at Samuil, Borysko snapped at him.

"Thought you were going let us drown, worm."

"Hey! That's Papa's rope!" Lauro yelled.

"How'd you get Papa's rope, worm?" Borysko snarled.

"He stole it!" Lauro yelled.

"You stole it?" Borysko echoed.

Borysko jumped up and shoved Samuil into the deep end of the pond.

"Drown, worm," Borysko snarled.

"Yes. Drown, worm," Lauro mimicked.

Frowning, Samuil swam to shore and walked over to Katya.

"You saved them, Samuil. You're my hero."

She kissed Samuil on the lips. A bolt of lightning shot through his body, and reflexively, he jerked. Katya smiled and then giggled. Samuil stiffened, turned red, and kicked the dirt. Teddy snickered.

"Stop Teddy."

"Samuil's in love with Katya."

"No. She's a friend," he mumbled.

"That was a love kiss, Sammy."

"No. It was a friendship kiss."

"Kissy, kissy, she's your girlfriend now."

"Stop Teddy, or I'll throw you in the pond to drown."

Sergey crashed out of the woods in a dead run. He stopped to catch his breath, gasped, and shouted.

"Boys!"

Shocked, they all turned and looked at Sergey. In the following moment, there was only the sound of children breathing. Walking up to his boys, he spoke again.

"Is everyone all right? What happened here?" Sergey asked.

No one spoke.

"Borysko, Lauro, are you alright?"

Both boys nodded. Samuil suspected if their Papa discovered they had been playing in the deep end of the pond, there would be a whipping.

"Samuil, are you alright?"

Samuil looked to the heavens for help, but none came. Then he looked at the pond, hoping to see blue mist. There was no help there either. So silently he looked at the ground.

"Samuil?" Sergey inquired again.

"Yes, sir I'm alright."

"What happened, boys?"

Sergey waited for an answer, but all he saw was a frightened look on their faces. He stared at the boys.

"Borysko what is going on here?"

When he didn't answer, Sergey raised an eyebrow.

"I heard your sister screaming, and when I got here, Alonya was crying. If you know what's good for you, you'll start talking right now. The truth, boy; let's have it."

Borysko swallowed hard and began his lie. "Uh…we were…uh…playing…in the pond. And uh…Samuil came. And he…uh. He had your rope. And uh…we…uh. Tried to take it from him."

He paused to think.

"He ran and uh…we followed him. And uh…we tried to get the rope. And…and…Samuil slapped me with the rope, knocking me off balance. And Lauro grabbed my arm to steady me. But uh…I slipped and grabbed Lauro. And…Lauro grabbed the rope, and we all fell in."

"Is that the way it happened, Lauro?"

"Yes, Papa."

Looking at Samuil, Sergey held out his hand.

"Let me see the rope, Samuil."

Reluctantly, Samuil handed it over.

"Yep," Sergey said after studying the rope carefully.

"That is my rope, all right. How did you get it, Samuil?"

Samuil didn't answer. He knew the odds were stacked against him. Sergey would believe his boys, not him, so Samuil did the only thing he could, he turned and ran into the forest. As Samuil ran, Katya grimaced.

"Papa!" She shrieked.

Startled, Sergey turned to face his daughter.

"It's all a lie, Papa. They were playing in the deep end, where they weren't supposed to be, and fell in the pond."

"What?"

"It's true, Papa. Samuil saved their lives."

Sergey walked to a tree and snapped off a switch.

"Katya, take your sister home. The boys and I will be along shortly.

Deep in the forest, Samuil stopped at a cliff by the river to catch his breath. Drenched in sweat, he sat on a stump, closed his eyes, and enjoyed the moist river breeze blowing across his face. He heard a twig snap, and with all his senses still on high alert, he jumped up and ran.

Slowing to a trot, Samuil decided to turn from the river and head inland. He was afraid that Sergey or the brothers were following him, so he headed to the haunted Southern Forest.

"Sammy."

"What?"

"Why are we headed to the Southern Forest?"

"Because no one will follow us in there."

"Papa won't be able to find us there either."

"Teddy, Papa doesn't know what happened. He won't be looking for us."

"But Sammy…"

Samuil explained to Teddy that Sergey would believe his boys' story, and that made him and Teddy thieves. He also explained that when a thief was caught, they cut off the hand that stold.

"So, we're going to hide in the Southern Forest forever?"

"Yes, and if we have to. Now come on. Let's cross the stream and enter the Southern Forest."

Teddy hesitated.

"It's live with the ghost and monsters of the Haunted Southern Forest or lose a hand."

Samuil shook his head.

"The ghost stories are true and so are all the other stories, It is all true, and that's why we are going in. No one will be brave enough to follow us in there. Now, come on."

"And if someone is?"

Samuil hesitated for a moment took a deep breath and let it out before replying.

"Then we'll go into the Bogs and hide. We have no other choice. Come on."

"Sammy, we can be killed in the Bogs."

"Teddy you can get killed anywhere you go."

"Yes, but the Bogs Samuil. They are the most dangerous."

"And we are not going there unless we have to."

Samuil turned to walk toward the hunted Southern Forest. Teddy was still reluctant and didn't want to go along. Samuil felt Teddy's anxiety; he really didn't want to go either, yet he felt they had no choice.

"Sammy, people go into the haunted Forest and disappear in there."
"Yes, they do."
"So—"
Samuil ran his fingers through his hair and sighed.
"Teddy, I promise I will keep you safe."
"You're going anyway, aren't you?"
"Yes, but only to the haunted Forest."
"You know people disappear there too."
"Yes, I have heard about the demons and monsters eating people in the Forest but you will be okay with me."
"Oh, I will? Remember what happened last time we were there?"
"Well, yes, but maybe we will see the mysterious magical snow owl."
"Well-okay, let's go."
Together they ran until they came to the border stream. There, Samuil stopped.
"Teddy, across this stream is the Southern Forest.
Ready to enter?"
"Yes. No. I don't know."
"Here we go anyway."
They walked into the Southern Forest that was keen with whisperings. The wind moaned through the trees. The water splashed along but didn't sing. Birds were silent, but the forest was alive with the sounds of buzzing insects.

Samuil was alert and looked for the snow owl, even though he knew it was the wrong time of year for it to be this far south. Walking into a meadow, he noticed a shadow fog slowly rolling across the forest. He watched it slide into the creek, making the water churn.
"We've got to go."
"Why?"
"Look at the stream."
"What?"
"Look closely. Look under the surface. Something in the water."
"What is it?"
"It's a shadow fog, and there are demons inside it."
As Samuil spoke, the fog began to bubble and rise from the water and roll out of the stream. It twisted and knotted through the forest and rose like a blanket into the sky. It spun and boiled and

spread through the sky thundering into an ominous dark cloud. When the dark cloud filled with red lightning and began flashing through the heavens, Samuil ran.

As he ran, a typhoon wind blew, caused him to veer off the path. Lightning struck the ground, forcing him to cut into the unfamiliar parts of the forest. The shadow cloud swirled, grew, and maneuvered through the forest, as if herding them to a specific location.

"Why are we stopping?"

"The shadow cloud is forcing us to go somewhere."

"Where?"

"I don't know."

"What are we going to do?"

"If we stay here, the demons will come. If we keep going, we will end up in the Bogs. And anything could happen in there but not anything good."

Suddenly, gale-force winds blew Samuil off his feet.

"We've got to go, Teddy."

Struggling to his feet he tried to run against the wind. Getting nowhere, Samuil turned his back to the wind and ran. The wind blew them in the direction of the Bogs. As they stumbled into the Bogs, the wind continued to blow them deeper and deeper into unknown parts of the Bog.

When the wind stopped, everything became eerily silent and still. A shadow fog menacingly tumbled and knotted through the swampy bog and hovered before them. Hanging in the air, the fog turned a light charcoal and lurched across the stumpy ground. The fog rolled across Samuil's feet. It was cold to his feet but warm as it rose above his ankles.

Samuil shivered.

"Come on, Teddy; we must keep moving."

"We better do more than move; we better run."

"No, Teddy, it's too dangerous to run. I don't know this part of the Bogs. I've never been here before."

"Don't tell me we're lost."

"Okay, I won't, but we are."

Slowly, they made their way across the sinister terrain, careful not to slip or step in a bog. As they walked, the only sounds were their footfalls and breathing. The bog was murky, deathly silent, and eerie. Ghostly images invaded Samuil's thoughts as beads of cold sweat accumulated on his forehead. Malevolent whispers rose out of the mire alone with muddy bubbles. Samuil stopped behind a large tree and looked around. He shivered at all the sinister things he heard lurking in the bog.

The fog rose above the treetops and boiled into the sky becoming a dark storm cloud full of red lightning that blocked out the sun making the Bog fade into gloomy shaded of darkness. Samuil wiped his clammy palms on his shirt and clenched his fists. Ready but frightened, he stood wide-eyed, struggling to see.

A moist breeze ruffled his hair. Seconds later, gale-force driven rain soaked and blinded him.

"Teddy, come on! We've got to find shelter!"

Hurrying through the Bog, Samuil saw a large tree with an opening in the trunk. He ran to it, crawled in—and discovered too late that there wasn't a bottom. He and Teddy fell. As they tumbled down, darkness swirled around him and the bounced off of streaking black and red lightning.

Finally, Samuil stopped falling when he splashed hard into muddy water. The world faded as he sank. He pumped his arms and kicked his legs and slowly began to rise—until a hand grabbed his foot and pulled him down. Surprised and shocked, Samuil instinctively fought kicking and squirming with all his might to get free.

Air! I need air! I need to breathe! I've got to surface! I've got to break free!

Then Samuil calmed his mind, relaxed his body, and commanded his muscles to go limp. No longer struggling, he became deathly still and a moment later, he felt the grip on his foot slacken ever so slightly.

Seizing the moment, he jerked. Freed from the death grip, he swam upward. He surfaced and dragged himself from the muddy swamp, fell onto his back, and filled his lungs with air.

Threatening sounds shocked Samuil back to reality. He jumped up and ran into a grove of pines, where he knelt behind a large fallen tree. Quietly, he labored to catch his breath.

"Teddy, look. The storm followed us."

"How can it do that?"

"I don't know."

"Why is it still pursuing us?"

"I don't know. All I know is, here it comes."

"Sammy, we need to find somewhere safe."

"Too late."

He jumped up and ran but the storm quickly overtook them and pounded them with muddy ran and dark hail. Coming to a dark waterfall, they stepped through it into a cove that sheltered them from the deluge.

Together, they watched the storm. Sheets of black-red lightning ripped through the sky, and deafening thunder shook the ground and echoed throughout the valley. The dark storm rapidly intensified.

"Sammy, how do we get out of this mess alive?"

"Don't worry. I'm working on that."

"Work a little faster please."

When the storm ceased, Samuil peeked out from behind the waterfall to see a shadow fog rolling over the swamp and hover. Dark flashes streaked through it, outlining hundreds of hideous forms that slowly twitched and dripped to the forest floor. Demons and monsters rose from the drippings.

"Teddy, open your eyes. The shadow demons are here."

"Did they come from the fog?"

"Yes."

"Can it get any worse?"

"Let's hope not."

The sky streaked with dry lightning, and thunder rumbled, but this time there were no clouds. A hot wind blew the fog into swirling eddies that grew dense and twisted through the Bog. By the light of the flashing lightning, Samuil saw a fiery whirlwind. The whirlwind crashed into the fog and spun out dark, malformed shapes that transformed into four-legged creatures.

"It's the crawlers again, Teddy."

"Yeah, and look how much bigger they are."

"And some of them have wings."

"We're in a lot of trouble Sammy. So, what are we going to do?"

"We'll stand and fight, like always."
"No, there are too many, and they're huge."
"If we run, they'll catch us. We'll stay here for now."
"Good idea."

With a knot of fear in his gut Samuil stood watching as shadow demon slithered out of the shadow fog and stood beside winged crawlers. When a demon with piercing red eyes turned and glared at Samuil all he could do was grimace and stare back.

The crawlers crouched, the demons mounted, and they sprang into the air. Samuil ran as a winged crawler quickly soared across a bog in pursuit and grabbed Samuil with its sharp claws. Samuil struggled, kicked, yelled, and swung his fists at the beasts but it was all to no avail. The monster was too strong. With Samuil in tow, the demon rider flew back into the fog, dropped Samuil and flew away.

Inside the fog, the air was thick and dank. It smelled of sulfur and death. Shadow strings were everywhere, wiggling around like worms. Discarded bones rose like mountains. Yellow eyes pierced the darkness, staring menacingly at Samuil. Screams, screeches and inhuman noise of terror echoed through the fog. Samuil shuddered. More red lightning fingered through the fog, and a molten monster dripped out of a lightning bolt.

Samuil stared in disbelief at the giant fiery leviathan. Closing his eyes, he mentally called for the hero hound. From somewhere beyond, a soft whisper touched the fog, stilling the turbulent atmosphere. A trickle of hope rose in his heart as the whisper vibrated into a soothing melody. Samuil closed his eyes and listened to the melody swell into rhythmic, angelic tones.

"Samuil," it called tenderly in his mind.

Samuil opened his eyes and tried to focus. Outside of the dark fog that encompassed him, he saw an angel riding on a blue cloud. Her silver wings glowed. Glittering golden flecks spun in a circle around her head like a crown. Radiant rainbow lights emanated from the area all around her.

"Haven't we met before? You look familiar. I think I know you." Samuil asked with his mind.

Softly, the Keeper answered with her mind.

"Yes, Samuil, you know me. I am your Keeper. Remember?"

"Yes, yes, I remember. The pond. I remember."
"It's time for you to meet your guardian and teacher."
"Oh? Now?"
"Yes, Samuil."
"Teddy and I are kind of busy right now, trying to stay alive and escape."
"Yes, so you say."
"We really don't know how to get out of this fog."
"So I have observed."

The Keeper extended her hand into the fog. Samuil took it, and the Keeper gently placed him on solid ground away from the menacing fog and its evil deadly creatures.

Unexpectedly, the fog twisted, knotted, and rolled. A red demon atop an ebony dragon slid out of the fog on a dark lightning bolt and soared through the heavens. The red demon's eyes glared and hot dragon fire blazed as they flew to challenge the Keeper.

The Keeper's eyes began glowing a blinding silver. Samuil heard a loud cry, and looking up, he saw a fiery phoenix flying toward her. The Keeper mounted the phoenix and flew into battle. Teddy shut his eyes and grimaced. Samuil covered his eyes and peeked between his fingers to watch as the two combatants collided and fought in the heavens.

Blazing black fire and searing silver light exploded in the hostile sky. Below, trees tumbled, smoke rose, the ground shook, and the earth cracked open. Shards of light and darkness rippled in the air as Samuil fell through the cracked earth.

CHAPTER 25

Tracking Samuil

As he fell through the earth, Samuil heard the Keeper's voice whisper, *"Remember when you need to remember."*

As her voice faded, so did Samuil. As he fell through the earth, he blacked out. When he awoke, he found that he and Teddy were out of the bog.

"Where are we, Sammy?"

"We are on the sandy bank of the border stream on the other side is the Southern Forest.".

"How did we get here?"

"I don't remember."

"I remember demons and shadow creatures."

"I remember…floating like in a cloud. Then falling. But it was so strange."

"Yes, and scary too."

"Come on, Teddy; let's get out here."

Samuil ran through the Southern Forest without looking back until he heard the singing river and smiled.

Excited he ran faster until they reached the bank of the singing Samuil and Teddy, both out of breath, stopped at the edge of the river. Spotting at an old tree that had fallen into the water, they walked out on it, sat down, and listened to the river melody. Samuil dangled his feet in the cool water.

"Strange things have happened today, Teddy, and I can't remember much of it. Can you?"

"No, not much. I remember running through the Southern Forest. And we were in trouble in the Bogs."

For a moment they silently sat and listened to the singing river.

"Let's go for a swim. That should cool us off."

"No, I don't want to get wet."

"You sure? The water's cool, and it will feel good on this hot day."

"I'm sure. I want to stay on dry land for now."

"Okay."

"Hang me in the tree, in the shade and I'll be fine."

"All right. I think I'll float down the river, but I'll be back soon."

"While you're floating, I'll take a nap."

Samuil hung Teddy in a secure spot in the tree and dived into the cool river.

"Be back soon, Teddy. Stay there. Don't wander off and get lost. You might get eaten by a wildcat."

Teddy grimaced at the thought.

Spotting a large piece of driftwood, Samuil swam to it, grabbed it, and floated off down the river. He slowly drifted down the lazy river, gazing at the sky. The hot sun began to melt his tension away. As he gazed at the scattered bank of opaque thunderheads gathering in the summer sky, he relaxed. The tranquil river breeze eased the shadowy quandaries of his soul. The cool water washed away the worries in his troubled mind. As one, Samuil and the river slowly meandered through the winding valley.

Drifting along, Samuil saw squirrels and beavers on one shoreline and a wildcat on the other. They had come to the river to drink. Further down the river, he came to a sandy cove. Thinking that it would be a nice place to rest, he pushed away from his driftwood and swam to it.

The sand on the shore felt as warm to his cool skin as the sun did to his face. Samuil lay back in the sand and breathed deeply. He sighed as the warmth of the sunny day sent waves of serenity over him. His tension eased, his mind slowed down, and his body relaxed. As his anxieties melted away, relief settled over him. Like the comfort of a cozy blanket, calmness embraced him, and Samuil unwound.

Now calm, his mind began trying to sort through the day's events. He quickly found that stringing the day together was all but impossible and trying to understand it was hopeless. There were just too many gaps in his memory. The day's activities had too many blank spots, and that which he thought he knew was hazy. Nothing fit together and nothing made sense.

What really happened in the bog? Who was there? Why can't I remember?

Again, Samuil struggled to recall the strange events of the unusual day until fatigue seized his body, and drowsiness disabled his mind. Stretching his weary muscles, he closed his eyes, breathed deeply, and slowly drifted away to dreamland.

Katya swam out of the river and sat in the sand beside Samuil. She tickled his upper lip with a blade of grass and giggled when he swatted at it.

Waking, Samuil rubbed his sleepy eyes.

"Katya? What are you doing here?"

"Oh nothing. I saw you in the river and decided to take a swim."

"But you can't swim."

"Yes, I can."

"Since when?"

"For a long time now."

"Really?"

"Yes, I practiced a lot, and I am good. Swear you will not tell Papa or anyone."

Samuil grinned and raised an eyebrow.

"Swear, Samuil!"

"All right. I swear on our friendship."

Katya grinned and blushed and Samuil smiled.

"Katya if you can swim, then why didn't you try to save your brothers at the pond?"

"Because I would have gotten in big trouble for knowing how to swim."

"Why?"

"You really don't know, do you?"

Samuil thought for a moment. Then puzzled, he rubbed his chin and shrugged.

"It's not ladylike, Samuil."

Samuil frowned.

"Oh, you would have let your brothers drown so you could continue to be ladylike?"

"No, Samuil, even though they are mean, stupid, and cruel, I would not let them die."

"Then what?"

"I knew you would come."

"Oh?"

"And you did."

"Yes, I did, but…"

"Heroes always show up in times of trouble and make things right, and you are my hero, Samuil."

Smiling, Katya leaned in and kissed him softly on the lips. Samuil froze, sighed, and opening his eyes he blushed. Katya smiled proudly at a job well done and winked at him. Samuil, stunned and not knowing how to react, smiled back. Then he reached out and gently squeezed Katya's hand. She blushed and giggled. After a long, somewhat awkward moment, Samuil lay back in the sand.

"I just love these warm lazy days, Katya. But they make me sleepy." He yawned.

Katya smiled. "Go back to sleep, and I'll wake you later."

Lying in the sand, Katya snuggled up close and gave Samuil a peck on his cheek.

Samuil blushed, not knowing what to do.

Katya's kisses are different from Mama's kisses. A lot different.

It wasn't the first time that Katya had kissed him. He was puzzled and wondered what that was all about, but down deep, he knew. Trying to doze, Samuil shut off his racing mind. He squeezed his eyes shut and lay still as an opossum.

She's doing it again. She's kissing me. Oh. Her kisses are nice. Her lips are soft, warm, and … and … Katya's kisses began intense. She was kissing him all over his face and neck. Suddenly, the kisses became sloppy, wet slobbers. Then she began licking him.

Too much. Too much. I have to move. I must get up.

But he couldn't move, speak, or even protest. Try as he might, his body refused to respond. It was as if he were paralyzed. His limbs tingled but wouldn't respond. His mind was sluggish. He struggled, trying to force his body to move. He couldn't even wiggle. His eyes wouldn't open. He screamed at his brain to work and his body to move. He pleaded and battled but to no avail. He was aware but couldn't move; he was breathing but couldn't respond.

A drooling tongue licked Samuil's mouth and a bolt of energy surged through his body. Startled, he jerked upright in the sand and woke up from his paralyzing dream. Still dazed, he pushed away and rubbed his face. Confused, he wiped the slobbers from his mouth and blinked his sleepy eyes.

What happened? Where is Katya? She was just here a moment ago… wasn't she?

Samuil looked around, and his eyes settled on a hairy creature. That wasn't Katya; it wasn't even human. His dreamy mind was unable to comprehend, and his body jerked in response. He jumped to his feet and stared at the thing, unable to conceive what his eyes were seeing. He closed his eyes, took a deep breath, and shook his head, hoping to focus his mind.

Opening his eyes, Samuil glared at the monster as his drowsy mind tried to focus. When the creature barked, Samuil flinched, and his mind suddenly engaged. With a shiver, he realized it had all been a dream. The mangy old mutt sitting beside him had been licking him all over, even on the mouth.

"Yuck!" Samuil murmured spitting and wiping his mouth. He made a face.

I dreamed of a nice girl and wonderful kisses but woke to mangy dog slobbers. That's disgusting. I wonder what he has been eating! Ugh! I really don't want to know.

Samuil frowned at the long-legged, lanky old hound with splotches of gray on his jaw and around his eyes and the hound gazed back, panting and barked. Then he realized that this was the rescue hound that had saved him numerous times in the forest.

Samuil tilted his head to one side and the hound barked and wagged his tail. Samuil sat down in the sand and the hound licked him on the jaw. His coat was a dirty brown, his eyes were knowing, and his expression was playful.

"I know you."

Woof, woof.

"Where did you come from, dog?"

The old hound sat, panted, and looked to the Southern Forest. "You're the dog from the forest?" The hound wagged his tail.

"I knew it. Why are you here?"

He stood and pawed the ground. "Do you have a home?"

He bowed.

"Where is your master?"

He howled.

"Show me."

The hound began running in circles, chasing his tail. When he stopped, he looked at Samuil and licked his hand.

"Too late. We have already been introduced in my dream. In real life, you are probably not any better a kisser than in my dreams."

The hound howled.

"Take me to your master."

He barked and walked toward the Southern Forest.

Leaving the sandy cove, the old hound led Samuil up a small embankment and into the woods. The pair continued until they came to a slope in the bend of a creek. Samuil knew this creek marked the beginning of the Southern Forest. Without thinking, he stopped. The hound stopped, turned, and barked at him.

Samuil remained motionless, except for his eyes, which searched the forest across the creek. This time the old hound howled, and it broke Samuil's spell. He looked at the hound and the hound barked and chased his tail until Samuil began to giggle. Regaining the boy's attention, the old hound walked into the Southern Forest and Samuil followed happy to be out of the Bogs.

There was an uncanny silence in the forest, and Samuil didn't like it. As they walked the boundary between the Bogs and the Southern Forest, Samuil noticed a knee-high shadow fog to his left. As it snaked along the edge of the tree line, the shadow fog inched closer to the trail. A twig snapped and to his right, Samuil saw a twisting blue mist keeping pace and edging closer to them. He watched as the mist and the fog met on the trail, entangled, and became a knee-high blue-gray mist. Now Samuil could only see the hound's ears and his wagging tail slapping the mist as they continued their mission. Samuil chuckled at the funny sight.

Strange and mysterious sounds began emanating from within the rolling mist. Some of the noises didn't belong in the forest. Many of the sounds Samuil knew as shadow creatures; others he didn't recognize. The trail of swirling mist puzzled him as it continued to become more and more eerie.

Why haven't the shadow creatures attacked? Is it because the gray and the blue fog mingled together? Are they canceling out each other's powers?

Samuil jumped when something brushed against his leg. He was on the verge of bolting out of the spooky forest when he saw the old dog's tail wiggling above the fog. When he barked, Samuil smiled, knowing he could trust the hound. After all, he had saved him and Teddy from a wildcat and a shadow creature and had helped at the battle of the Bog.

Teddy, I promise to come for you as soon as I get the hound safely home.

The hound barked, shocking him back to the moment.

"Oh, lead on, boy. Let's get you home."

As they traveled, the sounds in the woods intensified, but the hound never slowed down. They continued through the forest at a fast clip until they reached a small clearing. The hound stopped, and Samuil spotted a cave in the cliff, just up ahead. A silver-blue mist surrounded the cave. Above the mist was a blue cloud. In the cloud, there were golden flakes and a silhouetted figure of a woman. Samuil gasped. The hound barked.

I have seen her before. She was at the pond.

Samuil watched as the whole thing slowly dissipated and rolled back into the forest.

"You must live in that cave in the side of the hill."

The hound wagged his tail and barked.

Slowly, they maneuvered up the hill and neared the cave. Samuil wondered who lived there with the old hound. The narrow path they had followed gradually began to widen. The closer they came to the cave, the wider and better kept the path became. Slowly, the blue mist and dark fog began rolling away. Walking out of the mist, Samuil saw neat rows of colored flowers and even a cobblestone walkway. Someone had cleared the brush and boulders, making a smooth ascent to the mouth of the cave.

Bugs and lizards were scurrying around in the garden. The trees were filled with singing birds. Frogs croaked in a man-made pond. Clean clothes were hanging in the bush to dry. Everywhere, butterflies swirled and floated lazily. As Samuil watched them, they slowly swarmed around him. Two landed on his right shoulder and then two more on his left.

My welcoming committee. That's nice.

Turning around, he saw a dense wall of shadow fog rolling and knotting menacingly. It hung thick, like a wall between the cave and the forest. When the hound barked, it twisted, knotted, and slid back into the forest.

To Samuil, this new world was amazing. Captivated by the butterflies, he stood still, not wanting to frighten them off. Then the hound barked, and the butterflies flew away. Samuil turned and frowned at the hound. The hound walked up to Samuil and nudged him backward toward a boulder at the edge of a steep cliff.

CHAPTER 26

The Guardian Of The Southern Forest

S amuil heard footsteps to his left and turned to face a pair of bright green cat eyes. A stout old man with a twisted walking stick and a long, scraggly gray beard stood before him.

Samuil looked up at him.

"Oh. Uh. Hello."

"My, my. What has the dog dragged up? What, what?"

"Uh …"

"Well, well, to whom do I owe this pleasure?"

"What?"

"Who are you, boy? You have a name, don't you?"

Oh yes. I'm Samuil."

"Samuil. My, my. Does Samuil have a last name?"

"Fedorchak."

"Oh, yes. Samuil Fed-or-chak. Son of P'etro. Yes, yes. I knew it. I knew it. Yes, it has a ring. I like it. Yes, yes. You and I did a good job of this one, old hound."

The eccentric old wise man looked at Samuil with his catlike eyes. "Do you like your name, Samuil Fedorchak?"

"I haven't thought about it, but now that I do, yes, I like it. I like it very much."

"Wonderful, wonderful. I like it too."

"Woof, woof."

"Oh, so does he."

The old man rubbed his chin, as if in deep thought, and looked at the hound. Then he took a deep breath and looked back at Samuil.

"I knew you were coming. Yes, yes. The Keeper told me you would come when you come. Now you've come, you're here, and we can talk."

"You know the Keeper?"

"Yes, I do."

This was a shock and a surprise to Samuil. It was exciting to meet someone who knew the Keeper. Perhaps he would have answers.

"Who are you, and how do you know the Keeper?"

"I'm your guardian. My name is Nikolai of the Caves."

"You're my guardian?"

"Yes, yes, I am. In the flesh."

"I have a million questions."

"One at a time, one at a time."

Samuil didn't know which question to ask first until Wolf Killer barked, snapping him back to the present.

"Is this your hound?"

"When he's hungry and can't catch a rabbit."

"What's his name?"

"Wolf Killer."

"Wolf Killer! Wow! He must be more furious and braver than I thought. How many wolves has he killed?"

"Ha-ha! Him? Kill a wolf! Ha-ha-ha! If he saw a wolf, he would not know whether to pee or run!"

Nikolai laughed loudly, but Samuil frowned. Wolf Killer had come to their rescue in the forest on several occasions. The hound was always around when Samuil needed him.

"Wolf Killer saved me and Teddy from shadow creatures in the woods more than once."

Nikolai rolled his eyes and stared at the dog.

"Yes. He does that occasionally when he wants attention. He's spoiled, you see. Yes, yes."

"Why do you call him Wolf Killer if he doesn't kill wolves?"

"Oh. Well, well. That's a good question. Yes indeed. Because I'm a name-giver. Oh yes. Yes, I am. A good one too. Yes indeed."

Samuil rubbed his chin. This was something new. He had never heard of anyone naming things, but he was talking to his guardian.

Who knows what he can do?

"You name things?"

"Oh yes. If I didn't, who would? And it's lots of fun. Yes, yes. The plants and animals are the most fun."

"But plants and animals are already named."

"Oh no, Samuil. No. I am talking about individual names, Samuil. Not categorical names. No. No, indeed!"

"What?"

Nikolai tilted his head and looked at Samuil.

"A tree is not just a tree. No. Not at all, not at all. Come, Samuil, I will show you."

Nikolai walked to a tree and stopped.

"Samuil, this is my friend, Planky."

"The oak?"

"Yes, Samuil. This is Planky the Oak, to be exact. He says hello.

"They talk to you?"

"Oh yes. Everything does. Talk, talk, talk. The key is knowing how to listen. Yes, listen. The other key is knowing to make the be silent."

"Do you name everything?"

"Yes indeed. Oh yes, yes. But mostly the ones who ask. I named you also."

Samuil gasped in disbelief and wondered why his guardian had named him instead of his parents. "You named me?"

"Yes. I did, I did."

"But how?"

"Wolf Killer told me."

"What?"

"He helps, you see. We named you after we saved your father from the Southern Forest."

"You saved Papa from the Southern Forest?"

"Oh yes, yes, Wolf Killer helped too."

Woof, woof.

"Yes, all right. Wolf Killer reminded me that was not the only time we saved his skin in that forest."

"Really?"

Astonished, Samuil stared at the wizard with eyes of wonder as his brain struggled to comprehend what he was being told.

"Woof, woof."

"Oh yes. My, my. I cannot talk about the first time. Nope. Can't, can't."

"Woof."

"Yes. I agree. That's a story for another time, Samuil. Yes, later. Later, later."

"But—"

"No buts, Samuil. No, no."

"Woof, woof."

"Oh yes, yes, Wolf Killer. Very well, then. Very well."

Nikolai stroked his long white beard and looked around suspiciously.

"What did he say?" Samuil asked.

"He wants me to answer your question about his name. You see, Samuil, it is like this. Every caveman wants a good dog—a dog that is a lean, mean, killing machine. At the very least, every caveman needs a good dog with a lean, mean, killing-machine name. But not everybody gets what they want. No, no. Some of us just end up with what we need. So, there you have it. Yes indeed. That is how Wolf Killer came to be a dog with a lean, mean, killing-machine name. Yes indeed."

"Machine?"

"Oh yes. Machine. Indeed, indeed."

Pausing, the old man scratched his scraggly beard, cleared his throat, and took a deep breath.

"Machines, machines indeed. They are marvelous, terrible, magical things! And they do the work of many men! Oh yes, yes. Many, many. And they are more and better than man! Yes indeed. They have lots of them in America. Yes, lots and lots. Or they will have. Let me see. The Allied Shadow War was in the late 1840s. You came into this world shortly after P'etro was wounded and released. And France is machining up. Or have they started yet? Oh well, this is the beginning time of machines. Yes, yes, machines, machines."

Focusing his cat eyes on Samuil, Nikolai crooked his finger and beckoned him.

"Shh, come closer. Come, come. I'll tell you a secret."

The old man looked all around with his wild eyes, making sure no one was near enough to overhear.

"First, I saw them in my dreams. Yes, yes, my crystal-blue dreams with silver linings. Yes indeed."

"Blue dreams? Silver lining?"

"Yes, my boy. I did. Yes indeed. Yes indeed."

"Wow."

Samuil scratched his head hardly able to follow all that the old man was saying.

"Oh yes, Samuil. Wow, indeed."

Motioning Samuil closer, the caveman spoke in a whisper.

"I have traveled through time and investigated these things. Yes, yes, I did. One day I went there just to make sure. Yes indeed. To be sure, you see. Sure, sure. I stepped through time to the distant land's past and present. Yes, and there it was, just as I had seen in my crystal dreams. Yes, yes."

"You stepped through time into distant lands?"

"Woof!"

"Oh, very well, then. Wolf Killer said it is not the time to talk about that."

"Woof."

"All right, all right. Back to the machines. It's a revolution, son! Yes, yes. Or it will be. It's building momentum. Indeed, indeed. It will sweep through the whole world! Yes, yes! It will change everything! Yes, yes! Indeed, Indeed, it will. Yes, yes. In the future, mankind will call it the Industrial Revolution. And it will even bring war."

Samuil noticed that the trees appeared to sigh with sadness at this.

"War?"

"Oh yes, Samuil. War. War and more. More, more. Things, my boy. Awful things! Awesome things! Wonderful things! Yes indeed, yes indeed. Ah, but enough of that. Yes, enough. Later. Yes, later. Yes, yes, later, later. I'll tell you more later."

Refocusing his wild eyes, Nikolai motioned to Samuil to follow him.

"Let's sit under Piney, where it is cool."

Once they were comfortable in the shade of the pine tree, Nikolai screwed up his face, crinkled his nose, and looked at Samuil.

"Samuil Fedorchak, they say you are crazy. Hee-hee. Shh. Don't worry; we'll not tell. No, no. It's fine to be crazy. Fine. Yes, yes. So am I! Yes! Hee-hee!"

At that, Nikolai threw back his head and roared out a hefty laugh.

"I'm not crazy!"

"We're all crazy, Samuil! Oh yes. It is only a matter of degree, you see! Degree, degree, degree. Yes, yes."

"Degree?"

Again, the old man threw his head back and laughed loudly, waving his arms in the air. Taking a deep breath, the wise wizard of the Nieper River Valley looked at Samuil and winked.

"You will do, son. Yes, you will. Yes, yes. You will do just fine. I knew you would. Now come walk with me. Come, come. I have more things to tell you. Shh. Secrets, Samuil, secrets. No one must know. No, no, no."

"Woof."

"Oh, all right, all right," Nikolai said.

"What did Wolf Killer say?"

"He thinks it is time to go inside. So come along to our humble little home. Come, come."

Stepping in the cave, Samuil stopped to allow his eyes to adjust to the dimness. Nikolai's cave was huge. Samuil had never seen a cave like this one. He stood looking around until he heard running water.

"You have running water! Wow! Where does it come from?"

"Back there is an underground stream that rises to the surface and flows through my cave. Now pull up a rock, boy. Make yourself at home."

Samuil sat on a nearby rock, looking around with wonder and fascination.

"Tell me about your cave."

"It's just a cave. Cozy, don't you think?"

"Are there other caves like this?"

Wolf Killer walked over to Samuil, laid his head in his lap, and moaned. Nikolai made a face and rolled his eyes.

"Nikolai, you were telling me about the caves. I know you must have been in some of the caves. How many? Which ones?"

"Slow down, Samuil, slow down. Now let me see."

Nikolai sat quietly, staring off into space and thinking. Wolf Killer barked, and Nikolai looked at Samuil.

"What I am about to tell you very few people know. Few, few. And it must remain secret. Just our secret. Yours and mine, yours and mine. No one else can ever know these secrets and mysteries. However, they'll be a help and lifesaver to you in your journey."

"What journey?"

"Oh yes. Yes, yes. We'll get to that. Be patient."

Snarling, Wolf Killer jumped to his feet. He faced the entrance of the cave, growled, and barked. Samuil didn't know what to do, so he sat and watched. Both the old man and his dog ran around the cave, howling, jumping, and rolling in the dirt. Then, as suddenly as they began, they stopped.

"Hush, Wolf Killer. Samuil would never tell. Would you?"

"No, never. Promise."

"Then swear on your mother's grave, and spit on that rock of secrets over there."

Samuil did, and everything returned to a relatively normal state. Or at least as near to normal as possible under the circumstances and considering the occupants. Samuil whispered to Nikolai to get his attention.

"The caves?"

"Oh yes. The caves. Yes."

Nikolai told Samuil about the ancient network of secret caves, tunnels, and chambers that ran beneath the rolling hills of the valley. He described how they snaked, shallow and deep, through the white sandstone hills of the river valley in every direction, like spider webs.

The caves were referred to as the Far Caves and the Near Caves. Some of them long ago had been turned into catacombs. Some had famous bishops and monks entombed in them. Some of them had ancient frescoes and paintings dating as far back as the twelfth century. The cave in Bakota was an ancient orthodox monastery. The priests boasted that from their order of monks there arose twenty bishops in the twelfth and thirteenth centuries. Kings fought wars over the caves.

Others were known for their flowing springs of healing waters and renowned medicinal plants and herbs. Others near the Bakota cave monastery held the souls of dead warrior priests and ghost solders.

"Samuil the healing water and magic plants can save lives. Indeed. I'll show you how to find them."

Samuil's eyes were wide with excitement, as Nikolai paused for a breath.

"I feel as if I know some of this already but tell me more."
Nikolai curled his finger, signaling Samuil to come closer.
"The caves have many secrets—and magic. Lots and lots."
"Secrets?"
"Yes, bloody, spooky, golden secrets."
After a long silence Nikolai whispered.
"Maybe I will tell you. But you can never tell!
No, no, no. Not a soul, not a soul. Not even if they torture you!"
"I will never tell. I promise."
"Good boy, Samuil. Good boy, yes, yes. Indeed. But not now.
Not now. No, no, no. Not now."
"But Nikolai, just one secret. Please."
The wise old man paused and looked at Wolf Killer. The hound moaned.

"Well…all right. But just one. Then you must hurry along home. I have things to attend to."

"One secret, and I'll go."

"Yes. One and off with you, one and off. The caves have magic. Shh! If you tell, you will be cursed and die hundreds of awful deaths.
Hundreds and hundreds."

"My lips are sealed. Promise."

"Then follow me. I something to show you, and there may be something for you."

Together they walked through several connecting caverns and into a large chamber. In the chamber, a pool of water danced as sunbeams wiggled through rocks to tickle it.

"Over here, Samuil. Help me push the boulder."

Rolling the boulder aside, Samuil gasped as blue light filled the chamber.

"Wow! I have never seen anything like this. What are they?"

"Magic stones, Samuil. Magic, magic, magic."

"Where did they come from?"

"Mother Earth Cave gifts them to me for safe keeping."

"Wow!"

"Wow, indeed. Yes, yes."

"They are glowing light blue with silver around the edges. Why? How?"

"They are magical crystals. Each has its own secrets to tell. But they only reveal them to their individual prodigies. When the time is right, one will choose you."

Samuil didn't know what to say. He just stared in disbelief.

"Me? Really?"

"When you are chosen, we will talk more. I'll explain it all to you. Yes, all of it. All in all. But remember, not a word to anyone, or the deaths will come get you over and over again. You will live horrible, horrible, horrible. Fire and ice, fire and ice."

For a long time, there was silence in the cave as the crystals softly glowed. Suddenly, one glowed a bright silver. Nikolai took Samuil by the hand and walked to the glowing crystal. Looking down, Samuil saw his image floating in the crystal. His image was rippling as if it were floating in liquid.

"Samuil, that's your image. The crystal has chosen you. Pick it up and look inside."

When Samuil touched the crystal, his right eye turned silver and his left blue.

"When you look inside the crystal, it will look inside you and know you better than you know yourself. It will see your thoughts and know before you do. It will show you what you need to see. Think what you need, and the crystal will make it so."

Samuil gently picked up the crystal and looked inside. First, he saw the Keeper in all her glory, afloat on the blue mist. She smiled and spoke to Samuil's mind without moving her lips.

"So, it is time, Samuil. I know you have a lot of questions. And there is a lot you don't know, but your heart is pure, and we need your help. Trust the crystal; it has chosen you. The crystals are never wrong. It will guide and prompt you along the way."

Next, he saw the giant Snow Owl. It looked at Samuil and blinked. The blink told Samuil to be brave and have faith. Then the owl spoke to his mind.

"You are part of us now. We need you, and we welcome you. Be strong and brave. You have a lot to learn. Great battles and a long journey await you."

Samuil nodded.

"Now you must go, Samuil. Yes. Go, go, go. Your Papa is in the forest, looking for you. Yes. And Katya will be with you soon. Do not worry, Samuil. I will let you know when the time is right to talk. I will. Promise, promise. We will talk again soon. Soon, soon, soon. I will send Wolf Killer for you when it is time. Now that you are his friend, he can find you much quicker and easier, anytime, anywhere. Yes indeed, yes indeed."

Samuil sighed.

"But Nikolai—"

"No *but*, Samuil. No, no, no. It is time for you to go! Go, go, go!

"Woof woof."

"Oh, I see, I see. Well, then, we will just have to pick Teddy up on the way to Samuil's home."

"How did you know about Teddy?"

"Wolf Killer just told me. Oh yes. Time for Samuil to go. Yes, yes. Samuil, come sit beside me. It's time for you to go. Yes indeed. You have things to do. The shadows are gathering."

"All right."

Nikolai looked endearingly at Samuil.

"I will send for you soon, but now you must go."

As Samuil sat beside Nikolai, Wolf Killer laid his head in Samuil's lap. Nikolai pulled a crystal from his pocket, and his eyes glowed silver. Samuil stared. Nikolai grinned mischievously; then he giggled as his crystal began to glow and pulsate.

"One day soon, your training with me will begin. Yes indeed. But now, there is a conflict brewing that you must help stop. I'll see you on the battlefield."

As he squeezed the glowing crystal, a blue cloud materialized outside the cave, and a silver mist slid across the cave floor and rolled across their feet. Nikolai giggled, and Samuil smiled. Wolf Killer growled, barked, and began howling.

"Oh no, oh no," Nikolai mumbled.

"Something is wrong. Very wrong. Wrong, wrong, wrong."

⸺⸺◆⸺⸺

At the barn, P'etro heard someone call his name. It was Sergey. He walked out of the barn and saw him running out of the forest,

his rifle slung over his shoulder, his pistols stuck in his belt, and his sheathed knife strapped to his leg. He looked anxious. P'etro wondered what could have happened to upset his neighbor.

"P'etro, is Samuil here?"

"No, he's off playing in the woods. Why?"

Sergey explained the incident at the pond and showed P'etro the rope. P'etro examined the rope and agreed it was Sergey's. Then he wondered how Samuil got it and why.

"After I took the boys home, I started looking for Samuil, but I lost his tracks in the forest. So, I came here to tell you what happened and help you search for Samuil."

"Thank you for telling me, Sergey, but Samuil usually spends the weekend days in the forest. I am sure he will be home in time for supper. Or even earlier, if he smells Ilia's cooking."

"Well, P'etro if you are sure, you do not need me."

"I am positive, Sergey. Go home to your family. And thank you for coming all this way to tell me about Samuil."

Sergey nodded and headed into the forest at a trot.

P'etro went inside to tell Ilia about Sergey's visit. He could tell that she was upset. The worried look on her face disturbed him.

"We'll give him enough time to get hungry, and maybe he will come home on his own. You know how he loves the forest."

P'etro tried to sound optimistic, but inside, he was worried.

"Yes, but he's in trouble, scared, and alone. That concerns me. If he's upset, he might—"

"Ilia, pour me a cup of tea while I prepare for a journey into the forest."

Ilia smiled a weak smile and hugged P'etro's neck.

"Of course, my dear."

"Sergey said he lost Samuil's tracks in the woods south of the pond. He was walking on the west bank of the creek. So, he's probably going to the river."

"Do you think he would venture into the Southern Forest?"

"He knows better than to do that. But if he's scared of Sergey and does not want to be found …"

Ilia took a deep breath and covered her mouth.

"P'etro, you must find Samuil before—"

"Ilia, Samuil knows not to go into that part of the forest. But if I do not find him by the river or in the woodlands, I will go into the Southern Forest and look for him."

As Ilia mindlessly chopped onions, her heart filled with dread.

"He wouldn't go to the bog, would he?"

"I'm sure he wouldn't do that."

"Please be careful. You know how dangerous it is in the Bogs."

"I will, dear. If he returns before I get back, fire off two shots, and I'll know he's home."

"What if you're too far to hear?"

"The shots will echo through valley, and I'll hear them."

P'etro grabbed his weapons and rushed out the door. Moments later P'etro arrived at the creek, he stopped and leaned his rifle against a tree stump. He breathed deeply and stilled his racing heart. Calm and in tune with the pulse of the forest, he looked around for signs. He reached out with his senses into the surroundings, listening to the numerous voices of the river valley. The rhythms of the valley seemed to be harmonious, and nothing in the forest gave him the impression of being disturbed or endangered.

That's good. Peace and forest chatter are good. It's a sign that predators are at bay, and Samuil is all right. At least for now.

P'etro relaxed and his heightened awareness calmed. He didn't want to be in the woods any longer than necessary, so he grabbed his rifle and headed down the creek in search of Samuil's tracks. Finding Samuil's trail, he followed the tracks down the creek bed and into the Southern Forest. He tracked Samuil deep into the forest. Suddenly, his trail turned toward the river. P'etro wasn't surprised. Grinning, he followed the cold trail.

When P'etro arrived at the singing river, he noticed something unusual. There was another set of tracks. They were smaller than Samuil's and they followed Samuil to the fallen tree and then into the river. Yet only one set of tracks emerged from the river and walked down the bank.

Samuil must have floated down the river. But someone else was here. Those tracks are a bit smaller than Samuil's, and this person

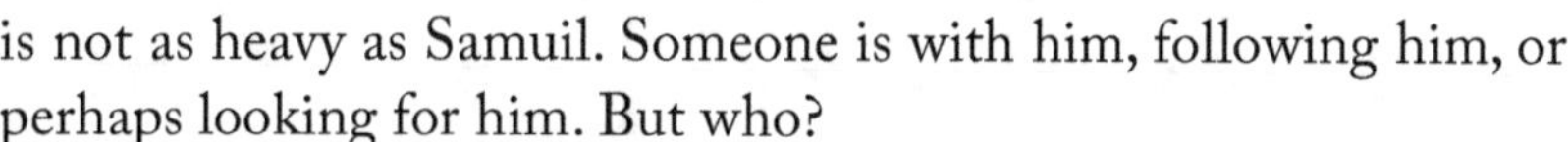

is not as heavy as Samuil. Someone is with him, following him, or perhaps looking for him. But who?

P'etro rose and followed the prints along the riverbank to a sandy cove. Now Samuil's footprints were back. And there were paw prints also but no sign of a scuffle.

A wolf is on Samuil's trail. It maybe stalking the child or just following Samuil? All three prints lead into the woodlands and straight to the Southern Forest.

With a sense of urgency, P'etro followed. When he stepped onto the bank of the border creek that signaled the beginning of the Haunted Forest, P'etro stopped. Sighing, he shook his head. All three sets of tracks led into the forest. Crossing the creek, P'etro disappeared into the ghostly timber.

CHAPTER 27

The Precipice Of No Return

At home, lost in her daydreams, Katya thought the best thing about the day was her kiss with Samuil. Then she wondered why they didn't do that more often. However, the more she thought about the day's events with Samuil, the more she worried about him. She realized that he'd run away because he knew Sergey wouldn't believe him, and now he was hiding in the forest and probably scared to go home.

I've been in the forest with Samuil. I know the places he might hide. I'll go find him, take him home, and explain everything to his parents.

Convincing herself of her hastily devised plan, Katya sneaked out a cabin window and ran into the forest. Her first stop would be the pond where she'd last seen Samuil.

Arriving at the pond she pushed her strawberry-blonde hair behind her shoulders and searched for his tracks. There were a lot of footprints at the pond, and they were everywhere. She immediately found and disregarded Alonya's small tracks. Next, she found Borysko's big boot prints and then her own. That left only Lauro's and Samuil's footprints. To her dismay she discovered that their footprints were the same size. One set of footprints led into the forest; she knew those were Samuil's. Quickly, she followed the tracks.

When Katya came to the border creek, she stopped and stared into the Southern Forest.

Papa told me to not go in there. And I remember that night with the wildcat that was more than a wildcat. But I must help Samuil. He saved my brothers. Sorry, Papa, but here I go.

She took a breath, stepped across the creek, and entered the Southern Forest.

Katya walked deeper and deeper into the forest. The further she walked; the eerier things became. She noticed that Samuil's footprints suddenly became farther apart.

He's running. Samuil must be in trouble. Something must be chasing him. But there are no other tracks.

Katya quickened her pace. Several times Katya lost Samuil's tracks, but with persistent searching, she always found them again. Following them deeper into the forest, she entered the Bogs without realizing it. Gradually, she noticed a bizarre change in her surroundings. She smelled sulfur on the wind and stopped, shook, and looked around. Before her, dark thick shadows bubbled up from a bog, and shadow strings dripped from the trees. Carefully, she backed away from the terrifying bog, unable to take her eyes off the menacing shadows.

When she was a stone's throw away, she turned and ran. She didn't stop running until she was free of the Bogs. Back in the Southern Forest, Katya sat down and rested.

I've lost Samuil's trail. I can't go back into the Bogs. How will I ever find him? The river. Samuil loves the singing waters. He might have gone to the river.

With renewed hope, Katya walked through the forest until she heard the singing river. Excited, she ran. As she neared the riverbank, Katya saw a fallen tree and walked over to it.

She was shocked to see Teddy hanging in the branches.

That's strange. Samuil has never left Teddy behind. Why would he leave Teddy behind now?

Katya walked up to Teddy and spoke softly.

"Hello, Teddy, you look lonely. Come with me, and we'll find Samuil. I could use the company. And I'm sure he will be happy to see you."

Katya put Teddy around her neck, squeezed him tightly, thought about Samuil, and walked to the river. Samuil's tracks disappeared into the river, so she walked down the riverbank, hoping to find his tracks again. At the sandy grove, she found Samuil's tracks and paw prints alongside of them.

Wolf prints! A wolf is on Samuil's trail.

Picking up a big stick, she walked on, determined to find Samuil and, if necessary, help him fight the wolf.

Katya tracked him through the forest. When she arrived at the border creek again, she stopped.

Why would Samuil go back into the Southern Forest, knowing the dangers? What is he thinking? He must be upset. Or maybe he's fleeing

from the wolf that is following him. I don't know, but I must find Samuil and make things right.

Katya took a deep breath and stepped back into the Southern Forest. As she followed Samuil's trail, she noticed that the forest was still and silent.

Where are all the creatures? The forest should be teeming with wildlife. Why have they all gone silent?

She decided to continue deeper into the forest and shook her head at the thought of its being haunted.

Losing Samuil's trail once again, she sat and palmed Teddy.

Why would Samuil come so far into the haunted Forest? He knows the ghost tales about this place.

Backtracking, she found Samuil's trail and continued until she was stopped cold by the sudden howling of wolves.

Wolves? What should I do? Climb a tree? No, hide. But where can I hide?

The wolves howled again, breaking Katya's concentration. Panic seized her mind, and for a moment, she was frozen in terror. She shivered as cold fear surged through her body making her unable to think for the horror that entrapped her. Katya ran until she realized she was lost deep in the Southern Forest. Out of breath and scared, Katya stopped. She sat on a stump, buried her face in her skirt, and sobbed.

I'm alone in this haunted place. I have lost Samuil's trail, and I'm hunted by wolves. Where are you, Samuil? How will I ever find you? How will I ever get out of here?

As if in answer, she heard an owl hoot. Startled, Katya looked up. Before her, on a large stump sat the legendary snow owl. Katya blinked and rubbed her eyes. The owl swiveled her head and looked at Katya with golden eyes. Katya couldn't believe what she was seeing. The snow owl was enormous. It was so huge she wondered how it was able to fly. P'etro and Samuil were the only ones she knew who had seen the snow owl. Plus, this wasn't the season for the owl to be this far south, but there she was. Katya wondered if this was the beginning of serious shadow trouble.

The magnificent owl hooted, flapped her wings, and flew into the heavens. Katya watched in awe as she soared. Then she swiftly dived toward her. Katya flinched as the owl landed on a nearby stump on the other side of her. The owl ruffled her feathers and looked at

Katya. Her eyes were hypnotic, and Katya could not look away. As they stared, Katya felt her fears melt away and a calm wash over her.

For a while, she sat very still, admiring the white snow owl. The owl fluttered off the stump and hopped over to Katya, where it observed Katya for a long moment. Katya broke the silence.

"Yor are a legend, and you are here."

"Are you here alone?"

The owl blinked.

"I am. I'm looking for a friend who helped me earlier. But he was betrayed by my brothers and ran away. I think he's lost, scared, and hunted by wolves. I must find him. His name is Samuil. Have you seen him?"

The owl blinked again.

"If you see him, tell him I'll not stop looking until I find him." Katya flinched when she heard the owl speak in her mind.

"Katya, I'm sorry you have not had time to find the Guardian and develop your powers. But we need you. Things have escalated. The shadows are striking out. Danger is ever present. P'etro is in danger. Samuil needs your help. Here—this is for you."

The owl lifted her wing, and under it was a glowing crystal. She handed it to Katya.

Katya took the crystal and her gray eyes blazed. Her right eye turned blue and her left silver. She gazed at the crystal and saw herself floating in it. She gasped.

The owl ruffled her wings and then settled them.

"This crystal has claimed you. It will be your help and guide. Have faith and believe. Later, you will understand. Take it. Look into it so that it may know you and your thoughts before you think them. It will lead you to the great conflict. I will see you there."

The owl hooted and took flight. Katya watched until she disappeared. For a long time, she sat thinking about the encounter that both had calmed and encouraged her. In the crystal, she saw a cloudy image of Samuil in a cave, and then she saw P'etro, alone on a bluff, staring at something. The crystal told her to go to the bluff. Rising from her stump, she put the crystal in her pocket. As her eyes changed to gray, she headed to the bluff. When she heard the wolf pack howl again, she ran.

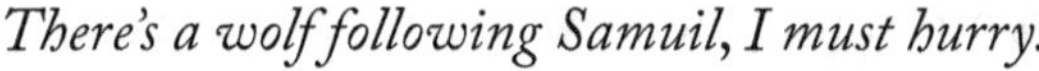

There's a wolf following Samuil, I must hurry.

Farther down the trail, all the tracks vanished. P'etro kneeled and studied the ground.

Something has destroyed the tracks.

Looking around, he found some unusual markings.

What are these? Snakes? But there are so many. And some are very large. But snakes do not travel in packs. Well, this is the Southern Forest, and I've seen stranger things than this.

P'etro flinched when a wildcat screamed. He remembered battling the shadow cats of the Bogs not so very long ago. Thinking about that encounter made him shiver. Moments later, he flinched again when a wolf pack howled.

The presence of the wolves intensified the situation and increased P'etro's concern for Samuil's safety.

I must find Samuil before the wolves do. They are close and getting closer.

P'etro frantically searched everywhere for the lost trail but found nothing. His best guess was to continue in the direction the trail had been going. Perhaps he would stumble onto fresh tracks farther into the forest. The distant scream of a wildcat persuaded P'etro that it was time to go, he continued his search until he heard another chilling cry of a wildcat.

That cat is very close.

Quietly, he looked and listened for the cat. To his right, a branch snapped. P'etro turned as the cat leaped into the air. The big cat landed on top of P'etro, knocking the rifle out of his hands as they tumbled to the ground. The impact separated them, and P'etro rolled into thick undergrowth. Standing quickly, he drew his pistol. The cat was nowhere in sight.

For several minutes, all was silent except for P'etro's heavy breathing. Behind him, the cat screamed. Turning, he saw two hungry eyes staring at him, and he slowly backed up. He ran to his rifle, stooped and quickly picked it up. The rifle appeared to be in good shape, so he aimed the rifle between the cat's eyes and squeezed the trigger. Nothing happened; the rifle misfired. Quickly pulling his pistol, P'etro aimed at the spot where the cat had been, but the cat was gone.

P'etro looked and listened, but everything was silent. After reloading his rifle, he walked carefully back to where he had last seen the big cat. The only thing there were paw prints leading farther into the forest. He followed the cat tracks and noticed that the cat was circling to prepare for another attack. Silently P'etro squatted and listened. There were no sounds in the forest—until P'etro heard a low growl. He quickly stood and fired at the growl. He heard a thump in the leaves.

Got you.

He walked over to inspect his kill, but he was shocked to find no dead cat—only drops of blood.

I only wounded the cat. A wounded wildcat is a mad and dangerous beast. And it's in here with Samuil. I must find it and kill it.

P'etro followed the blood trail into the Bogs, suddenly the Bogs turned dark, as if the sun had stopped shining. In the dimness, he felt an eerie chill fill the air. Walking into a small clearing, he looked to the sky. A dark shadow cloud had engulfed the heavens, blocking out most of the sunlight.

How can I find this cat, Samuil's trail, and Samuil in this shadowy light? I can barely see anything.

In the gray light everything began to change. A shadow fog surged through the trees. Reality shifted, and the Bogs transformed into a dark otherworld. The curling gray fog pitched forward, rose, and curled back into itself. P'etro heard hissing and growling sounds emanating from it as evil slithered along its edges.

Something was stirring deep within the fog. Two yellow eyes stared down menacingly at him. He shook his head, whispered a prayer, and fired his rifle into the fog.

⚒

Katya jumped and gasped when she heard the rifle shot.

Someone else is in the Haunted Forest. But who? Could it be Papa, looking for me? Or P'etro, looking for Samuil? Whoever it is, they are behind me. And so are the wolves. I'll have to be careful and circle around the wolves to get to the shooter.

With renewed purpose, Katya inhaled and took the first step in her quest toward hope and rescue. She ran through the forest and reentered the Bogs. She stepped on a fallen branch, and its snap echoed through the hills. Grimacing, she chastised herself for not being more careful and silent. All she needed now was for the pack to find her before she could find the rifleman. She carefully resumed her journey in the direction of the rifle blast. When the wolves howled, she ran faster, and as she did, the forest grew dark, and the wolf pack was getting closer.

I have to hurry, or they will catch me.

When Katya heard the second shot, and she ran even faster. Cresting a hill, she saw the shadow fog blanketing the Bogs below. The fog stopped near the edge of the bluff, and she watched it as it rose into the sky. It hovered above the treetops, as red lights flashed within. She breathlessly watched the shadow fog. She had never seen anything quite like this.

Katya sat down behind a fallen tree to rest and felt her crystal growing hot. Looking at her pocket, she saw that it was glowing blue. When she took the crystal out, her eyes changed. The crystal showed her a safe way through the fog, and a cave and a man on top of the bluff. Then the crystal stopped glowing, as did her eyes.

Katya glanced at the distant bluff and saw a lone figure running along the brim, chased by a large shadow snake. He stopped beside a tree, knelt, aimed, and fired. When the bullet struck the snake, it coiled in on itself and lay motionless. He raised his other rifle, aimed at the quickly encroaching shadow fog that towered above the trees, and fired into it. The shadow stopped.

Papa? It must be Papa. Oh no! What if it kills Papa?

In the crystal she had seen that the fog didn't completely surround the bluff. From the hill, she could see a path through the fog. Quickly, she headed toward the clearing. Stumbling through the Bogs, dodging trees, and climbing over rocks, Katya made her way toward the bluff.

Something behind her growled. She looked over her shoulder and saw a bleeding wildcat. She ran in a panic, and the cat pursued her. She watched, astonished, as the cat stumbled and fell into the fog. When it hit the fog, it didn't disappear. She could see the outline of the cat within the fog where it was struggling, fighting, and tumbling.

The tip of a huge claw pierced the fog. Katya watched as a giant paw appeared. The wildcat that had fallen into the fog began slowly reemerging from it. She couldn't believe her eyes. In the fog, the wildcat had changed into a monstrous cat as large as a horse, with long fangs and yellow demon eyes.

Frightened, she ran until she reached the bluff, and then Katya began to climb. The footing was treacherous. Rocks were slick, and the ground was moist. After only a few steps, she slipped and slid. When she came to a stop, she stood, and her eyes fixed on the cave she had seen in the crystal.

She had to make her way to the safety of the cave and with great effort she finally she did. Once inside, Katya sat and caught her breath. When the devil cat screamed, she jumped up and moved deeper into the cave. First walking and then crawling, she moved through the darkness, praying that the cave would bring her to the rifleman. Instead, it brought her to a large cavern with an overhang and cliffs. As she stood on the precipice, she looked up and saw light. Looking below, she saw jagged cliffs and dangerous rapids. White-capped water rushed angrily along splashing over boulders and uprooted trees until it disappeared around a sharp bend.

The cat screamed again. It was right behind her. Quickly yet carefully, she climbed down and under the overhang. She sat under it hugged her knees to her chest and waited fearfully. But she didn't have to wait long. In a matter of minutes, the monster cat walked to the precipice, stopped, sniffed the air, and roared. The cat had her scent, and Katya knew what she had to do.

I've dived in the river with Samuil from trees higher than this.

Taking a deep breath of courage, she jumped.

⸻◆⸻

Samuil was still in the cave, listening and learning from Nikolai, when he felt his leg burning. Looking down, he saw that the crystal in his pocket was pulsing blue. Instantly, he took it out, and his eyes changed to blue and silver. When he opened his hand, the crystal filled the cave with blue light.

"Nikolai?"

Nikolai laid his crystal on the cave floor and looked at Samuil with glowing silver eyes.

"Place your crystal beside mine."

When the crystals touched, their blue glow began to pulsate. Samuil stared in amazement as silver strings streaked to the crystal's center and bubbled hot. Steam rose from the crystals as they vibrated. Suddenly, they flared red, flashed yellow, and turned a smoky charcoal. Samuil stared in wonder.

"Samuil, there's a great disturbance in the Bogs. Something is happening. Something bad. Bad, bad."

Suddenly the air in the cave grew still and cold.

"What is it, Nikolai?"

"Not good. No, no. Not good. Evil is having its way."

Nikolai blew on the crystal. The smoke dissipated, and the crystal became clear. Blue and silver streaks floated like clouds across it. When the two colors receded to the perimeter, a blurry picture appeared, but it quickly came into focus.

"Look into the crystal, Samuil. Look, look, look."

Samuil stared into the clear crystal.

"Tell me what you see, Samuil."

"I see a man. And a girl."

"Look at the girl, Samuil."

As the crystal zoomed in on the girl, Samuil quickly inhaled.

"It's Katya! She's in trouble."

"Look at the man, Samuil."

"It's Papa! He's in trouble too. They're in the Bogs and in trouble."

"Look again, Samuil. There's something else in the Bogs."

"There's a huge shadow fog, and it's filled with something." "Yes, Samuil, something evil. Evil, evil, evil."

Samuil looked at Nikolai with worried eyes.

"Samuil, they are in trouble. Trouble, trouble, trouble. Come— we must go quickly. There is no time to waste. None, none. Wolf Killer, take Samuil to the bluff and help fend off the shadow creatures. I will be right behind you. Go, go, go."

Wolf Killer barked, and together, he and Samuil ran out of the cave.

They entered the Bogs and found it difficult to maneuver around the shadow fog. It appeared to be stretching out in every direction.

"Wolf Killer, wait here while I climb that tree and see if I can find a way around or through the shadow fog."

Wolf Killer groaned and sat.

Atop the tree, Samuil saw that the fog was everywhere. At the foot of the bluff, the fog was thick and almost black. He saw no way to get through or around it. When he took the crystal out of his pocket, it began to glow, and so did his eyes. Palming it, he faced it toward the ever-present fog. Silver light shot out of the crystal into the heavens.

Looking up, he saw the sky rippling like a mirage. Dry silver lightning flashed and rumbled through the rippling sky. Moments later, a blinding bolt streaked through the air and struck the ground in not too far away. It exploded and raced along the ground spewing dust, dirt, and rocks high and wide as it blazed a small wide silvery fissure all the way to the top of the bluff with a protective sealed.

Samuil quickly climbed down the tree, his silver and blue eyes shining, and he and Wolf Killer ran through the Bogs. Cautiously, they approached the sealed path that led through the fog. Samuil noticed lush grass growing in the sealed plus a stream ran through it and trees grew through it but everything else was sealed out.

Beasts rushed toward them as they entered the silvery pathway. Looking back, they saw the entrance shrink closed and seal behind them. He noticed that the path was bright and shimmering. The channel and everything in it glowed, as did his eyes. Even Wolf Killer was glowing and shimmering. There were no sounds or animals in the silver fissure, but through it, he saw giant eerie shapes in the fog.

The shapes looked like animals, but they weren't any animals that he had ever seen. Red eyes stared at him from the fog, and a second later a giant, malformed claw from an unrecognizable monster screeched and then pounded on the dome.

⋯⊰◈⊱⋯

Katya stood on a cliff, staring into the rapids. She prayed and then jumped, falling feet first toward the angry water. Just before she plunged into the rapids, she inhaled a lungful of air. She plummeted into the white-capped water and battled the intense force of the violent current until she forced her way back to the surface. Once she was above water, she fought the raging rapids that tossed her around like a rag doll. She dodged boulders and struggled to keep her head above the swift and powerful water.

Fear raced through her body when she realized that the rapids fell off into a cavern. She fought to swim to shore, but the rapids were too swift. She screamed as she was washed over the waterfall.

If the fall doesn't kill me, the boulders below will.

She splashed into the pool below. Luckily, there were no boulders, and Katya swam to shore in calm water. Barely able to move, she crawled out of the water and onto the shore. She gasped several times, collapsed, rolled onto her back, and closed her eyes. The sand ground into her back as she felt something warm on her face and looked up. It was light.

That could be my way out of the underground cavern.

She scrambled up and moved toward it. The light shined through a moderate opening above her. She climbed the rock face in the cavern and came to the narrow tunnel, through which a shaft of light shone. She placed her feet on the cave wall, pressed her back against the opposite wall, and inched her way upward. As she neared the top, she saw a small cavern and looked inside. It was dark inside the cavern, so she couldn't see anything, but there was an awful odor and a rustling sound.

As she continued her ascent, her foot slipped. She gasped and steadied herself as rocks fell. The noise disturbed the inhabitants of the small cavern, and the still air erupted with the fluttering of wings. Hundreds of bats began to swarm all around her. Panic-stricken, she screamed and swatted as they fluttered up and out of the cave. She watched as they flew straight into the shadow fog and transformed into giant, monstrous raptors. Katya climbed for her life.

She reached the top of the cave, pulled herself out, and ran. When she topped the bluff, she looked for the rifleman, but instead she saw lurking shadow beasts—and they saw her. She ran.

P'etro was struggling to stand his ground against beasts, monsters, and demons. Repeatedly shooting and reloading, he was keeping the evil horde in check. Hearing a rustling, he raised his rifle and aimed. He knew it was another monster, and he was ready to kill it. A stone's throw away, Katya stood from behind the underbrush and stared at him.

"Katya?" P'etro asked in shock.

"Papa P'etro!"

Katya screamed and ran to him. She wrapped her arms around his chest and hugged him.

"What are you doing here? How did you get here? How did you find me? I thought you never came into the Southern Forest, much less the Bogs?"

"Usually I don't, Mr. P'etro!"

"Why are you here now?"

"I sneaked away from the cabin to find Samuil."

"Why?"

Glancing at the shadow fog, Katya told P'etro the short version of the events at pond.

"So, the extra set of footprints were yours, Katya?"

"Yes."

"What about the paw prints?"

"I suppose it was a wolf."

Their conversation was interrupted by an unearthly sound coming from the fog. Both turned to look and saw a bat struggling to get out of the fog. Whatever was within the fog had transformed the escaping bat into a giant mutant bird of prey. P'etro raised his rifle and fired. The mutant fell back into the fog.

"Come with me, Katya. We need to leave."

"But what about Samuil?"

"We will keep looking, but now we have to get away from the shadow fog."

P'etro took Katya's hand, and they ran to the other side of the bluff, only to find that they were trapped. The fog had surrounded the bluff, and there was no way out.

"Katya, do you know how to load rifles and pistols?"

"Yes, I have practiced with Papa. But you can't tell Mama, or Papa or I will get in a lot of trouble."

"I promise I will never tell. Here is the ammunition. Take it and reload the rifle and pistols."

"All right."

"When the battle begins, you load, and I will shoot."

"All right." She grimaced as she took a pistol in her small shaking hands and reloaded it.

P'etro knelt beside her and spoke softly.

"Samuil tells me that when your brothers mistreat you, you pelt them stones. And he told me that your aim is as good as his."

"Yes, sir."

"Then you can be just as good with a pistol as you are with rocks. Katya, if you must shoot the pistol, it will be like throwing stones at your brothers. Aiming the pistol is like looking at your target. When you squeeze the trigger, it's like throwing the stone.

Aim at what you intend to hit and hit what you aim at."

Katya smiled and relaxed.

"All right."

"You can do this, can't you?"

"Yes, I can."

When the shadow creatures attacked, P'etro fired, and Katya reloaded. They continued until the barrels of all their weapons were glowing red hot. P'etro knew they would run out of ammunition very soon, and if the regeneration of the fog increased, they wouldn't be able to fend off the monsters fast enough. As if reading his mind, a massive nest of snakes began slithering up and growing into monsters. P'etro stared in disbelief and called out to Katya.

"Look!"

Within the smoky fog was a pocket of something rising. They stared in dismay as hundreds of demon bats materialized.

"Here, Katya," P'etro said, handling her a pistol.

"Remember it's like throwing rocks. Look at your target, pull the trigger, hit the target."

"Yes, all right." She took the weapon with some worry.

P'etro turned and fired, and a giant bat fell.

"Just like that, Katya."

Katya fired, and when a beast fell, she smiled.

Aiming again, P'etro fired his rifle and Katya fired her pistol. Bullets filled the air repeatedly, and shadow monsters fell. Gun smoke filled the bluff, yet the monsters kept coming.

Running backward, P'etro stopped and fired his rifle. Hitting a monstrous deformed snake it slithered back into the fog. Katya fired, and a wolf fell. Hordes of bats began emerging from the fog and closing in.

P'etro fired his pistol, and a bat fell. Katya fired, and two bats fell back into the fog. P'etro threw his hunting knife into the heart of a pouncing wildcat. He grabbed Katya's hand, and they ran as the cat fell back into the fog.

CHAPTER 28

The Shadow War

In the silver pathway, Samuil watched monsters' claw and beat on the dome until Wolf Killer barked shocking him back to the moment.

"Come on; let's get out of here while we still can."

The hound barked, and they ran. Dodging branches and crossing streams, they hurried toward the bluff. When they reached it, Samuil noticed that the pathway was thinning and weakening. He also saw that the shadow fog was darkening and growing stronger.

They hurriedly climbed the bluff as fingers and claws broke through the pathway, grabbing at them. Samuil heard a roar and looked over his shoulder. Horrified, he saw the pathway collapsing behind him. Beasts were pouring into it. He pulled out his crystal, pointed it at the approaching monsters, and thought of a shield. A thick barrier materialized in front of the beasts, reinforcing the collapsing pathway and stopping the invasion.

Samuil and Wolf Killer hurried to the top the bluff. He looked behind him and saw the pathway starting to collapse. To his surprise, it imploded, killing hundreds of shadow creatures.

Wow, did I do that? I didn't even think about it.

Atop the bluff, Samuil looked for his Papa and Katya. Not seeing either, he and Wolf Killer went in search of them. The bluff was crawling with beasts and demons. He and the hound had to move slowly and carefully so as not to be seen. They climbed to the top of an embankment, and he peeked over the edge. He saw his Papa and Katya, shooting at creatures that swarmed around them. However, as the shadow cloud engulfed the dead beasts, they gradually reemerged and attacked.

Samuil closed in and then stopped behind a tree. Wolf Killer sat by his side.

"Shh, Wolf Killer. Quiet like a mouse, invisible like a ghost. We're going to sneak closer."

Wolf Killer groaned.

Quietly, they crept closer to the mayhem. Samuil accidentally rustled the bushes, causing P'etro to spin around and aim.

"Samuil!" Katya squealed.

P'etro lowered his rifle.

"Katya!" Samuil yelled.

Katya ran to Samuil, threw her arms around his neck, and kissed him. Samuil turned bright red, and P'etro grinned.

"Oh, Samuil, you're alive and safe."

"How did you get here Katya? Why are you here?"

"That's a story for another time, Samuil. I have something for you. Something you left behind."

Katya smiled sweetly, took Teddy from around her neck, and looked at Samuil.

"You found Teddy!"

Katya placed Teddy around Samuil's neck.

"Thank you, Katya."

"You're welcome, Samuil."

"Good to see you again, Teddy. I am glad you are all right,"

"You didn't come back for me like you promised."

"Sorry."

"He couldn't, Teddy. He was with the Guardian." Katya mind-spoke to both of them.

"You can hear Teddy?"

"Yes."

"But how?"

"I think it is the crystals."

Samuil stared as she pulled her dimly glowing crystal from her pocket. Samuil retrieved his glowing crystal, and they smiled at each other.

"It's all right, Samuil, just remember I can hear."

"Now it's like a three-way conversation."

Before Samuil could answer, they were interrupted by Wolf Killer, who began barking furiously at the shadow cloud. They all turned to see a giant snake coiling upward through the fog. The snake grew into a hissing monster with giant fangs that dripped hot yellow venom. The snake stretched out of the fog and stared at

them with red demon eyes. P'etro raised his rifle and fired. When the snake was hit, it only flinched and then came for them.

Katya handed P'etro another rifle. He aimed and fired. Again, the snake only flinched, and Samuil knew they were in trouble.

"Samuil, I passed a cave over there when I was searching for P'etro," Katya said, pointing.

"We can hide and regroup there."

"Papa, come on; there's a cave near, and we can take cover in it."

Together they headed for the safety of the cave, with Katya leading the way.

Samuil heard his Papa yell. Turning, he saw him fighting off a six-foot-tall shimmering shadow wolf; he was hitting it with the butt of his rifle. As Samuil ran to him, the wolf circled and leaped through the air, knocking P'etro to the ground. Samuil reached in his pocket and held his crystal. Instantly, his eyes turned silver and blue, and a bejeweled poisoned silver saber appeared in his hand.

Samuil slashed at the wolf but missed his mark. The wolf jumped off P'etro and onto Samuil. They rolled in the dust, and Samuil dropped his saber. Wolf Killer came running and jumped into the fray. All three tumbled about, knocking Samuil free. Samuil grabbed his saber off the ground and sunk it to the hilt in the wolf. Instantly, the wolf collapsed, and Wolf Killer released his jaw from the beast's throat.

As the saber vanished, Samuil eyes returned to normal. He and Katya helped P'etro limp to the cave, where they all collapsed, exhausted and out of breath. Samuil took out his crystal, pointed it at the mouth of the cave, and envisioned a clear protective barrier. The barrier appeared and locked in place. P'etro and Katya looked at Samuil with shocked expressions. Samuil shrugged.

"Nikolai taught me."

"Samuil, where did you get the crystal?" P'etro asked.

"It chose me in Nikolai's cave."

"Where did the saber come from? And where is it now?" Katya asked with a raised eyebrow.

"I thought of a silver saber, and it appeared," Samuil explained.

"Oh. Can I do that?"

"My crystal has always responded to my thoughts. Yours should too."

Samuil looked at his Papa and noticed that he was bleeding.

"Papa, what happened?"

"The wolf gnawed my right calf pretty good. I can't put much weight on it."

As Katya inspected P'etro's leg, Samuil took off his shirt and tore several strips from it to wrap P'etro's wounds.

"Samuil, maybe your crystal can heal P'etro."

Samuil took his crystal and touched P'etro's wound. It glowed dimly, stopped the bleeding and the pain, but it didn't heal the wound. Katya took the strips and carefully wrapped P'etro's wounded leg.

"Stand Papa see how it feels to work."

He stood without pain, but his leg was weak.

"Look, Samuil," Katya said, pointing at the entrance of the cave.

A dragon lumbered past the cave, followed by a saber-toothed tiger, a giant lizard, and a wild boar as big as an ox. They gathered at the cave entrance as an endless number of monstrous animals and giant demons emerged from the shadow fog. The wooded bluff quickly filled with stalking shadow creatures, and the sky filled with various raptors and flying dragons.

"Papa, I think the barrier is failing. We'll have to leave soon."

"We have to find a way off this bluff and out of the Bogs," P'etro said with a frown.

Samuil and Katya nodded. They rose to get ready.

"Papa, since you don't need to run, we'll need to sneak through the undergrowth so the beasts can't see or hear us."

"But they can smell us, Samuil," Katya pointed out.

Samuil frowned and thought for a moment. Smiling, he looked at Katya.

"Maybe there's a way I can fix that."

He closed his eyes, held his crystal, and thought.

We need to look and smell like shadow beasts.

Samuil opened his eyes and looked at Wolf Killer. He looked like the giant shadow wolf they had just been killed. P'etro and

Katya looked at one another and then at Samuil, who was grinning from ear to ear and then he laughed.

"You both look and smell like red-eyed demons."

"So do you," Katya said.

"Let's get out of here while we still can."

When the barrier blinked and fizzled, they stepped out of the cave. They strolled through the bluff, looking and smelling like beasts, until they came to a stream. The stream was swift and deep, and they had to cross it.

"We'll have to swim," Samuil whispered.

"Can you swim in the swift water, Papa?"

"Yes, but it will take me longer. I'll meet up with you downstream."

They all waded in and swam. As soon as they crawled out of the stream, Samuil, Katya, and Wolf Killer changed back to themselves and hurried downstream to meet up with P'etro. They helped him to his feet and hurried to a stand of reeds not far from the stream. They splashed into the shallow water and squatted out of sight. Samuil peeked out and saw a demon riding a ten-foot-tall horse with tusks searching the reeds.

Samuil suddenly jumped to his feet and ran, leading the demon away from Katya and Papa. Something hit Samuil from behind, and he fell. As he rolled to a stop, he heard a hideous laugh and saw the demon. It hissed and circled. Slowly getting to his feet, Samuil held his crystal and thought of the saber he'd used earlier. Nothing happened.

In a blink, the demon attacked. Samuil grabbed a stick, and it instantly became a double-edged sword. The horse barreled into him, thrusted its head, and its tusks threw Samuil back into the reeds. He splashed into the water, scrambled to his feet, and swung the sword at the stampeding horse. The horse's head skipped across the water as the demon splashed into the reeds. Katya's eyes were shining silver and blue as she slammed the ten-inch blade between the red eyes of the demon.

P'etro looked at her and smiled. "Well done, Katya."

"Don't tell Papa."

"Your secret's safe with me."

Hobbling off the bluff, they continued through the Bogs. Samuil felt something eerie and strange. He noticed that all the bogs around them were bubbling. Shadow strings were slithering out of bogs and racing into the forest. Tree leaves rustled, but there wasn't a breeze.

The air was pungent. Samuil and Katya helped P'etro into the safety of a small cave. While he rested, they stepped back outside to look around.

Samuil felt his crystal warming up. He looked at Katya, and she nodded. They took their crystals out of their pockets and their eyes changed. Both sensed a message and laid their crystals on the ground. Nikolai's grave face appeared in the crystal.

"Meet me at Devil's Island. We can make a stand there. We—" Suddenly, a pair of large talons grabbed Nikolai, and the crystal went dark.

"What was that?" Katya asked.

"Some kind of monstrous feathered creature has grabbed our guardian teacher and flown away."

"Oh. And what kind of bird did those large talons belong to?"

"I'm not sure."

"I hope he's all right."

"We'll know when we get to Devil's Island."

"Where is Devil's Island?"

Though Samuil had never been to the island, he knew where it was. He also had overheard his Papa and Ivan talking about their visit to the island. Samuil explained to Katya that Devil's Island was farther south in the Bogs, and it was in the middle of the river, where the Bogs crossed the river and extended farther south toward the Black Sea. Steep, tree filled, cliffs encircled it and only one narrow path on the south side of the island wound through the cliffs. The path opened into a lush but swampy meadow. Inland there was a thick forest filled with rotting trees and lots of bogs.

Samuil looked up and saw gray clouds racing through the sky.

"It's time to go. The Bogs is changing."

As they moved through the Bogs, the shadow fog thickened, and it became harder for them to see. That meant it was harder for the monsters to see them, and that was an advantage that Samuil liked.

However, the temperature variant of the fog changed as it rose to touch the shadow cloud just above the forest canapé. It was hotter and colder in the fog than it had ever been before. One moment they were hot enough to pass out as red lightning popped above them. The next their teeth chatter in a blizzard as black lightning exploded through the cloud.

They helped P'etro through the Bogs toward Devil's Island. Before reaching the river, they walked out of the dark fog to a clear blue sky and singing water. Without any trouble they crosse the river, reached the island, and ascended the narrow, winding pass.

At the top of the pass, they propped P'etro up against a boulder, and Samuil gripped his crystal. A scimitar sword appeared, which Samuil handed to his Papa. P'etro smiled and nodded his head.

"Nothing will get past here alive."

Samuil smiled and nodded.

"I know it won't, Papa."

Lightning flashed through the clear blue sky, followed by rumbling thunder. Samuil saw the heavens flicker, ripple, and sway as a silvery mirage appear. In the blink of an eye, giant snow owls flooded through the mirage. Then Nikolai appeared, riding on a snow owl with blue-tipped wings; he held a silver saber in each hand.

Once they were free from the mirage, it shattered, scattering blue-sky-fragments into the surrounding feathering clouds. The clouds gathered and rolled into a giant blue cloud with a silver outline that erupted into a thunderhead that filled the sky as blue and silver lightning streaking through it.

Samuil heard something rumbling in the forest. Turning, he watched a shadow fog explode into the sky and quickly plume into a shadow cloud. Racing through the heavens, it threatened to swallow up the blue cloud. As the clouds collided, the sun shook, the ground buckled, and the island trembled. Samuil watched as Nikolai and the owls flew through the blue cloud gathering strength. Momentarily they exited the cloud on blue lightning.

Then flashing out of the shadow cloud on black lightning were red dragons ridden by gray demons. With sword in hand, Nikolai cut a blood trail through them. Most of the owls fought with Nikolai but a few flew to the meadow.

The owls landed near Samuil and Katya, and the legendary Snow Owl spoke to their minds.

"We came as soon as we heard the conflict with the Shadows was escalating. The shadows caught us off guard by moving sooner than expected. It was a long journey, but we are here now to help you with the final battle."

The owl extended a wing, and Samuil climbed onto her neck. Katya mounted an owl with black-tipped wings, and they flew. Suddenly, the heavens were filled with demons riding dragons. Samuil and Katya circled, flew high, and dived into the middle of the demons.

Blazing fire from dragons and owls shot through the sky filling the air with burning feathers, scorched scales and dripping blood as the spoils of war fell through the battle torn sky.

Samuil watched Katya as she shot an arrow. It flew true and pierced the heart of the dragon which tumble out of the sky. As she continued firing arrows, Samuil flew to a dragon and thrust his French saber into its brain. He felt the strong wings of the owl beneath him as she turned and flew into the monstrous flying horde of beasts pouring out of the shadow cloud. Silver light exploded from his sword as he slew dragons and demons in the sky while the owl roasted others.

A demon riding a giant bat dived at Samuil and his snow owl. They soared, rolled, and fought in a life-or-death struggle. Samuil wielded the silver sword with the deadly accuracy of a supernatural knight of the royal guard, and he slew the demon and bat. Glancing around he saw dead devils, bats, dragons, and winged monsters tumbling from the heavens.

Samuil glanced down and saw herds of monstrous shadow creatures lumber from the forest toward the meadow, as the fog twisted, knotted, and rolled. Then he saw Nikolai fly down, pick up P'etro from the path and fly into the fray. Hungry for blood shadow beasts charged P'etro and Nikolai, who, with sabers in hand, readied themselves.

As the ground battle began, snow owls dived from the sky. Flying just above shadow beasts, they roasted monsters faster than the fog could generate them.

A herd of burning bulls stamped toward Nikolai. The owls breathed fire, but it didn't faze them.

Samuil and Katya landed next to Nikolai.

"Nikolai, leave the bulls to Katya and me."

"Oh, oh. But first me touch your sabers, Samuil."

He touched Katya's saber and turned it into a silver bow and a quiver filled with silver ice coated magical arrows. Then he turned touched Samuil's saber and infused the tip with the same ice coated magic.

Samuil turned and looked at Katya. She smiled.

"Are you ready, Katya?"

"Yes."

"Alright, time fill the sky with your arrows."

Katya nodded, Samuil yelled, and with weapons in hand they ran head-on toward the fiery bulls.

They stopped and Katya fired volley after volley of arrows, three and four at a time. Bull after fiery bull fell to her deadly aim. When their numbers shrank, Samuil yelled and charged. He leaped into the air and sank his sword into the leading bull. Sliding to a stop, he slew bull after bull as they encircled him. When he disappeared from her sight, Katya screamed, "No!"

She ran toward Samuil while continuing her aerial assault, praying that he was all right. From the middle of the herd, a blue light flashed bright, blinding Katya for a moment. Blinking from the brightness, she stopped. With a crooked grin, Samuil emerged from the slaughtered bulls. She ran to hug him.

"You're quite the archer, Katya." "Someone has to keep you alive."

Samuil smiled.

"The light Samuil how—"

"Well—"

"Samuil!"

He turned quickly at the sound of his name and saw Papa and Nikolai being overpowered by herds of monstrous land beasts. The beasts poured out of a fog that hung in the southern cliffs and Nikolai was casting fire spells, lightning spells, wind spells, poison spells, bone breaking spells, heart stopping spells and more as fast as he could think.

"We could use some help!" P'etro yelled.

As Samuil and Katya ran to help, there was a rippling mirage in the meadow, and General Kovalski and his men appeared, standing by P'etro's side.

"P'etro, Nikolai called me to save your skin again and his too."

P'etro saluted.

"General, sir, your bullets and bombs will be ineffective against the new shadow creatures, Only swords and arrows and magic works now."

"Who needs bullets and bombs when you have star sabers, lightning bullets, and sun bombs?"

"Where did you get all that?"

"Nikolai."

P'etro looked at Nikolai.

"Wolf Killer said it was necessary. He did, he did."

P'etro smiled and all three men saluted. The general turned to his ghostly troops and yelled.

"Charge!"

The general and his twelve men rushed into battle as star sabers flashed, sun bombs exploded, and lightning bullets filled the hostile air in the most horrific ground battle of the day. The troop beat the beasts down the path and into the river. Nikolai cast a drowning spell and they sunk.

Behind them, monsters filled the pathway blocking their way back up the path to the meadow.

"General, sir, we have depleted our supply of sun bombs and lightning bullets," a ghost soldier reported.

The General looked at Nikolai, who grimaced.

"Then, by the heavens, until we are resupplied, we'll beat these monsters back with our star sabers!"

Turning to his men, he shouted, "regroup for an uphill battle!"

For the second time that day, he yelled, "Charge!"

The ghost solders and P'etro fought on furiously in hand-to-hand combat along with P'etro and Nikolai magic while Samuil and Katya flew through the meadow, slaying beasts from the air with their bows.

Then, flying low, the owls roasted the horde of beasts in the pathway. Although they had been massively outnumbered, they once again had secured the footpath and meadow.

A dark fog boiled above the river, and shadow creatures splashed into the river and raced up the path.

"P'etro, my men and I will hold these creatures at bay while the rest of you and find a bulwark from which we can fight. Hurry! It's our only chance against this horde."

P'etro saluted and watched his brave comrade's advance. He knew he would see them again, either later in the day or in the next conflict.

"Samuil, you and Katya take Papa to the cave, while Wolf Killer and I help the general buy you some time. Go on, go on."

"Come on, Papa, we'll regroup at the cave. From there, we'll search the island for a fortress."

As they ran, they heard the scream of an eagle. Samuil turned to see Nikolai atop a giant magical eagle, fighting demons and dragons in the pass and in sky. Alongside him were the fighting snow owls.

When separated from the owls, Nikolai and the eagle were suddenly attacked by several demon riders on dragons. Smoke filled the sky as flames engulfed the eagle. Nikolai and his eagle plummeted from the sky and splashed into the river. Samuil and Katya stared in disbelief, but having secured Papa in a cave they took the lead in the vicious battle to secure the pass again.

"Samuil, a bat!" Katya called out.

Samuil looked up just in time to see the bat soaring toward him. Side-stepping, he swung his sword, cutting off a wing. The bat crashed, rolled, and died. He turned to see Katya ram her sword into the skull of a giant lizard with a spiked tail.

"Katya, if we stay here any longer, we'll be encircled. We have shadow beasts in front of us and behind us."

"Where can we go?"

"To the cliffs!"

Together, they ran to the cliffs. As they retreated, the fog rolled through the pass and filled the meadow. Maneuvering their way through the steep, jagged cliffs, they came to a spot where they could climb up and be hidden by the cover of the forest. There they skillfully fought and ambushed monsters until they heard a baying.

Wolf Killer! Samuil thought.

Samuil looked at Katya. She smiled and nodded. Both turned and ran through the forest toward the baying. When they came to a stream, they saw Wolf Killer sitting and panting. They ran to the hound.

"I wondered where you'd gone," Samuil said, scratching him behind the ear.

The hound turned to the stream and barked, Samuil saw a giant beaver dam. He and Katya splashed into the stream and swam to it; then they dived down and came up inside the dam. Crawling on top of rocks they sat down and caught their breath.

"Samuil, can we use the crystals to get out of here?"

"I don't know how. Nikolai didn't have time to teach me."

"I hope he's all right. We need our guardian teacher."

"Yes, we do. We need to go to the meadow. We can see the river from there, and maybe we'll see Nikolai."

When they held their crystals, their eyes changed, and French sabers appeared in their hands. They left the dam and the river and sneaked through the forest, dodging beasts, until they came to the meadow. The meadow was a scene of carnage. There, they mounted their snow owls and flew back into the sky battle.

Winged beasts tumbled from the shadow cloud faster than the two warriors could kill them. A red-eyed demon on a dark winged horse attacked from Samuil's blind side. In the battle, Samuil was knocked off his owl and fell into the river. Looking up, he saw the sky horde overwhelm Katya. A demon sliced at her head. She leaned away, but the sword grazed her shoulder, and she also fell into the river. Both swam back to the island.

Halfway up the narrow path, Samuil saw Nikolai leaning on a boulder.

"You're alive!" They both yelled.

Samuil ran and threw his arms around the old man neck.

"Oh, happy to see you as well. Yes, yes. But you two still have work to do. School is not out yet. No, no. Finish, finish, finish. Give me your hand and help me hobble up this path."

When they reached the top of the pathway, Samuil saw Papa limping, battling, and giving ground as he backed toward them. With their eyes blazing and weapons raised, Samuil and Katya ran to P'etro's side. The three battled bravely on the ground, while the owls fought in the sky, but the beasts had them surrounded in the meadow. Nikolai cast a protective dome over them. Beasts crashed against it but couldn't penetrate it.

Though he was exhausted and overwhelmed, Samuil felt his crystal glow. Sensing a message, he took it out and laid it down, and everyone looked at the message. The legendary Snow Owl gave instructions, and everyone looked at one another and nodded.

Katya secured her crystal to an arrow and nodded at Samuil. Nikolai made a fissure at the top of the dome, and Katya shot her crystal through it. Then he closed the fissure. When the crystal hit the shadow cloud, nothing happened. However, a moment later the sky twisted, the shadow cloud stilled, and the forest became silent.

Suddenly, the heavens erupted in fire, smoke, and deadly fumes. Demons, dragons, and flying monsters were killed instantly, and the shadow cloud vanished. As the island rumbled, flaming skeletons, burned shadow flesh, and bone shards rained from the sky.

After the rain of death ceased, Nikolai opened another fissure. Samuil took his glowing crystal from his pocket, squeezed it, and threw it into the approaching shadow fog. The explosion shook the island, sending fire, dirt, and rocks flying high in the sky. The ground trembled violently and split open. Trees fell, cliffs tumbled into the river, and fires raged. Shadow creatures and beasts were instantly consumed. Some tumbled into the abyss of the smoking chasm, some were crushed, and others vanished into a silver swiveling mirage.

Abruptly, sheets of silver lightning filled the heavens and thunder shook the forest. It felt as if the world was coming to an end as an earthquake buckled the ground, and the island began to sink. Sulfurous fumes boiled up from the underworld. The dome shook and cracked, the top broke open allowing the underworld fumes to seep in.

Gasping, they fought for air and life. First P'etro fell, then Wolf Killer, and then Katya. Samuil looked at Nikolai. Nikolai winked and cast a small protective dome around them, just before he blacked out.

Samuil looked at his fellow warriors and mumbled, "Papa? Katya? Wolf Killer? Nikolai?"

All lay breathless and still on the cool bloody ground.

"No!"

A blue cloud rolled into the sky, and once again the heavens thundered. Samuil saw the snow owls take flight from the forest. As they flew, he heard the Snow Owl's voice in his head.

"Samuil, it is over, but it has not ended."

As owls vanish, he hears another voice.

"Keeper?"

"Yes, Samuil. It is I. You and Katya fought bravely beside your comrades. We are in your debt. Now you must be vigilant, my child. I will see you again."

In the calm blue sky, Samuil saw the heavens ripple, and he watched them disappear through a mirage. He took a breath and looked at the carnage. The island was torn apart and sinking. River water flooded the path and poured into the meadow. Then, suddenly, everything went black.

Thunder rumbled in the distance as three ghostly glowing hooded figures with red-black swirling eyes mysterious weaved their way through the carnage of Devils Island. They glided inches above the war-torn sinking island as their cloaks ruffled in the wind. They surrounded P'etro, Nikolai, Wolf Killer, Katya, and Samuil and raised their hands to the heavens. Magically, their hands began to glow as blue, red, black, green, and white colors of magic flared like fire from their fingers.

A hot wind swirled dirt, blood, bones, burned flesh, feathers and the ash of the battlefield into eddies that spun through the island toward Samuil and friends who laid deadly still on the sinking island. The hooded figures swirl the powerful colors of magic into the eddies along with black, gray and white magical smoke and the engulfed sinking island disappeared.

ACKNOWLEDGMENTS

Samuil and the Legendary Snow Owl would not have been possible without my sons' interest and support. Nor would the novel have come to life without the encouragement of my 1970 high school classmates.

A big thank you to my wife for her patience and support.